JOHN D. MACDONALD DESCRIBES CAPTAIN KILPACK'S SHIP:

||||||||||||||||||||||||||||||||||||||||||||||||||

"She was a hotel with over three million miles of travel in her old steel bones....On shipboard, because the large group was assembled through almost random selection, there had to be a small percentage of nature's oversights.

"The fat man who cannot understand why anybody would object to his lighting his first black cigar of the day at the breakfast table. The woman who slips silverware into her purse and takes it back to the cabin and hides it. The child who reaches into the elevator and pushes all the buttons...

"However, the ship's geography provides refuge from the pests and the peculiar..."

Fawcett Books
by John D. MacDonald:

ALL THESE CONDEMNED
APRIL EVIL
AREA OF SUSPICION
BALLROOM OF THE SKIES
THE BEACH GIRLS
BORDER TOWN GIRL
THE BRASS CUPCAKE
A BULLET FOR CINDERELLA
CANCEL ALL OUR VOWS
CLEMMIE
CONDOMINIUM
CONTRARY PLEASURE
THE CROSSROADS
CRY HARD, CRY FAST
THE DAMNED
DEAD LOW TIDE
DEADLY WELCOME
DEATH TRAP
THE DECEIVERS
THE DROWNER
THE EMPTY TRAP
THE END OF THE NIGHT
END OF THE TIGER AND OTHER STORIES
THE EXECUTIONERS
A FLASH OF GREEN
THE GIRL, THE GOLD WATCH AND EVERYTHING
JUDGE ME NOT
A KEY TO THE SUITE
THE LAST ONE LEFT
A MAN OF AFFAIRS
MURDER IN THE WIND
MURDER FOR THE BRIDE
THE NEON JUNGLE
ONE MONDAY WE KILLED THEM ALL
ON THE RUN
THE ONLY GIRL IN THE GAME
OTHER TIMES, OTHER WORLDS
PLEASE WRITE FOR DETAILS
THE PRICE OF MURDER
SEVEN
SLAM THE BIG DOOR
SOFT TOUCH
WHERE IS JANICE GANTRY?
WINE OF THE DREAMERS
YOU LIVE ONCE

NOTHING CAN GO WRONG

John D. MacDonald
&
Captain John H. Kilpack

Fawcett Crest • New York

A Fawcett Crest Book
Published by Ballantine Books

Library of Congress Catalog Card Number: 81-47232

ISBN 0-449-24551-9

This edition published by arrangement with Harper & Row, Pub-
lishers

Printed in Canada

First Ballantine Books Edition: October 1982

S.S. MARIPOSA

NORTH CAPE, RUSSIA, AND NORTHERN EUROPE CRUISE
(May 2, 1977—July 13, 1977)

SAN FRANCISCO—Sail Mon., May 2, 11:00 A.M.

LOS ANGELES—Arrive Tues., May 3, 8:00 A.M.—Sail Tues., May 3, 1:00 P.M.

SAN DIEGO—Arrive Tues., May 3, 8:00 P.M.—Sail Tues., May 3, 11:00 P.M.

TABOGA ISLAND, PANAMA—Arrive Tues., May 10, 9:00 A.M.—Sail Tues., May 10, 4:00 P.M.

PANAMA CANAL—Tues., May 10 (Evening Transit)

SAN JUAN, PUERTO RICO—Arrive Fri., May 13, 9:00 A.M.—Sail Fri., May 13, 4:00 P.M.

HAMILTON, BERMUDA—Arrive Sun., May 15, 1:00 P.M.—Sail Mon., May 16, 6:00 A.M.

SOUTHAMPTON, ENGLAND—Arrive Mon., May 23, 8:00 A.M.—Sail Tues., May 24, 10:00 P.M.

LE HAVRE, FRANCE—Arrive Wed., May 25, 8:00 A.M.—Sail Thurs., May 26, 6:00 P.M.

ZEEBRUGGE, BELGIUM—Arrive Fri., May 27, 8:00 A.M.—Sail Fri., May 27, 6:00 P.M.

AMSTERDAM, NETHERLANDS—Arrive Sat., May 28, 8:00 A.M.—Sail Sun., May 29, 4:00 P.M.

HAMBURG, GERMANY—Arrive Mon., May 30, 12:00 noon—Sail Tues., May 31, 6:00 P.M.

LENINGRAD, U.S.S.R.—Arrive Fri., June 3, 8:00 A.M.—Sail Sun., June 5, 6:00 P.M.

HELSINKI, FINLAND—Arrive Mon., June 6, 8:00 A.M.—Sail Mon., June 6, 5:00 P.M.

STOCKHOLM, SWEDEN—Arrive Tues., June 7, 9:00 A.M.—Sail Wed., June 8, 5:00 P.M.

COPENHAGEN, DENMARK—Arrive Fri., June 10, 8:00 A.M.—Sail Sat., June 11, 4:00 P.M.

OSLO, NORWAY—Arrive Sun., June 12, 10:00 A.M.—Sail Mon., June 13, 8:00 A.M.

BERGEN, NORWAY—Arrive Tues., June 14, 8:00 A.M.—Sail Tues., June 14, 6:00 P.M.

GEIRANGER, NORWAY—Arrive Wed., June 15, 10:00 A.M.—Sail Wed., June 15, 4:00 P.M.

TRONDHEIM, NORWAY—Arrive Thurs., June 16, 8:00 A.M.—Sail Thurs., June 16, 2:00 P.M.

HONNINGSVAG, NORWAY—Arrive Sat., June 18, 6:00 A.M.—Sail Sat., June 18, 12:00 noon

LEITH, SCOTLAND—Arrive Tues., June 21, 9:00 A.M.—Sail Wed., June 22, 5:00 P.M.

PONTA DELGADA, AZORES—Arrive Sun., June 26, 10:00 A.M.—Sail Sun., June 26, 6:00 P.M.

ST. CROIX, VIRGIN ISLANDS—Arrive Sat., July 2, 8:00 A.M.—Sail Sat., July 2, 6:00 P.M.

PANAMA CANAL—Arrive Tues., July 5 (Daylight Transit)

LOS ANGELES—Arrive Tues., July 12, 8:00 A.M.—Sail Tues., July 12, 12:00 noon

SAN FRANCISCO—Arrive Wed., July 13, 9:00 A.M.—*ALOHA!*

CAPTAIN J. H. KILPACK, Commanding

J. M. COCO   S. A. GLAROS
Chief Officer   Chief Engineer

The Officers and Crew Welcome You Aboard the
S.S. MARIPOSA

J. P. YONGE	Chief Purser
J. ABRAMSON	Chief Steward
R. E. McGUE	Chief Radio Officer
R. L. STEVENS	First Assistant Engineer
A. GRAYSON, M.D.	Surgeon
W. D. McDONALD	Senior Assistant Purser
W. J. KELLY	Tour Escort
W. B. ZAMBRESKY	Paymaster
D. E. G. GORMAN	Cashier
K. YOSHINAKA	Second Steward
JOHN MERLO	Executive Chef
MAURICE HEROD	Headwaiter

CRUISE STAFF

ALAN SCOTT	Cruise Director
KAUI BARRETT	Cruise Directress
ANNETTE ALIOTO	Mariner Hostess
MICKEY MENDITTO	Orchestra Leader
RICHARD SEDERMAN	Organist
R. C. STANLEY	Art Instructor
GARY AND JOYCE MARTZOLF	Bridge Instructors
SUSAN CASHMAN	Cruise Entertainer
ART AND DOTTY TODD	Cruise Entertainers
JAN MUZURUS	Cruise Entertainer
JOYCE STANLEY	Cruise Entertainer
ROSS AND MARGE WERNER	Dance Team
HAL WAGNER	Cruise Lecturer
JACK STANTON	Thomas Cook Escort
JAMES McFARLAND	Thomas Cook Escort
ANDREW DAMIA	Thomas Cook Escort

PREFACE

This is the true story of the last long cruise of an American passenger ship. The S.S. *Mariposa* of the Pacific Far East Line sailed out of San Francisco Bay on Monday, the second day of May 1977, and returned July 17, 77 days later.

There are long digressions from the actual cruise, incidents and adventures garnered from the maritime career of Captain John Kilpack, which should serve as antidotes to the "Love Boat" mythology.

After much experimentation we decided the best way to do the book was to let me speak in my own style, and John Kilpack in his.

Whenever you see this type used, it is John Kilpack speaking.

Whenever the use of actual names might prove an embarrassment to the passengers or staff, or a source of glee to their attorneys, the names have been changed.

There is no list here of people we should thank. It became far too long. You all know who you are.

John D. MacDonald

||||||||||||||||||||||||||||||||||||||||||||||||||

Leaving San Francisco

When we sailed under the Golden Gate Bridge on a bright, cold, windy morning, a friend who had been aboard to say goodbye, went to park on the San Francisco side of the bridge in time to walk way out to a point above the ship channel and take pictures of the *Mariposa* below. Dorothy and I are among the tiny figures clustered on the weather decks. The white ship is dressed and gleaming, cutting through the dance of blue water. We waved and waved.

The *Mariposa* and her twin, the *Monterey*, were twenty-five years old when we sailed and were coming to the end of their years of government subsidy. They had been laid down as high-speed freighters but had been converted to passenger ships: single-screw vessels, 20,000 tons, cruising speed 21 knots (24 miles per hour), able to accommodate 365 passengers, with a crew of 276. Though of course not mentioned in the brochures, two aspects of the *Mariposa*'s increasing obsolescence were clouding her future.

Modern freighters, tankers, container ships, and passenger vessels have bow thrusters which come into play during docking and while maneuvering at slow speeds in close quarters. They are controlled from the bridge and can push the bow of the vessel to the left or the right, as needed. Their use, in conjunction with twin screws, eliminates much of the need for assistance by harbor tugs. Tugs are very expensive and become more expensive with each passing year. The *Mariposa* needed them badly at all ports. At dead slow speeds, the torque made it almost impossible to turn her to starboard in a flat calm.

The second major handicap served to restrict her ports of call rather than increase the expense of operation. Unlike contemporary passenger vessels, she had no sewage holding tanks and was thus barred from an increasing number of harbors around the world, such as Tokyo. And where she was permitted to enter, the habit was to assign her to a berth out in the boondocks, an inconvenience for all aboard.

The confusions of sailing are compounded by the fact that many of the passengers on any cruise are boarding a ship for the first time. They have no idea where anything is. They clot around the "you-are-here" maps, trying to figure out which way to their cabin, which way to the purser's desk, which way to the bow. They are made helpless by anxiety. Where do I sit in the dining room? What sitting am I on? Which is my room steward? Should I unpack now? Where's my big red suitcase, Martha?

But there are always the ones who have been there before. We had sailed three times aboard the twin ship, the *Monterey*, and so the internal geography was completely familiar. We knew what to do to get settled in, and the best times to do it. Long ago Matson founded a passenger group called the Mariners, awarding repeat passengers certificates of rank and little pins based on their miles at sea, with presentation ceremonies during every voyage. We were among those so anointed and found ourselves among many old friends, both passengers and staff.

During the first day at sea I happened to pass a man who had been pointed out to me as the captain, talking to an elderly lady. He was a slight man of middle height, dark-haired and balding, with an engaging grin and a showman's voice.

I heard him say, "Ma'am, if you are looking for the pointy end of the ship, it's up that way."

It wasn't sarcasm. He said it with fond good humor. An immediately likable man. I told Dorothy about it, and because he was such a change from the tall austere Captain Caldwell with whom we had sailed before, I wondered how he had become the captain of a cruise ship.

In 1941, just before the war started, everybody my age knew they were going to have to go into something. My good friend and I were checking into all kinds of programs in the Navy and the Army and the Air Force. One day I saw an ad in the newspaper that showed a fellow steering a ship. He had on sort of a yacht uniform, with his necktie blowing in the breeze, and it said, JOIN THE MARITIME SERVICE. *I had never heard of that one. I always liked ships, so I went down to investigate. It was a brand new program handled by the Coast Guard. I asked the recruiter for all the facts. He said they were opening up a school in Port Hueneme, California, and the course would be about nine months long.*

I said, "Well, if I signed up now, how soon would I be likely to be called?"

And he said, "Oh, hell, they're just building the school. It'll maybe be close to a year before the thing is really functioning."

I asked where Port Hueneme was, and he said it was down below Santa Barbara. I was living in Portland, Oregon, at the time, in all that cold and rain.

I said, "Gee, that's nice. Will this keep me out of the draft?" When he said it would, I said, "Let's run through this thing one more time. It will probably be more than a year before I'm called, the school is going to be nine months long, and it's down by Santa Barbara. What happens next? How long do I have to enlist for? What happens after I finish the school?"

"Then you are on your own," he said.

After running through it two or three more times, I said, "I'll take it." I signed up and went back and told my best buddy that I had something better than the Navy, Marines, Air Force, or anything. I gave him the pamphlets and brochures. He went down and got the same story and signed up too.

A few months later, along came Pearl Harbor. They short-ened the course from nine months to three, and I was called in the early part of 1942. I went down to Port Hueneme with a group of about thirty, all of us sworn in at the same time. It was a military camp out on a lonely sandspit with a high

*barbed-wire fence around it. They gave us denim pants, tur-
tleneck sweaters, and watch caps and started marching us
around in formation.*

*Two weeks later my good buddy was called up. He was an
only son and his family's pride and joy. He was really spoiled.
When he reported, there were only three or four others that
day, so they sent them down on the train by themselves, and
when they arrived at Oxnard they were picked up by a station
wagon. Our group had been picked up by an old bus. The
station wagon drove into our training camp around noontime.
We were all lined up like a bunch of convicts, waiting to go
to lunch. When he got out of the station wagon he had a
portable radio and a beach umbrella and his golf clubs. He
took one look around at that dreary place and all of us guys
lined up in formation, and he muttered something like "Screw
you" and tried to get back into the station wagon.*

John Kilpack shipped out as a sailor and, with the exception
of a training period at officer's school, served through the war
years and ended up with a second mate's license. He stayed
ashore for about ten years and then went back to sea with
Matson Lines, sailing on freighters, mostly to the Far East,
before moving to Pacific Far East Line. In the early seventies,
PFEL acquired the Matson South Pacific run, taking on a couple
of old freighters and the two remaining passenger ships, the
Monterey and the *Mariposa*. They brought over the major part
of the Matson personnel with the passenger ships because PFEL
had no prior experience in passenger-ship operation. By this
time John Kilpack had been working for PFEL for many years.
The line wanted to work some of their own people into the
passenger-ship operation, but none of the freighter officers were
very enthusiastic about going over onto what were commonly
called the White Ships. On average, at 20,000 tons they were
smaller than freighters and carried a bigger crew. Merchant
Marine pay structure is based on the size of the ship; the big
crew meant less available overtime.

*They asked me a few times to go over, and I declined. Then
I finished a long trip on a freighter and went off on vacation.
When I was due back, a lengthy stevedore strike began and I*

*was out of work. I sat around for several months. The White
Ships kept running; they were not struck, just the freighters.
There were all these guys who came over from Matson, still
working. I remembered what my friend Doug Reid kept telling
me, after he had gone over as chief mate on the* Monterey.
*"Boy, you're missing a real bet. You walk around in a uniform
all day, and you can pick up the phone for cocktails, and it's
really great." I had taken this with a grain of salt, but I finally
went down to the company and said that I'd changed my mind;
I was interested in working on the White Ships. There wasn't
anything open at the moment, so they sent me over to a little
training program as a second mate. I dug out some moth-eaten
old uniforms and bought one set of whites—enough, I thought,
to get along until the strike was over and I could get back onto
a freighter where I belonged.*

*At the time I went over, in 1971, the Matson retreads were
beginning to worry about the security of their jobs and thought
everyone from PFEL was a threat to their livelihoods. When
I was assigned to the* Mariposa *as second mate, I knew I would
be about as popular as a case of smallpox, but it was worse
than I had imagined it would be. Few people would even talk
to me.*

*Unbeknownst to me, one of the other junior mates on the
ship was a practical joker. He was not an old Matson man,
and he was glad to see me come over. He enjoyed baiting the
others. He told them confidentially that in a very short time
I would be taking over the ship. He told them I had a locker
full of expensive new uniforms ready for the occasion. He told
them I had a tape recorder and I was dictating full reports to
the home office on personnel problems aboard.*

*It happened that I was using a tape recorder for my cor-
respondence. I despise writing letters. This helped confirm the
rumors.*

*On that trip, coming back through Hawaii, a man named
Leo Ross boarded with his wife and some friends. He was the
president of PFEL. When I came up out of the stern of the ship
one morning after breakfast and walked across the Pool Terrace, he waved me over and said, "John, what are you doing
here?" I had no idea he was aboard. I said that I was just
marking time until the strike was over. He introduced me to*

everyone and invited me to sit down. As we talked about the steamship business, I looked out of the corner of my eye and saw the steward's-department lined up—whispering, I found out later, about the stool pigeon and the president.

Mr. Ross was a very polite man, and when I got up to leave, he hopped up and shook hands again. The story of how he greeted me by my first name and shook hands twice went all over the ship. When it got back to the junior mate who had started all the rumors, he said, "Of course! That's when Kilpack slipped him the tapes."

At last the strike ended and I received a wire aboard advising me at the end of the trip to proceed to New Orleans to pick up a freighter. The heat was off.

I recall one small satisfaction. Before being second mate on a White Ship, I had been sailing as relief captain and chief mate on freighters for several years. I had not stood a regular bridge watch in some time and hadn't really done any actual navigating. A big heavy old man named J. J. Lard was my junior mate on the watch. There are a lot of little Mickey Mouse things they want done on the White Ships, such as figuring sunrise and sunset for several days ahead so it can go in the ship's newspaper. It takes time to get your feet on the ground if you haven't been navigating regularly. It's something you don't completely forget, but you forget the routine. I fumbled around, and J. J. Lard wasn't a bit of help. He was a perennial old third mate who liked to stand on the bridge and do nothing. That's why he liked the passenger ships.

After I received word of my transfer back to freighters, J. J. Lard, who had watched me struggling for a couple of months, said, "Well, Mr. Kilpack, it has been a real pleasure sailing with you. Hope I have an opportunity to sail again with you sometime. You must be a crackerjack skipper or chief mate, because you sure are a lousy second mate." He felt free to say this because he thought he'd seen the last of me. A year or so later I showed up on that ship again. He was still the junior mate and I was captain.

I went over to the White Ships a second time because the company pressured me into it. One captain had died and another had moved over to Matson freighters, and they had to have somebody in a hurry. They promised me it would be *temporary. But after I got back to the freighters, another emergency came along, and they wanted me as relief captain on the* Mariposa.

I thought it over and told them two days later that I would do it, but I wasn't enthusiastic about it. There wasn't much future in the job, it was less money, and I was really turned off by the protocol, which was a hangover from the old Matson days. I told them that unless they had a training program for Matson captains showing how to get that pained, serious look on the face and keep it there all day, I was going to do the whole thing my way. They agreed. By then I had served under three Matson captains, each one rigid and stuffy in his own special way, each acting as if he had the power of life and death over everyone under him.

This seemed ridiculous to me. I was used to big freighters that are operated with just three people on the bridge, you and the man on the wheel and one more mate. On a White Ship, you've got quartermasters and mates—three mates altogether—up on the bridge, running back and forth, to handle a ship smaller than the ones I'd been running.

Actually, in the old Matson days the captains did have a kind of life-and-death power over all those under them, and so did the old-line chief mates. They had the power to fire and the power to turn in bad reports. Either event could ruin your career. Those days were over, but the captains were not willing to admit it.

I got off on the wrong foot with Captain X. He was a pompous fellow who seemed to think he was commanding the Queen Mary. The first morning with him, when we were just getting under way, I looked out from the bridge toward the forecastle and said, "It sure is nice to be back on a small ship again," and he spun around and snarled at me. It was the beginning of a strained relationship.

I made it a point to try to get along with him, but it was difficult. The captain liked to go on inspection of the ship, and he marched us around belowdecks almost every day. In navy fashion, he wore his hat. I could never figure out why he wanted to wear a hat inside the ship. That meant we all had to wear hats in our little parade. He went first, and I walked behind him, carrying the flashlight, and behind me was the chief steward, and behind him another man from the steward's department, depending on which department of the ship we were inspecting.

I could never take it seriously, this business of looking around for little spots of dust. Sometimes, as I followed along, I would pull my hat down over my eyes and turn on the flashlight. I don't think he ever figured out why the passengers were always laughing at the inspection tours.

Part of the routine was to inspect an empty stateroom. Empty staterooms had to be ready for inspection, with each drawer pulled out to a measured distance, the bunk cracked open, the toilet paper folded back just so, the closet doors open. He had to find something wrong. He always could, because there is no such thing as a perfect room. He'd find some flaw in maintenance or housekeeping. One day we went into a room and he looked around and everything seemed to be in order until he bent down and picked a little object up off the floor, held it in the palm of his hand, and peered at it. He did not have very good close-up vision. He turned to me and demanded, "What's this?"

I bent and looked at it and said, "Gee, I don't know. It looks like somebody's toenail to me." Whereupon he flipped it up in the air and we got the hell out of there.

I don't remember how much time I put in with Captain X, but with every passing day I found myself less able to take the pompous routine seriously. During all port arrivals and departures, he wanted to be out on the wing of the bridge where everybody could see him and know who he was, and he wanted me standing behind him. So when I stood there I always did little things to break the monotony. Finally it got so the crew would come out and watch us to see what I would come up with next, whether I would blow up little balloons and release them, to go fizzling away, or just run my zipper up and down.

Before I finally agreed to go over to the passenger ships as captain, I had a long talk with Gregory Price, one of the vice presidents of the line. He was a very hard-working individual, always trying to maintain the schedules and services. The job was a constant strain. I said again that I could not conform to the rules and traditions they seemed to expect from a master.

Price said, *"You'll be fine. The passengers like you. We know that. We know you'll do a great job."*

"Okay, I'll take it," I said. *"But I'm going to make a few changes around here, and I'm going to do it my way."*

"That's okay, John. As long as everybody is happy. That's the main thing."

So I assumed command of the *Mariposa*. And whenever I had that vice president to call I'd try to add some small detail to shake him up, things like, *"Which deck should I set aside for nude sunbathing?"*

"Jesus!" he'd say. *"What are you trying to do to me?"*

During the old Matson regime the schedule was of top importance, and rightly so. They wanted the ships to arrive on time and leave on time. I questioned the practice of very early morning arrivals. They caused a lot of overtime. I was told they had always arrived at that early hour and would keep right on. So, though I was shot down, I said not to yell at me about the overtime we ran up.

On my first trip to Alaska, the schedule called for one of those early dockings. We went up the coast and picked up a pilot early in the morning at Victoria. At Vancouver, we dropped him and picked up two others to take us as far as Prince Rupert Island. Then I was to proceed to Ketchikan.

I studied the schedule: After I dropped the pilots at three in the afternoon, I was not due in Ketchikan until noon the next day. It was a run of only a few hours. How was I going to use up all that time?

Most of those little towns on the Alaska cruises have facilities for only one ship at a time and there were a lot of ships running, so the schedules were planned months in advance, so that two or more cruise ships would not try to hit the same port on the same day.

I called the agent in Ketchikan to confirm my berthing and said I had all this time to kill, and could I come in earlier? She said, *"Why not? There's no problem. The berth's empty."* I said I would get there early in the morning. It stays light almost all night during the cruise months up there. I went up slowly and was all tied up by 7A.M., and everybody went ashore. The woman went from the ship back to her office in the agency and received a phone call from my vice president. He was firming up last-minute details for the arrival of the ship and telling her all the things to watch out for and take care of—the gangway and the shuttle bus and do this and do that. She kept saying, "Mr. Price...Mr. Price...Mr. Price..." trying to break in. Finally he paused for breath and she said, "Mr. Price, I'm trying to tell you, the ship is already here, it's been here since seven o'clock."

And Gregory Price said, "Jesus Christ! Tell the captain to call me."

"I hear you got there kinda early," he said when I did call him.

"Yeah, Mr. Price. There was nothing to do. We'd have just had to kill time. The water is too deep to anchor and the berth was empty, so here I am."

"Well, try to keep to the schedule!"

"Hey, this is just a cruise. People aren't embarking or disembarking here, so what the hell's the difference?"

"The difference is we want you should keep to the schedule. Understand?"

On the following trip the same thing occurred. Only this time I called the agent earlier and asked her, after she told me the berth was empty, if it was okay if I speeded up and got there by nine at night, seeing as how it didn't get dark until eleven. She said it was up to me, and if I wanted, she would call the local saloon where they had a floor show and ask them if they would like to put on a late show for the passengers.

It was the first time one of the ships had stayed overnight in Alaska, and everybody had a ball. I phoned Gregory Price the next day, and when he found out I had arrived a whole day early, all I could hear on the line was a sort of panting sound. When he recovered he said, "Kilpack, I know what you're doing, but for the love of God, please stick to the schedule!"

We continued our trip and went up into Glacier Bay and came back down and arrived at Sitka, where the agent told me that the vice president wanted me to phone him as soon as we were tied up. There is an option of several ports in Alaska, and you can't make them all because of the coordination with other cruise lines, the length of the voyage, and other factors. One such port, Skagway, was not on our schedule that trip.

I went to one of the waitresses—she was very smart and

quick-witted—and asked her to pretend to be a long-distance operator.

  · *She got on the phone and said that she had a collect call, person-to-person, to Mr. Gregory Price from the master of the* Mariposa *in Skagway and would he accept the charges. She did a great job. Then she handed me the phone and I said,* "Hi, Mr. Price."

  "Skagway!" *he yelled.* "Good God! What are you doing in Skagway?"

  "Well, I went by Sitka and took a look at the place, and the crew told me it was a real bummer, no action at all, so I said to myself, What the hell, and I came on down here to Skagway."

  He made a lot of animal noises, and it took a long time to convince him that we really were in Sitka. He used to dread my phone calls, but he admitted that, yes, it was a change from the old Matson Line captains.

  When this long cruise to the North Cape and Russia was in the planning stages, I tried to avoid being assigned to it. I don't particularly like long cruises, especially to places where I've never been. I like to sail to ports I know. It's like driving home.

  I complained to Gregory Price various times, but he was optimistic and very confident. "Hell, you won't have any problems. Nothing can go wrong. I've researched everything. It's all in this big book."

  And he would pat the big book and tell me it held all the details about every port: the situation for docking, and pilots, and agents, and medical help—everything I might possibly encounter.

  "You won't have any problems at all. Nothing can go wrong. Just take this book along and read through it. It covers every question you might have: all the time changes, the routes, the distances, fuel consumption, where you can take on more fuel, and how you take it on. Everything is right in here."

  So finally I came to believe in the magic book, and there I was, out in the Pacific, heading south, telling some nice little old lady how to tell the front end of the ship from the back end. The front end is pointy.

2

||||||||||||||||||||||||||||||||||||||||||||||

San Francisco to Los Angeles and San Diego

The short hop down from San Francisco to Los Angeles was
a predictable confusion. Those of us who joined the ship at San
Francisco were, for the most part, taking all or a major portion
of the North Cape cruise. Still aboard were lots of people
ending up a Pacific cruise. We found some old friends aboard
and were disappointed to find out they were leaving the ship
at Los Angeles.

The passage down to Los Angeles was smoother than most
train rides. We were settled in and slept well. Up early in the
morning because a good friend was due to come aboard for a
visit. She was on the dock at eight, but because Customs and
Immigration took their own sweet time about clearing the ship,
all we could do was wave at her from time to time until they
let her come aboard at eleven.

*If Immigration stood at the gangway and checked everybody
on and off the ship to make certain that nobody was a stowaway
or was smuggled in, they would be performing a useful service.
But to come aboard and make a big important show of checking
the passports of all the passengers, which have already been
checked by the purser's staff, and of checking the crew's papers—this is time-wasting, bureaucratic nonsense.*

13

Take a freighter, for example, with a crew of forty. They are all signed on by the Coast Guard when we sail, and there's no crew change, and the same forty guys come back. Then an Immigration officer has to come down, with a great huge book he can hardly lift. For every name, he has to go through his big book and look it up and see if he can find it in there. Suppose you have a cook named Wong. There are thousands of Wongs in the big book, and maybe fifteen Arthur Wongs, so the bureaucrat looks sternly at our Arthur Wong, who can't possibly be over thirty-five years old, and says, "Did you jump ship in New Orleans in 1922?"

Once this ridiculous routine is finished, the ship is pronounced cleared and from then on there is no control of who comes and goes. It makes jobs for a few thousand people, I guess, and irritates all the rest of us.

But compared to Customs, Immigration almost makes sense. I have been dealing with U.S. Customs for years, and all I can do is shake my head. They are absolutely unbelievable. They go through their fantastic production, trying to use their creepy regulations to shake down U.S. citizens for about one tenth of what it costs to run the U.S. Customs Service, while two docks over, thousands of tons of Toyotas, Datsuns, and Sony televisions sets are being off-loaded at about 10-percent duty. Go abroad and buy a few knickknacks and come home and face the Spanish Inquisition. Everybody knows that billions' worth of hard drugs and marijuana come in every year, while the U.S. Customs is bugging tourists with knickknacks.

Suppose a cruise ship comes into Hawaii on a weekend. Any place on a weekend is very bad because the steamship company has to pay for the Customs people to come down and service the ship. (If you can arrive between nine and five on a weekday, the government furnishes the inspection, but if you can't manage that and come in on a weekend or after five, you are privileged to pay double time to be harassed.)

If another ship happens to come in at the same time and they have to go over and work the other ship as well, then their charges—a full day's overtime for any part of a day—are prorated between the two ships. One full day of overtime equals two days of regular pay. In Hawaii they usually get lucky and have just one ship to service.

Many times I have brought cruise ships back from a South Pacific cruise. There is nothing you can buy in Australia or New Zealand that can't be bought cheaper in San Francisco. In Fiji you can buy some crude wood carvings, grass skirts, bead necklaces, shell jewelry, and so on; Tonga and Tahiti likewise. All the passengers buy knickknacks, and if you come in on a weekend, the U.S. Customs people who come down act as if they are being put upon by being asked to draw two days' pay for two hours of work. So they check all these chick-enshit purchases item by item, going through all the luggage. I have seen people with flights to make lined up at the Aloha Tower like convicts, waiting for hours for some boob to say with a lot of cynical hilarity, "Well, open up everything. I want to see all *the loot."*

We had a man named Nichols aboard who taught lost wax casting to the passengers, so they could make little doodads to hang around their necks. He also made jewelry during the cruise which he would sell to the passengers, welding and brazing and casting and so on.

On this South Pacific cruise there was a very quiet, conservative couple who wanted to do everything in a law-abiding way. Before they left the States the husband had taken his wife's jewelry down and had it inspected by Customs, who gave him a receipt attesting to that fact, so they would have no trouble coming back through customs.

During the trip he decided he wanted to have Nichols make a ring for his wife. Nick drew a sketch and the couple liked it, but Nick didn't have time to do the ring during the voyage. So it was agreed that Nick would make it later and deliver it to them. They lived in the Los Angeles area. The price was $250, and the man paid Nick in advance, and got a receipt.

We arrived in Hawaii on a Sunday, and all the passengers streamed off the ship. An hour or so later, when I walked out to see somebody in the parking area, most of the passengers were still lined up at Customs. The Customs agents like to pretend that they hate to have to do this weekend work, and they hate being assigned to a hellhole like Hawaii, and they are nearly always brusque and nasty to the passengers.

As I walked by I could see that there was a hassle going

on between a Customs officer and the conservative couple.
Somebody said, "There's the captain over there. Ask him."

They waved me over and I said, "What's the problem?" I
had changed to a sport shirt and slacks.

"Are you the captain?" the Customs guy asked.

"Well, I am unless you know something I don't know. What's
the problem?"

He showed me Nick's business card and said, "Do you
know this guy?"

"Yes."

"Is he legitimate?"

"To the best of my knowledge, his parents are married."

His face got redder. "Is he one of your crew?"

"Not exactly."

"Well, what the hell is he?"

"He is what we call a guest art instructor. We don't pay
him anything at all. He gets his food and his room, and he's
entitled to sell his wares to the passengers."

"Well, these people have a two-hundred-and-fifty-dollar
ring from Nichols, and I demand to see it!"

The Customs officer had picked out this couple to hassle.
They looked like money, and they looked nervous: perfect tar-
gets. He had been all set to make a score on the wife's jewelry
and the husband's camera equipment, until they produced the
receipt from Customs predating the sailing date of the cruise.
So he had demanded the woman's purse and gone through it.
They have that right. They have the right to have her taken
away to a private room to be stripped and body-searched by
matrons of the service if they so choose.

In the purse he found the receipt for the ring and Nick's
business card. The man had tried to explain about the ring,
but the Customs officer had said, "What do you take me for?
Nobody pays for a ring that isn't made yet. You've got that
ring and I want to see it, and I want to see it right now. Do
you understand me?"

So I said, "I still don't see what the problem is. What if
they did have the ring? It would have been made aboard ship
by Nichols out of materials he bought in San Francisco and
brought aboard. He carries gold stock and silver stock, wire
and little plates and so on, and he bends and melts and makes

things aboard an American ship and sells them to American tourists."

But by then the Customs man couldn't let go of it. He called his office on the pier and went down and looked it up in the big book and came back with the ruling that even if an object is made of American materials on an American ship, it is done on the high seas and so it is susceptible to duty, and he wanted to see Nichols. This ruling meant, of course, that the doodads the passengers had bought and made for themselves were also subject to duty, and the people should have declared all these things.

They found Nick and took him to the Customs Office there, to the boss man. Nichols was big and strong and had a short fuse. A lot of yelling went on. He said he had been doing this work for years and had never heard of such a stupid damn thing. But the Customs people were stern and nasty and triumphant. They had just broken the Brink's case. They had uncovered a veritable nest of smugglers.

Of course, the pleasant conservative couple—the wife redeyed from tears of anger and frustration—missed their plane, and Nichols had to go up to the main Customs Office in San Francisco to get a reasonable reinterpretation of the ruling.

Dorothy and I have come back into the country at many places and encountered many varieties of behavior in Customs lines. Each port and airport seems to be a fiefdom, where the behavior is a product of the quality of leadership of the Customs Agent in Charge. Arrogance, indifference, insolence, and contempt flourish at some stations, while at others there seems to be an attempt to help the returning citizens make the best of a clumsy situation.

The worst we know of is Miami International Airport. Coming back through Miami is a degrading and exhausting experience. Politicians and officials are hustled through and never get a chance to see how wretchedly the incoming people are treated. As the carousels pile luggage into the stifling room, long lines of people shuffle toward the inspection stations, pushing all their luggage along on the dirty tiles, sometimes for up to five hours.

Miami is the gateway to the United States for much of Latin

America and all the Caribbean Islands. By the time foreign nationals reach Customs, they have been cleared through Immigration. In Customs, foreign nationals, unless of middle years and fashionably dressed, are considered guilty until a search proves them innocent. Bored inspectors make them dump all the contents of suitcases on the counter and unwrap every gift being brought in, and then they exhort the visitors to "hurry up, hurry up, get that stuff packed and move along."

U.S. Customs has built up over their years in the Miami International Airport a heritage of hate and resentment that no amount of official Good Neighbor acts in other dimensions can hope to outweigh. It is in Miami that the most obvious discrimination against the poor and the dark-skinned persists.

Customs inspectors are border guards, secure in their authority and their seniority and their immunity from any kind of discipline which might arise as the result of a citizen's complaint. In any confrontation, they have the ultimate weapon, that big book of rules. Their goals are the proliferation of paperwork and the avoidance of any decision which might get them into trouble. At their very best, their beefy jocularity is patronizing, like a prison guard who tries to be a nice guy.

More friends and familiar faces joined the cruise at Los Angeles: Dick and Anne Lund, Addison and Ruth Moore, the Frank Hursts, all settling back into the routine of the ship, prowling, looking for old friends among passengers and staff, partying, unpacking, checking dining room reservations.

We sailed shortly after one in the afternoon for the slow seven-hour run down to San Diego.

I never did figure out why we stopped at San Diego for a few hours at night. Vice President Price and some of the office people had driven down to Los Angeles to take care of some last-minute details. I looked at the schedule of the previous European cruise and discovered they had stopped at Acapulco. This breaks up the long haul down to Panama.

I said, "Gee, May third to May tenth is a long time. Even when we make a four-and-a-half-day run, the natives get restless. What are they going to be like after a week aboard with no break?"

"Oh, you won't have any problems," they said.

"I've been looking the schedule over, and I think we could work in a stop at Acapulco."

"Goddamn it," the boss said, "the trip has hardly started, and here you go again! Listen. We spent months making up that itinerary and working everything out. I want you to arrive when it says and leave when it says. Please don't start screwing around with the schedule!"

"Okay, okay! San Diego to Panama. Six and a half days. Okay. But I'll get back to you later. I've got some great ideas for some little side trips we can take farther along."

The Vice President walked away, waving his arms.

3

||||||||||||||||||||||||||||||||||||||||||||||||||

San Diego to Panama

The *Mariposa* sailed through warm seas, bright sun, a gleaming of blue water, down the coast of Baja California, a tan and brown escarpment on the distant eastern horizon. And the people moved about, looking around, conjecturing, making tentative alliances.

Passengers on cruises sort themselves out into groups and subgroups with a speed and precision worth sociological investigation. On short cruises careful discrimination is not important. Should you become stuck with someone who becomes more boring with each passing day, you will soon be rid of him. But on the long cruise, where the age of the passengers is directly proportional to the length of the voyage, the wary passenger will spend from ten days to two weeks in careful survey of those around him, being adequately cordial, of course, reasonably polite, but not invitingly warm and open.

As soon as the folding metal screen is rolled up out of the way, one group called the Booze People heads for the bar, smiling winningly at the bartenders. There they find joy, and there they will stay.

We had a little old judge from Texas on one of those forty-two-day South Pacific cruises. He had been a general during

World War II, and we didn't know whether to call him Judge or General. As soon as he boarded the ship he found his way to the bar and took over the end stool, where he proceeded to hold court and tell stories, either about courtroom trials or World War II.

When the bar opened he would duck under the grating as it was rolled up, take his usual seat, and order his usual drink. Once someone like this judge nails down a seat, nobody else is welcome to sit there; the bartender protects it. The judge would stay until they closed the bar at night and then wobble off to his room. At one point the seas got rough enough to warrant taking the stools away from the bar. This is a usual precaution. But he wouldn't let them take his. On one roll of the ship he fell off and cut his head. They wanted to take him to the doctor, but no way. He wasn't giving up. The nurse came up and slapped a bandage on him, and they put him back on his stool and he was fine.

The old boy never left the ship. He saw Tahiti and he saw New Zealand and he saw Australia through the back window of the bar. When people came back aboard from shore excursions, he would agree with them that whatever country we were in was a fine place and he was mighty happy to be there.

When we finally got back to Hawaii on the way home, he decided to look up an old crony of his who had been in command of a submarine during World War II. He got down as far as the lobby. As I walked by he said, "Hey, young man, can you help me here a minute?"

"What can I do for you, General?"

"Don't call me General. I am a judge."

"Okay, Judge. What can I do for you?"

"I want to find out what submarines are in town. An old friend of mine is skipper of one of those things."

He was looking at the bewildering pages of navy numbers in the Honolulu phone book. I looked at the listings. "Why don't you try the operations office?"

"No, I don't want to fool around with that. Can you find a number there for the admiral in charge of the whole thing?"

I found the number for him and he called it, and when

somebody answered he said, "This here is General So-and-So, and I want to know all the submarines you have in town today."

Apparently they hung up on him. He muttered something about the goddamn Navy and went back to the bar. That was as close as he got to seeing Hawaii.

Finally, when the trip was over he packed up, shook hands with everybody, and staggered down the gangway, saying it had been a mighty fine trip he had made and he wanted to come back and do it again. He said travel really broadens the mind. And that is the last we saw of him.

The *Mariposa* was admirably designed to enable passengers to spin off into groups of kindred interests. When you boarded at the Main Deck lobby, starboard side, the purser's office was immediately at your right, the foyer or lobby straight ahead, chief steward's office on the far side. The dining room was at your left, and through the open doors you could see into the "Pit," the sunken center portion, three steps down from the rest of the dining room, with its six banquettes along the side, two tables for four, two tables for six, and the captain's table for nine at the far end of the Pit, the captain's chair facing the double doors, and behind it a long polished cupboard area, a mural, and, as often as possible, fresh cut flowers.

Forward of the foyer on the Main Deck, corridors led to twenty outside staterooms and nineteen inside staterooms, as well as to the doctor's office, beauty shop, barber, photo lab, and ship's shop. The outside staterooms on the Main Deck were, apart from the suites and deluxe bedrooms, the most desirable because overhead were the staterooms of the Upper Deck. Thus there were no overhead morning joggers, no free-striding walk freaks in combat boots, no resounding clang, thump, and crash or work details at nap time. The wise passenger always checks the plans of the ship's deck areas to see what will be overhead. We were in an outside cabin near the shop. The lower decks amidships have demonstrably less roll-and-pitch movement than the highest decks and the forward accommodations.

The Upper Deck was all cabins, forty-two outside rooms, forty-eight inside rooms, and four deluxe bedrooms.

The Promenade Deck, counting from the stern forward, contained: open deck space, then the Outrigger Bar, then the Polynesian Club (dancing and entertainment), next a foyer with elevator and stairs; next, on the port side, a "gallery," usually the focal point for handicrafts, costume making, money changing (in port); on the starboard side, the cardroom, both rooms opening into the Southern Cross Lounge (lectures, concerts, teas, and church services). After that the forward foyer and then the high-rent district: two lanai suites, two deluxe bedrooms, eight outside rooms, six inside rooms. Unfortunately for the walker, the weather-deck areas of the Promenade Deck stopped at the forward foyer, so if one wanted to make a complete circuit, one had to wrestle open the heavy doors and go through the foyer and back out to the deck. This did, however, guard the privacy of the high-rent district, as no pedestrian could peer through the portholes at luxury.

When the ship is at sea at night, the wheelhouse is in total darkness except for the very dim lights on the dials of the controls. This provides good forward vision. You can pick up lights on other ships and shore lights. It is not like driving a car. You have no headlights facing forward, and when your eyes have adjusted to darkness, a small distant light will show up well.

So we must have all the thick draperies drawn across the stateroom portholes in the forward part of the vessel. The lights shining out along the side do not bother you on the bridge. But even the side lights forward and the running lights are shielded so they do not affect night vision. At dusk the room stewards who have the passenger rooms up forward on the Upper Deck and the Promenade Deck, below the bridge, always close the draperies. If this is not done as soon as it gets dark, you can see the lights shining out from the rooms, reflecting against the white mast. Sometimes the room steward will miss one. Sometimes the passengers come back and open the drapes. Then we have to send word down from the bridge to correct the situation.

Sometimes I forget, especially when I've had guests in my quarters on the Boat Deck forward, and I do not realize it has gotten dark so quickly. They have to call down and ask me to pull my drapes. This is embarrassing, because I know better.

On one particular trip a woman had one of the forward rooms on the Promenade Deck. They are a little larger and more expensive than the others. She was in one that had a dressing-room area. The first night we were out at sea, she came back from dinner and opened the draperies. We sent a steward down to ask her to close them again.

She said, "I'm not pulling the drapes. I want them open."

"Ma'am, it bothers them up on the navigation bridge."

"I don't care about that. This is my room and I'm not pulling the drapes."

He relayed this to the bridge, and one of the junior mates was sent down. She said, "I'm not pulling any drapes. I told the other person. This is my room, and I want the drapes open."

"Madam, it's pitch black out there. You can't see anything anyway."

"That's my business, isn't it?"

He went back to the bridge and called the chief mate, who called me, and I called the purser to get some background on this passenger. Then I went to her room and talked to her. She didn't seem very tightly wrapped. She was some sort of psychologist or psychiatrist. She told me one of the reasons she had taken the outside room was so she could look up at the tropical stars.

I showed her that it would be pretty difficult to see many stars out of a porthole and told her it would be better to look at them from the open deck.

"I paid for this room and it is an expensive room and I want to look at the stars at night from my room and that is what I am going to do."

I gave her a lecture on the safety of the ship. Nothing. I offered to have her moved to a room on the side of the ship. No way. I asked her to come to the bridge so I could show her what the problem was. She wouldn't think of it.

I knew what we were going to have to do, if I couldn't reach her. We were going to have to rig something out of plywood and canvas and drop it over her window at night, and I did not care to get into that hassle.

Finally, exasperated, I said, "With these room lights on, the bridge can't see to navigate, and you can't see the stars if you look out."

She looked surprised and said, "Oh, I don't have to have any lights on! I just want to be able to look at the stars."

That became the deal. She could keep one little dim light on over the bed. She could watch the stars and we could navigate. We became fairly good friends. During the last few days of the trip she wanted to know if she could come back aboard as a guest lecturer and give psychology lessons, but I didn't really push for that program.

The next deck up was the Boat Deck, with the swimming pool and sunbathing area aft of what was called the Pool Terrace. This was a roofed area, open across the aft portion but with canvas flaps which could be lashed across the opening in bad weather. It was filled with rough tables and chairs, a long food-service table along the port side and a bar in the starboard forward corner. Here was the early buffet breakfast, with pecan rolls if you were early enough. Here was coffee and bouillon and sherbet and conversation among the unaffiliated—the non-bridge players, non-lesson takers, those who skipped the lectures, the demonstrations, the dance classes. Here was free beer before a buffet lunch, and off-duty entertainers and ship's staff, and the suntan crowd. And private cocktail parties in the evening.

Just forward of the Pool Terrace on the port side were the nine single cabins known to the staff as Swinging Singles, or Maiden Lane.

Prices for the entire cruise, California to California, ranged from $18,114 per person in the Lanai Suites to $5,150 in an inside four-berth room. This was 1977. The price included the same menu, the same service, the same freebies, regardless of where you were living aboard. A conditional democracy at work.

Quite a few years ago *The New Yorker* magazine carried an article about a little old lady who made her home aboard the *Ile de France*. Her stateroom was her home, cluttered with her prized possessions. She was allowed to keep her little dog with her. Whenever the ship was scheduled into dry dock for maintenance and repairs, the shipping company would move her into a convenient luxury hotel and move her back aboard for the next sailing.

For a trust-funded old lady, there could be no better life. Gourmet food, personal services on request, luxurious quarters, afternoon and evening entertainment, free movies, live-in medical care, parties every day, exotic shopping, and the best climate the shipping line can find.

One woman who spent a lot of time on the ships, and lived on Maiden Lane, sat near us in the dining room: a Mrs. Crouse from Akron. She was a small woman with thick glasses, prominent teeth, and a shaggy gray haircut. She looked like a friendly elf. Cruises attract champion shoppers, and Mrs. Crouse proved herself to be one of the all-time greats. She used to spend so much time in the gift shop aboard, they had a special stool there for her. She bought items every day. She had one naughty habit. She would sit on her stool and listen to some woman trying to make up her mind whether or not to buy a dress, blouse, skirt, or whatever. If the woman said she would think about it and come back later, Mrs. Crouse would hop off her stool, buy the item, regardless of size, and carry it off to her cabin. At the end of any long cruise it was said she had items in enough styles and sizes to start a shop of her own.

Though she was a small woman, and seemed at times to totter, she was a durable walker and shopper and could carry an impressive number of shopping bags and parcels around the downtown areas of Hamburg, Oslo, Helsinki, Edinburgh and San Juan studying every window display.

She had a quiet, reflective dignity about her. She said she always had the same table, a banquette against the forward wall, port side. She preferred eating alone. Breakfast was an open sitting because so many people went up to the Pool Terrace to eat. Sometimes when Mrs. Crouse came in she would find the woman from the first sitting at her private table—a spindly, jittery little person who seemed to live on papaya and yogurt. Rather than sit elsewhere, Mrs. Crouse would go back out into the foyer and sit in quiet steaming indignation in a wicker armchair until her table was available.

She finally began to talk to us. She had an odd, slow, gritty little voice. She said one day, "You know, when I came to get aboard this ship in San Francisco, the airplane stopped in Los Angeles, and without thinking, I got off. I didn't want to tell my friends about it because they would think I was senile. I went to the desk and arranged to have my things taken to the ship and I stayed up in the airport all night long, and I took a taxi to the dock and got on at Los Angeles."

Another time she told us that she was an only child, the daughter of a railway executive. She said that she had been premature, born unexpectedly and suddenly, judged too small to make it, but had been put in cotton in a shoe box on the back of the stove.

"And I lived," she said solemnly.

Another time she said she had been engaged to a man for nineteen years.

"Nineteen years!" we said:

"Oh, yes. Mama and Papa didn't approve of him. I lived at home. After they died, I married that man and he died a year later."

"My God! How tragic!"

"Not really. I really didn't care very much for him."

There were frequent discussions among the other passengers as to where Mrs. Crouse could find room in her small cabin for all her purchases. Her room steward would admit that it was possible for him to get in there and make the bed, but that's all he would say. From time to time he would take cardboard boxes and twine to her and then stow the packages she packed belowdecks.

She was a dandy little person, a true eccentric—the kind who considers herself to be just like other people, but isn't. We saw her lose a little bit of dignity only once. She came to dinner one night with her short gray hair in disarray and confessed to young Sandy, her favorite waitress, that she had tried to tidy her cabin and lost her hairbrush in the process.

Near the end of the trip, when everybody was feeling sad and nostalgic about it soon being over, she said to Sandy, "I hate to leave. I hate to go back home."

Sandy said, "Why don't you just stay on, Mrs. Crouse?"

"Well, I have to go back to Akron and get some more

money. But I'll see all you people in November, when we go to Alaska."

"But Mrs. Crouse," Sandy said. "We don't go to Alaska in November. We're going to the South Pacific."

"That's nice. I'll go there, then."

4

||||||||||||||||||||||||||||||||||||||||||||

San Diego to Panama

The slow pace of ocean travel eliminates that sense of diso-
rientation associated with jet lag. When time is changed in
thirty-minute chunks, the transition should be imperceptible.

But in the transit from west to east, toward the oncoming
sun, as clocks march forward, a half hour at a time, stomachs
march to a different drummer. People come to meals later and
later. Many miss the word, no matter how prominently it is
posted. Some take it as a personal affront.

*I had a couple aboard one time named Roger and Norma
Brennan. It was fairly obvious that Norma had the money.
Roger was a nice, dapper, good-looking guy, who catered to
Norma's every whim. Norma was a chronic complainer. Every
time she would start yammering about some part of the cruise
she didn't like, Roger would pat her arm and tell her that
everything was going to work out just fine.*

*We were heading out on a South Pacific trip, changing the
clocks every night, and Norma couldn't get used to this. She'd
show up everywhere an hour early, forgetting to change her
watch at night and bitching to me about it every time she saw
me. She'd say she felt like an idiot peering into the dining room*

for breakfast at seven when they didn't open up until eight fifteen. Roger would stroke her arm and get her settled down.

Finally, heading toward New Zealand, we crossed the International Date Line and lost Tuesday. She got all upset. She thought it was some kind of a conspiracy. "What happened to Tuesday?" she kept asking. I tried to explain to her that it was all going to work out fine.

Pretty soon we started back, changing the clocks the other way, and Norma started missing breakfast every morning. When she missed her art class she was more upset than ever before. Roger kept saying to her, "Honey, don't you worry your little head about a single thing."

So we had two Thursdays. She came to me and said. "What's with two Thurdsays? Why didn't we get that Tuesday back?"

"Are you hung up on Tuesday or something? You're getting two Thursdays. What's the difference?"

She was one of those single-minded people who brood about something they cannot understand. And she was getting more and more troubled, so one day I sat down with her and, using an orange to represent the earth, gave her a half-hour dissertation on time and showed why the Greenwich Meridian is in London because the other side of it comes through the middle of the Pacific where it doesn't bother anyone. She did not buy this at all. She said it was an absolutely terrible inconvenience, and why did I have to screw around with the clocks all the time?

Finally, the day before we got back to San Francisco, we made our final time change, and when I saw her I said, "Okay, Norma. No more time changes. We're back on California time."

She stared at me and said, "Captain, this whole thing is ridiculous. Going out you changed the clocks one way and I was early for everything and you skipped Tuesday, and coming back you changed the clocks the other way and I missed everything and we had two Thursdays, and now you're telling me the whole thing comes out even? You did the whole damn thing for nothing! You could have left it alone. You didn't have to change a thing. You sailor people must be crazy."

"Norma," I said, "I swear. I'll never change the clocks again."

* * *

So here was the *Hotel Mariposa* cutting her way down through the shining sea, with some creaking, sighing, rattling, some areas of vibration. She was a hotel with over three million miles of travel in her old steel bones. A day warm in the sun, cool in shadow. Walkers walking, drinkers drinking, the lonely looking cautiously for new friends, none of them particularly aware of the dynamics of propulsion, the refinements of navigation.

The basic strength of the *Mariposa* was the inner structure of an oblong steel box divided into watertight compartments. This box had to be so strong that the entire weight of the ship could rest on a center point of the box, on the crest of a giant wave, without twisting, bending, collapsing. The skin of the vessel was composed of the welded steel plates of the hull, strengthened by vertical ribs, a few feet apart, called frames. These were strengthened by horizontal ribs called beams when they are near the top of the ship and floors when they are at the bottom. There were two bottoms, the real bottom of the hull welded to the underside of the floor framing, and the false bottom above that, divided into sections and used for storing the Bunker C fuel, drinking water, and water ballast.

The simple propulsion system was a process of preheating the heavy fuel to that thinness which could be squirted into the furnace combustion chamber, where continuously circulating boiler water in the tubes was converted to superheated steam at about 900 degrees Fahrenheit, which was used to turn the high-pressure turbine rotor shaft at thousands of rpm. This energy was converted by heavy and carefully machined reduction gears to the slow rpm's of the propeller astern. Water loss, in the creation of steam and its recondensation into boiler water, was made up by adding desalinated seawater.

This primal energy source was the takeoff point for most other energy use aboard: generators, winches, air conditioning, cold rooms, pumps, hoists, machine tools, and bed lamps.

The ship was a spiderweb nightmare of electric cables and lines, three communication grids, pipes for bath water, toilet water, chilled drinking water, sewage. These were laced behind and through bulkheads throughout all crew quarters areas, passenger cabin areas, common areas, control points. In areas open to the weather, as in the Pool Terrace, lines and pipes led behind bulkheads painted so many times over the years that unused fittings had become unidentifiable white blobs.

Were a ship to sail forever at a constant temperature, quartering into a sea of a constant wave height of X, and a wind strength forever Y, research engineers could then feed to a powerful computer all those factors about longitudinal stress, lateral load, weakening of welds, and potential metal fatigue and get specific answers.

But she had been on the go for twenty-five years, breasted hundred-foot swells in the Tasman Sea, taken astonishing stresses caused by gales, air-pressure differentials, temperature changes. There was no way to predict what might go next. All that was known was that she met all the requirements for seaworthiness set up by the Coast Guard and the Bureau of Ships, had the requisite number of lifeboats and firefighting equipment, adequate pumping facilities, medical facilities—and had passed sanitary inspections with high grades. And it was known, of course, that she did creak and shudder, had spells when she made odd banging and moaning sounds, and, due to the slow degradation of her propulsion equipment, could no longer make her avowed 21 knots for any sustained length of time, especially with one or both of her stabilizers outthrust from the forward hull. Then she couldn't make it at all.

To those loyal Mariners who had sailed aboard her many times, her crankiness and fussiness were endearing. Her crew and staff were old friends. The paintings and decorations belowdecks were of Pacific motif and in exceptionally good taste. Whenever the Mariners had a chance in port to board another cruise ship anchored nearby, a new ship of foreign registry— say, one of the Royal Vikings—they would return to the good old *Mariposa* (or *Monterey*) muttering about Hilton Hotels.

On the evening of the fifth, at the Captain's Champagne Party in the Southern Cross Lounge, it all seemed to come together. Sparkling lighting, dinner jackets, long dresses, jewels, ice sculpture, a long reception line of the ship's officers, with Alan Scott, the cruise director, and Kaui Barrett greeting the passengers first, sorting out the names of those they didn't yet know and passing them along to the captain at the head of the reception line.

* * *

We used to have a lot of fun in those receiving lines. It was a duty thing we had to do, all stand there and go through two of those cocktail parties, one for each sitting, but enough funny things happened from time to time to keep us alert.

When the line was moving so slowly that people would become stalled in front of me, I would, of course, try to make some conversation, such as, "Where are you nice people from?"

I took many trips with Hal Wagner as chief purser. On one North Cape trip he was on as cruise lecturer. We used to call him Daddy Warbucks: a big tall balding man, very big with knife and fork, he was gifted with an absolutely fabulous memory—total recall of faces, names, dates, places. He could lecture entertainingly on thirty or forty different ports without ever using a note, all the way from the ancient history of the place right up to the names of the best shops and their addresses and the best things to buy. The passengers were always very fond of him. He was a proper sort of fellow, considerate and helpful and socially correct at all times.

I remember a time when the cruise director introduced me in the line to quite a frail-looking old lady of at least seventy-five. It was a bit bumpy out. Not too bad, but enough to keep quite a few away from the party. It was the second night out. Later on, the same amount of motion wouldn't have bothered anyone.

We kept little packages of Marezine or Dramamine available for seasick passengers at the purser's desk and at the doctor's office.

Just as I was about to pass this old lady on to the next officer the ship gave a lurch and she seemed to be losing her balance, so I reached out and grabbed her again and said, "Hey, is everything under control?"

She gave me a sweet smile and said, "Oh, yes, thank you. I'm on the pill."

"Well, hang in there, baby," I said, and passed her along.

Another time when the line was moving, I was introduced to a man whose name and face were familiar to me. So I said, "Where are you nice people from?"

"Someplace you never heard of," he said. "Seaside, Oregon."

"Hell, I know it well. You owned the hotel down there. I worked for you once and you fired me."

He looked shocked, and about that time the line started moving again. Later on, on that trip, we had several conversations. He was a nice man. He had owned the hotel in Seaside, a small Oregon beach resort. When I was young my elder sister and her husband lived there, and I used to go down and freeload. At one period of time I actually worked at the hotel, either in the kitchen or as a busboy. I can't remember much about it, even whether I quit or was actually fired.

He had the ship's photographer get a nice picture of us together, and I heard later that he kept it in his desk, and when people came to the office, he would haul it out and say, "Here I am with the captain of the Mariposa. He used to work for me and I fired him."

Sometimes in the reception line you can get an inkling of future trouble aboard. We rarely have any violence on the ship. Once in a while a couple of drunks at the bar will snarl at each other, but that's usually all it amounts to. This story concerns one of the more memorable events of my seagoing career. I always refer to it as the Indian Uprising.

We had started on a nice peaceful trip to the Islands, and when we had the champagne cocktail party, this couple passed through the line. I guessed that they might be from Central America. The wife was extremely heavy-set. I would say she was about 270 or 280 pounds. Both of them wore denim outfits, Levi pants and jackets, to this party on a formal night aboard. She had black greasy braids and was, as I have said, very large. The husband was somewhat smaller, maybe only 240 pounds, with the same denim outfit but short black hair and, as I remember, some sort of tattoo.

They shook hands and went through the receiving line and everybody did a double take. They didn't stay long. From then on I didn't see much of them around the ship, but I heard they were pretty steady customers down at the bar.

A couple of nights later the phone rang after I was in bed. When the phone rings any time after ten o'clock at night, it is *never good news. This time they told me there was a big fra-cas—a big pier-eight brawl—in the bar.*

I put on some clothes and went down there, and this couple was really beating hell out of each other. I mean they were not fooling around. The barstools were tipped over and everybody was standing way back and the two of them were really going at it, using language that would shock a stevedore.

I was not about to get into the middle of that, so I went over to the phone and called the chief steward, who on that trip was Si Lubin, a little bit of a guy who looked like a shrunken version of Henry Kissinger. I told him we had a real Donny-brook at the bar, and to get somebody to come break it up. At this point we usually blame it on the bartenders for letting people get this far gone to begin with.

By the time I got off the phone, the two fighters had left the area. We went after them. They went through the Poly Club and through the lounge and were up in the forward part of the ship, in the alleyway by the big expensive rooms up there, and they were purely beating hell out of each other. You could hear the smacking sounds when the punches landed. And they were using all the words. They were yelling them. "You rotten damned bitch! I'm going to break your ass! Take this, you $%&¢#☆!" And the cash customers were cracking their cabin doors open a little bit and cautiously peering out to see what could possibly be going on.

By now I had my reinforcements! Si Lubin, who was a little bit over four and a half feet tall, and a potbellied mate name of Robin Lindsey, a fairly short fellow, very heavy at the dinner table. He was quite a stomper out on the dance floor. We used to call him the Roadrunner, and sometimes Robin Redbreast. With those two is about a seventy-year-old sailor.

By great good fortune we managed to get the brawlers onto the Mariners' Lounge on the side deck. Out there we tried to break it up. We tried to grab them and hold them apart. Poor little Si got in between them and said, "Now, lady. Now, lady. No fighting."

"Get out of the way, you little son of a bitch," one of them said, "or we'll kill you."

At about that time the husband took a pretty good belt and suddenly had had enough for the time being. He was the smaller of the two anyway. In the process of trying to grab him around the middle, I found out he was not a fella. So I told her to come with me to an empty room, and I put her in there and said, "Now you stay in here and don't leave this room, and we will sort this thing out tomorrow."

I went back to the Mariners' Lounge, where Robin and the sailor were keeping an eye on the big one. She was sitting there, filling up one of the big wicker chairs.

I said, "Your friend is bedded down for the night, so now you go on to your room and we will straighten this out tomorrow."

No. She was not going to budge. She had to see her friend. We argued a little but I could see I was not going to budge her, and there was nothing we could do with all 280 pounds of her, so I said, "Robin, you and the sailor stay here and keep an eye on her. I don't want her back in the public rooms. The bar is closed now, and if you can talk her into going to her room, fine. Otherwise, keep an eye on her and if you need assistance, call the bridge."

I went to bed. About half an hour later, the phone rang and it was Robin. I asked him what the problem was.

"Oh, everything is going fine. I got her some coffee and she seems pretty sober now and she is really a very nice person. She is studying for her master's degree in child psychology. But what she wants is to be reunited with her friend."

"No dice, Robin. Only I know the room where her friend is stashed away. I couldn't lock her in, but I told her to lock the door on the inside and stay in there, and that is it."

"Well, what should I do?"

"You said she is such a nice person, you can just stay there and entertain her and you will be relieved by the watch at four o'clock—unless, of course, you can con her into going back to her room."

About an hour later the phone rang again, and when I answered this time Robin said, "We really got trouble."

"Robin, we have had trouble all night. What the hell have we got now?"

"I finally conned her into going back to her room, and went up and let her in with a passkey, and when she went inside, lo and behold, there was her friend, who had probably sobered up and gone back to her own room, and when the two of them saw each other they went right back at it again, and they are really busting the place up."

I called down and got the chief purser and the doctor, and I called for about five sailors, and we went up there. Those two had one of the big expensive rooms at the front of the ship, the ones that at that time went for three hundred bucks a day. You could hear them all the way down the alleyways, and once again all the doors were open a crack, listening to the two of them demolish the stateroom.

We went charging in there, and I yelled, "All right, you goddamn blankety blanks! I've had enough of this crap. You've got everybody on this deck up. I've got a nice jail down there, and one of you is going to spend the night in jail."

The room was a mess. Chairs were tipped over, broken glass all over. They were snarling at each other, and I wondered what in the world I was going to do if they called my bluff. I knew we could jump them, but I could not see us trying to pack the big one all the way down to the brig, which was at the other end of the ship down on the Main Deck.

When the big one stared at me, the little one charged her and gave her a really big clout with a boot. The big one staggered and wobbled and the doctor stepped right in there and said, "That was a very hard blow, and you might have a concussion. I see you've got some other bruises there. And abrasions. And lacerations. I'm going to take you down to the hospital and check you over. Come on, now."

And away she went. We followed along. After he checked her over, he locked her in a detention room he has down there. End of the fight.

The next day I got hold of a purser named John Bender, a very nice, ultra-polite man, and told him he had to accompany me to that smashed-up room to shake it down, confiscate all the booze, and try to get the smaller one sobered up. She didn't give us any trouble. We moved her to a single while a crew got the room put back in shape. We kept the big one locked up for a day or so.

Then I got them together and said that, in the interests of everybody aboard, including them, I was making the very *strong suggestion that they pack their clothes and get off as soon as we got to Hawaii.*

They agreed meekly and sent off a wire to an Indian reservation somewhere up in Oregon. Somebody aboard remembered reading that that particular Indian tribe had just received a big settlement from the government, and by adding two and two it became clear to us that these were two Indian lesbians on their honeymoon.

One of them had said to the other, during a pause in the combat, "You goddamn bitch. I brought you along on this trip to show you a good time, and you act like this. People are going to think we're a pair of fucking savages!"

Anyhow, that was the Indian Uprising.

After a dinner of great shrimp and Alaskan crab, and soprano Susan Cashman's concert, we went out on deck, into the soft sweet sea air of a Mexican night. We could make out no lights on the distant shore; it was a low dark shape against a pallor of stars. The ship lifted, sighed, subsided, lifted again, the wake creamy behind us in the running lights.

5

||||||||||||||||||||||||||||||||||||||||||||||||||

San Diego to Panama

There is an absolutely unique flavor to the shipboard nap, especially for those Calvinists who, like myself, can crank up a ton of guilt for each pound of weakness. For a long time I could not imagine why the nap aboard was so much more enjoyable. Then, on the cruise before this one, I finally realized that something was being accomplished while I slept. I was traveling. I was moving. I was going from here to there. Napping was not in any way circumventing or slowing that preordained, purposeful dotted line across the globe. I do indeed know how stupid this is, but waking up twenty-something miles from where you fell asleep gives one the feeling that the hour was not entirely wasted.

The guilt—all I needed—had been established at lunch on the Pool Terrace. A couple of planter's punches, then some free beers with the hot dogs and beans, topped off with a peanut-butter sundae made with macadamia-nut ice cream. A total indulgence. One cannot keep this up for the entire cruise . . . but some do—and must end with a wardrobe purchased along the way, because they no longer fit into the clothes they brought aboard.

A portion of the blame, or credit, must go to John Merlo, the executive chef. He is a master of the art, a very hearty and outgoing man, at home with the cuisines of many peoples: Chinese, Mexican, Indonesian, German, French, and Pure Merlo, a combination of all.

Merlo is not only one very good chef, he is also a real showman. Lots of gestures and expressions and arm-waving, and a thick Italian accent. He was always invited to most of the cocktail parties aboard. I used to hold my breath when he started telling jokes. He knew about seven, all of them long and raunchy, but he always seemed to get away with it. He told dialect jokes in other dialects, but they all came out Italian.

On one trip there were two wealthy couples traveling to- gether sharing a table for four in the Pit. I don't know exactly how it got started, but they began asking John Merlo to cook up special fancy items for them for dinner. Each night the waitresses would bring in these special dishes under big silver covers, and when the covers were whipped off, those people would oh and ah at the look of the special items, and then yum and ah and oh at the taste.

Right behind them, at the table closest to theirs, was another group who had to sit and watch this ritual and these gyrations every night.

It was a long cruise, and after a week or so of this they went to John and said they would like to have a special dish too. And Merlo thought, Oh, my God, what has started here? First one table, then another, and pretty soon the whole dining room. How do I stop it?

"We want big deluxe cheeseburgers," the people said. "And we want them brought out under those silver covers, and we don't want them unveiled until we give the waitress the signal."

So it was done, and the covers stayed on long enough to create a lot of suspense at the neighboring tables. And when they gave the word, Merlo himself came out in his yard-high hat and whipped the covers off. There were cries of ecstasy, shouts of delight, ohing and ahing and gasping like you never heard before.

And that was the end of the special orders from both tables.

On another trip to the South Pacific we had a self-appointed gourmet aboard who kept bothering Merlo, asking him when and where they would take aboard some fresh snails. As in most famed hotels, the escargot aboard was canned; it was stuffed into the shells before serving, and then the shells went through the dishwasher, ready for the next stuffing.

"Fresh escargot," the man kept harping. "Really fresh, John."

Finally Merlo had had enough. When they got to Tahiti, he took aboard some fresh escargot for the gourmet pest and, on second thought, he asked the vendor to give him some live ones in good shape. That night, just before he served the man's special dish of fresh escargot, he dropped some live ones on the top. When the lid was lifted, the man stared in disbelief at the live snails moving around. And that was the last John Merlo heard about fresh escargot.

Merlo was fantastic in that big galley on the Mariposa. It looked like total confusion, the waitresses pushing toward the service counter, shrieking their orders, the chefs and helpers bustling around, steam and clatter-bang of pots and pans. But it was really better organized than it looked. Merlo would stay in motion up and down the whole area, keeping things moving, spotting the trouble areas and straightening them out. He was in his element, and all the time he was moving he would keep up a line of chatter, giving orders, waving his arms, patting the waitresses and saying, "Okay, I get you, baby. Your number is coming up. Next week is your week, baby. How you like a little bit of the old Italian como-say-yahma?" He had been going on like that for years, always the big talk, the big Italian lover, and everybody took it with a grain of salt.

Out in the back they make a big scene about crew birthdays and such, and on one trip John Merlo's birthday came up, and they had a big party for him, long after dinner, with a big cake and lots of booze. In the midst of all this, John is coming on strong with his talk about baby-I'll-see-to-you-next, so after a few more drinks and some more of John's bragging, four or five of those big strong old waitresses said, "Okay, Merlo. You've been talking so big all these years, let's see what you've got."

This quieted him down, but they decided it was the right time to find out. Those waitresses grabbed him, pulled him down onto the deck, and, even though he was really fighting for his honor, proceeded to take his pants off. Because of his *fright, and the resistance he put up, and the number of people watching, poor John's manhood had shriveled up to almost nothing. The waitresses looked at him and said, "This is the como-say-yahma you've been bragging about all these years? You've got to be kidding!"*

Poor Merlo was so embarrassed, so humiliated. For weeks he sulked around, chin on his chest, saying very little. But after a couple of months there was a crew change, and little by little his spirits picked up until finally he was right back to his old self again.

I remember a famous cake Merlo baked for the doctor we had aboard at that time. I'll call him Doctor Buglebalm. He was an eccentric old duck. He wanted to be a guest lecturer and give little talks and show slides of places he had been. The slides were pretty bleached out, and he had a sort of monotonous delivery, so we would keep putting him off. One time one of his fans in the crew slipped a special slide into the projector. He had purchased it in one of those specialty shops in Japan, I think it came on the screen right after one of the cathedrals of Rome. It really woke that audience up.

Buglebalm had great faith in suppositories. He had them in all colors. This was a well-known joke around the ship. No matter what was wrong with you, you were going to get a suppository. If you went in there with a hangnail, you had to bend over and get your suppository. He prescribed them for headaches, fallen arches, anything that came along. Finally when the day of his birthday came along, they brought the big cake into the dining room, right to his table, with HAPPY BIRTH-DAY spelled out in suppositories.

On one long Pacific trip we had an attractive woman from Canada who had just gone through a divorce. Apparently because it was so traumatic for her, she had decided to take this long cruise to get away from it all. But after she boarded the ship, she began to have second thoughts, and I heard that she was thinking of canceling. She wasn't what you'd call morose, but she wasn't very good company. She had built a wall around herself.

Somehow it was discovered that her divorce was going to be final on a certain day, so some of the passengers set up a little celebration party for her at the Pool Terrace. Merlo heard about it and baked her a cake. It was carried to the party, with John following along behind with a sharp knife. I think that only he and I and the ship's photographer knew what was going to happen.

He gave the new divorcée that sharp knife and said, in his heavy accent, "What you do now, you pretend you're sticking the knife in that rotten husband."

She stabbed it a good one, and the balloon Merlo had put into the middle popped and blew icing all over the woman and the guests. The photographer got a great action shot and the woman went into hysterics, but it was the turning point of the whole trip for her. She came out of her shell and had a fine time from then on.

For other special occasions, Merlo had a plywood cake to which he would apply very elaborate icing and messages and then watch the passenger try to cut it.

Practical jokes seem to flourish aboard ship—aboard mine, at least. They did not go over too well under old-line Matson discipline. One time one of the entertainers aboard was a female vocalist named Pam Cavanne. She was full of hell, always organizing late parties in the Poly Room, playing jokes on people, and so on. I was serving under Captain Y on that trip, an old Matson captain a little less pompous and self-righteous than Captains X or Z, but still pretty rigid.

During this South Pacific trip, Pam had been kidding me about my bald head, and one day as we were approaching Honolulu and everybody was out around the Pool Terrace, she said she had a present for me, if I'd promise to use it. She had been saying this for days. She went to her room and came back with this scroungy wig. She had tried to shape it or cut it, and it hadn't worked out at all. I had to close my eyes as she put it on my head, and everybody broke up.

So I went on down to the purser's desk, wearing my wig, and the boys behind the desk thought it was hilarious, and they challenged me to wear it up onto the bridge.

I tend to take dares, so I wore it up to the bridge, and there was Captain Y, who looked vaguely like Lord Mountbatten did in his fifties, staring out the window toward Honolulu. So I took the next window and put my elbows on the sill and stared out.

Pretty soon he glanced over at me and did a double take and said, "John? Johnno? What happened to you?"

I said, "Well, Captain, I thought this would add something to arrivals and departures."

"No. Not really. It won't, really. I liked you better the way you were."

I was off the White Ships for a while and when I came back, I had Captain Z to contend with. And good old Pam was aboard and she had another wig for me, a silver-gray job she had trimmed so that it would do wonders for me.

I said, "No, Pam. Not this trip. No more wig episodes."

She kept after me, daring me to wear it to the first champagne party, and I said, "Absolutely not! Not with Captain Z. He doesn't go for that kind of stuff. It's out."

But she kept at me until finally I heard myself agreeing that what I would do, I would put it on in between the two champagne parties for the two sittings and just walk into Captain Z's room. I knew it would really shock him, but I agreed to it.

I came up to my quarters from the first party, and she had left the wig there on top of my ice bucket on my chest of drawers, all shiny and clean and brushed out.

Just as I was trying to get up the courage to put the thing on, Captain Z thought of something he wanted to tell me and came walking into the room. He looked over and saw the wig on the ice bucket and said casually, "Oh, is this what you wear when you're in the room by yourself?"

That blew the whole thing, so I left the wig sitting there on the ice bucket for several days. This drove my room steward absolutely out of his mind. He used to clean the mirror for hours, staring at the wig, staring at me, wondering if it was in truth my wig and I went ashore in drag, or if some woman had left the wig there by mistake, and, if so, why hadn't she come after it? God only knows what rumors were going around down below.

We pulled one nice little joke on a very affected heavyset woman from San Pedro. Her name was Alice something, and her family owned or had owned one of the big tugboat companies in the Southwest, so we quickly nicknamed her Tugboat Alice. She was actually sort of nice. I do not know, nor would

I care to try to guess, where she got her Bostonian accent. She wanted to be one of the in-group aboard, and when there were any officers sitting in the bar area, she would contrive to join us.

One night when we were having some drinks and she had joined us, she took a big heavy ornate ring out of her purse and showed it to us and told us it was a family heirloom. She said what the stone was, but I forget its name. A sort of green-blue, and large. Her trouble was the ring had been mashed out of round; I guess it was 18 to 20 karat gold, and quite soft. She asked me if anyone aboard could fix it so she could wear it.

Sitting with us was the chief engineer, Bob Tompkins, so I said, "The chief engineer right here is the guy to talk to."

I passed the ring over to Bob, and he took a look at it and said, "Yeah, I can fix it." And he stuck it in his pocket.

Tugboat Alice sort of gulped and reminded us that it was a real genuine family heirloom, and irreplaceable.

For some reason Bob didn't surface for a few days, and Alice sought me out and asked me where the chief was; she hadn't seen him since he pocketed her ring. I said I would go check.

I went up to Bob's room, and because he was the typical chief engineer, his desk was a mess of papers and odds and ends of junk fittings and pieces of metal stock.

"Bob," I said, "Tugboat Alice is concerned about her ring. She says she hasn't seen you since you took it to repair it. Did you ever fix it?"

"Sure," he said. "I've got it here someplace."

Pawing through the stuff on his desk until he uncovered it, he handed it to me, and I saw that he had gotten it back into round again.

"I've got this here little gift box," he said, "and I was going to put it inside and present it to her."

It was a tacky little plastic box with a see-through top. "Wait a minute, Bob," I said. "Let me think. Have you got any brass scrap down in the engine room? You must have."

So he worked up a brass ring of about the right size, and we broke a Coke bottle and put a couple of chunks of the broken bottom in with the brass in the tacky little box.

Then Bob had a bunch of people up to his room for a drink, including Tugboat Alice. At the opportune moment he took the little plastic box out and said, "By the way, here is your ring. I think I squeezed it too tight in the vise, but you can have it fixed when you get back to Portland." He tossed her the box; such a spine-chilling scream I have never heard before. Then he gave her her own ring, all fixed. It took more than a little while to get her settled down.

6

|||||||||||||||||||||||||||||||||||||||||||||||||

San Diego to Panama

Although at noon on the seventh we were still 1,180 miles from Taboga Island, Cruise Lecturer Hal Wagner felt it was the right time to give his talk about the place. Listening between the lines, we agreed that if we happened to feel like going ashore at that time, we'd give it a try—but no great urgency. If one came from the mountains of Montana and this was the first look at a tropical island, fine. But we live on a semitropical island, and Dorothy is never eager to go bouncing around in lifeboats and launches.

People scrambled to get their free tickets at the purser's desk. This is usually a waste of time and energy. When the time comes, there is always room for a few more.

One of the most irritating aspects of ship travel is the compulsion of most of the passengers—I would guess seven or eight out of every ten—to stand in line. This same idiot tendency can be observed at any airport. Even though all the passengers in the lounge have been issued seat assignments, at the first hint that maybe soon the boarding will begin, they hop up and scuttle over and line up. When the aircraft has landed, long before the doors open, they clog the aisle, straining to get off and enjoy the twenty-minute wait for the luggage to come off.

49

On a cruise ship there seem to be far too many chances to line up. No matter how many times the public-address system says to stay out of the foyer and lobby until the ship has been cleared, there they are, restless, nervous, bobbing and weaving, standing on tiptoe to see over the people ahead of them, grousing about the delay. One of the most shameful demonstrations can occur when, in port, people come aboard to change passenger dollars into the local currency. It should be obvious that this service is not performed out of goodwill. If the official rate of exchange is, say, 21½ umlouts to the dollar, the people who come aboard will be giving 20 to the dollar. People line up way ahead of time and stand for an hour waiting to change money. If you try to tell them that they can stroll off the ship and walk to a downtown bank and get 21½ umlouts to the dollar, or get 20½ or 21 at most hotels and shops, they become furious with you, and they will stay in line. If they change more than they use ashore, they can stand in line again before sailing, and this time trade in their currency to the same small clerical people for 22½ or 23 umlouts to the dollar, thus losing 5 or 6 percent both ways. In other words, if they change $100 and then change $50 worth of umlouts back to dollars, they have paid $8 or $9 for the pointless privilege of standing in line.

Aboard ship they will line up for the captain's cocktail party, line up for a lecture, line up for movies. I have decided that the disease is the product of an anxiety of the middle years. There are always a few people who feel absolutely compelled to line up. They are so terribly afraid they might miss something, they are willing to stand for hours, barefoot on broken glass if need be.

If some very secure people walk by and see the beginning of a line forming, five or six nervous souls standing there, they will shake their heads in disbelief. But if insecure people come along, a few of them will join the line. When there are a dozen people in line, the line becomes more persuasive to the insecure, and the more people who add themselves to it, the more plausible the line begins to appear. Can all these people be wrong? By the time there are a hundred in line, any man walking by on his way to his cabin is electrified. They must all know something he doesn't. So he scurries and finds his wife and brings her back to stand there with him, nervously waiting for the line to move. Being in a strange environment seems to compound anxieties. Nobody wants to be wrong about something, to miss out on something. Standing in line seems less risky than not standing in line.

The line I found most offensive was the chow line for the twelve-thirty buffet lunch at the Pool Terrace. The buffet lasted for an hour. There was always more than enough of everything. One could go to the long buffet table at twenty-five past one and get the same hot food in the same quantity and diversity as did those who began lining up at twenty past noon, waiting for the clang of the signal gong. Some of them even darted to the head of the line to grab silverware, napkins, and plates and take them back to their place in line, so that no precious microsecond would be lost. These chowhounds were always the same group: about twenty of them, forming a line that extended back between the tables, so that if you happened to be at a table near where the line formed, you could anticipate having a massive behind standing in bovine patience seven inches from your right ear. Caustic comment did not sway them. They didn't even know what you were trying to say. Or care.

The most persistently offensive chowhounds were a couple of huge, jolly, elderly Australians. They were very bluff and muscular and extraordinarily ruthless about going for the groceries. When they came back for seconds (or thirds or fourths) of some specific item, they would shoulder into the line of people moving along the table for the first time, stab at what they wanted, and carry it away. So elemental and uncaring a force were they that it was possible to imagine them standing on your foot and impaling your ear on the fork on the way to the goodies, without ever noticing what they had done. This same frontier heartiness was evident when people were lined up at the rail, as when coming into port. They would physically shoulder you out of the way in order to make a place for themselves. If you objected, they would stare at you with a look of total incomprehension. "Wot's wrong with you, mite?"

On shipboard, because the large group was assembled through almost random selection, there has to be a small percentage of nature's oversights. The fat man who cannot understand why anybody would object to his lighting his first black cigar of the day at the breakfast table. The woman who slips silverware into her purse and takes it back to the cabin and hides it. The child who reaches into the elevator and pushes all the buttons. The husband who whiles away the idle hour by thumping his wife all over the stateroom. The ship's geography provides refuge from the pests and the peculiar. One begins to move in a pattern which minimizes irritation and, like the bull in the bull ring, seeks that *querencia* where one feels most assured.

The pests I have to worry about are the ones who really begin to disrupt everything. Sometimes you can nip it in the bud. One time three hotshot Texans from Houston flew out to Hawaii to join the vessel there and make the thirty-day round trip from Hawaii back to Hawaii. They arrived the day before the ship got in, apparently after a good flight, first class, with plenty of booze. They checked into one of the better hotels downtown and went on from there, and in the course of the evening they managed to get thrown in jail.

I never found out what they had done to get arrested. They got themselves bailed out the next day and came aboard ship with their gear. The arrest hadn't dampened their spirits or slowed them up much. As soon as they boarded they threw their gear in the cabins, found the bar, bellied up to it, and said, "Hey, nigger. How about a little service here?" At that time we had a black bartender, quick, pleasant, and well-liked. He took this abuse for an hour or so and then called the chief steward and said he wasn't going to put up with it any more.

The chief steward tried to settle them down, and they told him to bug off. The chief steward got hold of the chief officer, quite a young guy, and he went down and they called him sonny and drove him off. So he called me into the act, and when I came down they told me to get off their backs, for Chrissake, and go drive the boat.

So I said, "You get your gear and be off this ship in ten minutes, or I will have the police come and take you off." And when they took a long look at me, they knew I meant exactly that, and they left. So, in essence, they took the shortest trip on the Mariposa *ever known to man. Flew out from Texas, spent almost two hours aboard at the dock, and flew back. But it saved thirty days' worth of trouble.*

There was one woman from Tulsa who liked to swing her weight around. Let's call her Mrs. Porter. She had married and outlived a couple of old boys with oil wells. I think the first one must have hit oil when he went out to dig a new site for the three-holer, because she was not what you would call a real high-class lady. But she had lots of scratch, and she knew how much leverage that gave her.

She had traveled often on the ships before I ran into her, and I had heard stories about her. A pretty little Mexican maid named Pancha usually went with her. Sometimes she came on with other people, once with a couple of young men she introduced as her nephews, another time with a man she never explained. On one of the trips before I met her, she had fallen madly in love with her room steward, a dashing Puerto Rican fellow, and when she rebooked for another trip it was with the stipulation he would be taking care of her stateroom.

She always picked up an entourage that followed her around the ship, and apparently she paid for everything. On that trip she had her room steward and a deck steward, the organist on the ship, the drummer, and Pancha. Mrs. Porter always led the parade. She had a distinctive walk. As her boobs swiveled to port, her behind swiveled to starboard, and then this action was reversed. It was interesting to watch her go. She moved right along.

I was made aware, by people who'd traveled with her before, of the troubles she'd caused. I was told of the knockdown drag-out fights in her stateroom between her and Pancha, the screams of "you rotten spic bitch," and so on, and the next morning Pancha would be found sleeping out on one of the davenports in the lounge, and the purser would have to have a chat with Mrs. Porter about the noise and the complaints. But, they said, it didn't seem to do much good.

So I was aware of who she was, and I was keeping an eye on her. She seemed to hold forth at the bar most of the time with the hard-core drinking crowd, which was fine. Outside of the occasional complaint about noise and shouting and so on, things were going pretty good.

I was heading up to my room one night about ten thirty or

eleven when things were beginning to wind down in the Poly Club. We had a nice bridge instructor aboard, and she intercepted me and said, "Captain, can I talk to you?"

The poor woman looked to be practically in tears. "Sure. What's the problem?"

"We had a very bad scene today at the bridge class. This lady came in—she hadn't been there before, even though she seems to play very good bridge—and she played and she used foul and abusive language and she disrupted everything so badly that my players said, in effect, if she came back another time, they wouldn't play bridge any more."

"Who is this woman? Who are you talking about?"

"Her name is Mrs. Porter."

The next morning I located Mrs. Porter and took her into a quiet corner, and I said, "Mrs. Porter, you have made several trips on this ship, and we value your business and respect you as a customer. We need the business. We are always glad to have you and Pancha aboard. I would like to see you have a good time. You are more than welcome to hold court at the bar and really swing and have a ball. But there is one group of people on this ship that I never bother with. They never bother me. They rarely complain about the air conditioning or the food or the tours. They sit in the card room and play bridge day in and day out. Even if we went and saw all seven wonders of the world, they would still be in there playing that stupid game. But, God bless them, they never bother me, and I don't bother them. Mrs. Porter, feel free to have a ball out at the bar, but do not screw with the bridge club. Have you got my message?"

She just cocked her head a little and stared at me.

"Mrs. Porter, I am not kidding. The very next time I hear of you disrupting the bridge club, you and Pancha are going to be standing on the dock with all your luggage at the next port of call when we sail, and I will be waving goodbye to you. Now do you understand me?"

"Yes, I do," she said.

And that was the last problem I ever had with Mrs. Porter.

It is useful and desirable that the captain should be able to order the unmanageable passenger off his ship. Passengers who know very little about the chain of command aboard seem to accept this ultimate authority.

Aboard the *Mariposa* during this first stage of the voyage, J. M. Coco, the chief officer (or staff captain, as called by Matson Lines) would take over if anything happened to Kilpack. He was in charge of all the maintenance of the deck of the ship, the outside portions of the ship, some of the alleyways, the looks of the ship, and the maintenance and operation of the safety features.

The second mate under Coco was called the navigator, but in effect all the mates navigate. There were two third mates and three junior third mates. They stood watches, four hours on and eight off, four to eight, eight to midnight, midnight to four, etc. There were always two mates on the bridge each watch, and the senior mate never left the bridge. He could send the junior mate out to check problems and then alert the chief officer if he deemed it necessary.

Next down the line was the bosun, who, like a sergeant, was in charge of all the sailors and made sure that work ordered was properly done.

The quartermasters steer the ship, maintain the bridge, and stand the gangway watches in port. Also under Coco were special categories such as the ship's carpenter and the joiner, who fixes small broken objects all over the ship, except in the engineering department. Incidentally, the sailors stand watches, as do the mates, except for those classified as "day workers."

Under Chief Engineer S. A. Glaros, the line of authority was through a first, second, and third engineer, down through plumbers, electricians, air-conditioning people, and sound and communication engineers, to the wipers, oilers, and firemen. Glaros was also responsible for making fresh water aboard and had a couple of men called evaporator operators. The *Mariposa* used about 250 tons of water a day, and took on fresh water in port to augment the supply, because it is an expensive process to evaporate fresh water from seawater. They evaporated enough to try to keep the tanks full at all times. In the tropics where the boilers are a little less efficient, and on-board consumption goes up—drinking, showering, ice cubes—there sometimes wouldn't be enough fresh water to permit washing down the side of the ship, washing off the encrusted sea salt.

Being completely in charge of the engine department and mechanical department of the ship, Glaros would not confer with Kilpack unless it was a matter of such importance that it might result in a slowdown of the ship or a compromise of safety. There was, of course, the constant good-natured tension and rivalry about whether the chief was doing his best to squeeze out the knots the captain wanted to have. On a lower level, between the mates and the engineers, there was always friction because, in truth, the engineers do work a little harder, and they work in noise and heat, and when they come up they see the mates in clean dry clothes.

The steward's department, under Chief Steward Jack Abramson, was the biggest department on the ship, because he had to run what was called the hotel section. He had a yeoman to do the paperwork. The Second steward was in charge of all room stewards, the maintenance and cleanliness of public rooms, bar, and lounge, and the servicing and scheduling of passenger cocktail parties. The third steward took care of A Deck, where the crew lived and had their own mess rooms, galley, quarters, and so forth.

John Merlo, the executive chef, as part of the hotel section, was in charge of the galley, food preparation, and all the storerooms and storekeepers. In theory he was also in charge of the dining room, but that was handled by the headwaiter, Maurice Herod, and the head waitress, Pat Logan. Merlo had an array of special chefs: baking, pastry, salads, soups and the like.

Chief Steward Abramson was also responsible for the telephone operators, beauty shop and barbershop personnel, lounge stewardesses, bartenders, wine waiters, and the ship's laundry.

In the purser's department there was Chief Purser J. P. Yonge, Senior Assistant Purser W. D. McDonald, and three other pursers to man the front desk. The department was responsible for all room assignments and changes; the ship's daily newspaper, the *Polynesian;* the paymaster for the ship, the cashier, and all passenger and crew charges; the ship's photographer, and all public relations functions affecting passengers; tour escorts and tour booking; all entertainments, lectures, and instruction classes (motion pictures, bridge, Bingo, music); and the scheduling and manning of all passenger entertainment functions, as well as deciding which nights would be formal nights.

It is obvious that there is an overlap between the steward's functions and the purser's functions, areas which can only be handled through cooperation. Kitchen versus dining room can be a source of friction. Deck maintenance work versus passenger convenience can create problems. On all cruises there are always a few people aboard who have been on too long without a break and are becoming stale and cross, and they foment friction and tensions.

When a captain holds himself aloof from internal frictions and tensions, depending on the lines of authority and responsibility to keep things orderly, there can be such intense emotional trauma between staff members, such spite and hatefulness, that passenger relationships and services suffer. We have seen this on other ships.

On the *Mariposa*, Captain Kilpack held staff meetings of all department heads, the purser, and the doctor, once a week, oftener if there was a major change coming up, such as a change in schedule or a late arrival. In these meetings he encouraged the airing of every possible gripe, and by eliminating trouble spots before they grew larger, he operated what is usually known as a happy ship.

7

|||||||||||||||||||||||||||||||||||||||||||||

San Diego to Panama

Unlike other cruises we had been on, there seemed to be no men of the cloth on the passenger list this time. On this Sunday, Purser Yonge was conducting one service and Alan Scott, the cruise director, the other.

Quite often on the trips, particularly at Christmas or Easter, they would put a minister on the ship. Sometimes we'd have one as a passenger. But quite often it would be a Catholic priest being given a free ride, and he would handle the services.

Some of them were a real asset. Some of them were really great about working with the social staff. We had a really cute little priest one time, a delightful guy who had spent most of his life working with under-privileged and handicapped children. Someone had recommended him, and he was absolutely enthralled at the whole thing. It was unbelievable what the trip meant to Father Kern.

In my little talks I give to meetings of the Mariners, there was a gag I would always pull if we had a priest or a minister aboard. I would say, "I don't want to hear any complaints about the weather. I know you people paid a big price and expect to lie out in the sun all day, but really I have no control over that. However, we do have a priest on board." And I would introduce him and go on to say, "Father so-and-so is in charge of the weather because, after all, he has a direct pipeline to the Boss." I had been made gun-shy by one memorable trip where we had foul weather for the whole forty-two days. This is bad enough for everybody who works aboard, listening to the constant griping from every side, but it is pure disaster for nice people who have saved for a long time to take one big wonderful cruise to the tropic seas. They get cabin fever. I think that cruise was responsible for four or five divorces.

When we sailed with Father Kern aboard for the South Pacific cruise, we had unbelievably good weather. We followed along behind several storm fronts, always arriving after the skies had cleared. And after we left port, another front would move in behind us. So, of course, in a spirit of fun, Father Kern was taking the credit for all this. And when people would mention the fine weather we were having, I would tell them to go thank Father Kern, and add, "Remember, now, if the weather goes bad it's still his responsibility, not mine."

On one stretch, heading south from Hawaii, we did have several overcast days. I said to the little priest, "Father, you'd better get busy and talk to the Boss, because this weather isn't all that great and we're depending on you."

Sure enough, the weather turned fair again. Because we had left two days later than our scheduled departure time, we had to make a change in the stops. We had been going to go into Apia, British Samoa, but because of the two days lost, we were knocking heads with a Russian cruise ship, and it didn't look good for Apia. But we were playing it cool, waiting until the last moment, and if it didn't work out we would go to Pago Pago, to American Samoa.

Early in the morning of the arrival day, we got word that Apia was out, so we changed course to Pago Pago. Everybody was on deck. It was a beautiful morning. The entrance to the harbor in Pago Pago is beautiful but very narrow, with big green mountains on either side that go right down to the water. You make a long slow turn to port to get inside. Once you are committed and head up in there, there isn't a lot of choice.

I was sliding in very slowly when the pilot boat came alongside and the pilot came aboard. Just then a Samoan rainsquall *hit us, and the rain came down in sheets. The pilot came running all the way up to the bridge. "Boy!" he said. "It doesn't look good at all. I can't see anything. There's a buoy right over there someplace and I can't even see it. I don't think we can get in."*

"No problem at all, pilot," I said. "I have a Catholic priest on board who handles the weather. I'll call him." I stepped over to the P.A. system, flipped all the buttons, and said, "Father Kern, please report to the bridge on the double."

A few minutes later the little old father came racing onto the bridge. He had on a floppy golf hat and a startled look; I guess he thought there had been some sort of accident and somebody wanted the last rites.

He had probably been sitting down there in one of the deck chairs, looking out at the rain, with people needling him about not taking care of the weather. I said to him, "Father, you had better do something. I can't even see the buoy. What happened to you?"

"Gee, Captain, I didn't know we were coming to Pago Pago. I've been working on Apia all morning. They've got good weather over there."

"Well, you better do something right here at Pago Pago and do it quick, because we are in real trouble."

And so help me God, a great big blast of wind came down off the mountains and blew that rainsquall away, and it all opened up, and we were right on course. The pilot stood there with his eyes bugging out. Father Kern said to me, "You're welcome, captain. Now I am going back down there and make them all eat crow." And off he trotted.

Toward the end of that trip, after fine weather almost every day, we came into San Francisco in a beautiful pink dawn and one of the passengers said to me, "You know something? That little priest is beginning to believe he's done it all himself."

Another time we had a Catholic priest aboard who wanted to give a full communion, and he wanted everything to be just right. He had brought aboard all the needed paraphernalia, and he had procured the red wine; the final thing he asked for, in lieu of wafers, was some bread cut up into very small squares. He told Jim Yonge, the purser, of this requirement, and the purser advised the chief steward, and the chief steward advised the executive chef, and the chef told somebody out in the galley that they needed some bread cut up into little squares up in the lounge.

Somewhere in that chain of command the wires got crossed, and the guy down in the galley had a lot of garlic croutons all made up out of hard pieces of French bread, so he gave them a quick toast and sent them up. Jim said he caught a scent of the heavy garlic as they were carried in through the cardroom toward the lounge, but he said it was too late then to stop it, and he thought the best thing to do was to walk away and try very hard not to think about it again.

I really could have used Father Kern on one island cruise. We were docked at Nawiliwili in Hawaii. It's an intricate little harbor. They have two breakwaters. You have to make an S turn to get in there, and you need two tugs to tie up and to get back out.

Early on a Sunday morning, about seven o'clock, I got a call from our agent in Honolulu, and he said there had been an earthquake down in the vicinity of Samoa which had set off a big tidal wave, and they predicted it would hit Hawaii sometime around noon.

I said, "Well, what do you want me to do, get out of port?"

He said, "No, we just wanted you to be aware of this thing so you can take the necessary precautions."

"If you want me to get out of here, you'd better tell me now. I can only get hold of one tug to work my way out."

"No, no, we just wanted you to be advised."

"Okay."

About half an hour later the Coast Guard called me up with the same story, that the tidal wave was going to hit around noontime.

"What do you want me to do? Should I try to get out of port?"

"No, we just wanted you to be aware of it."

"Okay. I'm aware of it." We put out some extra lines, but I was still wondering if I should try to get out of there or not. Another half an hour later the Civil Defense people called up with the same story, that it looked as if we were going to have a tidal wave.

"What the hell do you want me to do?"

"We just wanted you to be cognizant of this."

"I'm aware. I'm cognizant and I've been advised, but what the hell should I do? Do you want me to get out of here?"

"No. We'll let you know."

In the meantime there had been reports on the newscasts, and some passengers had heard them, and in seconds it was all over the ship. People were very concerned about what was going to happen. They were looking out to sea, waiting for the big wave.

At eleven thirty the Coast Guard called back and said the whole thing had fizzled out and there wasn't going to be any tidal wave. So on the way home, when we had a Mariners' Club party and I was recapping the highlights of the cruise, I said, among other things, "You passengers were aware that there was a potential tidal wave going to hit Nawiliwili during our port stay there. We were right on top of this thing every minute. But due to the fact that it would have conflicted with some of our shoreside tours, the tidal wave was canceled for lack of interest."

This is a reasonably typical example of my contacts with the bureaucracy. Let me tell you about the Quarantine officials. They are almost in the same league with the Customs clowns.

Back in the old days on the freighters we would have to drop anchor and wait for one of these guys to board the ship and check us out. Usually he was a carpenter's mate or a machinist or a yeoman who knew nothing about health or medicine. He would go have a couple of drinks with the purser, and the purser would tell him that everything was fine. And then he would go get back into the boat that brought him out, usually a great big hairy cutter with a crew of ten. He wouldn't know dengue fever from athlete's foot. As a health inspection, it was a waste of time.

On the passenger ships it is easier because there is a doctor aboard. We can send a wire ahead testifying that there are no contagious diseases on board. They still come down to the ship, but they accept the doctor's word. These quarantine people are also part of the Public Health Service, and for the last several years they have been inspecting all ships periodically and grading them on a point scale. I am proud of the fact that the Monterey and the Mariposa were very clean ships. I've

*never seen a passenger ship of foreign registry that would meet
our standards. We did a lot of our own inspections as well,
with even the doctor inspecting the refrigerators.*

*Well, they went on a new program, I guess to keep some
jobs for the men in Hawaii or make new ones. These guys
would come down to the dock with a ten-page checklist devised
by the Disease Control people back in Atlanta, those same
medical geniuses who took so long to diagnose Legionnaire's
disease, the same ones who couldn't find the cause of hundreds
of cases of severe diarrhea on an Italian cruise ship. They
came on with all these recommendations of what we had to do.*

*When we would take aboard water from shore, it would
come from a regular city source, and we would get a certificate
each time verifying the potability. That water has to be good
because some of it goes into the boiler, and the boiler water
has to be more pure than drinking water, and one hell of a lot
better than the shower water. So the water aboard is probably
much better than the water in almost any city in America.*

*But it is not good enough for the Quarantine people. They
recommended we buy a certain kind of chlorination plant available in Hawaii, something with a black light and other great
features. We bought it and installed it and never could make
it work properly. When we were inspected in Los Angeles or
San Francisco, the inspectors would look at the chlorination
plant and say, "That thing's a piece of junk. Why did you buy
that?" And I would tell them that their own teammates in
Hawaii had told us to buy it.*

*The water in the swimming pool is pumped directly out of
the ocean, and the pump runs continually. It is a continuously
circulating system, with overflow. Every couple of days, after
dark, they drain the pool, wash it out, and fill it again. When
we get into port we naturally shut off the circulation valves.
We don't pump any harbor water in, and as soon as we leave,
we dump the pool and start again. That's the way it has always
been.*

*But that's not good enough for the Quarantine guys. They
want us to put a chlorination plant on the salt-water pool. Not
being an engineering person, I could not understand how you
could expect to chlorinate seawater at enough strength without*

turning every swimmer's hair bright green. But they were very hard-nosed about it, saying, "That's how it's got to be."

We finally arrived at a compromise. We can run the pool out in the ocean, but we must dump it as soon as we get into port. The water cannot sit in there even one day. This upset the people who had traveled with us a lot. In port when they don't go ashore, they like to sit around the pool and have a little nip and a little dip from time to time. But that was the way it had to be. The Quarantine officials did a marvelous job of protecting people, against their will, from a danger that never existed in the first place.

They had a big checklist for the galley. Temperature in the dishwashers, all dishes covered in the refrigerator, and so on. The same things we had always inspected ourselves. On the Mariposa we had one big box which, years ago, had been converted to a chill box, and when they made all the cold dishes for the buffet in the forenoon, they would put them in the chill box as soon as they were made, so the salads and all would look nice and fresh. On one inspection day I was walking around with this inspector. In the chill box there was a big dish of potato salad, all set to go up to the buffet. He took out what I thought was a thermometer and shoved it down through the potato salad and said, "Oh, oh. You're going to get two demerits for this."

"Why is that?"

He pointed to the mark on the ruler he had stuck into the salad. "This salad is over three inches high."

I said, "Gee, I didn't realize that would create any problem."

"Nothing in the refrigerator can be over three inches high, and your potato salad is three and a half inches high!"

"My God, I'm glad you found that. A three-and-half-inch-high potato salad could destroy us all."

That is the kind of meaningless stuff they did, and still do. I got so I would dodge them whenever possible. They always came down and ate a hearty meal aboard the ship. They'd have a nice table, a nice long lunch with wine, and a lot of laughs. Apparently our sanitation didn't keep them from enjoying the free food.

One time we were on our way out from California to Hawaii,

and we had the usual little run of diarrhea going around. Between the crew and the passengers, there were thirteen reported cases. We always have to send a wire ahead stating health conditions on the ship, and the doctor, being a conscientious guy, reported this: not dysentery, but just diarrhea, where one has it for twenty-four hours or so and it goes away.

When we tied up in Honolulu a bunch of Quarantine people came storming on board to find out all about the epidemic. I told them we didn't have any epidemic, and they said they had sent the figures back to the headquarters in Atlanta, and the computer had said tilt: Thirteen cases per 474 people equals an epidemic.

"No, no, no. We have absolutely no problems at all. In fact, most of the people who had diarrhea and got over it have gone ashore."

"Well, we have to take action."

"What do you mean, action?"

"We want you to distribute these questionnaires at everybody's door to be filled out, and these stool-sample containers and instructions, and then at six o'clock tomorrow morning, you muster all the passengers, and for the ones who can't provide stool samples, we'll procure them rectally with a sterile tube."

"You have got to be kidding!"

"No. This is what Atlanta says we have to do, and this is what we do."

"Look. This is a cruise ship, and nobody here is paying less than a hundred and something dollars a day, and the only way I will wake them up at six in the morning is if the ship is on fire or sinking. Now you better go back and call Atlanta and tell them Captain Kilpack is not going to cooperate. And find out if you have enough juice to hold this ship."

"No, I don't believe we have."

"Then I'm definitely not going to do it."

I went ashore and called John Bell, the company vice-president for passenger ships in San Francisco. I can still remember the sound of his voice on the other end. "They want to what?"

San Francisco called Atlanta, where it was about two in the morning, and finally Atlanta backed down and said they wanted everybody to fill out the questionnaires, but they would settle for stool samples from X number of people on a voluntary basis.

So we went ahead with the questionnaires, and of course one question said, "What is your last foreign port?" and a few wrote Los Angeles, and others wrote San Francisco. Some of the crew were not Phi Beta Kappa quality and neither were some of the passengers. These were complicated forms with, as is usual with all government forms, several questions written in babblegobble. When one crewman wrote on the form he'd had diarrhea for two weeks, the inspectors jumped on that. "Hell," I said, "nobody in this crew is ever sick for over a day without going to bed. The first thing they do is stop working, and this guy is working."

They hunted him up and got their sample. He said he felt fine. Then, as part of the survey, they set up card tables in front of the dining room and up on the Pool Terrace and tried to stop passengers going in and out to question them about their stool habits before they went to dinner. You can imagine how far they got with that. People just stared in disbelief and walked away from them.

They tried to check out the cause of the diarrhea. I tried to explain it to them. "Hey, these people are eating four and five times a day. They're eating rich food and drinking a lot of booze, and their stomachs aren't used to this. It's nothing uncommon. It goes around on every single voyage. Any group of people, particularly these older people, they're used to a more bland diet. We don't have any epidemic. This is a farce. You're wasting your time." But they kept checking the water supply and the food and asking questions all day, checking people's bowel habits.

By the time we were getting ready to sail, they were still fooling around, so I went down and said, "If you guys don't want to go to Hilo, I would suggest you get off the ship."

"Well, we can't find anything."

"I'm not surprised."

"We have to do our job."

"Yeah, everybody has to make a living somehow."

"You know, this ship has come up a lot since we took it over."

I was almost but not quite speechless. "This ship has not

come up at all. You people have done nothing useful in the past or in the present, and I doubt if you'll come up with anything useful in the future. I am going to sail in exactly three minutes whether you are aboard or ashore."

But they never gave up. They were back every voyage. They would go through the whole inspection, over and over. Ships are the helpless victims of the bureaucracy. Ships can't vote, and the owners pay the fees.

8

Monday, May 9

San Diego to Panama

There was to be a pre-lunch meeting of the Mariners' Club members aboard. The invitations had been slipped under the stateroom doors the previous evening. Certainly, forming associations of passengers is not a unique public-relations gambit. The airlines have had them for years. Little lapel pins and wall plaques and, the customer hopes, some special treatment. The special treatment is far easier to provide afloat than in the air. The traditional meeting of Mariners on the *Monterey* and *Mariposa* consisted of free Mai Tais—gigantic lethal drinks of fruit juices and rum—some remarks by the captain, and a presentation of new certificates of rank in accord with the total miles traveled—including the total of the current voyage—along with little gold-metal bears and also lapel pins of rank, with one stripe, two stripes, three stripes, etc.`Presentations were made in inverse order of rank, and the Mai Tais tended to make it a jolly gathering.

This was the largest Mariner meeting ever held. There were more than two hundred and ninety people who had sailed on the White Ships before, and only twelve people aboard who hadn't. Dorothy and I remained Commodores, as before, but with a new certification of 58,745 miles and two more little golden bears. And that sense of unreality which one too many Mai Tais can induce.

That party was so big that the steward's department thought we should have it in two sections, but I vetoed that because how could we divide them? By rank? By alphabet? So instead of having it in the Poly Club, they worked out a way to get all the people into the lounge. It was set for 11:30 A.M., and they started moving the chairs in and setting it all up at about 10:15. But these Mariners are noted for being on time or a little ahead of time, so as soon as they would get one area of the room set up, a bunch of little old lady Mariners would move in and sit down and start looking around for the Mai Tais. By eleven, when it was all set up, every chair was occupied, so they called me up and said, "Everybody is ready, so you might as well come down now."

The party lasted a couple of hours and I gave out over 290 certificates, great big parchment things in envelopes fastened with a big gold seal. Matson had started it out with Navigator, Captain, and two kinds of Commodores. Eventually they had so many Commodores they had to go to three categories of Admiral. There was one little old lady there named, I believe, Mrs. Andersen. She got a little gold pin with a diamond in it, to signify she had become an Admiral of the Fleet. She said she had first gone from San Francisco to Hawaii many many years ago as a very young girl, in a sailing ship.

One time there was a very small Mariner party. We were making the Hawaiian trip, five days out, five days back, and seven days around the islands. We had a party for the Mariners who were going the whole way on the trip out, and would have another one for them on the way back to California, but there were ten or twelve of them who were just making the island segment, so rather than try to have a full-scale event, I said I would have a little party for them up in my quarters. I told Jim Yonge and Kaui Barrett to set it up for six o'clock when we were in port, in Hilo.

So it was all arranged, and the hors d'oeuvres, the diplomas, and the Mai Tais were sent up. Jim Yonge and Kaui arrived, and we sat around, and at six o'clock no one had arrived.

I thought this very unusual, because when passengers are invited to the captain's quarters they arrive right on time, even standing around outside in the corridor so they can come in right on the dot. At quarter past six I said, "This is amazing. I can imagine some of them being on tours, but I can't imagine nobody showing up. I wonder if the invitations went out."

Kaui said, "I can find out. I know some of these people personally. I'll call and ask them if they were invited."

She called them and lo and behold, they knew nothing about it. Upon investigation we found out that the invitations had been made up and put on the bellhop's desk for him to deliver to the various rooms, but since he was about to go off duty, he didn't bother with them, and before the next bellhop reported, somebody put a stack of newspapers on top of the invitations. We found them still sitting on the desk, under everything.

We got them all on the phone and had them up to a come-as-you-are party. It worked out. One woman in curlers. Men still in golf togs. Everybody had a good time. I think Jim Yonge gave that cheery little bellhop a real blast, because for the next few days if I saw him coming down a corridor toward me, he would about-face without missing a stride and be out of sight in seconds.

I knew nothing about the Mariners when I first came over to the White Ships. I did not know the old-time Admirals and Commodores, but let me tell you, when they had enough miles, they expected the captain to know who they were, and the other officers too. One time Jack Abramson invited me to his room for cocktails. He was chief steward, and he said he had some other people stopping by. When I got there, there were two women present. One of them was Mary Beth Webber and the other was Mary Jane Harris. I had no idea they were the top two Admirals in the Mariner fleet, probably at that time with well over 100,000 miles each, and very proud of it.

I got my drink and sat down and said, "It is certainly nice to meet you ladies. Is this your first trip?"

Poor Jack. The ice cubes went up in the air, and he had to hastily explain to me the status of these guests. I became good friends with both of them later on, and they forgave me for the bad start.

Another morning when I had not been on the White Ships for very long, I walked out onto the Pool Terrace early, and saw this pleasant-looking old lady sitting alone having a cup of coffee, so I walked over with my coffee and said, "May I join you?"

She looked up and batted her eyes and said in a syrupy deep-south accent, "Well, I would dearly love the pleasure of your company." I sat down and we introduced ourselves and after a bit she said, "Now tell me. Is there much goin' on, on the ship?"

And I said, "Well, Mrs. Greyson, there's the usual things. We have the art classes and the dance lessons, the Bingo games—"

"I don't mean that," she said. "is there much goin' on?"

And I said, "Well . . . Mrs. Greyson . . . I really don't know."

She said, "Well, you know, I'm too old to par-tic-i-pate, but I still like to hear about it."

This old gal was really fantastic. Come to find out, she had been traveling on the ship for a good many miles and a good many cruises. She was a real favorite of practically everyone on the staff. She had one of the rooms up on the top deck, port side, aft of the radio room, in that row called by the staff Swinging Singles, or Maiden Lane. She very seldom went down to dinner. She just shuffled back and forth from her room out to the Pool Terrace and back, and even wore bedroom slippers most of the time.

From time to time, after having coffee with her, I would walk her back to her room. There were red emergency lights spaced at long intervals along that corridor. I got her back to her room one time, and as she was fumbling around, trying to find her key, she said, "This is my room. Whenevah I travel, I always have this room. It's got this little red light ovah the doah. It's mighty convenient."

I really cultivated Mrs. Greyson. She and I became pretty close friends, and whenever I had other guests on board, I would call down and ask if I could bring them down for a drink. She was always all snugged down in her room. At either end of the beds in those single rooms there is a large nightstand. These were always stacked with bottles, anything you wanted, at least twenty different brands.

Always when we would go in, she would say, "You all have a drink now. You all just he'p yourself."

She had an acquaintance named Mrs. Suggs, who stayed in the same area on many of the same cruises. They were not really good friends, but they had traveled together for many thousands of miles. On the trip where I met Mrs. Greyson, Mrs. Suggs had the room next to hers.

Mrs. Suggs was pretty heavy on the Smirnoff. For a time Mrs. Greyson was unwell and confined to her cabin. All the Pool Terrace habitués were inquiring about her. I stopped in to find out how she was getting along. She said she was getting a good rest, but she said, "Every night that Mrs. Suggs comes over to see me. And I say to her, 'I'm tarred, and I want to go to sleep.' And Mrs. Suggs says to me, 'I'll go, just as soon as I finish my drink.'" She sighed and said, "You know, I have to buy that Mrs. Suggs a new bottle ever' single day."

One night I had a pretty good-sized cocktail party in my quarters, so I invited Mrs. Greyson. There were five couples, as I remember, so they were pretty well jammed in. I told my guests they were really going to enjoy this old lady, that she was something special. When she didn't arrive and didn't arrive, I phoned down and asked her if she was coming to my party. She said, "Well, I'm having a little problem with my zipper." I said I had an engineering officer there and I'd send him right down. She said she didn't think that would be necessary, but I said that he was right there, and after all, he'd been trying to get into her room the whole trip. She said, "You tell that boy my doah is always open." I sent the man down, and pretty soon he reappeared, escorting Mrs. Greyson.

I sat her in the swivel chair at my desk. I gave her a drink and she got her cigarette going, something that always seemed to be quite a chore for her, and then I introduced her to everyone at the party.

After that was over, she apparently wanted to get the names straight, so she turned to the nearest woman and said, "Let me see now. You're Mrs. Smith and this is your husband."

The woman smiled and said, "I'm Mrs. Smith, but this is Mr. Jones. That's my husband over there sitting with Mrs. Brown."

So she turned to a woman on the other side of her, and said, "Now you're Mrs. Robinson and this is Mr. Robinson."

That woman said, "This is Mr. Robinson, yes. But I'm Mrs. Butler. And that's my husband sitting over there with Mrs. Jones."

So she asked Mr. Robinson where his wife was and he said, "Right over there with Mr. Brown."

There was one of those party silences while Mrs. Greyson looked them all over, and then she favored them with an incredibly sweet and lascivious smile and said, "Well, it certainly looks like you're all having a good tahm!"

Some of the older hands who dated back to the Matson days on the Mariposa and Monterey told me some of Mrs. Suggs's prior history. She and her husband made numerous trips, and they were both pretty heavy on the Smirnoff. There are some wild stories about those days, such as the long Mediterranean cruise where neither one of them ever set foot ashore, anywhere, which certainly avoids any problem with Customs when one returns.

Finally the old boy died of cirrhosis of the liver. She came back aboard to travel as a widow, and after a trip or two she met this eligible bachelor who didn't drink. So Mrs. Suggs went on the wagon, straightened up, and nailed the guy. As soon as they were married she converted him to Smirnoff and picked up where she left off. The new husband tried to hold up his end of the deal, but after a couple of years of it, he also died of cirrhosis. She came back on the cruises, widowed again and going as strong as ever. I sincerely feel that if she ever passes away, the Smirnoff distillery should put their flag at half mast.

Mrs. Suggs lived alone in a big house in a town not far from San Francisco. Once when the Mariposa was in port, she invited a purser, Frank Ellery, for dinner. He went down and they had some drinks before dinner and during dinner and after dinner. When Frank got ready to leave around midnight, she decided that he should not try to drive in his condition. He protested, saying he could make it just fine, but she said, "Frank, I can't let you drive like this. You are too drunk to drive." She said she would feel terrible if anything happened to him, and there was no reason why he couldn't stay all night. So he went to bed in a guest room.

At about three in the morning, Frank got up and went to the bathroom down the hall, found the light, used the bathroom, flushed the toilet, turned the light off, and made his way back to bed. The noise woke Mrs. Suggs up from deep sleep, and she used her bedside phone to call the police. The next thing Frank knew, he was waked up by bright lights shining in his face.

"Who are you?" they asked.

"I'm Frank Ellery. Who are you?"

"What are you doing here?"

"I'm a houseguest."

"Sure you are. Get dressed."

They got him dressed, muscled him out of the room, and were about to haul him down to the station. There was Mrs. Suggs standing in the hallway in her robe.

She stared at him and said, "My God! It's Frank Ellery! What are you doing here?"

Mrs. Suggs was a passenger when I was making some thirteen-day summer cruises to Alaska. She would come aboard, and as soon as she got to her room, she would pick up the phone and order a couple of fifths of Smirnoff. She rarely surfaced around the ship, except to come to dinner. She was a room drinker, and she had friends always dropping in to see her, a steady parade of old cronies.

So each day she would call down for two or three more fifths. More than halfway through the trip, when we were on our way back to San Francisco, she called down and asked them to send up a case.

They said, "Mrs. Suggs, we've only got a few days to go. Why do you want a whole case?"

She said she had called several times and hadn't gotten service, and she had run out of booze when her friends were there and it was embarrassing.

They sent up a case, and she went to work on that. We arrived in San Francisco a couple of days later, and there were about seven bottles left. This made a problem for her. It was hard to take ashore because of the duty, and the shipboard accounts had been closed so there was no way to buy it back.

We asked her what she was going to do, and she said, "Well, if I can have the same room, I'll just stay on for the next trip." And so she did. It began to worry us that she might not come out even this time either, and we might have her aboard permanently. But at the end of the second trip she had no unmanageable surplus and was able to go ashore.

9

Tuesday, May 10

Taboga Island and the Panama Canal

A morning of fog and soft rain, thick warm air, and a silvery sea. We were at anchor off low tropic islands. Though the sea looked almost flat calm, the nearby tugs and tenders rolled steeply in the slow swell. The rain and the threat of more rain discouraged many who could and would have gone ashore.

Taboga, discovered by Balboa in 1513, had been a shipping center in the middle of the eighteenth century. During the gold rush, 49ers trekked across the isthmus and boarded Pacific Steamship Navigation Company vessels there. It was a rest area later for the sick and weary during the canal construction. In World War II, PT squadrons trained there. No vehicles are now permitted on the island, and bicycles must be put away by 6 P.M. The beach is a sandbar between Taboga Island and Morro Island, covered at high tide.

Around noon it began to rain so heavily that launch service was discontinued for an hour.

At Taboga we had to put our little float in the water. It is a hollow metal platform decked with wood. It's carried lashed down on the afterdeck, and we winch it up over the side and lower it, then free up the ladderway that leads down from the main foyer doorway. There is a plug on the float so that it can

77

be drained. Even though, the company told me, nothing can go wrong, they hit it against the side of the ship somehow and knocked the plug out. Nobody noticed this, so all the time the launches were coming and going, the float was slowly sinking. We couldn't figure out why it was listing to one side.

Then it really rained hard, and the wind came up and we had to move the float around to the other side of the ship. By the time we were ready to pick it up and get moving, it was about one third submerged, and the big fat Hawaiian sailor we sent down to hook it on had a lot of trouble with it, the way it was flopping from side to side. But we got it up, with a ton of water in it, and it finally drained itself empty, somewhere during the canal transit.

It was a minor and unimportant mishap, but things always happen in threes, and there is no way to tell ahead of time if the next two will be minor also. I remember particularly the triple whammy that occurred when I made my first long South Pacific run, not long after I became captain of the Mariposa. Leaving Los Angeles, I had an old harbor pilot aboard I was not too enthusiastic about. At Los Angeles there is a gantry-type platform that extends from the upper story of the dock structure right across to the ship. It is on wheels so that it can be rolled up and down the dock to exactly the right place where you want it on the ship. As we were leaving the dock, we had one tugboat up on the bow and one on the stern. The tug on the bow was supposed to pull the bow away from the dock. When your ship turns at the dock, it is obvious your bow will overhang the dock, and there was some chance, if he didn't get it far enough off, that it could hit that gantry platform.

The wind was blowing a little, not much, and we started to slide back. I told the pilot he'd better have the tug pull the bow off. In the meantime the tug captain had taken it on himself to get around the bow and get between the bow and the dock and push instead of standing off and pulling. But now our bow was up against the dock and he couldn't get in there to do any good. I looked down, expecting to see him out there pulling, but instead he was trying to wedge himself in between the ship and the dock. So just about then the bow hit the big gangway gantry a good thump and sent it running down the dock. I *didn't think at the time there was much damage, but later we got a bill for $10,000.*

It was initially the fault of the tug captain, but he was under the pilot's orders, and the pilot couldn't understand how such a thing could have happened, so in the final analysis it came down to me. It was my responsibility. I had some words with that pilot, but it didn't do any good. The ship lost a little paint, and we were on our way.

In Tahiti, in the harbor at Papeete, on that same trip, we came in in the normal manner—which is to come in, get turned around, and be facing out with the starboard side of the ship against the dock. But this time the dock we normally use was occupied. The harbor people said we could dock at the other end of this long pier complex. We would be port side to, and our bow would overhang quite a way. In other words, there was not enough room for the whole ship. They asked me and I said I was agreeable. "I don't see any problems. Let's go there."

I'd been aboard in other capacities when we had this same pilot, a young French Tahitian, and he had seemed competent. There wasn't much breeze blowing, but as we approached the berth I thought we were setting sideways a little bit too much. I called this to his attention and he said, "No, it looks okay to me."

I said, "Look aft, because this bridge is so far forward, you don't get the right perspective on the whole thing unless you look aft."

Then I called the stern and asked how close we were to the French freighter who was tied up right behind our intended berth, and he said, "Captain, we are very close and closing fast."

I said to the pilot, "You better give it a little more speed and put the wheel to the left to kick the stern away from that ship."

At this point I had decided I would rather go into the mud up ahead than have a collision with a French ship in a French port. The litigation could go on for months. He did as I suggested, put quite a bit of extra speed on the ship, and as soon as I realized we were just going to clear the freighter, we kicked it hard astern to take the momentum off the ship.

Well, they had strange fenders there on that dock, consisting of a whole bunch of old tires with a big timber through the middle of the tires, probably about ten to twelve tires in a row. We made hard contact with those fenders, and it caused a very loud screeching sound, and some blue smoke came up from the points of contact as we went by. The ship stopped, and we worked back to where we belonged and tied up, and I said to the pilot, "At least we missed the other ship, and anything you can walk away from is a good landing." I hadn't felt any sensation of hitting anything, except I knew we had hit the fenders, but that is what they're there for.

He left the ship and I went down to my room, and just as I got there, I got a call and they said, "You better get down to the laundry room right away."

"Why should I do that?"

"The laundrymen are all rushing out of there ready to abandon ship."

The laundrymen were all Chinese. So I went down and looked, and then I went out onto the dock and looked at the side of the ship. In making contact with the rubber fenders, we had definitely stove in the side of the ship. The indentation was only a few inches deep, but it was about twenty feet long.

This created a new problem. We had to do a very careful inside check to see that there was no structural damage. We had actually bent a couple of frames and buckled the plates, but a careful survey indicated that there was no significant structural damage to the ship and we'd be able to go on. There was no facility to have anything done in Tahiti anyhow. We would have had to take off some of the sheeting in the laundry to examine more carefully what our damage was, and work like that in a foreign port, particularly a French port, can result in a quantity of paperwork you wouldn't believe.

We proceeded to New Zealand with no problem, and there we had some ship surveyors come down and look at the dent. They agreed with our analysis that nothing had to be done until the ship went into dry dock, scheduled in six months. They recommended we be surveyed again at the next port to make sure there was no continuing damage, and we were to take off some additional sheeting at that time to get a better look. And, of course, it was going to be expensive to repair it in drydock.

*Then we were in a port in Australia, with a noon sailing.
The stevedores were finishing up the cargo work, using the
winches to lower cargo into the hatch and bring stuff up and
swing it out and lower it to the dock. The passengers always
enjoy this. Some of them will stand for hours watching the
stevedores when they could be ashore sightseeing. They get so
they are real critics. They would tell me if the men were being
rough with the cargo, or handling it too slowly, or if they were
working fast and efficiently. I would always get a full report
from the passengers. They could watch from the after portion
of the Boat Deck and the Promenade Deck, and from up on
the Sports Deck.*

*I was having breakfast at about eight-thirty in the dining
room. I usually go in and grab a bite in the officers' mess, but
at that time I had some nice people at my table and so I was
enjoying breakfast. Suddenly I heard a big crash, and all the
passengers looked startled. So I said, "Nothing serious.
They've just closed the hatch at number seven. Big steel thing;
they drop it the last couple feet. When they get careless, it
makes a big racket. It's nothing serious at all."*

*A few minutes later I saw a mate out in the lobby beckoning
to me. I excused myself and went out and he said, "You won't
believe what happened."*

"At this point, I'll believe anything."

*He explained as we hurried up on deck. They had been
picking up a big piece of steel fabrication that weighed almost
a ton. It was in two wire slings. They had picked it up and
swung it aboard and started lowering it toward the hatch.*

*In most places one stevedore runs the controls for both
winches, but in Australia they are very big on featherbedding.
There was one stevedore on each winch, a nonsensical arrangement at best. As they began to lower it, there was a
malfunction with one winch. So one of them started to go up,
and the other one was in doubt as to what was going on, and
between the two of them they shot this thing back up into the
air clear to the top of the boom, flipped it around like a sling-
shot, and threw it all the way over onto the Boat Deck, just
aft of the swimming pool, where it came crashing down,
smashed one of the benches there, and made a big ugly hole
in the steel deck.*

By great good fortune there was nobody there, no critics, no little old ladies by the pool to faint dead away as that chunk of fabricated steel came crunching down. Aside from some damage to the booms and a repairable hole in the deck, we were home free. That was number three in the sequence, and I knew we'd have no further incidents. But the paperwork on those three little happenings went on for almost a year.

After the last launch came back, and the gangway and float were stowed, we circled the area until six and then headed for the canal. A boat came and took off officials, briefcases, and a stretcher containing a young crewman, a carpenter's helper. In a roll of the ship, a crate had fallen over on him and crushed his leg.

We sailed under the bridge. The line handlers came aboard, a man began lecturing over our P.A. system on the wonders of the Panama Canal. Passengers altered their routines to the extent that one was constantly seeing faces so totally unfamiliar it did not seem possible they had been aboard all week.

I watched the process of locking the ship through the first set of locks, with an eye to seeing how readily the locks might be sabotaged. There were tensions at home, the beginnings of the long and bitter debate about returning the Territory to Panama. Choleric and indignant men were proclaiming that the canal could and should be defended at all costs. The honor of America. We built it. It was a frontier bravado clashingly out of tune with the realities of contemporary nationalistic fervor. Were we to hold the ground, with difficulty, we couldn't hold and operate a working canal. It is a rainfall canal. Billions of gallons of heavy rainfall are held in the lake and used, in effect, to flush the ships up and down the two slopes, into the Pacific and into the Atlantic, the fresh water flowing out into the sea through the final locks.

The giant gates are hollow structures, so that when they need repair they can be dismounted and towed to a repair area. They are the points of greatest vulnerability. The diesel mules, made in Japan, on tracks beside the channel and atop the locks, pull the ships in and out of the locks and stop them short of the gates. Braking is done in much the same fashion as a brake on a reel on a fish rod, except that the braking becomes more intense as the cable is paid out. The *Mariposa* went through with two mules forward, port and starboard, and two aft. They are enormously heavy, carrying tons of lead just above the tracks on which they ride.

To cripple the canal for a long time it would be necessary only, through bribery or sabotage, to let the enormous weight and momentum of any large ship carry it forward and through the gates while about to begin its passage down to sea level. Or a charge could be dropped from any ship to rest near the base of the gates for detonation from afar when next that lock was loaded with a ship in transit, floating in the rainwater of Panama.

I spent a long time up toward the bow, watching the navigation aids as we cruised the lake and the cuts. It was so silent, burbling along through the stillness of the night, that I could hear, directly above me, the conversational tone of the pilot on the bridge, telling the quartermaster how much left rudder or right rudder to give the ship. I amused myself by looking ahead at the beacons and buoys, trying to read them and anticipate what the orders would be, giving myself merits and demerits depending on how well I anticipated.

We had been invited to a cocktail party at the Pool Terrace at quarter to midnight. When we got there we found out that it was a birthday party. The ship's orchestra was up there, and Art Todd with his banjo. The birthday wife had no inkling of the party. She had taken a sleeping pill and gone to bed and had to be shaken awake to get dressed and be led up to the Pool Terrace and the birthday singing. There was dancing, drinks, do-it-yourself sundaes, and a huge cake baked in the shape of and decorated to resemble the husband's Social Security card—because it was the wife's sixty-fifth birthday, an event the card made abundantly clear to all.

In the small hours of the morning the changed motion of the ship awakened me, and I knew we were out in the Caribbean heading northeast to San Juan.

10

||||||||||||||||||||||||||||||||||||||||||||||||||||

En Route to San Juan

One of those rare days at sea when, in intense heat, the following breeze is making just about as many knots as the ship, thus leaving all the decks in a sooty swelter.

I became involved in gathering material for a petition to Congress regarding an extension of the subsidies on the *Mariposa* and the *Monterey*. Both John Kilpack and Jack Abramson gave me interesting material. The actual computation of a subsidy is too complex to explain here. It involves refunding to the ownership a percentage of wage scales in different categories over and above an international norm. This amounted to many millions of dollars per ship per year.

By law, subsidies last for twenty-five years, deemed to be the statutory economic life of a vessel. Subsidies go with the vessel, regardless of changes of ownership. The subsidy on the *Monterey* would expire in January 1978, on the *Mariposa* in April 1978. The ships could not be operated at a profit without subsidy, under the flag of the United States, so if all efforts for an extension of subsidy failed, ours would be the last long cruise through the Atlantic for either of them.

It would take an act of Congress to extend or renew the subsidies. As I went about that day, checking my facts, I could not imagine any Congressman seeing any political advantage in approving fifty or sixty million in subsidies so that these two last passenger ships under the American flag could continue to tote predominantly elderly Americans from island to island and from shore tour to shore tour for five more years. The same trends and the same reasoning had eliminated ships such as the *Argentina, America, Brazil, Constitution, Independence, Lurline, Matsonia,* the several *Presidents* and the *United States,* and would wipe out the last two White Ships, I thought, without fail.

But for any Congressman willing to look a few inches past the end of his vote-seeking nose, there were some major policy questions needing long-range deliberation, over and above the estimated $40 million a year which suspending the two ships would take out of the economy.

The spring issue of *The Mariner,* a six-page tabloid-size newspaper distributed quarterly to the 40,000 members of the Mariners' Club, was flown down to Panama to be distributed aboard to all. It estimated losses at $20 million payroll for 1,000 persons, $1.15 million for other services, $2.4 million annual maintenance and repair at California shipyards, $2 million worth of ships stores, $2 million in travel agency commissions, $1 million in passengers and freight brought in from Australia and New Zealand, and some $11 million in other related expenditures.

The problem was and is and will continue to be the dreadful dwindling of our total commercial fleet of freighters and passenger ships. As the number of ships dwindles, shoreside services for new construction and repairs are pinched off. Skills are forgotten. The cadre of seamen and officers shrinks constantly. Air services cannot meet national needs. How many air freighters would be needed to carry one shipload of bauxite, forty thousand tons, to this country?

We now depend on foreign bottoms to bring in over 90 percent of our essential commercial requirements. We cannot force them to service us if, for some commercial or political reason, they choose not to. How many years would it take to make back all the ground we have lost?

The U.S.S.R. has not only an expanding commercial fleet but an expanding fleet of cruise ships. Of her twenty-seven in service in 1977, ten were in service on internal waters and the other seventeen were, in that antique phrase, "showing the flag" in all the world's oceans. Lord Mahan's seminal work on sea power was concerned primarily with ships of war. Today's wars can be waged in cold commercial terms, and are being waged in that manner, as our difficulties with the OPEC nations reveal. In the face of this new kind of war, we are disarming ourselves and becoming a bit more helpless each year. Billions upon billions are expended on warships, which at best are sitting ducks in this age of the new weaponry—as outmoded as knights in armor. The vast sums could better be spent in rebuilding our fleet of freighters and container vessels and bulk carriers, in preparation for the inevitable crisis of commercial blackmail which is not far down the road.

So I got the facts together and typed up a petition which was at once both solemn and fervent and turned it over to the people who had talked me into doing it. They made changes, as do all committees, and then it was circulated, signed by practically everybody aboard, and mailed from a foreign port back to some sort of Maritime Affairs Committee of the Congress. I thought it most useful to mention in the petition that both ships used a heavy fuel oil so far down the list of refinery products that it constituted a disposal problem rather than a resource. But, of course, the price was going up on that too.

Perhaps we should have been attempting to achieve a more lenient interpretation of the end of the subsidy period from the Honorable Robert J. Blackwell, Assistant Secretary for Maritime Affairs, of the Department of Commerce. The ships had spent their first five years as cargo vessels before being rebuilt as passenger ships. Perhaps the twenty-five years, by stretching a point, could have been computed from the first day of passenger service. In the absence of such an attempt, Mr. Blackwell went by the letter of the law.

The trusty old Mariners really fought to keep the thing going, but all their letters and petitions were written to no avail. When the subsidy ran out, it was absolutely impossible to operate the ships under an American flag, at acceptable standards. The company did some research on whether they could run to the islands with a greatly reduced crew and a lot of the frills eliminated, but the price of fuel made it impossible.

The unions brought a lot of it down upon themselves. For years the operation was heavily featherbedded. We always had a lot of people we didn't need at all, and they managed to make their overtime charges excessive in certain crew categories. Whether or not a lot more restraint could have saved the thing or not, it's hard to say. At the bitter end, when the unions were willing to make concessions, it was just impossible to meet the competition from foreign lines.

Take the British Princess line, for example. They use all English mates, engineers, and key people. But they use an Italian steward's department, which has a less expensive union agreement, and they use Goanese for the actual crew, the sailors and wipers and such.

On the Royal Viking line, the key people, the captain and the mates and even the sailors, are well paid, but in their hotel section, they hire as waiters and stewardesses people from maybe twenty different nationalties, on the basis of no union, no unemployment benefits, no retirement benefits, and very limited sick benefits. Down below in the laundry they have, in many instances, people who have fled from Red China by way of Hong Kong and are paid very little.

As long as an American ship is subsidized, one of the rules is that all people employed aboard must be American citizens, and that means, of course, that they have to belong to the particular union which covers their job. There is no way PFEL could hire cut-rate labor.

Now you've got all these cats and dogs working the Caribbean: Russian ships, and the Greeks, and some Norwegian. They all hire anybody they can, and there is a going labor market in all the tourist ports around the world. At one time the Japanese worked very cheap, but as their standard of living went up, they were priced out of the cruise-ship labor market. This applies, of course, to freighters and oil tankers as well. Then they went for Chinese crews out of Hong Kong, and then the Koreans became cheaper. At one time they could hire Spaniards at a very low cost. Even on the supertankers, where the crew is very small and where payroll can't really be a big item in relation to total cost, they still go out and shop for the cheapest possible crew. The people you get that way are not really competent or well trained. This can account for some

*of the accidents, collisions, and spills they have. They get an
absolute minimum per month.*

*We were definitely locked into a maximum wage scale over
many years, and we were able to drop only a very few people.
And in every meeting the union reps would scream loud and
long. Over a period of years we took off two quartermasters,
one sound electrician, and a few more minor stand-around
jobs, and they never let us hear the end of it. We were op-
pressing the loyal American workingman.*

*I get widely varying feedback on the foreign cruise ships.
Some of them are terrible. There was a cruise to nowhere out
of New York where they had sewage in the corridors, and
everybody sued. On one of the Italian ships they once had
hundreds of cases of diarrhea which nobody was able to track
down as to cause. On the Russian cruise ships, it seems to be
a good idea to use some of your shore time buying food to take
back aboard.*

*When these ships stop at U.S. ports, where are those health
bureaucrats who made our lives so miserable over the years?
They couldn't have applied the same standards to those ships
which they applied to ours. Why not?*

That evening at an estimated 42 degrees west latitude, we
went to a cocktail party celebrating a couple's 42nd anniversary. We have gravitated toward people who have similar interests and disinterests: a market analyst and his wife, some
retired State Department people, a retired general, a grain
and feed merchant, a Washington researcher, a labor-relations
attorney and his wife, a ball club owner and his wife, a
physical education teacher, a photographer and his wife, an
eye surgeon and his wife, a real-estate broker and his wife.
Most of these people had other circles of contact. The pattern
of contact could be drawn with overlapping larger and smaller
circles. Were I to try to pin down what made our particular
group cohesive, I would say it was a shared irony, a greed
for conversation, and agreeing about what to laugh at and
when to laugh. Of the ship's complement, the Abramsons,
Cashmans, Todds, Stanleys, and the captain were the ones
who most closely shared our view of reality. Far away, in

other corners, in other circles or alone, were passengers who seemed to us totally out of touch.

On one trip I took, one of the fifty Mariners aboard was a little old lady who looked so frail and old I wondered how she could get on and off the ship. She would spend hours staring out at the ocean, all alone. So I made it a point to speak to her whenever I saw her. I'll call her Mrs. Merlin.

On the night of the big costume party aboard, I do not know whether she actually applied for one of the categories or whether she saw people walking and just fell in behind them. Anyway, she was wearing one of her regular dresses, which wasn't exactly subdued, and she walked around and around and ended up with first prize in the Most Colorful category. So the captain (not me that time) came out and gave her a gift, and the ship's photographer took her picture with the captain, and they escorted her back and sat her down in her chair.

As soon as the awarding of prizes was over I ran over and said, "Mrs. Merlin, congratulations! I'm so proud of you."

She stared at me and said, "For what? What did I do?"

"You won a first prize in the costume party."

"I did? I didn't know that. What did I get?"

"You got this nice set of place mats that you're holding here on your lap."

She looked down and said, "Oh, aren't they nice!"

Another time we were way out in the middle of the ocean, on our way to Hawaii, when a nice old lady who had apparently done the tour through Disneyland before she boarded the ship came up to me and said, "Excuse me, captain. Is it true that the ship is attached to a cable that runs along the bottom?"

And I said, "Well, I sure hope so. Otherwise I wouldn't have taken the job."

Sometimes there is a question that really stops you. There is absolutely no answer. A woman got on at Hawaii to take the South Pacific trip. A couple of nights out, I was attending a cocktail party and this woman came up to me and said, "Captain, just how many people are employed on the Mariposa anyway?"

"Right now, two hundred and seventy-five, give or take a couple."

"Oh, my! And do they all sleep aboard?"

I keep thinking of better answers every year. All I could say then was yes.

Sometimes, of course, it is obvious there is nothing you can say, when the best response is a hasty retreat.

One hot day on a Circle Pacific cruise, I walked past the pool where a group was basking in the sun. One was a special friend of mine, a Hungarian lady named Eva Sommers, who had a very heavy accent. I stopped to chat and they suggested I change to swim trunks and come back for a swim with them. Eva said, "Please, sveetie, you come back and ve can mess around in the pool a little bit."

When I got back to my quarters there were some calls and some messages, so I didn't get back to the pool as soon as I had hoped. By the time I did get back, the rest of the group was gone, but Eva was still there. I recognized her by her blue and white swim suit. She was stretched out face down with a towel over her head. So I went over and bent over her and whispered in her ear, "Come on, sveetie, now ve can go mess around in the pool a leetle bit."

An absolute stranger sat bolt upright and stared at me in shock, anger, and disbelief.

11

||||||||||||||||||||||||||||||||||||||||||||||||||||||

En Route to San Juan

A bright day, high wind, a lumpy sea. At noon, San Juan was 298 miles away. It seemed to be jock day. People were playing off the games they'd signed up for. Paddle tennis in the wire-enclosed court up on the Sports Deck. Ping pong, quoits, deck tennis with the high net and the rubber ring—one of the most energetic and frustrating games known to mankind. Lots of fast walkers, living up to their pre-cruise vows. And a lot of the very old ones, sacked out in the deck chairs, head collapsed on a shoulder, mouth agape, being shifted slowly as they slept by the motion of the ship.

Every cruise has its makeshift Lothario, often more than one, but there is usually one very obvious one. It will be a man in his forties, divorced or a widower after a quarter century of marriage. He will have recently changed his plumage: dyed hair, snappy clothes, recent dieting. He, by God, has come aboard to make out, and he has a nice single outside cabin, with booze and ice, and he has taken bridge lessons and an Arthur Murray refresher course to help him prepare for romance. Unless he can find his exact counterpart in a

93

female in her middle years, with the same yen for escape, romance, and transoceanic lovemaking, he is not going to do well at all. The lithe young things travel with a watchful set of parents and are more interested in officers in their twenties than in randy old passengers. The other bunnies in the suntan group are waitresses, who can be observed down there on a deck off limits to passengers. He has believed the advertisements, the posters, and the brochures. He has expected to make out like a rabbit dropped into the cabbage patch, but he finds to his total dismay that on this long cruise, of the three hundred passengers aboard at any given time, nearly two hundred are women, a hundred and sixty of these women are over fifty, and of the forty remaining, thirty are too young or too weird, and quicker fellows have already moved in on the remaining ten. As his search becomes more despairing, his hunger becomes ever more obvious to the passengers at large, and as his ventures continue to fail, they begin to watch with a certain cruel glee how, even as he becomes less discriminating, he continues to be rebuffed. He blunders about with a frozen smile, nodding and humming and wondering how he got into this.

One time at my table, I got this real dude from Kansas City or someplace, and he is really primed for the trip. He was a divorced accountant named Stanley something. He had a brand-new mod tuxedo and quite a few ruffled shirts. The first couple of nights aboard there was a cute little blond entertainer who sang: Linda Wilson. Stanley met Linda, and he was really enthralled and came on very strong.

About the third night they put a new passenger at my table: an attractive woman, a little older than Linda but sharp and well-groomed, traveling alone. So all during dinner Stanley was making a big pitch to the newcomer.

That night we went up to the Poly Club to see the show, and all of us at the table sat together. Stanley wanted to be right in front so he could cheer for Linda and make the big pitch, but he also wanted to keep in with the new one in case things didn't work out.

They put extra chairs on the floor along the edge of the dance floor and we were all seated in a row. There wasn't room for all of us, so Stanley had a chair out in front of those chairs. He was virtually a part of the floor show, he was so far out front. The new woman was sitting right behind him, and I was sitting next to her.

Linda Wilson came on, the lights went down, and she sang a couple of ballads. He was clapping like crazy, but he also managed to turn around now and again, with a big smile, to have a little conversation with the woman behind him.

Then the lights went down again, and Linda was singing a very sentimental ballad. Stanley very casually hooked his arm over the back of his chair and put his hand on the woman's knee, keeping time to the music with little light pressures. She nudged me and pointed to his hand. I reached over and took his hand. He squeezed and I squeezed back and he squeezed and I squeezed back, and everybody sitting along our row could see this. They were giggling and getting a big charge out of it.

At about that time Stanley looked around with a big silly sentimental grin on his face. The woman smiled back. Suddenly he noticed that she had her arms folded across her chest. He looked down and saw that he was holding my hand. He let out a blood-curdling yell and threw my hand up in the air, and everybody who had been watching collapsed laughing. Poor Linda couldn't imagine what was going on. The rest of the audience was shushing our group. As I remember, Stanley missed dinner a few nights.

When passengers have mating problems, the captain can be an innocent bystander, but when problems arise with the crew, they create a lot of trouble.

Like with old Bernice, the nurse. She came aboard the ships when I first came on and she was desperately looking for a man. I think she had been an army nurse at one time. She had been married but had been a widow for a long time. Her family was grown, and she wanted a man so obviously that she scared them all away. She never knew when to keep her mouth shut. We called her Sarge, because she looked like a top sergeant. Also Flannel Mouth, Muscle Jaw, and other names less delicate, because she was a genuine pain in the ass. One time when she came down to the dock in boots and hot pants, somebody said all she needed was a whip.

After about a year aboard she found her big romance, and it was with Joseph, a deck hand. Joseph was a big dumb Hungarian about fifteen or twenty years younger than Bernice. He bought her an engagement ring; if you looked real hard, you could see the little diamond there. Everybody had to listen to Bernice talk about all his virtues, how he would come up and do all the heavy work around some little place she had up in the Nevada mountains, and how her whole family liked Joseph, and it was the big thing in her life she had been waiting for. In any foreign port you would always see Bernice and Joseph strolling down the street, hand in hand.

We were on an Alaska trip. I really didn't care for those trips to begin with. They require me to be up on the bridge a lot of the time, and I am not all that crazy about staying up there and going down all those narrow channels where weather can be a real problem.

We were coming to the end of one of the Alaska trips. We had arrived at Victoria early in the morning, which meant I had been up since four o'clock, and we were going to sail in the evening. So I had gone up in the afternoon after the formalities had died down and stretched out to take a little rest. I didn't like to tell the operator that I would not receive any calls, because in the event that something happened, maybe something not all that serious, I would rather know about it than find out two days later when somebody said, "Well, we didn't want to call you because you were taking a nap."

I was about half asleep when the phone rang. It was Bernice, the nurse.

"Captain, I hate to bother you but Joseph has just struck me. I have had a fight with Joseph."

"Where are you now?"

"We are down in the doctor's office."

On that trip John Bender was chief purser. I ran into him on the way and asked him to come along, as I might need a witness. We went into the doctor's office, and Bernice was sitting behind the desk and Joseph was sitting where the *patient would normally be, and they were glowering at each other. In the middle of the desk was the ring. She had thrown it at Joseph and he had given it back to her, and she had thrown it in the wastebasket and he had dug it out and put it in front of her.*

I went in and said, "Listen, I don't have time to settle domestic disputes and I don't want to listen to all the whys and wherefores of this thing, so let's knock it off right now. Joseph, in effect you are an enlisted man. You are an unlicensed person and you have no right to be up here at all associating with Bernice. What you do ashore is your own business. I know what has been going on, and as long as everybody kept cool I preferred to look the other way. But now you are rubbing my nose in it. From now on, until the end of this trip, you two stay apart from each other. When we get to San Francisco you can go ashore and settle your differences, and that is all I want to hear about it."

I left, but Joseph followed me out into the passageway. "Captain, do you think I would hit Bernice? I love Bernice. Bernice is the only woman in my life. Since my wife died I have never had anything to do with any other woman, and Bernice is the first one who has turned me on." I looked at him to see if he was kidding. He had to be out of his mind.

"Joseph, I am not interested in that. As I told you in front of the chief purser, I want you to stay the hell away from each other until this trip is over. Do you understand me?"

"Yes, Captain, I do."

I went back to my nap.

We left that evening, and just as we were leaving the breakwater, after I had dropped the pilot off, and I was doing one of the few things that I am really paid to do, be the master of the ship and take it out through the breakwater and out through the traffic, the phone rang. It was for me.

Bernice said, "Captain, I am sorry to bother you, but Joseph has just hit me again."

"Jesus Christ, Bernice! I am trying to get this goddamned ship out of port. What the hell is the matter with you?" I slammed the phone back onto the hook.

I turned to Coco, the chief mate, and I said, "Joe, go on down to Bernice's room and see what is going on and tell them that when I get out of here, get this ship cleared of the port and the traffic, we will get this thing settled once and for all."

He went down and came back and reported that Bernice was alone in her room.

So I told him, "All right. I will be clear in about an hour, and at that time I want Bernice and Joseph and the doctor and the union delegate and everybody else up in my room, and I will settle this thing once and for all."

When I got clear, I went down to my room and was told that nobody could find either Bernice or Joseph. The first thing I thought of was murder and suicide. That would be bad news for me, because after I have been advised about potential violence and I don't take action, anything that happens is my fault. So I told them to break out some more people and search again, search everywhere.

Finally they flushed Joseph out of a friend's room. He was in there playing cards. They brought him to me.

"Where is Bernice?"

"I don't know."

"Joseph, you are in the soup right now. If you have done anything to Bernice, you had better talk right now because this is a bad situation."

"Captain, you know I wouldn't hurt Bernice. I love Bernice. She is the only woman in my life. After my wife died—"

"Shut up, Joseph, and go help find her."

All my spies went out. Finally they found that dizzy nurse dressed up in a formal gown, attending a passenger cocktail party in the Poly Club. They brought her up to my quarters in her formal. She had a mouse under one eye, so it appeared that Joseph had indeed belted her.

I proceeded to rip into both of them. "God damn it, both of you have disobeyed a direct order. I told you to stay apart and—"

"Captain, after he hit me the first time I asked to have the lock changed on my door because he has a passkey."

"Captain, I wanted to give her back the ring, that's all."

"I don't want to listen to all this. I told you two to stay absolutely apart. Bernice, why the hell did you let him into your room?"

"Well, he said he just wanted to talk to me."

"Joseph, you leave me no choice but to lock you up, because if anything happens to Bernice between here and San Francisco, my neck is really out a foot."

Bernice said, "Oh, Captain, please don't lock Joseph up."

So I got her out of there and I said to Joseph, "You've got me over a barrel. I was willing to let the matter drop and not say anything about it, but now, with all this stuff, the whole crew is stirred up and I have no choice but to put it in the official logbook that you assaulted an officer. Bernice is, in effect, an officer of this ship and you struck her."

"Captain, do you think I would hit Bernice? I love Bernice. Bernice is the only woman in my life. After my wife died—"

Finally I put Joseph under what you might call a peace bond. He agreed he was not to go near the woman, near the doctor's office, near Bernice's deck. I sweated it out until our arrival in San Francisco, knowing that I should have locked him up.

I called ahead and said I wanted the Coast Guard down there on arrival. I wanted them to take over and settle the thing. When I talked to the office I said I wanted a replacement for Bernice too. I said I wanted them both off the ship. I had had enough of this, clear up to my ears.

During the last hours of the trip, Bernice kept trying to see me, to discuss the whole thing. I said, "I don't want to talk about it. It's out of my hands now. You can talk to the Coast Guard when we get to port."

"Well, under the circumstances, I think maybe I'd better get off."

"I'm way ahead of you, Bernice, I've ordered your replacement."

When the ship arrived, the Coast Guard investigators came down. They interrogated one person at a time and took color pictures of Bernice's mouse. They never seem to do much, actually. When they learned Joseph had no past record, I guessed they would put it in their computer and forget about it. But at least Bernice and Joseph were both fired off the ship and I was rid of them.

Later in the day Joseph came to me and said, "Captain, I wonder if you could do me a favor."

"What's that?"

"I've worked for PFEL for three years, and I have always been a hard worker. Could you give me a letter of recommendation?"

"No, Joseph. I don't give many of them anyhow."

Then Bernice got hold of me and told me she feared for her life. Joseph, she pointed out, was a big husky guy, and she's got this place up in the mountains and Joseph knows where it is, and he could go up there and do her bodily harm.

"Bernice, if you feel threatened, take it up with the police. I'm not concerned in any way. I just want you and Joseph to hurry up and get off the ship."

Joseph came to me again and said, "Captain, I wonder if there's another favor you might possibly do me?"

"What is it, Joseph?"

"All my clothing and stuff are up at Bernice's place in the mountains. I wonder if you would intercede and ask Bernice if she would drive me up there to get my stuff?"

"No, Joseph, I don't think that's a good idea anyway. Why don't you drive up there and get it yourself?"

"I don't have a car."

"Why don't you take the bus?"

"There's no bus goes up there."

"Joseph, you have a problem. Go rent a car. Go do something, but don't bother me any more. I have no interest in your problems. I don't care how you get up there. Just leave me alone!"

The next time I walked down past the dock, Bernice came running out and snagged me. "Captain, Joseph asked me to take him to my place in the mountains. Do you think I should do it?"

"Honestly, I don't care what you do! Just leave me alone! A little while ago you were telling me you feared for your life. Now you want to take him on a six-hour ride to Nevada. Please just get the hell away from me. Both of you. Get off my ship. That's all I want."

Finally, finally, they got all their gear together and

got it off the ship. And somebody told me that they saw the two of them at nine o'clock that night, wrapped up in a very tender embrace on the dock, and then the two of them went and got into Bernice's car and drove off into the sunset.

12

||||||||||||||||||||||||||||||||||||||||||||||

San Juan, Puerto Rico

So many cruise ships stop at San Juan that the whole area near the docks has somewhat the flavor of a big bus station. The passengers are processed by tour guides and bus drivers who have seen so many hundreds of thousands of Americans they have all begun to look alike. The little quips and jokes built into the standard spiel have become as automatic as a facial twitch.

Dorothy and I take organized shore tours when there is absolutely no alternative, as in Russia or China. We have found it far more agreeable to read up on an unknown area in advance, decide where we want to go and what we want to see, and then go out and establish a firm price with one of the ever-present taxi drivers. It must be made quite clear that the agreed price is for two people, or four, and not a price per head. And in most ports more foreign than San Juan, one must guard against the driver who *seems* to be able to speak English. "Have nice car here, boss. Show you everything. Nice day, go to nice places. Get in, boss. Get in, lady." And that can be all the English he knows. So before you get in, you smile at him and ask him if he is married, if he has children, how old they are. If you draw a total blank, look for another driver. Properly planned and executed, you can avoid what promises to be dreary, spend as much time as you wish at what you want to see, eat well, and end up spending less than people spent for their tour tickets.

We are not enthralled by Puerto Rico. We had driven around during a previous trip. There are urban areas where the tourist is not welcome, areas of an intense hostility, despite the island standard of living and mean average income, the best in the Caribbean area. It will probably become the fifty-first state, a partial solution to the unrest fomented in part by the Cubans, in part by the stories of the mainland brought back by self-repatriated Puerto Ricans, and in part by the overpopulation of all the islands of the semi-tropics, where increasing millions of bare feet are stamping a rich fertility into dust and hunger. So, there is a rain forest, and there is El Morro fortress, and there is a tourist-type shopping area.

We got off and walked about. Went up to the place in the fort where you can look down between trees and buildings and see the ship. Walked out of the fort to the place where we had looked over a wall the last time and seen several horses feeding on a gentle slope of rock and scraggly grass and debris that reached down to the sea. Yes, the horses were still there, picturesque and improbable. We walked several blocks along the coastal street above the rocks and then turned inland and found our way down into the center of the city. Bought news-papers, magazines, a necklace of three Chinese porcelain beads on a blue cord, debated taxiing out to one of the beach hotels for lunch, then walked back to the ship instead. The older beach hotels, the ones nearest the city, have changed hands so many times they would feel at home on Miami Beach. And they look as if they belonged there, with an overall decor, a friend once said, like unto a dental plate.

Aboard we found a new couple, friends from other cruises who had flown over from St. Croix to join this one: a peppery, crochety, sour, funny old boy who had retired from the printing business a long long time ago and his tolerant wife, with a freshly broken toe. He planted himself in front of us, beamed at us, and said, "Thought I was dead, didn't you?"

"We sure did."

The buses unloaded the shore-tour people at the gate on the street, and they came straggling onto the dock to climb the gangway, laden with cameras, camera bags, and purchases. A staple of every shore tour is a stop at a souvenir shop. All over the world the shore-tour people dicker with gift-shop operators to obtain the best deal in return for stopping with their loads of pigeons. It is either a flat fee or, in cases of mutual trust, a percentage of the take.

It has always amazed me, really amazed me, that people who wouldn't travel anyplace on a bus in the states except under threat of death will take all these shore tours. At home, if they had to go from A to B, they would fly, drive, rent a car, or con a friend into driving them—anything in the world but a Greyhound.

I know passengers who have probably never in their lives ridden on a bus who come aboard and pay two hundred dollars a day for a cruise, and when they get in port they are willing to be herded onto a bus and taken for a ride somewhere. And some of these all-day bus rides are very expensive.

Some of them come back bitching about how they rode on a bus all day and the driver was rude. Others will come back with high praise and what a good time they had, and if there were several different buses making the same tour, which is quite common, I'll hear them in the bar later, arguing about who had the best driver, and which driver told the best jokes, and which guide you could understand and which one you couldn't.

Then on every bus tour there are always the little old ladies who demand a certain seat right in the front of the bus, and the ones who seem to be frail and walk with a cane, but don't try to get too near them when they are standing in line to get on or off the bus because they'll puncture your ankle. Some of them have the little canes with four prongs on the bottom, a four-prong walker, or whatever they call them. They are really dangerous. They can get four tourists with one shot. People learn to stand back and give them the right of way when they take a tour. Then there are the ones who carry a big shoulder bag full of rocks on a long strap, and if they want to edge by you they give that bag a nice big swing and catch you just under the belt buckle and then step into line ahead of you when you fall back.

On one trip there was a couple with the wife in a wheelchair, who wanted to attend everything aboard and see everything ashore. Let's call them the Hobarts. The husband was a very quiet meek little guy, really beaten down. I don't know why she was in a wheelchair, an accident or polio or something, but anyway he had to push her everywhere. She had a voice like a saber saw, very whiny. And for her, everything was wrong. "Look out, Howard! You'll bang me against that post. Watch it! What are you trying to do? You're going too fast!"

"Yes, dear. Okay, dear. Sorry, dear. Excuse it please, dear."

I had them construct a couple of little ramps so he could push her up over the doors that have raised sills, like onto the Pool Terrace and onto the Main Deck. They had a room at the end of one of the forward ship alleyways, and she complained bitterly that they couldn't make the turn with the wheelchair and get into their room. I guess he had to carry her in and go back and fold up the wheelchair and carry it in, and then reverse the process when they left the room. We tried to move them to another room, but no, she liked the room they were in, only why did they have to build the ship that way?

At all the functions aboard, at anything in the Poly Room or out on the Pool Terrace, she expected a place right up front because she was in a wheelchair. The other passengers were very kind to her. They always left an aisle for her, and she always arrived late. They always moved their chairs to make a place for her right in front. I made a point of avoiding her because every time I saw her she had a complaint. We've had lots of other people aboard in wheelchairs, and they are almost always patient and considerate and grateful for any little thing you can do for them.

Before we would arrive in the various ports, he would arrange ahead for a limousine. They would get her down the gangway in her wheelchair, or down the ramp, and at least once they took her down and out through the Crew Deck port because that side port was level with the dock. But there was always some squawking in advance about what the arrangements would be.

Then we arrived at Moorea and anchored in Cook's Bay. At this particular port we use our own gangway. We rig it up to the side of the ship, and it leads down to a very small float, and the launches come alongside and pick up the passengers and take them ashore.

She cornered me. "How am I going to get ashore?"

I said, "Mrs. Hobart, I'm afraid that this is one you are going to have to skip. Even the people quite able to get around, some of the older people with canes and walkers—I worry about them and we escort them down the gangway. And then the float at the bottom is subject to bobbing around because we are in a big bay here. I have a lot of very anxious moments about getting everybody on and off, but it's the only way it can be accomplished at this particular port because there is no way to dock."

She said, "Well, I go ashore at every port. That's why we bought tickets for this cruise, and I am going to go."

"Mrs. Hobart, I would be happy to see you go and I don't want you to miss anything, but I don't know what we can do. There's just no way we can get you down there."

"Well, when I made a trip on the Statendam, the captain carried me down the gangway."

"You've got to be kidding. There's no way I could carry you down the gangway. I have this old war wound and a hernia. And I am not going to let any of my crew do it. It is too dangerous. I'm afraid you just won't be able to go."

She wasn't buying this at all. Finally we anchored and the people were all jammed into the main lobby waiting to go ashore. We always announce that there is no rush, and you will be paged, and please don't block the lobby, but they are always there, all jammed in, breathing hard, each wanting to be the very first one ashore in every port. I looked into the main lobby, and people were standing ten deep waiting for the first launch. Over on the outskirts of this scene was Mrs. Hobart in her wheelchair. I could hear her loud whine about people having no consideration for people in wheelchairs.

I went back up onto the wing of the bridge where I could get a good view of the whole operation, and where I could put an immediate stop to any arrangement she made to have anyone try to carry her down that steep gangway. When it was time for the second launch load, I saw her husband push her out onto the little corrugated steel platform at the head of the gangway.

Right there, she got out of her wheelchair and walked down the gangway and across the float and got into the launch, with her husband following her with the folded wheelchair. She went very slowly, but she went.

That really blew it. That ruined her case for the rest of the trip. Everybody had been bending over backward to show her consideration in spite of all her bitching and whining, but from then on she was in the back of the line for everything.

To get back to the shore tours, for years I never went on any of them. I would listen to what the returning passengers would report, and then the next trip, when somebody would ask me about a tour, I would repeat what I had heard.

On one trip when my wife and son were along, I succumbed and made several of these bus trips. And from then on I could speak with more authority.

On the Alaskan cruise one of the highlights is a trip on the narrow-gauge railway from Skagway up to the top of the pass. It was built during the Alaskan gold rush days at a considerable cost of life and limb. They sell a package tour where you ride up on this little railway, and at the top you are served a lunch of beef stew, beans, and sourdough bread. I thought I had better take it so I could speak with authority from then on.

There was a good turnout, several hundred people all from the ship. We all got on funny little coaches on the narrow-gauge railroad train. Right after I boarded, an old man and his wife got on. He was really old, perhaps in his eighties, and nattily dressed. She looked like Gravel Gertie. She had a pin holding her sweater together, and she had bobby socks hanging down over her saddle shoes. And her lower teeth were missing.

They immediately got into a loud argument. She was hassling him because she couldn't find her sister, who probably got onto another car. "Why didn't you keep better track of my sister, hah?"

And the old boy said in a loud voice. "Well, goddamn, I've had it up to here with her!" He ran his finger across his throat. "I've had it with that old broad. For one thing, she's stone deaf. She can't hear a thing. You have to yell everything at her, and you try to talk to her for two or three minutes and all she wants to talk about is Jesus Christ. I've had it up to here with your sister."

They found a seat, and as soon as the train started she went into this fantastic lecture to everybody on that car. "Everybody should go to the toilet on this train," she said. "You take my word for it. I made this same trip nineteen years ago, and I told my husband here to go to the toilet on the train and he wouldn't do it. And I'm telling you what's going to happen. We get to the top of the pass and five hundred people are going to pour off this train, and they only have one toilet up there and it's a one-holer. I'll tell you it was a real hassle up there like you never saw before. All you people, you better take my advice and go to the toilet on this here train."

About a quarter of the way up the mountain she decided to take her own advice. The seating was two long bench seats running the length of the car, with everybody facing each other, and a narrow aisle down the middle. She announced what she was going to do, and went in and did it and came back to her seat, with people reaching out to steady her on account of the rough roadbed.

She sat down next to her husband and said, "It's really great. You all ought to go. When you flush it, the water turns blue."

The old doll turned out to be absolutely right. Everybody got off the train and headed for the bathroom, and it was a one-holer, and they spent most of their time at the top of the pass standing in line. On the way down she told us all that the next time she prophesied anything on this trip, we'd better damn well listen.

There was another couple on that train trip, very old and very tall and slim. Whenever I would talk to them, and the old boy would start to say something, he would only get a few words out before his wife would start going "Ssh ssh ssh ssh" until he would stop.

The old boy wasn't that loud. I guess it was a habit she had formed over the years, an unconscious nervous habit, indicating he was either talking too much or too loudly.

My wife, Kay, heard this and thought it was hysterical. She doubled up laughing. I didn't think it was all that funny. I thought it was sad, that poor old boy never being able to finish *a sentence for the rest of his life, unless he was saying it only to her. But Kay explained that in China and Taiwan, where she was born, that was the way they had always instituted toilet training with tiny boys and girls. They would sit them on the potty and go* Shh shh shh shh shh *in exactly that same way until they learned.*

At four we went up on deck to watch the departure. The channel needed dredging. We churned up the bottom all the way out, big boiling clouds of mud staining the green water and tailing out behind us. When we went past the old fort on the starboard side, we looked along the steep shoreline for the barrio we had seen on the previous trip, picturesque at a distance, a festering ugliness at close range. Squatters had moved onto the slope and built shacks of tin, scrap plywood, tarpaper, and cardboard and had painted the shacks in bright colors. It looked at a distance as if children's toys had been spilled down a rocky slope. We had been told on the previous trip that the government was going to force the people out and clear the slope, but the settlement looked larger than before.

This is, of course, one of the primary problems of Latin America, the migration from the countryside to the cities, made more critical by explosive birthrates. It makes for squalor, hopelessness, degradation, and violence. If unchecked, the population of Mexico City will reach thirty million in the year 2000, making it the largest city in the world. Caracas, São Paulo, Rio: all are scabrous with the shacks of the squatters.

A cruise is a sanitized affair. We see the barrio from afar. It has bright colors and seems to sparkle. We passengers do not wish to know of the sick children dying in the barrio shacks. We do not want to know how much hate is being born of despair in all the barrios of the great cities to the south of our nation. Hunger stunts the minds of two generations. We do not want to see hunger from our tinted bus windows. In effect the cruise is a trip to what used to be, a voyage by twilight people in an obsolete ship, off to visit museums and souvenir shops. The sores and bandages of the world would depress us, and we have paid money to be amused, not depressed.

So we sail on into the Bermuda Triangle on Friday the thirteenth, into that area created by magazine hacks to chill the blood of the ignorant. Being scared is harmless fun. Witness Halloween.

There is a joke aboard that evening. "Remember the kid who got taken off the ship with a smashed leg down there in Panama?"

"Sure, why?"

"Well, he might get on a lot of talk shows this summer."

"How? Why?"

"He missed the mysterious disappearance of the *Mariposa*."

13

|||||||||||||||||||||||||||||||||||||||||||||

En Route to Hamilton

Hot muggy morning, turning to chilly rain in the afternoon.
Hal Wagner lectured on Bermuda at eleven in the morning.
Full house. We are to be part of the six-hundred-thousand-plus
tourists they will attract in 1977. Eighty-eight percent of all
tourists American. Tourism the biggest source of income.

Businessmen in the audience sat at attention when he talked
briefly about business on the island. No income, sales, inher-
itance, or profits tax. There are 3,400 foreign-owned (many
U.S.-owned), exempted companies—exempted from having
to obey the stringent laws of Bermudian ownership and em-
ployment.

Many groups of people who come to the lectures have some
little woman bird-dog the seats for them. She will come scut-
tling in early, grab choice seats, put hat in one, purse in another,
scarf in another, camera in another, and plunk her aggressive
little bod in another, half an hour before the scheduled time.

On another cruise the practice became so virulent that management had to step in and make some rules, putting a notice
in the ship's paper. "From this day hence the only thing in a
seat that will reserve it for an upcoming event is a behind. A
purse, a book, or an item of clothing is not a behind and may

be removed by the stewards and turned in at the purser's desk."
Applause.

Many rumors this day about somebody having missed the
ship or been put off the ship or falling off the ship. Related
somehow to Bermuda Triangle. Nothing to it, we decided.

*The source of that rumor was a very old lady traveling alone
who had become pretty sick on the way up from Panama, so
we wired her people to come meet her in San Juan and fly her
home.*

*Of course, people do die aboard. Carrying so many old
ones, it's bound to happen. On one world cruise I understand
the* Kungsholm *lost seven and kept them all refrigerated until
they reached their home ports. This is often easier than the red
tape of off-loading a body and flying it home.*

*On one island trip we had a millionaire about a hundred
years old traveling in a Lanai Suite with his much younger
wife. I think his name was Wirebacher, something like that.
On the morning we got to Hawaii they found the old boy had
died. He was in his pajamas on the deck between the twin beds.*

*I talked to the doctor and the chief steward about it. The
doctor said it was either a massive coronary or a stroke.*

I said, "Was he smiling?"

*The doctor looked puzzled, "Well, he didn't seem to have
died in any pain. I guess you could say he appeared to be
happy enough."*

*"In that case," I said, "let us all prefer to think that it
happened while he was trying to get back to his own bed."*

*Another time, on a fairly routine trip when we were on the
long run south from Hawaii to Tahiti, a woman passenger
became quite ill from a respiratory problem. The doctor was
concerned about her. She wasn't responding to routine treatment, and we didn't have the facilities aboard to make the tests
he felt she should have. He told me that unless she showed a
very substantial improvement, he wanted to hospitalize her in
Papeete.*

*I said he was the doctor, the authority; whatever he advised,
I would agree to without question. The doctor told this to the
woman, and she told her husband.*

I don't know what the man's profession was, but I had

learned that no matter what the topic of conversation happened to be, he was the ultimate expert in whatever it was, and his opinions were carved in stone. He came boiling to me. "What is this I hear about a hospital in Tahiti? You are not going to hospitalize my wife in Tahiti. They don't have decent facilities there. The hospital is a pigpen. It's not sanitary. You have to bring your own linens and towels and soap."

I wondered where he could have gotten his information, and then the light bulb went on over my head. Good old big-mouth Bernice, the nurse. "I have to go along with what the doctor advises," I said. "That's what we have him aboard for. I respect his opinion, and he is genuinely concerned about your wife."

"Well, we planned this trip for a long time and I have no intention of terminating it in Tahiti. Besides, what would we do with all our luggage?"

"Let's worry about that when we come to it. Maybe they can take her right away and make the tests the doctor wants made, and she can come right back aboard."

He wanted another opinion, and he kept talking about the problem of the luggage. He more or less indicated that if she did go to the hospital in Papeete, he was not going to stay there with her. He would continue the trip because of all the problems they'd have with the luggage.

I said, "Make your decisions about what you do. We're out here in the middle of an ocean. We do the best we can. When we reach a port with adequate medical facilities, we take advantage of them when necessary."

I had to go through two or three more sessions with this man. The closer we got to Tahiti the more enraged he became. I finally got him and the doctor together in my cabin for a three-way talk.

I said, "We are now going to have a calm and reasonable discussion about this. If we can't get the tests done in time, and if the doctor feels your wife's condition is such she cannot continue this cruise, then she will stay ashore in the hospital."

"And if that happens," he said, "you are going to get slapped with the biggest lawsuit you ever saw in your life. Do you read me? My ticket entitles us to take this cruise, and you are not putting us off anyplace."

"In that case," I said, "you had better read the very very fine print on the back of that ticket. I have an option on these things, and if I don't take advantage of other medical facilities and care and opinion, I would really be open to a lawsuit. We have a seven-day run from Tahiti to New Zeland. How would you feel, sir, if we didn't do anything and continued on and your wife passed away?"

And he said, "Well, after all, she is sixty-three years old and she's lived a full life, and that's the way the ball bounces."

Both the doctor and I realized at that moment we were not dealing with a rational person. I don't know what he had in mind.

We had wired ahead to Tahiti regarding what we wanted done. They got her to the hospital, confirmed the doctor's treatment as the correct one, and said they really could do no more than that for her in the hospital. She was brought back aboard and continued the trip and finally regained a reasonable state of health before the trip ended. Naturally, the husband wanted to tell the doctor and me that we were needlessly alarmed. I don't know if he spoke to the doctor. But there is nothing in the fine print on the back of the ticket that forces me to talk to any son of a bitch I do not care to talk to. Had I wanted to say anything to either of them, I would have told his wife, after she recovered, not to lean over the rail on a dark night.

Sometimes the doctor aboard can run into a situation nobody can anticipate. We were on a special Mariners' Cruise to the South Pacific, and we were stopping at new ports wherever possible because most of the people aboard had been to all the others.

Our first stop after Hawaii was Christmas Island, an operation where nobody goes ashore. We anchor out and admire the view, and the locals come out and put on a show and sell souvenirs. We do the same thing at Rarotonga. A day before we arrived, we had a wire from Christmas Island asking if we were capable of doing any eye surgery aboard; a boy there had a fishhook in his eye. We wired back that we didn't have that type of facility aboard, but we would be happy to examine him and see if there was anything we could do for him. I assumed it would be one of the native boys.

We anchored, and out came this young blond kid, with his father and a woman and another man traveling with them. They were around-the-world yachtsmen from Canada, planning to sail for a couple of years, and about the time they got to Christmas Island the kid was fishing and got this hook in his eye. They went ashore, and the local doctor tried to take care of the situation. (He had had some training, but I don't think it was at Johns Hopkins.) When the accident had first happened, the father had taped the top part of the hook, its eye, against the kid's forehead. The local doctor had cut off the shank of the hook as near the barb as he could manage, whereupon the barb disappeared into the kid's eyelid. And at that point he was afraid to try to go any farther.

Our doctor wasn't very anxious to try to do anything either, but it was obvious that the wound was festering, and if the hook didn't come out the kid was going to lose his eye or even his life. So he and the two nurses and the hospital technician worked all the time we were at anchor. I think the doctor did a hell of a good job, though I am no authority on the medical profession. He got the barb out, cleaned the wound, and sedated the kid. The two men and the young woman were there, standing by.

The younger of the men, an uncle or an older brother of the kid, decided he'd had enough of this romantic cruising around in a sailboat and needed to get back to Canada as soon as possible—to close a big business deal, he said. He wanted to book passage.

On this trip we were completely booked. It doesn't happen too often, but we were. In fact, we'd been overbooked from Los Angeles to Honolulu. The chief purser told him there was no space available.

"I've got to get out of here. I've got to make connections back to Canada. I'll sleep anyplace. On a davenport or a cot or whatever. All I want to do is get somewhere where I can catch a plane."

The purser took a look at the man's passport and found he had no visas whatsoever. "Sorry, I can't book you," he said. "Our next port is a French port, and they won't let you off there to catch a plane without a visa. We know that from experience."

We'd had a bad time on a previous cruise with a couple and their two kids, trying to land them at Papeete to fly home. We discovered that her passport had expired en route, and even though she had a valid visa in the expired passport, the French kicked up a fuss, and it went practically up to the international diplomatic level before we could get her off just to board a plane with her family. The French make a whole life's work out of picking nit. They are as bad or worse than the authorities in Calcutta and Karachi and Leningrad and Shanghai. They do not want you to confuse them with logic. Thinking clouds their minds. If it isn't in the rule book, it can't be done.

The fellow demanded to see me, and I said, "Sorry. Can't help you. I don't know where or what port we'd be able to get rid of you, and you would be our responsibility for all that time." He got nasty, so I ended the discussion.

He went out to the Pool Terrace, where the show was going on, and ran into one of my constant passengers, who, like Bernice the nurse, never knows when to keep quiet. The fellow told Sam his problem, how he had to get back to Canada, and of course Sam was going to fix the whole thing. "Hey, I know the captain. He's a personal friend of mine. I'll talk to him."

So Sam came to me and I said, "No, Sam. No! I know the whole story. I know the visa problem. No way. Look, it was his choice to go along on this wonderful romantic yacht trip lasting several years, right? It seems so glamorous, but when anything happens, they want all the ships at sea to start circling around looking for them. Sorry, but I'm not sympathetic. If he was planning to be gone so long, how come all of a sudden he has to get back?"

Because nobody was going ashore at the island, and we weren't leaving anything off, there was no need for customs or quarantine or immigration clearance. Sam got back to the fellow and said that he was sorry, he hadn't been able to do anything with the captain. The man was disappointed and told Sam he had been stuck on the island for quite a few days with nothing to eat but coconuts and breadfruits and fish, and he would like to buy some food to take back ashore. It had been announced over the P.A. system that nothing was to go ashore. And the same notification had been published in the daily Po-

lynesian. *But good old flannel-mouth Sam said, "Hell, don't worry about it. The captain's a good friend of mine. We'll fix you up and it won't cost you a thing. We'll get you a big bag of food to take ashore."*

Sam came to me again and I had to go through the whole thing for him: The ship has no clearance. The guy can take ashore all the food he can carry—in his stomach. He can have the biggest meal he can hold. By then the yachtsman was very snarly about it, and Sam just couldn't understand why I wouldn't pitch in and help him out.

Before they all left the ship, the doctor showed that young woman how to treat the eye. He gave her antibiotics and the necessary medicines and dressings. We sailed away, expecting to hear how the boy made out. It had been an operation for free, a courtesy to people in trouble, and he'd seemed like a nice kid.

Would you believe it, we never heard one word from those turkeys? No note, no thank-you, no nothing. Nobody connected with the ship has ever heard from them.

As far as people missing the ship is concerned, it happens, of course. Every once in a while the two ships, the Monterey and the Mariposa, would hit Hawaii at the same time, one of us outbound and the other heading for the barn. It always made a big afternoon for the crew running back and forth, seeing old friends.

On one of those afternoons we had some kind of Hawaiian entertainment going on in the big lounge. A lot of the passengers were in there and the Hawaiians were doing their hula thing, when at about that time the Monterey sailed. She backed out away from the pier, and as she went by we blew three blasts on the whistle and she answered back, and everybody looked out to wave to the ship leaving, and somebody said, "Well, there goes the Monterey."

And this little old lady said, "Oh, no! There goes the Mariposa. This is the Monterey."

"Excuse us," the people said, "but this is the Mariposa."

"Oh, my God," she said. "I'm supposed to be on the Monterey."

Finally they got word to me, so I dashed up and got on the VHF radio and called Jim Stafford, who was the skipper over *there at the time. By this time he had pulled out of the break-water, dropped the pilot, and was moving on up to full speed ahead.*

I said, "Jim, we've got a Mrs. Wilson, Room Two-twenty-seven, who is supposed to be on your ship, and she is over here."

And he said, "Well, tell her to have a nice cruise on the Mariposa."

Another time on the way back from the islands the pursers told me that a couple had managed to miss the ship when we left Honolulu. It was an island cruise, and I guess I had met them but I couldn't recall their faces. When we tied up in San Francisco four and a half days later, I passed down through the public rooms saying goodbye to people, telling them to come back soon, and so on. I ran into a couple down in the gallery where they have the ship's photographer's pictures on display. We'd had an incredibly smooth and cloudless run from Hawaii, in an area that can get lumpy indeed. So I said, "Did you folks enjoy that run from Hawaii?"

She gave me a very frosty look and said, "It was unfor-gettable."

And he said humbly, "We're the people who missed the ship. We flew back. We just came down today to get our lug-gage."

Once we were getting ready to sail from Los Angeles at six o'clock, and at five thirty I got a call from Delta Airlines. They said they had a flight coming in from the East somewhere, and there was a party of three on board who were to join our cruise and would I hold the ship?

"How long?"

"The flight is late. But it's due to land at six, and they should be down to the ship right away."

"That means about an hour by the time they get their bags and get transportation down to the dock. At least an hour."

"Oh, no. It won't take that long at all."

"Don't give me that, I've flown into L.A. on your airline, and it's impossible to get your luggage within half an hour, and it's another thirty to forty-five minutes at best, and they'll be in heavy traffic. They'll never make it."

"Will you hold the ship for them?"

"*If I called you up and told you my ship was late coming in and I had some passengers for you, and your flight was due to take off, would you hold the flight for them?*"

"*Well, no, we really couldn't do that.*"

"*Well, then, you've got my answer. I can hold the ship for a few minutes, a reasonable time, up to fifteen, but that's it.*"

By coincidence I got a call from another airline as soon as I hung up, and they told me they were on the ground and my passengers were starting for the ship and could I hold. I said I was taking on fuel and could maybe hold for a little while, but they would have to hustle.

The passengers were an elderly couple and the wife's aunt. Pretty soon I got a phone call from them and they said they were on their way and were calling from the corner of Sepulveda and something, and would they make it?

I told them to hurry right along and they would probably be okay.

Ten minutes later the phone rang again and it was the same people, this time calling from another corner, Figueroa and something, and they wanted to know if they were going to make it.

I said, "Look, don't call me. Don't give me progress reports. Just keep coming and you should be able to make it."

I told the purser's office the situation. The passengers were out on deck throwing streamers. We left the gangway up as long as possible. It was fifteen minutes past sailing time when the limo pulled up on the dock and a bunch of stewards ran out to grab the luggage. The late arrivals got a big round of applause from all aboard.

The people on Delta never did make it. They flew on to Hawaii and joined the ship there. They were not especially upset. They knew I couldn't hold the ship for them. We figured that they would have gotten to the dock at about seven thirty, when we were an hour and fifteen minutes out to sea.

As for people disappearing at sea, I never had one of those, thank God. There were times I thought I had one, but they always turned up, sometimes in the wrong cabin.

There are, of course, many instances of passengers disappearing off cruise ships in the middle of the ocean. One woman fell or jumped from the *Monterey* during one of the ship's final cruises.

Another was Carla Iris Bodmer, the sixty-nine-year-old widow of Leo Bodmer, president of the Swiss newspaper *Neue Zurcher Zeitung* and a director of the Brown Boveri Engineering Group. After her husband's death she lived for a time in the Palace Hotel in Lausanne and was considering emigrating to Australia.

She read an advertisement for a ninety-six-day QE2 "Great Pacific Cruise," booked passage from New York to Sydney, and flew to New York from Lausanne with eighteen trunks, several fur coats, and a fantastic collection of jewelry. She boarded in New York on January 16, 1978, a lively, forthright, gregarious woman, with hair dyed brilliant red.

Postcards she sent to friends in Switzerland reveal that at first she did not like the ship. Her cabin, 4207, was not as luxurious as she had hoped. That cabin, with its fare of $8,-5000, did not entitle her to eat in the Queen's Grill, the most elegant dining room aboard, and she was unable to purchase permission, as the available spaces at table in the grill were filled.

But soon, apparently, as she entered into the social swing of things aboard ship, the games and contests, dances and parties, she began to enjoy herself. On several special occasions she appeared wearing over a million dollars' worth of precious stones, which she kept in one of the safety deposit boxes provided by the purser's department.

Instead of leaving the ship at Sydney to emigrate, as she had planned, she decided she was having too good a time. She was able to take over a vacated cabin at a higher cost, $10,500, for her passage from Sydney to Honolulu, an arrangement which entitled her to eat in the Queen's Grill. (The total cost of her passage from New York to Honolulu via Sydney for $19,000 can be placed in context by explaining that the most expensive accommodations aboard ship, the duplex penthouse, was available on that cruise from New York to New York for $165,000.)

On March 27, Mrs. Bodmer checked her luggage through for disembarkation at Honolulu. On the evening of the twenty-sixth, when she had turned in some jewels she was wearing, she had, for some reason, left her lock-box key with the purser. On the morning of the twenty-eighth, before the ship arrived in Honolulu, the room maid found the cabin empty, the bed still made up. Captain Peter Arnott ordered a search of the ship. She was not aboard.

The QE2 was built with passenger safety in mind. It is highly improbable that anyone could ever slip and fall overboard by accident. She was not depressed, nor did she take drugs or drink to excess. Friends say she was a cheerful person. On the way to Honolulu she talked with obvious anticipation about flying back to Australia to live. As there was no inventory of her jewels, no one can say if any are missing. All her jewels and furs and trunks are in storage at the Queen's Warehouse in Southhampton. There are no claimants. No one has been able to find any living relatives.

The wry footnote is that her possessions *have,* in one sense, been imported into England. They are there, though she never intended them to be there. And the tireless tax collectors of Her Majesty's Customs and Excises are looking for some legitimate owner of the dead woman's goods so they can levy a charge for the import duties. No one else in an official capacity seems to have any remaining interest in the fate of the old widow with the bright red hair.

14

▊▊

Sunday, May 15

Hamilton, Bermuda

Though there were some cruise ships tied up at the Bermuda docks, there seemed to be room enough left for the *Mariposa*, but we anchored out. Possibly it was a decision made ashore because of our lack of sewage holding tanks. Or it could have been a San Francisco decision based on the cost of anchoring out versus tying up and paying dockage charges. The third possibility would have been a flaw in the coordination arrangements of the several cruise companies involved, but in that case I suspect that we would have been able to come in, had some other ship failed to arrive on time.

Launches are a tiresome nuisance. One hopes to be able to wander back and forth from ship to shore at will. And we were there on a Sunday. We went ashore by launch and wandered for a time up and down the main street, looking at the expensive goods from all over the world displayed in the windows of closed shops.

On long cruises, your ship will often arrive in port on a Sunday, a national holiday, election day, or during a strike. This is particularly true of those ports where the stay is short. It was a long time before we realized why this was so. There is an enormous amount of preplanning involved. The schedule of the ship must be established early enough for the shore tours to be set up and published in a lengthy brochure far in advance of sailing, so that interested passengers can make paid reservations early. Shore facilities must be given a firm commitment to set up their buses, drivers, guides, dining facilities, and so on, from six to eight months ahead of time. In a "popular" tourist port, dock space is so limited that arrivals must be staggered.

So look at the commercial logic involved. The *Mariposa*, with its less than 300 passengers, stops at Port Enchantment once every two years, if that, and may never be seen there again. But the *Stella Solaris* (630 passengers) and the *Vistafjord* (700 passengers) and the *Fairsea* (830 passengers) and the *Calypso* (740 passengers) call there every few weeks or months. Moreover, it is no secret around the world that the American passenger fleet has dwindled to a pair of small old ships, and they too will most probably disappear. So despite the clout of the Thomas Cook travel service in setting up peripheral arrangements, guess who is going to get the off days?

We had the good fortune to find a car with an agreeable and imaginative driver. We wanted a look at the best residential districts, the best hotels and beaches, the best view, and we wanted to find a nice place to have a late lunch.

We drove through a reckless welter of tourists on motor scooters, and our driver said that out of the twenty-five motor scooters hit by automobiles the previous year, nineteen drivers, all tourists, had been killed. Only two of the six survivors had been wearing crash helmets. He said they fly in, climb onto an unfamiliar machine, and go chugging off into an entirely unfamiliar traffic pattern on narrow roads with no shoulders and lots of traffic. He said he had lost count of the times they had turned directly in front of him. But there was no attempt to dissuade the tourists or publicize the carnage. After all, renting the scooters is a profitable business. Tourism is a profitable business. Shades of *Jaws*. Had sharks grabbed nineteen visitors, the flights to Bermuda would soon have been almost empty. It is a tourist area syndrome. Don't advertise the drawbacks. Keep them quiet. Never tell the travel writers that over forty tourists drown each season in the dangerous tidal currents at Cancún.

He drove us up to the lighthouse for the view: a wide sweep of islands, marinas, sailboats, beaches, and our small white ship out there with a water-beetle launch drawing a white V on the blue water, heading out to her. It is a handsome and tidy island, with its white-roofed pastel houses nestled into niches in the volcanic rock, surrounded by an opulence of flowers and greenery.

We stopped at the Waterlox Inn, with its great gardens, owned—as are the Princess hotels—by the mysterious Mr. Ludwig. Then we had the driver drop us off at the Hamilton Princess, where we had a rum punch and then walked back to the docks and took the next launch out to our white ship, sitting inside because the late afternoon was turning chilly. There were some tour-bus people on the launch, wearing Bermuda Triangle sweatshirts purchased at the ubiquitous bus-stop souvenir shop.

We had started losing our Hawaiian sailors in Puerto Rico. Most of our sailors were Hawaiian, and many of them had never been that far from home before. I think they thought they were going on a trip to Hilo or Kailua, and when they found out how far from home they were, they began to panic. From Puerto Rico on, we were losing one Hawaiian at every port.

Prior to our arrival in Bermuda, I had been following the company's instructions to the letter, checking everything out in the big thick book and making the time changes as ordered. So as we approached Bermuda I was confident I was on their time. Some passengers with radios tuned to Bermuda told me that the island was an hour ahead of the ship, but I told them it couldn't be so; it wasn't in the book.

When I contacted the port authorities, they told me I was an hour late. Unbeknownst to the book, and me, they had gone onto daylight time. It was embarrassing; a ship's captain should know what time it is. There were people up around the Pool Terrace, having a little pre-lunch nip at eleven o'clock, ship's time, so we made an announcement that it was twelve noon, and the chief steward got the kitchen staff busy rushing the lunch up to the Pool Terrace, which came as a shock to the early drinkers and the late breakfasters. But on the whole, most passengers seem to be able to eat at any time food happens to be served.

So two things had gone wrong: the plug getting knocked out of the float and the time of arrival in Bermuda fouled up. I wondered what the third was going to be. At least we did not lose the drummer and the cute little assistant cruise hostess. Our departure was scheduled for six in the morning. We picked up the anchor, and the pilot took us out along a reef. It was about an hour and a half from the anchorage to the pilot boat where we were to leave him. I was on the wing of the bridge looking down to watch the pilot transfer, and I saw the drummer and the hostess duck quickly back inside the pilot boat. They came aboard when the pilot stepped off. When I saw them later in the day, I told them they were very lucky they made it back, and please spare me any involved story about not being able to get a cab back to the dock.

Musicians often create extra static aboard. Ashore too, so I have heard. One time we were having our back-to-back champagne parties before dinner, the second night out. The first party went off okay. It's the older set at the first sitting, and you have a lot of canes and a few wheelchairs. Then we have a fifteen-minute break—we call it our half-time period, when we all tell each other we're doing a great job and we'll go out and really take them in the second half, like the L.A. Rams. Then we go charging out of the dressing room and line up for the second party, which is usually livelier.

That night, after the main bunch of people had already gone through the line on the second half of the party, this woman came rushing in wild-eyed. She started to go past the receiving line, so I used the little joke I always seem to use when that happens. I say, "Hey, you have to shake my hand. If you don't shake my hand, you don't get any free booze."

She said, "I already shook your hand. I'm on the first sitting. I just came back up here to make a complaint." She said this very loudly.

"If you have a complaint to make, madam, you came to the right place. What's your problem?"

"That goddamn organist. Who the hell does he think he is?"

"Oh, if you have a problem with the organist, why don't you discuss it with Mr. Scott, here, the cruise director? The organist works for him."

I signaled to Alan Scott to get her out of there, because she was being very noisy and upsetting the other passengers. He hustled her out, and that was the last I heard of the problem until the next day when Jim Yonge briefed me.

The woman and her husband and brother were on the trip together, on the first sitting. I didn't recall their going through the line; it was early in the cruise. She had quite a few glasses of the free champagne, and they went on down to dinner.

The organist, Paul, was playing in the dining room. He is a mild-mannered man, doesn't bother anybody, always co-operative, but he'd been on board for several months and had begun to get a little irritable.

He was playing quiet dinner music and the woman decided she would go up and ask him to play a request. She was middle-aged, but she asked him for some kind of rousing rock tune, "Sock It to Me, Tiger," or some such. He said he didn't know that tune, sorry. She then asked him for "Four O'Clock Rock," or something like that. He said he didn't know that one either and kept noodling away on "Tea for Two"-type music. A few minutes later somebody went up and requested "Tie a Yellow Ribbon," and he decided that wasn't too much of a rouser to fit in, so he played it.

The woman went charging back up to him, demanding loudly to know that if he knew and could play "Yellow Ribbon," why wouldn't he play her requests? I don't know what he said next, or what she said to him, but apparently he told her that the music she wanted was out of order for the older crowd on the first sitting, and he would continue to play music suitable for them.

At that point she apparently had something to say about his ability to play the organ at all. And he said that if she didn't like the way he played the organ, she could go sit down and stop making requests.

At that she continued to chew him out, so he put his left hand over his ear—she was standing on that side—and continued to play with his right hand. This so enraged her that she hauled off and belted him across the head with her purse and came running to complain about the whole thing.

Jim Yonge took the woman and her husband into his office to discuss the incident, and got Paul, the organist, in there too. Paul said that if he had been rude he wanted to apologize on behalf of the ship and the company, and he hoped that would end the matter, even though she really shouldn't have belted him with her purse. They more or less accepted his apology but were really not very happy about it.

The next night I was attending one of the passengers' cocktail parties before the second sitting, and they pushed the panic button and called me out. Jim Yonge was there. "You won't believe what just happened!"

"What happened, Jim?"

"The lady went back down to dinner tonight, and Paul was in there playing the organ again, and somebody had put a hard hat, one of those construction hats, on top of the organ, and when they saw her coming through the doors into the dining room, they ran up and put the hard hat on top of Paul's head. She has really freaked out."

I found out later that the other passengers had been needling the woman about belting Paul with her purse. He was well-liked. A big-mouth waitress told her Paul would probably sue. The woman had absolutely no sense of humor, so the needling built up a head of steam, and the hard hat was the final straw.

I went into a huddle with Si Lubin, then chief steward, in the empty cardroom off the lounge. I sent him to locate the woman and her husband and bring them to the cardroom. When they walked in, I could see the wife was close to hysteria. I made a very sincere apology. "As to what happened the first night, there is some room for discussion. I don't know the true story of that incident. But what happened tonight is absolutely inexcusable. We are supposed to have professional people down there. This never should have happened."

She said, "You don't give a damn about us. We're just small people. All you do is cater to the rich people. You don't care if we're a laughing stock."

"Madam, I try to make it a point to spread my time around as much as I can. There are so many people aboard I can't get a chance to know them all personally. But I care about everybody. Everybody bought a ticket, and I try to do everything I can to make their voyage pleasant. I am very sorry this thing happened, and I hope you will accept my apologies. I know it's small consolation to you, but for what it's worth, I am going to take some disciplinary action over this incident."

"Against who?"

"There is a headwaiter down there, and a head waitress, and a second steward. If I find out this thing was instigated by ship's personnel, or if they connived in it, encouraged it, or even stood by and let it happen when they could have stopped it, heads will roll."

"I don't care about those people. I want that goddamn organist."

"Okay, let's see if we can work that out right now."

I walked out of the cardroom to the phone beyond the glass partition and told the operator I wanted the organist. She took several minutes to come back and tell me he was on his break. I told her I didn't care what he was on, I wanted him.

When he came on the line, I said, "Paul, this thing is completely out of proportion. It's ridiculous. It never should have happened. I'm up here in the cardroom with these people, eating a load of crow, and I want you to come up here and really apologize."

"For the hard-hat incident?"

"No. Just a general overall apology."

When he walked in he had a smirk on his face, and when he walked up to the couple, all of a sudden he and the woman were screaming at each other about who started the whole thing.

"Hold it! Hold it!" I yelled. They stopped and I said, "Let's not have a replay of the whole thing. We want to hear your apology, Paul."

So he stared at them and smirked and said, "If it will make you feel any better, I apologize."

I thought the husband was going to belt him in the mouth. I told Paul he could leave, and he went swaggering out. Of course I had to apologize again. "I'm flabbergasted," I said. "I thought I had more rapport with my crew. I feel as if he really shot me down. All I can say to you is that I most sincerely apologize and I hope I can do something to make up for this."

Finally I got her calmed down. I told the cruise director to pay special attention to them and make sure they were having a good time. The next day I wired the company to accept the resignation Paul was tendering. He was off the ships for about six months. The whole thing was unlike him. It shows what can happen when an entertainer spends too much time at sea. Also, there was some very bad chemistry involved; the two apparently hated each other at first sight. But I must confess I wish I had seen her face when she walked in and saw the hard hat on Paul.

15

||||||||||||||||||||||||||||||||||||||||

Monday, May 16, through Sunday, May 22

En Route to Southampton

The passengers settled into the routine of a seven-day run more readily than on our first long run from San Diego to Taboga Island.

Three of the nights were formal, one casual, three informal. There were travel movies about Paris, Antwerp, Holland, and Denmark—as well as *Robin and Marian, Seven Percent Solution, A Song to Remember,* and *The Amazing Dobermans.*

There was craft time with Kaui in the lounge, bridge lectures, bridge competition, deck sports, art lessons, ukulele class with Art Todd. There was headdress assistance in preparation for the Mad Hatter's Ball. There was trapshooting, a golf driving range, slimnastics and the dance with Ross and Marge Werner, and cocktail-hour serenades. There were port discussions and lectures by Hal Wagner. There were shows by Art and Dotty Todd, a concert by baritone Jan Muzurus, a piano recital by Joyce Stanley with introductions by R. C., an art show in the lounge, paintings by R. C. Stanley and his students. There was deck walking, deck sitting, barstool sitting—and visits to the laundry, the hairdresser, and the barber. And always a quick look at the shop, because they kept bringing things up out of storage to keep interest keen. There was the parade of the funny hats, and a British dinner, dancing every night until past midnight. No packing and unpacking. No airports. No traffic to fight. And, best of all, no obligation to attend any of the entertainments or instructions.

It was a pleasant ship to walk around in and merely look at the designs. According to literature published by Matson, the sister ships contained 763 pieces of art by twenty-three artists, commissioned by the designer to create the color and culture of the South Pacific. The swimming pool mosaics contained 600,000 pieces of unglazed tile representing South Seas marine life. In the dining room of the *Mariposa* were six large inlaid wooden panels in warm tones of walnut veneer and gold-flecked tiles depicting various workday activities of the South Sea Islanders. There were hundreds of plants spotted about: kentia palms seven feet tall, tree ferns, philodendron, and bamboo. The big mural across the front of the Southern Cross Lounge was a stylized representation of the skies of the southern hemisphere, done in inlaid glass and tesserae in glazed walnut panels.

It was disturbing to think that this entity, this presence, could cease to exist. No national commission could designate it as a monument to anything. A ship, more alive than a building, can die as a building does not. The petitions, the efforts to keep the ship in service, were as futile as rearranging the deck chairs on the *Titanic*. And indeed one thought of the *Titanic*, the *Lusitania*, the *Andrea Doria*, of a barnacled splendor in the deeps. I thought of two ships I had been on years ago, the *General Von Steuben* of North German Lloyd, sunk by a Russian submarine in World War II in the Baltic Sea with 3,000 refugees from East Prussia aboard her, and the original *Statendam*, burned at the docks in Amsterdam in an air strike; of the *Conte Biancamano* of the Italian Line, captured in the Panama Canal while the Italian crew was trying to torch-cut her drive shaft, converted to a troop ship, which, in convoy with the *Argentina* and the *Brazil*, took me from Los Angeles to Bombay a life ago.

Years later we took a two-week Costa cruise out of Port Everglades to the Caribbean, Venezuela, and return aboard the M.S. *Franca C.*, captained by one dynamic chap named Emilio Zonka. It was a little old ship, held together by countless coats of paint. Captain Zonka, on warm afternoons, would stride the deck wearing his Mediterranean swim briefs, a white towel turbaned around his head, and a vivid smile. The small swimming pool was exceptionally deep. There were two vacationing stewardesses aboard. Captain Zonka loved to play "Cheeken!" with them. That involved grabbing one of them, descending to the bottom of the pool, involving her in tender embrace until one of them, out of air, would have to fight free and come bursting to the surface. This entitled the other one to come up for air and yell "Cheeken!"

The big single engine stopped one afternoon about eight miles off Aruba, where the sea breaks against boulders at the foot of hundred-foot cliffs. A cylinder had cracked. They carried a spare. It was a question of waiting until the engine had cooled sufficiently so they could use an overhead hoist to pull out the cracked cylinder, about a hundred pounds of it, lower the new one into place, and make all the necessary connections and attachments. One could look down through slanted gratings from the main deck, down into the Dante-esque engine room where excitable sweating men ran back and forth, yelling at each other.

As the long hours passed, we drifted closer and closer to Aruba. One of our group, Gordon Palmer, ducked under a chain and reached up and spun the gleaming brass propeller of one of the lifeboats. It spun freely, and kept spinning for some time. "Just as I thought," he said bitterly. "It isn't fastened to anything."

Night fell. The people on Aruba built bonfires atop the cliffs to warn us of danger. At three in the morning the familiar vibrations started up, and everyone sighed and went to sleep. In the late afternoon Captain Zonka had been on deck, playing cheeken. We wondered if he was trying to hearten us with his unconcern. We would have preferred to see him up on the bridge.

The *Franca C.* had a very low overhead belowdecks. If you were six feet tall, it was all too easy to crease your scalp on one of the protruding sensors for the sprinkling system.

Early in the trip the dance team aboard gave a show. It was a combination of ballroom and adagio. The man was very muscular and hearty, and the woman was quite slender and nimble. At one point she came scooting toward him, and he caught her by the waist and swung her up and thudded her head against the overhead with such enthusiasm that when he put her down her knees slowly bent and he had to grab her and hold her until she revived. Then he danced her slowly off the floor and into the wings, leaving the band to finish the number as best they could.

Some of the acts we've had aboard have been unbelievable. We used to shake our heads, wondering where the guy who booked the shows for the two ships found these people. We knew there was a lot of good talent available, certainly better than what he was putting aboard.

One time we had a troup called the Funelli Family. I can't remember their credits, but their routine was to be a lot of nostalgia from the last days of vaudeville. This was a show-biz family that had been out of work for maybe a year, and here was their big chance to lock on to a steady job.

The family consisted of a mother and father, two daughters, a son, and a son-in-law. There was supposed to be one more, but on final count there were six of them. The publicity pictures went up around the ship, with the tag line, Fun and Laughter at Sea with the Funelli Family.

When I am checking the ships out I like to take a look at the new talent rehearsing. They had a scroungy old trunk open, and the mother and daughters were wearing leotards with holes in the legs and skin bulging through the holes. I assumed these were their practice outfits and they would have some nice costumes for their opening show. I was wrong.

Some of the people in the dining room told me about their first breakfast aboard. They were assigned to a table by themselves, over on the starboard side forward. They came trooping in and picked up the menus. These menus are big: a full page of everything from waffles to breakfast steaks. As the waitress stood poised to take the order, the father handed her back the menu and said, "This looks good. We'll take it."

She brought it all, and they put it all away.

When their big night came, it was total disaster. The sea had been a little bumpy. There is no dressing room up in the Poly Club, so they put a screen around the closet by the door where the band keeps their stuff. They would dash in and out for their costume changes. The mother and daughters were trying to do soft shoe or tap dancing, but all three were seasick. They were trying to keep the big show-biz smile in place, but one or another of them kept making the forty-yard dash to the ladies' room.

We had to stop the father from starting his fire-eating act until we could get some people standing by with fire extinguishers, in case he set the overhead crepe-paper decorations alight. At the finale the father dashed off for a quick costume change and came back with his fly unzipped and sang, "You Are Going to See More of Us." It got the only laughter and applause of the evening.

It was an eighteen-day Island cruise, and the Funellis were into the groceries at all times. They would go to the buffet on the Pool Terrace and hit that line three times each, heaping the plates every time. Some of the passengers figured out that during the eighteen days the six Funellis gained weight equivalent in total to the Funelli who had missed the trip.

Another time we had a female organist, probably in her forties but very naive. She was the kind of person who believes anything you want to tell her. I don't think she had ever been married. We were docked in Sydney and she and a girl singer decided to go together over to the opera house and look at it, on their own, not in any tour. They went out onto the street and caught a cab. The cabdriver was a real hustler, playing every angle at all times. He was, I guess, more or less of a part-time pimp, looking for a couple of gals to put on the line. The singer was very pretty and the organist not bad-looking at all.

The cabdriver established that they were working on the ship, and he had worked on a ship too, so they had something in common, he said. The singer was wary of this clown. She sensed some kind of an approach coming up.

Finally he got to it. "Say, how would you gals like to have a date tonight?"

The naive organist said, "Gee, I don't know. Is he tall?"

And at this the singer broke up entirely.

We have almost always had a dance-instruction couple on board. They are supposed to have two duties. One is to teach dance lessons and give exercise sessions in the mornings, and *the other is to help the cruise staff at all social functions, mingling and mixing and giving special attention to the unaccompanied and obviously lonely passengers.*

Some of the couples were very good at this second responsibility, and some of them, who didn't last longer than one cruise, came aboard thinking they were Fred Astaire and Ginger Rogers, there just to perform and then disappear.

The line experimented and found that if they got their instructors from a school of dancing, there was a tendency to hustle the passengers for private lessons. But the ones who worked out well, like the Werners, came on cruise after cruise.

I remember in particular one pair of instructors from Santa Cruz. He was a very unlikely type, a contractor by profession, a slender spidery guy with a red beard. He and his wife really loved dancing. They took the job seriously and circulated around the Poly Room every night. He danced with every old lady up there; I was amazed at the way he would go around and around the room. I told him that if we'd been paying him by the pound, he would have made thousands that trip.

I remember another couple where the husband must have had very serious misgivings about the whole thing. He looked a little bit like Teddy Roosevelt, mustache and all. I think she must have told him that he wouldn't have a bit of trouble if he just kept smiling. Smile at everybody and look happy and it will all work out. All the time they were aboard, he was smiling: a whole bunch of teeth showing in front, no matter what was going on. It got to be a joke around the ship that maybe someone should get a passkey and see if he smiled in his sleep.

Speaking of teeth, sometimes there was inadvertent entertainment aboard the ship. We had an old Limey bar waiter named Gay Bentley who had been around for a hundred years and had supported horses all his life.

He was a very jovial, happy little guy, with a tendency to go up to new passengers, smiling, and say, "I'm Gay. I'm your waiter."

A woman who had traveled with us many times was having a little bon voyage party with old friends. They were in the bar area having drinks and Gay was their waiter. He had apparently been out the night before and was a little the worse for wear this morning. In fact, he was really suffering, and when he brought the drinks, he was not his usual spry and happy self.

When he brought another round, the woman, who had known him for years, said, "Gay, you don't seem very cheerful this morning. Come on, show your teeth."

All she wanted was the big smile, but Gay complied by whipping his teeth out and laying them on the tray. Fortunately the woman and her friends took it in good form, but she said to me later, "For God's sake, don't ever tell Gay to show his teeth, because he will."

You never know what they are going to put aboard as instruction or entertainment. Usually R. C. Stanley was the one aboard for art instruction, or Edie Meyers, who instructed in cloisonné, helping the passengers cook pendants and things in her little electric furnace up on the Pool Terrace. Sometimes it would be Nichols with his jewelry and lost wax method. Then there would be guest lecturers, maybe stocks and bonds, real estate, precious gems, and so on.

After each trip we would have a meeting. All the brass would come over from the office, and we would all discuss the bad things that had happened on the trip, and what the plans were for the next trip, and how about keeping that overtime down a little further, and that sort of thing. These meetings were held in the cardroom at eleven in the morning or one in the afternoon. At one point I had been up since four or five in the morning because of an early arrival and all the business of getting the ship secured, cleared, and so forth.

We were having one of these meetings and all the brass was there. I was having a hard time staying awake while they kept droning on and on about the previous trip. They were discussing the merits of the last lecturers and entertainers, and somebody asked, "What do we have lined up for the next trip?"

I had my head on my hand, trying to keep my eyes open, and I heard somebody say we were going to have a course in gargling.

I popped up wide awake and irritated. "Gargling? This is ridiculous. How the hell many ways can you gargle?"

"Not gargling, John. Gardening."

"Gardening?" I said. "Aboard the Mariposa?" It was almost as incomprehensible as gargling.

But sure enough, some clown came aboard, and they lugged on about fifteen boxes of dirt and set it all up in the lounge, and he gave courses on gardening. They did indeed grow flowers in the lounge.

I remember that on our long run from Bermuda to England we had our wheel of fortune at the Outrigger Bar one evening at cocktail time, to keep people amused. When I first heard of it, I thought it was an absolutely ridiculous idea. The wheel was set up above the bar with numbers from 0¢ to 75¢, and it was spun every half hour from five thirty to seven thirty. The place it landed would be the price of drinks for that half hour, from free to seventy-five cents. Any drink.

When we first used it on a prior trip, I was dead set against it. They said it had gone over big long ago when Matson owned the ships, and they wanted to revive it, as something to liven up the cocktail hour.

I said, "Why the hell should these people get all itchy over cut-rate drinks? Maybe if there was a real prize offered on the spin of the wheel, it might work. But this Mickey Mouse thing won't work at all. It's tacky."

They talked me into it, so I went down there to watch the fiasco. The night before this particular revival, we'd had the champagne party, where people can order anything they want for free, and they had seemed to enjoy it, and everybody said they had a nice time.

So I went down and learned something brand new about human nature: People would rather have a nickel drink or a dime drink or a two-bit drink than a free drink. On the first spin of the wheel, the drinks were forty cents, and everyone thought that was great. They were buying drinks back and forth, and the next time when the drinks went to twenty-five cents there was a big cheer, and everybody wanted to buy everybody else a drink. People who normally drank the regular bar brand were buying Johnny Walker Black Label and Chivas Regal. Nice old ladies who rarely drank at all were ordering Mai Tais because they were only twenty-five cents.

At that time Si Lubin was the chief steward, and we had one of the auditors at the bar stamping the cards so we could keep track of the whole thing from a bookkeeping point of view. I think at that time the drinks were usually sixty-five cents, so *the wheel was set for sixty-five tops, and here Lubin was selling drinks for twenty-five cents. He paced back and forth, looking highly nervous. At the next spin they went, I think, to a dime. A big cheer went up. Si's stomach was in knots. He looked as if he wanted to cry. On the final spin the pointer landed on zero, and Si went off to his room and locked himself in.*

I was wrong about how it would work. And after that first time, we used it off and on, to liven up a trip. The only danger, of course, was that people would get too sloshed. When drinks are a dime, it is a rare pleasure to buy all your friends a nice big drink or two.

We had a week of rumbling up a long northeast slant, from warm to cool, from sun to gray winds, from opposite Atlanta to opposite Gander. And every evening there were the cocktail parties given by passengers—in a corner of the Poly Room, or in either wing of the Outrigger Bar area, or in the cardroom, or up on the Pool Terrace. Mighty easy to give a party aboard. Go to the second steward, Ken Yoshinaka, and find an open date and a suitable place for ten, twenty, thirty, forty, a hundred people. He gives you the invitations. Make them out and put them on the bellboy's desk. Show up at the right place a little before the stated time. Greet your guests. Drink with them. Bid them, finally, farewell. All drinks ordered have been noted down. John Merlo's marvelous galley has provided the spread of free hors d'oeuvres. All you have to do is pay the drink total and tip the bar waiters. And walk away from the dirty glasses, ashtrays, and remnants of the feast. In 1977 on the *Mariposa*, a fine party for sixty people would cost you somewhere between a hundred and a hundred and fifty dollars.

If one attends many of these, survival techniques are soon learned. Ice and an olive in a glass of water look convincing. Do not sit down or you will become trapped. Do not attempt to eat and drink at the same time, especially in lumpy weather; one is not provided with enough hands for that. Arrive as late as possible, consistent with courtesy. Do not have a drink in your room first. Leave as early as seems plausible. At the party do a lot of nodding and listening. What you will hear will fall into two categories: excruciatingly boring, or so fantastic as to be almost unbelievable. Couples should split up and roam the crowd. You come up with twice as many unbelievable things to relate to each other at dinner. If it is a long cruise and you attend all possible cocktail parties and take them seriously, you will destroy your liver, your sense of balance, and your memory for detail.

16

||||||||||||||||||||||||||||||||||||||||||||

Monday and Tuesday, May 23 and 24

Southampton, England

When Dorothy and I had been in London in November of 1976 on a publicity junket for Pan Books, we had been driven about by Ken White, a driver-for-hire employed by Pan Books to take us to and from rail stations, airports, and luncheon dates with newspaper people. He was a good driver, conservative and competent, and always turned up on time, so we had asked Anthea Doyle of Pan Books if she could line up Ken White to pick us up at the Southampton docks for two days of sightseeing in the south of England.

We did not wish to go up to London. My most vivid memory of London is of endless waiting in a cab in dank drizzle, while some fifty thousand people marched through the Hyde Park area carrying big banners and yelling in unison, "Black and white. Unite and fight. Black and white. Unite and fight." It seemed to have no significance, except as a kind of dreary mischief.

Monday was a lovely spring day. The Albion Brass Band thumped and oompahed on the dock while the passengers were getting their landing permits and the ship was being cleared. We found Ken White smiling on the dock, and as the first priority was shopping for some warm clothing, we went off to Winchester, where in that pretty old city there is a shopping area where automobiles are not permitted, and at least half the populace seems to be towed about by large dogs on leashes.

From Winchester through Stockbridge and Middle Wallop to Salisbury, through valleys between spring-green hills, past yellow fields of mustard like islands in the green, past cattle and sheep, great old trees, birdsongs, horse chestnut trees in bloom, golden rain trees, lilac, tulips, iris, buttercups. Inside Salisbury Cathedral were huge bouquets of apple blossoms and lilacs.

From Salisbury to Stonehenge. Dorothy, a rock freak and texture freak, was totally unhinged by it. The stillness, she said, was like that at Monte Alban near Oaxaca in the early morning, or like the stillness around the Great Tree at Tule. Many people, influenced perhaps by photographs taken of Stonehenge which exaggerate the proportions, find it disappointingly small, this silent circle atop a gentle slope. They anticipate football field dimensions and skyscraper stones. In and of itself, it is enough. It seems as carefully arranged as if Henry Moore had stage-managed the presentation. Part of its brooding look derives from our knowing so little about it, what it represented, where the fifty-ton stones came from, how they were moved to this place and erected, what words were said here when it was finished.

It was 1977, and we were able to wander around inside the magic circle, between and around the stones. Now that is forbidden. So many millions of tourists visit the place that finally it became evident that the pebbles they kicked as they walked were wearing away the bases of the old lichened rocks. Now one must stand outside. Look, but do not touch. This prevents the usual activities of the initial freaks, the same mentalities which carved Chinese ideographiti into most reachable inches of the Great Wall. There is a special corner of Hell reserved for the Rod-loves-Cathy set, where demons stand in line to carve their initials in the hides of the imprisoned.

Many of the magical places of the world have been closed to tourists. Marble stairs centuries old have recently been worn down to glossy chutes. Everybody picks up a pebble and a mountain is gone. Tourism will be the death of travel.

When we got back to the car and told Ken White how great we thought it was, he said, "I can see stopping if one is in the neighborhood, but I don't think it's worth coming all the way down from London to see it."

After lunch in Salisbury, we went back to Hampshire County. The roads were narrow, the traffic intense, the speed harrowing. Near Ringwood we saw old white cottages with very thick thatched roofs overhanging, in some places, almost to the ground. Thatch must last longer in that climate. In Yucatán, where the Mayan thatch man will cut the fronds only when the moon is full, the best thatch is good for about six years before the bugs and the dampness have eaten it away. Took a look at Bournemouth mostly because my writer friend John Creasey had lived there. Once, when he was driving around the world in his Humber Super Snipe, he and his first wife had stopped with us in Florida, and he had astonished me by saying that the highway traffic in the United States seemed to him to be cautious and law-abiding. I had not appreciated the truth of his statement until today's drive.

Bournemouth reminiscent of pre-casino Atlantic City. An old and tacky resort, full of fresh sunburns, funny signs, fast-food stands, and antique hotels. It had a coarse and gravelly beach and seemed a sad place for Holiday.

We were so tired of traffic by then that Ken tried to find, without success, a quieter way to go home. Southampton one of the better looking port cities. Not as grubby industrial as most, with trees and parks to spare.

Up early and off again with Ken White, easterly, to Chichester, and then kept to small roads, to stay as near the sea as we could. Found a sparkling clean village and a beach to walk upon, a windswept beach of worn pebbles, with an earthen breakwater just behind it. After that there were many roads where the branches of the big trees met overhead, a tunnel of cold shade on a windy sunny day. Went through Bognor Regis and past a huge Butlin's resort development where a thousand people could come for regimented play. Ken White said that it used to be a family place but had become too expensive to bring the kiddies.

On to Brighton, with old gingerbread hotels, incredibly ornate, reminiscent of old Cannes. There were huge Victorian creampuffs at the ends of long piers extending into the shallow sea, and there were rows of little green dressing houses along the beach like so many doghouses. Ate on the second level of a giant modern shopping plaza, with open areas containing abstract sculpture, fountains, benches, pigeons, children, and picnickers. From there went to "The Lanes," a warren of little winding alleys walled by junk shops, antique shops, jewelry shops, craft and art shops. Looked for netsukes, found none worth buying. Bought rocks in a rock shop—or, as the locals would have it, pebbles in a pebble shop.

Came on back home through West Sussex on smaller roads. Many PUBLIC FOOTPATH signs. Huge old black trees covered with the pale green lace of spring. A quiet, contoured land. Saw one freehouse (a freehouse is a pub that sells more than one brand of beer) called, most humbly, "The Good Intent."

Back to Southampton to meet Anthea Doyle down from London on the train, bringing tea and chocolates, arriving to have dinner aboard with us. At ten, after the warning groans on the ship's whistle, we waved goodbye to Ken and Anthea on the dock, and then we sailed off across the channel and he drove her back to London.

Southampton was a bad scene for the crew. The customs officers were very arrogant and nasty. When you arrive in port, the crewmembers have to make out a declaration of anything they might want to take ashore, but they also have to list their valuables: watch, radio, camera, projector, binoculars—anything that could be black-marketed and would be subject to customs duty. They must also list their booze and their cigarettes. Many countries have the rule that you can only "bring in" one or two cartons of cigarettes and two or three quarts of liquor. But the sailor is not "bringing it in." He has his bunk and his stowage space, and he buys cigarettes and booze for his own needs, and it does not seem to him to be the business of the customs people of any country whether he happens to have two and a half packs of cigarettes on hand or two and a half cartons. They are not smuggling, and so they tend to get careless about filling out the list of what they have on hand.

This time the customs officers came on in force. They made a clean sweep of the crews' quarters, confiscated all cigarettes and booze not reported, and, in addition, fined the crew members they found guilty.

The customs official in charge of this daring raid was an arrogant little rascal. He came up to my room and wanted to talk to me. I said, "Fine. Talk."

In a very officious voice he said, "I am going to fine you, Captain, and I am going to fine the vessel for what has happened."

So I said, "Tell me what it is, and I'll pay it."

This surprised him. I guess he expected an argument.

I then went to the agent in Southampton and said, "Why are we getting this big hassle? What the hell is the reason for all this? Is there some kind of big black market in liquor here? Your liquor is just about the same price my people paid for theirs. Has somebody been caught trying to take anything ashore?"

"Not that I know of."

"Then why are we being treated like this? It seems rather ridiculous. After all, we're supposed to be allies."

He said, "Well, there are no other passenger ships in port. You are the only one. In fact, very few passenger ships ever come to Southampton any more." I didn't tell him that it wasn't hard to guess why. "Also," he said, "it is about time for promotions in the Customs Service, and these people are taking every opportunity to make themselves look good."

I spent a great deal of my time there trying to get that mess straightened out, but unfortunately I wasn't able to do a thing.

Afterward, the crew got together and composed a very bitter letter of protest about the shakedown and sent it to the head of Her Majesty's Customs Service in Southampton, attesting to the unfairness and the ugly attitude of the customs officers in dealing with the crew, and mentioning the fact that the customs agent left aboard as boarding officer had gotten so smashed on free liquor at the ship's bar that he had to be taken off feet first. This was signed by several of the officers and evidently must have caused some kind of furor when it arrived. The ship's agent at Southampton came all the way up to Scotland to intercept us on our way home, to ask me to please *rescind the letter because it was going to cause all kinds of trouble and unpleasantness. I pointed out that I hadn't written the letter, hadn't signed it, wasn't in a position to rescind it, and agreed with everything it said. We got far better treatment in Scotland.*

Captain Kjel Salbuvic of the *Royal Viking Sea* told us that he wished every port operated in the same fashion as Shanghai and Leningrad. There the customs people are not interested in the items aboard the ship. They are interested in what comes off the ship and what goes on the ship. All such items are checked. He said that by far the worst ports for cruise ships are United States ports.

In New York the U.S. Customs officers came aboard the *Royal Viking Sea* on one occasion and inventoried all the stock in the gift shop and in gift-shop stores. Where they found any discrepancies they impounded the goods, took them ashore and put them in a bonded warehouse, and in addition levied a large fine on the vessel.

This is, of course, a typical example of bureaucratic idiocy. They expect that each cruise ship will inventory—on their approved forms—every scarf, lipstick, T-shirt, postcard, and pottery polar bear aboard, will also inventory all supplies in all departments, and will be able to withstand a vigorous spot check of these items at any time while in port. The items are not coming ashore. There is no intention of bringing them ashore. The gift shop is closed when the ship is in port. So how, by any stretch of the imagination, can it be the business of the United States Government to inventory gift-shop stores aboard a Norwegian vessel? This is nit-picking on the same level as that of the Hindu clerks in Calcutta. This is departmental government gone mad. All our national public-relations efforts in which we term our country the bulwark of freedom, the functioning democracy, run counter to our actual practices when it comes to dealing with foreign nationals.

Captain Salbuvic said that it required pressure through diplomatic channels to secure the release of his goods and the refunding of part, though not all, of the fine. Such a waste of time and effort, he said. Such a nuisance.

If I remember correctly, the value of the goods impounded came to about $3,500. Were these goods to have been imported and duty paid, the duty would perhaps average out to $350. Who inspects the inspectors? Who has the authority—and the motivation—to rein them in? Who ever weighs the costs of the entire Customs Service against the monies received in duty? Who was it who decided that the service should be punitive? What power of law is it which gives the cop on the beat the authority to determine guilt, the size of the fine, and when it shall be paid? Why is there no machinery of appeal from such arbitrary and, quite frequently, malicious persecutions? Our ports and our borders and our international airports are the front doors to our country. It does us all a disservice to have these doorways manned by people who, in their labyrinthine bureaucracy, have warped their original mission to suit their own purposes.

We had a little hard-working port electrician who would come aboard to work on special electrical problems we couldn't handle. Call him Dave. I was on a freighter at the time. We asked for Dave as soon as we tied up, and he drew one of the cars the company leased, drove around to where we were docked, and worked all day.

When he drove out of the gates that evening, there were the Customs guys spot-checking the cars. He showed his identification and explained that he was an electrician working for PFEL and had just come over to work. So they asked him to open the trunk and he did so.

Unbeknownst to him, the previous fellow who had drawn that car from the pool had passed a farm-and-garden supply store where they were having a sale, and he had bought a big paper sack of manure and hadn't had a chance to move it over to his own car. There was no writing on the bag. Just a big brown sack made of some kind of tough paper.

"I thought you said there's nothing in the trunk."

"I didn't know there was anything in there. It's not my car. It's a company car and I just borrowed it to use for the day, and I'm on my way home, and that's it."

"All right. What's in the bag?"

"I don't know. I don't have any idea. It's not my bag and I don't know what's in it."

"What do you mean, you don't know what's in it? You're driving this car. You're the one who said there's nothing in the trunk. Now come on. What's in the bag?"

"I don't know anything about it."

So they had him brace against the side of the car. They frisked him, and they looked in his tool bag, and the man in charge says, "All right, fellow. We've got you dead to rights. What's in the bag?"

When he started to go through the whole thing again, they lost patience with him. There were more customs people by that time. They gathered around the trunk and cut the bag open. They looked at it, and then one of them said, "Gee, I don't really know, but it sure looks like bullshit to me." And pretty soon they let him go home.

It isn't only the Customs people who can give you fits. In port in San Francisco when the engineers were transferring oil from one tank to another, a couple of buckets of oil came up through one of the vent pipes and went into the bay. The people aboard ship weren't aware what had happened. Nobody saw it. But it was seen from one of the helicopters that fly around the bay looking for pollution. They have special lenses that make oil spills show up, even oil on the water that is not visible to the naked eye. They spotted this bit of oil and somehow traced it back to the ship. Soon a couple of Coast Guard and ecology people arrived and questioned the engineer on watch, and it was admitted that we had been transferring some oil, although we were unaware that any had been spilled.

They gave us a citation, and there was some kidding aboard the ship as to who should be the one to go to jail, and who was going to have to pay the ten- or twenty-thousand-dollar fine. But nothing happened. It was just a citation.

Each ship has to carry a book called the Oil Pollution Log. If you transfer oil from one tank to another at sea, or clean out a tank, or if you have an oil spill of any kind, you are supposed to make a dated entry in this book. I could never figure out what we were supposed to do with it. The instructions in the front were ambiguous. It didn't say whether you should *remove the pages and turn them in, or make copies and turn them in, or turn in the whole book to the Coast Guard. On short runs we'd often have no need for any entry. It seemed to be a book that tankers would have more reason to carry and use.*

I made no entry, nor did the engineer, regarding the alleged oil spill at San Francisco. After all, I was in theory reporting to those people, and they had been the ones who came down and told us about it.

One trip later we came in and tied up late at night, and what should have been a short fifteen-minute docking lasted, because of the stiff wind, for about forty-five minutes before we got the ship all fast. I was standing out on the wing of the bridge with the wind blowing and my nose running. We were more or less tied up along the dock, but not completely secured to my satisfaction.

A young Coast Guard officer came out onto the wing of the bridge to wait for me, and I assumed he was aboard to talk about some of the disciplinary problems we'd had, which are supposed to be handled by the Coast Guard.

Finally I got everything straightened away and we went down to my room and I asked him if he'd like a drink. It was about nine o'clock by then, and he seemed irritated at having to wait so long for us to get tied up.

He declined the drink and said he had to get moving and then said, "I'd like to see your Oil Pollution Log." I couldn't find it. I fumbled around for a time and then said that it was probably in the chief engineer's cabin. I went and looked there and couldn't find it, and came back and looked around my place one more time, saying, "I know I have it here someplace. I saw it just the other day." He was getting more and more edgy. Finally I came upon it, sighed with relief, and handed it to him.

He opened it and looked and said, "There's no entry in here for your oil spill."

"What oil spill?"

"The one you had right here in San Francisco three weeks ago."

"Oh, that oil spill. I'd forgotten about that thing. Why should it be in the log? We weren't transferring from tank to

tank at sea. And as far as the spill is concerned, you already knew about it, because you were one of the ones who came down and told us about it. Why report to you what you already know?"

"Nevertheless, you have to make an entry in the Oil Pollution Log."

"Okay, give it here and I'll make the entry."

"No, you can't. I have to give you a citation for not making the entry."

I actually had to go down and appear at a kind of kangaroo court. There was a regular judge there. I was told I was allowed to have an attorney represent me. I threw myself on the mercy of the court, told the whole story, recited my record, said I had never been properly informed of what I was supposed to do about spills we never knew we made, and confessed that I had, indeed, failed to make an entry in the Oil Pollution Log. They sentenced me to an Admonishment. That is when the judge says, Go thou forth and sin no more.

They get very childish about radio procedure too. We have our VHF radio, which is a line-of-sight thing, good for fifty to sixty miles at the very most. You have to send in and get a little license to operate one of these things. We use it to talk from ship to ship, ship to pilots, ship to agent, and so on. There is one channel that is used strictly for ship to ship, and by agreement you can switch to some other designated channel. These channels are monitored by the Coast Guard and the FCC. There is a certain protocol you are supposed to use. You are supposed to announce your ship's name and your call letters whenever you have any conversation.

This can get to be ridiculous. In Puget Sound it is completely disregarded. They have a traffic reporting center, and they refer to you by the name of the ship, nothing more. They want you on and off the air as fast as possible, to make way for other traffic. It's the same at Alaskan ports. You just say what ship you are.

We were coming into San Francisco very early one morning, about 4 A.M., and I got on the radio and said, "This is the Mariposa, KFCP, calling the San Francisco bay pilots." They answered and told me to go to Channel 12. I switched to 12 and said, "This is the Mariposa, KFCP, calling the pilots."

When they answered, I said, "Gentlemen, we're off the Far-
allon Islands now and we should be at the pilot station at oh
six hundred. On what side do you want us to pick you up, and
is there any other traffic?" He told me what other traffic was
coming up and he wanted to be picked up on the starboard
side, and he said, "This is the pilot boat, off and clear, returning to Channel Sixteen."

And I said, "This is the Mariposa, off and clear, returning
to Channel Sixteen."

A month later, I received an official communiqué from my
government: a transcript of the entire conversation with the
pilot boat, taken from a tape. The accompanying letter said
that when I was returning to Channel 16, I said Mariposa,
instead of Mariposa KFCP. Because of this omission, I was
subject to fine, reprimand, revocation of license, and so on.
I had to write a long humble letter begging forgiveness and
trying to explain how come I had done this unforgivable thing.
It amazes me that they haven't got anything better to do. I
think it comes from being overstaffed and trying to seem important.

Also, they seem to attract a certain kind of mentality. One
time I was on my way from Los Angeles down to San Diego.
It was a nice clear day, and we were going right along. I went
up to the bridge to check on our speed and arrival time. We
were ten to twelve miles offshore. Something caught my eye
off the port bow, so I picked up the binoculars and had a look
at it. It was a small, approximately seventeen-foot fiberglass
outboard motorboat. I didn't see anybody in the boat or anybody around it in the water.

I altered course to get a better look at it, and as we got
closer I saw the outboard motor was uptilted, with the prop
out of the water. The other mate on watch looked also, and
we were able to see that there was no one in the boat. It was
a little speedboat with a windshield.

I picked up the VHF radio and called the Coast Guard.
They responded instantly. I said, "This is the Mariposa,
KFCP," and I gave him my position, a very accurate position
off such and such a point of land, because we were in good
radar range. I said, "I've just passed a blue, approximately

seventeen-foot fiberglass outboard motorboat with no occu-
pants and the motor tilted up."

At this point he started going through the protocol. He had
to ask me what ship I was and my call letters and so on. Then
he relayed this information to somebody else and came back
on and announced himself as Coast Guard station so and so,
and he asked me to tell him again what ship I was, and the
call letters. Next he wanted to know my home port. Then he
wanted to know where I had left from. Then he wanted to know
my destination. Then he wanted to know my speed. While all
this was going on, I had long since passed the little blue boat
at full speed and was on my way to San Diego. He went and
conferred and came back and said that they wanted me to stand
by to render aid.

"Look, there's nobody there. If I'd seen somebody in the
water or anybody in the vicinity, or anything else, I would have
done that automatically without waiting to be told. I'm quite
sure this boat has drifted loose. It was probably tied up somewhere, or somebody beached it and it drifted loose."

He relayed all this and then came back on the air and said
that I was to stand by to render aid. In the meantime some
other boats—fishing boats and pleasure cruisers—had heard
all this, and they kept trying to break in and volunteer to go
look, but the Coast Guard paid no attention. He said there
would be a Coast Guard cutter or a Coast Guard plane coming
out, and in the meantime I was to stand by and render aid.

By this time I was out of sight of the boat.

I said, "This is a passenger vessel, and I am on a schedule,
and I have to be in San Diego at a certain time. There isn't
much I can do. I reported the boat."

"You are definitely to turn around and go back and render
aid."

"By the time I can stop this rascal and get turned around,
I am going to be halfway to San Diego. If you insist that I do
it, I'll do it. But let's try to make a little sense here. If I had
planned on stopping in the first place, I would never have
called you, and I would have had myself a nice little blue

seventeen-foot fiberglass outboard motorboat. Think that over."

He contacted his superior, and he finally came back with the order that I could proceed, and that's the last I heard of that.

17

▏▎▍▌▋▊▉█▊▋▌▍▎▏▎▍▌▋▊▉█▊▋▌▍▎▏

Wednesday and Thursday, May 25 and 26
Le Havre, France

Before we even arrived in Southampton I was advised that they were going to have a tugboat strike in LeHavre. I didn't pay too much attention, hoping the thing would resolve itself. In Southampton, they told me that there really was a tugboat strike, and what did I want to do?

I would have been happy to skip Le Havre, but the company did not want to start readjusting the schedule at this point. I phoned the company, and was told that if it was at all possible, we should go into Le Havre. I talked to the agent in Southampton and the agent in Le Havre and the harbor master in Le Havre about the problems I might encounter: how the berth situation looked, and how much room I would have to approach the dock, and the anticipated wind conditions. They assured me from Le Havre that I would have 150 meters at either end of the vessel, and that I would have two small line-handler boats to take my lines ashore for me, and I could then breast the ship in and winch it in broadside, using the lines fore and aft.

I said it sounded okay and I would go with that. Just before we left Southampton a nice little British pilot named Captain Rowles came aboard to be with us for the whole North Cape trip. He was knowledgeable about all the ports we were going

*to visit, and he said we shouldn't have too much of a problem
at Le Havre.*

*So we came in in good shape. Imagine a duck in profile,
swimming to the left. We came in down the duck's neck, and
our berth was along the duck's back. A very solemn and silent
French pilot came aboard. I told him the characteristics of the
ship. They usually assume we have twin screws, and they are
surprised to find we have only one. I always tell them we're
lucky to have one.*

*The space they had promised me had shrunk. We had very
little clearance between the ship ahead and the ship astern. As
we were on our way down the harbor toward the berth, a small
workboat full of French harbor workers cut across our bows,
so close that they were invisible from the bridge, waving their
fists and yelling French labor slogans: liberty, equality, and
more money right now.*

*There was one rowboat to handle the lines instead of two,
but the French pilot was pretty good and we got the vessel
breasted in in good shape.*

When the ship was cleared, Dorothy and I got on the shuttle
bus and went to the station and bought round-trip tickets to
Paris, first class. One of the tours was on the same train. Hal
Wagner, Dolores Abramson, and a couple of other strays were
going separately too. We sped through a green world. Trees
in extra-neat rows. Towns reminiscent of Pennsylvania, up-
state. Cobblestones and bricks set among gentle hills. Lots of
tunnels. Lots of apple blossoms. And cows lying down. We
never did figure out why the cows in Europe spend such a great
part of the day lying down.

We shared a cab to the Ritz with Dolores. No attendants
appeared, so I carried her bag in to the desk. She seemed to
think this not the thing to do at the Ritz. Always do whatever
saves time and irritation. Nothing more irritating than standing
guard on a suitcase, waiting for somebody you can overtip.

Went to the International Bank and changed some money.
Did some shopping. Back to the Ritz for a pre-lunch drink with
Dolores. Went for a walk. Picked the absolutely wrong place
for lunch but was too dumb and stubborn to walk away from
it. Came out into rain. Served me right. Found a store and

bought an overpriced English umbrella. Did some more wandering. Toward Tuilleries and the river. Restroom became imperative, so we went into the Gallerie L'Orangerie and stumbled upon a magnificent Henry Moore show. Stayed a couple of hours. Rain had stopped. Found our way back to the Ritz, had a couple of drinks, and then it was time to head for the Restaurant Taillevent for the eight o'clock reservation made for us by a Sarasota friend who had been a loyal customer of the place all the way from no stars to one, then two, and at last three stars.

Arrived on time, met in foyer by owner, wringing hands, saying, "Oh, but M'sieu, you deed not reconfirm your reservation."

Instant anger. "How the hell do I reconfirm from a ship, or even find out I was supposed to? We have come here directly from Le Havre. Mr. Westmoreland is going to be very very angry and embarrassed."

So he went away and came back in a few minutes, smiling, and said that if we could wait twenty minutes, they would be able to serve us. They moved a little round table out to the service bar in the rear of the foyer and gave us a complimentary aperitif. Half an hour later we were taken into the attractive dining room, where we had a hot paté of seafood and truffles stuffed so tightly into a sausage skin that when the headwaiter stuck it with a knife, it shot hot grease up the front of his starched white shirt. He had very little sense of humor about that. It was served sliced, with hot melted butter. Green salad with house dressing. Sliced boned leg of lamb with round inserts of kidney and truffle stuffing. Purée of spinach and purée of celery. Bottle of wine. Bread, cheeses, complimentary liqueur, and petits fours. Espresso. All this for only $155. In 1977.

They called a taxi for us, and we left with a comfortable margin to catch our 11 P.M. train. It was posted on a big board over its track. Eleven o'clock. To Rouen and Le Havre. No train at hand at twenty to eleven, and no train at eleven or at five after. No officialdom in sight. No ticket windows open. With timetable in hand, I searched the big station, and finally way up at the top of two flights of stairs I found three men in railroad uniforms sitting around with cigarettes and coffee in a small room with a large dirty map on the wall and several bulletin boards, file cabinets, stacks of documents, and the like. I have no French. I pointed to our train on the timetable, pointed to the little symbols which indicated it was to run on that day. And they laughed. All three of them. Ho ho ho. Hah hah hah. Funniest damn thing in the world—another stupid tourist looking for a train that isn't running. Hee hee hee hah hah.

Had told Dorothy I hadn't cared for the French in 1934 and wasn't expecting much from them this time. Such prejudice is unseemly. I had been trying to like them, from the woman at the gallery who became gratuitously ugly about my checking my umbrella, to a woman in a shop who refused to admit to herself that we were indeed standing in front of her trying to attract her attention, trying to get her to sell us something. But the railway fellows brought it all back again.

I have this fantasy. France was once inhabited by a race of people who deserved a land so lovely. They were generous, talented, warm, intelligent, thoughtful, helpful. On a faraway planet there was a race of gnarled, rodentlike creatures, permanently angry, contemptuous, miserly, aggressive, egocentric, and selfish. When their planet was about to be destroyed by a cosmic explosion they emigrated across space, landed in France, took over the bodies of those noble French people, and have ever since pretended to the heritage of the real French. And that is why Frenchmen seem like such unlikely inhabitants of la belle France.

There were five members of the *Mariposa*'s crew in the station, misled by the same false timetable. I told them that we would support their account of the fiasco if their superiors doubted their word. They had no passports, just the card that they carry ashore, inadequate for renting a hotel room. We had passports. We knew that the tour was staying at the Hotel Intercontinental. Took a taxi there. No room at the inn. A nice English desk clerk phoned around for us, located a room at something called the Madeleine-Palace. They did not mind us having no luggage, as long as we paid our $40 in advance. An extremely dingy room with no pillows. An attempt to acquire pillows fell upon indifferent ears. They had the money in hand.

Back to the station in the morning. Had to find out if timetable was accurate on the day trains, and if our ticket was good. Long long lines at the windows which dispensed both tickets and information. Became angrier and angrier as small French persons continued to wedge into the line ahead of me. A non-French person is a lower form of life, willing to submit to any indignity a French person can heap upon its dull suffering head. So when the next one slid in there, I took a backhand swing with the furled umbrella and rapped him smartly across the outside corner of his left knee, and at the same time roared, *"Pardon!"*

He leapt five feet to the side, eyes wide, eyebrows up to the hairline, hands upraised, palms outward in submission and defense from further attack. "Monsieur!" he said in a high voice, and went back toward the end of the line.

A very uncharacteristic act. Satisfying at the same moment, though. Only afterward did I feel shame, realizing that I had picked a rather small Frenchman. Settled ticket problem. By then so much time had passed we decided not to leave the station for fear we would not get back in time and would miss the train and, of course, the ship as well. Were among first to board. Dorothy thoughtful on ride back to Le Havre. Finally said, "Well, they really are quite *mean* little people, aren't they?" Seemed to cover it.

When it was time to pick up and leave, I had a discussion with the French pilot about the characteristics of the ship. He was a pretty good sized Frenchman, with a black seaman's cap with a bill, and a dark scarf tied around his neck. He looked like the young Robert Mitchum playing a Parisian nightclub owner. He had a very rich accent and a lot of assurance.

I told him that this ship has a right-hand wheel, so when you try to move ahead from a dead stop, the torque makes it want to turn to the left. It is very hard to make it turn to the right. It pulls definitely to the left from a dead stop at all times. Yes, yes, yes, he said; he understood all that, of course.

"By the same token, the ship wants to back to the left. It's almost impossible to back it to the right from a dead stop. If there's no wind factor, it will definitely back to the left." Yes, yes, yes, he understood all that.

There was a big Russian freighter very close astern of us, and a big French bulk carrier ahead of us, facing toward us. We were bow to bow with the French ship, and stern to bow with the Russian ship.

I asked him what his plans were, and he said we would hold onto the spring line, the line that leads aft from the bow, and go slowly ahead with the wheel hard left and this would cause the stern to come out. And when it was out sufficiently, we would back away from the pier. I told him fine, because this was the only way we could have gotten clear. I asked him if he wanted me to take a couple of more lines and put them on the dock so we could really go ahead on the lines and get the stern way out, and he said no, that wouldn't be necessary.

We let go all the lines except the one spring line and came ahead slowly on the engine, and the stern moved out okay. The wind at this point was not a factor. The stern came out at what I would estimate as a 20-degree angle from the dock.

He said "Okay, you can let the line go now."

"Why don't we kick it out farther, get the stern out farther?"

"No, this is all right."

So I thought, Well, you're the pilot, and you supposedly know this port. And that was my first big mistake at Le Havre, letting the line go. He called for the stern bell—at which time, just as I had predicted, she started backing over to the left and toward the Russian ship.

I said, "Hey, we're getting into trouble."

He wasn't watching the stern enough. On that ship the bridge was so far forward you couldn't see the turning quickly enough by watching the bow.

I said again, "Hey, we're getting into trouble. Let's get this thing back alongside the dock, and we'll get a line out and do it over again." At that point, we could have done just that and then wedged the stern out a lot farther.

"No, no," he said, "I think we're okay. Put the wheel hard right. And slow ahead."

"Look, it will take forever to turn to the right at this speed."

"So we'll go half ahead," he said. When it didn't seem to want to respond, he ordered full ahead. It was a nightmare. We began to pick up speed but the ship didn't turn, and we were heading right at the French bulk carrier. I was certain we were going to hit him. It wouldn't be a major disaster, but *we were going to go scraping and grinding along the side of that ship, and the paperwork would be unbelievable.*

The passengers were lining the port rails watching the action, and I turned on the horn and shouted for them to get back from the rail. First I was certain we were going to hit big, and then I was certain it was going to be a glancing blow. And finally, picking up speed all the time, we passed so close that one of those awestruck officers on the carrier could have leaned over and lighted the pilot's cigarette. We missed by inches. When a ship is in motion there is a complicated pattern of pressure and velocity changes in the water all around her. As our hull neared the Frenchman's hull, the velocity of the water between the two hulls increased. It climbed higher on the hulls and the pressure of the water increased, turning us just enough more to keep us clear. And don't try to tell me the pilot was counting on that effect.

Then we were heading toward the tail of the duck, heading toward the end of the harbor at a good rate of speed. I said, "We better stop this mother right now, pilot, or we're going to run out of room." So we kicked it into full astern and tried to stop it, but it had picked up too much headway.

I said, "We better drop the anchor."

He said, "Good idea."

Normally if you drop one shot of chain, which is ninety feet, plus the anchor, that will really slow you or stop you under normal maneuvering conditions. But this had no effect at all. I looked down and I could see the chain was bumping, which means the anchor is not holding. So I said to let another shot go. This time we really had plenty of anchor on to stop this thing, but it wasn't stopping us.

I turned to the pilot and said, "I can't understand this."

"In this harbor, it is a very poor holding ground," he said.

All I could think of was that maybe at some time they had paved the bottom, because the anchor would not hold at all. But with the stern bell and the anchor down and a hundred and eighty feet of chain, we eventually got it stopped. By then we were down at the narrowest part of the harbor, and he proceeded to try to turn the vessel around. I had told him earlier that slow or dead slow bells have very little effect on the maneuverability of this ship. You have to give it a half bell to get it turning. So he would try to turn it and say slow ahead and say hard left or hard right and get nothing at all. So I was indicating to the man on watch to give it a half bell, but all we were doing was working our way farther and farther down into the dead end of the whole pier complex, down where they keep the rowboats.

I have been in situations in the past when I wasn't very happy with what the pilot was doing, when I didn't think he was taking the best action under the circumstances. But I've always been reluctant to take a ship away from a pilot—to say, "You're finished; I'll take it now"—the reason being that when you do that, you lose the tugs. The pilot has rapport with the tugs, and they won't take orders from an outsider.

All of a sudden it dawned on me that this pilot couldn't do me any good because we didn't have any tugs anyway. He was still bound and determined he was going to turn her around to the right. So I told him that there was no way on God's green earth she was going to turn to the right, and the sooner he backed her away and gave her a half bell and turned her around to port, the quicker we'd get out of the narrow end of the harbor.

We picked up the anchor and went back and dropped it. I think we dropped it six or seven times until we finally got it swinging the other way and turned the ship around and got out of there. When we were right in the midst of one of the crucial turning maneuvers, a ferryboat loaded with people came shooting out of nowhere and crossed dead ahead of us. Very interesting.

I was embarrassed. It was a very poor piece of seamanship. It was about two hours from the time we cast off the lines until we got turned around and headed out.

I was ashamed to go to dinner that night and face the people at my table. But when I walked into the dining room, they gave me a big round of applause for getting the ship out of port. They didn't know they had just witnessed a classic example of poor seamanship.

That evening after dinner as I was walking through the foyer, I saw Captain Kilpack standing near the stairway and heard a nice sincere little old lady ask him, in view of the delay, when we were going to get to Zeebrugge.

He reached out to brace himself against the bulkhead as though faint. "Where? Zeebuggy? So we have to go *there? Where is it?"* And then of course he relented and said, "Yes, we'll be at the pilot station on the dot. Six tomorrow morning."

18

||||||||||||||||||||||||||||||||||||||||||||||||||||||

Friday, May 27

Zeebrugge, Belgium

With ports coming up so frequently, the motorcoach junkies were beginning to show the first signs of strain. It is a sudden change of life-style for elderly sedentary Americans to spend all day clambering on and off buses, trotting through gardens and cathedrals, trying to listen to the guide and change film at the same time, eating the semi-digestible tour lunch at the tour tables, fighting to get waited on in the gift shop before the bus leaves, always wearing something too heavy for the day that turns warm, or too light for the day that turns cool, fighting the constant head cold, popping down Lomotil to quell the endemic diarrhea, dragging back up the gangway at last to change for dinner and then attend an educational film about the next port, the next tour.

Captain Kilpack was mildly distressed at the berth they gave us in Zeebrugge. It was way out along the breakwater, next to a mountain of coal. It was a gray icy day with a strong wind blowing, and Belgium looked flat, dried-out and dreary.

There was shuttle-bus service from the ship to the middle of Bruges, and we took the earliest one, with a surly and uncommunicative driver. The countryside was less than charming.

Suddenly we turned in through a gate in an old city wall,

where swans floated on dark water under the curved shelter of willow. We were unprepared for the ancient magic of Bruges. It is curiously analogous to Pompeii. One was slain by ashes, the other by silt.

Bruges was a very important city in the fifteenth century. It contained the first stock exchange in Europe. In 1430, Philip the Good celebrated his founding of the Order of the Golden Fleece in Bruges with a fair and tournament of legendary splendor. It was a center of commerce. But then the Zwyn River began to fill with silt, and by the middle of the sixteenth century the city was cut off from the sea. In Korngold's opera it is called *Bruges la mort*, the dead city. Three hundred and fifty years later, work was begun on the new port of Zeebrugge, nine miles north of the city, and the two were evenutally connected by a canal. English tourists began to come to Bruges in the early part of the twentieth century. It has now become, alas, a rail and canal junction and a center for printing and light manufacturing. The Chamber of Commerce is busy.

The transit bus took us through narrow tidy streets to the Markt, the main square, where there is a huge bell tower, a civic monument with a famous forty-seven-bell carillon. There were restaurants with bright awnings and outside tables. There were horse-drawn carriages for hire, the drivers wearing derbies. There were chittering flocks of children in town for the holidays, being guided about—all in the coolness of early morning shadow as the sun came out, but did not yet reach down into the cobbled square.

From the Markt we walked along Breydelstraat to the Burg and a second square with a gothic town hall, a smallish church built in eleven hundred and something to house the relic that Thierry of Alsace brought back from the Second Crusade in 1150, and a fantastic flock of gingerbread Flemish buildings. We paused on the bridge across the Groenerei to watch the children, and to see the reflections of old houses in the canal, and to watch the bright canalboats go by, chock-full of tourists. We walked through the clean, open-air fish market.

We found the Hoogstraat, the best street for shopping, and bought blue canvas shoes, lace butterflies, a netsuke, a miniature oil lamp—and, in another place, just before catching the shuttle back, big strawberries and a bouquet of cut flowers.

Knowledgeable friends had recommended the Duc de Bourgogne at Huidevettersplaats 12 for lunch, and it was superb. A luxurious ten-room hotel operated by a family with daughters in school in California. Pâté, fish soup, fresh salmon, and wine, elegantly served. And better, even to the wine, than the three-star adventure in Paris.

Travel by ship is an easy way to discover those places to which you wish some day to return. We shall go back there one day and stay in Bruges. And cross the lovely St. Elizabeth Bridge and feed the swans on the banks of the Minnewater where once was the inner dock when Bruges had its natural access to the sea. And, with more courage than on the first visit, try a drink named *mort subite*, sudden death.

We learned there another quirk of the unreal U.S. Customs. In one shop we visited they sold marvelous little chocolates filled with liqueur. A polite sign warned American tourists that is was forbidden to take them back to the United States. Thus, back home, we are all spared the spectacle of American tourists, just back from Belgium, gorging themselves on chocolates, weaving about on the streets, falling down, singing bawdy ballads, and in general making fools of themselves. Or, even more paternalistically, we are protected from a dire plot whereby the chocolates would be pierced and the liqueur poured out into bottles, labeled, and sold *untaxed!* It is good to know we have such organized diligence protecting us from ourselves.

We found our way back to the Markt, to a crowded little corner café to have a beer while waiting for the shuttle bus. Most of the people on the bus back to the ship were crew, and it always makes for a cheerier ride when that happens.

We went aboard and changed for a cocktail party in the Poly Room and there said goodbye to Dr. Grayson, the ship's doctor, who was leaving us soon—in Amsterdam, I think.

I guess my best relationship with a ship's doctor was established when I was sailing as a chief officer with Captains X, Y, and Z. I am very bad at remembering names. When I would go in and eat as chief officer in the officers' dining room, I found myself right across the table from a real stodgy, antsy old kraut named Dr. Gienger. Starts with a hard G and rhymes with linger.

*He was so grumpy and remote, he was a challenge to me.
So I started calling him Dr. Schweitzer. He was a mean old
German with steel-rimmed glasses and steel-gray hair. He was
the Herr Doktor, and don't you forget it. Nobody messed with
him aboard, and when he was ashore he terrorized his house-
hold. Aboard, the two nurses gave him a wide berth. They were
nice people and I couldn't remember their names, so I called
them Trixie and Bubbles.*

*After I had called him Schweitzer a couple of times, he
grudgingly introduced himself, and I said, "Oh, you are the
doctor on this ship? How come we have a chiropractor this
time? I thought we had to have a regular doctor aboard."*

He glowered at me and said, "I am a doctor. I am an M.D."

*Whenever I had a chance to introduce him and his two-
nurse staff, I would say, "And this is Dr. Schweitzer, with
Trixie and Bubbles."*

*The nurses got a kick out of it, and old Dr. Schweitzer was
wary at first, but as I continued to needle him in front of the
nurses and the staff, he began to unbend a little. He was getting
a different kind of attention from what he was used to, and he
liked it. His attitude had always been: I am the doctor. Don't
fool around with me. Soon we got to be pretty good friends,
and he began to learn to needle the needler.*

*We used to meet up on the Pool Terrace and generally insult
each other every morning. We would pretend it was serious,
and one morning it got so hot and heavy, he reached over and
prodded me on the shoulder.*

*I said loudly, "Don't you ever touch me, Doctor. You only
have three stripes, and I have four, and that is all you are ever
going to have is three stripes."*

*One of the nice old ladies who was walking by went right
down to the purser's desk and said that ship's officers should
not be fighting in the passenger areas. It didn't look nice.*

*At one point we had a quartet on board, the John Cook
Quartet, the usual guitar, trumpet, piano, and drums. They sat
at Dr. Schweitzer's table in the dining room. Incidentally, on
many trips we had one little lady who insisted on sitting at the
doctor's table. She was a very good and very dedicated dancer.
She traveled alone. One time I asked her why she always sat
at the doctor's table and she said, "It's the best way to find*

out which wives are sick and which husbands will be free to dance." Anyway, the quartet really enjoyed the mock quarreling and the needling that went on between Dr. Schweitzer and me. And one formal night, after dinner, back in the Polynesian Room, we were sitting in a group, and one of the entertainers went by the big late buffet and picked up an apple as he went by and started munching on it as he walked. And I said to our group, "What kind of class is that? Here are all these people in formal clothes, and this turkey walks through munching an apple."

So the night the John Cook group was going to put on a special show in the Poly Room, I got everybody at our table to bring an apple up with them, with the idea that when a special solo number came up, we would all start munching our apples. But the people got carried away and started tossing the apples out onto the dance floor. It broke up the show and was good for a laugh. But unbeknownst to me, Captain X had come down to see the show, and he was sitting behind a glass partition over by the organ. He couldn't see me because I was way down at one end of the line. Dr. Schweitzer was at the other end.

The next morning I went to Dr. Schweitzer and I said, "Boy, we are really in hot water."

"What is the matter?"

"The captain is really hot. He is really unhappy about that apple-throwing episode last night."

"I didn't throw any apples."

"Well, I didn't either, but you were the only one of the officers he could see there, sitting with the apple throwers, and he wants us up in his office at ten o'clock."

He sweated it out until ten o'clock and then went up to see Captain X, who could be as savage as a crocodile when he was upset.

"Captain, you want to see me?"

"No, what about?"

Schweitzer came back to me and said, "You son of a bitch, you got me that time."

A few days later I went into the dining room. My assigned table was two or three tables away from the doctor's, and I had to pass his table to get to my own. Usually I paused long enough to make a few comments about the unseemly conduct of the people at his table, and why not keep the noise down, and let's be respectable and so on. On that day we ran out of hard rolls at our table in the middle of dinner. I faked a big scene with the waitress, saying, "How come we never have enough hard rolls at this table? The doctor always has plenty of hard rolls. He's only got three stripes and I've got four. How come we never have enough hard rolls here?"

The waitress apparently passed this story on down to the doctor's table, because when I looked over there a few minutes later, I saw one of the men at his table, a very mild-looking guy, possibly a bank manager, stand up at his place and wind up and rifle a perfect shot with a hard roll over the tables in between. I got the barest glimpse of that thing coming, and I stuck my hand up and snagged it. Willie Mays could not have done better. If I had missed, it would have continued on down the room and killed somebody. I think the guy startled himself, giving way to an impulse like that. But he put both tables into hysterics. It wasn't likely that too many people in the big room would have seen anything like that, but as it turned out, over against the wall at a table for two was a nice little old lady who had been on the White Ships many times. She went into hysterics and kept saying, "I can't believe it. I can't believe it."

Somebody said, "What can't you believe?"

"I have been traveling for thirty years on ships and I have never never seen ship's officers throwing rolls in the dining room."

In a matter of minutes that information was all over the room, and there was a good deal of commotion. I could look down into the Pit and see Captain X scowling as he wondered what all the noise was about.

The next day I went to Dr. Schweitzer and I said, "Boy, we are really in hot water now."

"What's that?"

"The old man is really hot over the roll-throwing episode."

"I didn't throw any rolls."

"I know you didn't throw any rolls, but the old man thinks you did and he wants to see us up in his office at ten o'clock."

That gave him an hour and a half to think about it. At ten

o'clock old Schweitzer trudged up there and said, "Captain, you wanted to see me?"

"No. What about?"

"That son of a bitch, he got me again!"

"What? Who, what?"

"Please excuse me, Captain," he said, and left in a hurry.

On that same trip I developed a cold, which I often do on the ship, and I was coughing and sneezing and vowing that I would never let that old veterinarian treat me. But finally I was conned into going to him. He took my temperature, made me say ah, gave me two aspirins, and told me to come back in the morning. Later the cold moved down into my chest, and old Schweitzer listened to my chest and said, "That's good. The cold is beginning to move down. It's going to break up. Here are two more aspirins. Call me in the morning."

A few days later the cold went up into my sinuses, and when I saw Schweitzer he said, "That's good. The cold is beginning to move up. It's going to break up."

"Which way do you want it to move, doctor? Up or down?"

By the next day the cold reached a point where I completely lost my sense of taste. Usually I am a martini drinker, but for some reason I had switched to Dubonnet on the rocks. I had a cocktail party in my room, with some of the passengers and Dr. Schweitzer. I had a mouthful of Dubonnet and I began to cough, so I let myself fall slowly out of the chair. I lay on the deck and went into a death spasm, and let a little trickle of Dubonnet run out of the corner of my mouth. I should have gotten an Oscar for that. I gave it everything, even the death rattle. The passengers were twitching and staring and saying, "Oh, my God!"

But old Schweitzer, he just sat there and beamed at me and beamed at the guests and clapped his big old hands and said, "Isn't he great? Isn't he wonderful?"

Just as that cold was leaving, it turned into a monstrously stiff neck, very very painful. I had to use both hands to lift my head off the pillow so that I could get out of bed. I was tottering around the ship in obvious agony when Bubbles saw me and said, "Why don't you go see Dr. Schweitzer"—by then everybody called him that—"and let him manipulate your neck? He's very good at it."

So finally I gave up and went to him. We were both in blue uniforms. He had me on the examining table on my back, and he went to the head of the table and worked on me from there.

As he manipulated my neck it began to feel better. In the course of his doing this, I kept sliding toward the head of the table until finally my head was pressed against his stomach. He worked for about ten more minutes and then let me sit up. He asked me how the neck felt and I said, "It feels a lot better, but what is this hole I've got here in my forehead?"

I went to the mirror and looked and there, high on my forehead, was the deep imprint of one of the brass buttons on the front of his uniform jacket, so deep and clear you could see the eagle.

It lasted about a half hour, which gave me a chance to cover most of the ship and point out what that quack Schweitzer had done to me.

One time Schweitzer brought his wife along on a trip. He was really set in his ways. He played golf whenever we were in port. By that time he and I always had breakfast together. I didn't expect to see much of him that trip, but that mean old rascal didn't change his ways at all. He would see his wife at various times, maybe have a drink with her on the Pool Terrace, have dinner with her in the evening, and maybe take her to the show after dinner. So the other ladies aboard traveling alone would see her in the company of the doctor, but not consistently enough for them to figure out they were man and wife.

She was sitting up on the Pool Terrace one morning and one of the other ladies joined her uninvited and said, "We were wondering about that officer we see you with sometimes. The one with the three stripes. What does he do?"

"I don't know what he does. I'm just sleeping with him."

On another trip we had one of those transfers at sea of a sick sailor from a freighter. We have gotten a lot of those in Pacific waters. There is an international reporting service hooked into a computer which will tell immediately the nearest ship with a doctor on board. We are usually the only ship within a thousand miles which can provide the service. We had an emergency call in the morning, and I got Dr. Schweitzer up there to check out the condition of the man aboard the other ship. It was finally decided that it was enough of an emergency *to bring him aboard. So at about noon, after we changed course, I got on the P.A. system and told the passengers that we were heading for a rendezvous with a British freighter, and at approximately three in the afternoon we would be transferring an ill seaman over to our ship for treatment.*

You can imagine how all the passengers liked this. Romance, adventure, a rescue at sea. From one thirty on, they were all staring into the distance. Everybody had their cameras and their binoculars. This particular transfer was a piece of cake. A flat-calm sunny day, and we brought the two ships close together to the minimum safe distance, and the fellow was put into a boat and brought over to our vessel. I think that during this process he had his picture taken ten thousand times. We got the man aboard, waiting until the other ship had its boat back, then blew the whistle and took off on a heading that would get us back on course.

By then it was about four o'clock. I went down through the lounge and there was Nick Nichols, the fellow who does the lost wax castings and the gold and silver jewelry, putting his artifacts away. He'd had them all spread out, nicely arranged, for his show, when he would reasonably expect to sell quite a lot of items to the passengers.

I stopped and said, "Gee, Nick. I forgot all about your show this afternoon. How did it go anyway?"

He straightened up from his packing and said, "It went dandy, Captain. Thanks a lot. It went great. The only guy I saw was one man who came through and said, 'Which way to the rescue?'"

I made a couple of other trips with Nick, and whenever he had an art show planned, he would look me up to ask if I had any rescues scheduled for that day.

19

Saturday and Sunday, May 28 and 29
Amsterdam, the Netherlands

At 4:45 A.M. we entered the locks of the North Sea Canal. By dawn's early light it was a scene like unto 1927 Pittsburgh or the Ruhr. An incredible vomit into the pale slant of sunrise. Ochre clouds from tall stacks. Billowing black. Gases of a strange fluorescence being burned off, in a spectrum from orange to green. Huge industrial installations along a polluted horizon. Nightmare of an environmentalist.

After the locks we moved along into a canal of such black filth it was astonishing that the few ducks we saw could live in it, or that the few fishermen we saw had hopes of catching anything other than sea slugs.

Indeed, the Dutch admit to throwing every possible expendable into their canals. The main Amsterdam canal is a toilet which is flushed every evening by letting in water from the North Sea. But that is effective in changing only the top few inches of the heavy pollution. Venice, with its flotillas of dead rats and orange peelings, is a twinkling paradise compared to the Dutch canals. One wonders how they can continue to live next to such monstrous stinks without being taken ill.

Our berth was at Oostelijke Handelskade, and we were tied up there by eight o'clock as promised. Took Tour 21, the motor-launch part, through the old city, and then by bus to the

177

Royal Palace, Bourse, and Rijksmuseum, which was the second half of it. Launch had a sliding glass roof overhead. Rainwater was trapped in it somehow, and it leaked upon us most of the short trip. Canal vistas interesting. Tethered houseboats, with plants and cats. There was a catboat (pun) with 150 resident strays, fed by the cat lovers. Lots of tall narrow pastel houses on the old streets, four and five stories. At the museum we looked at the Halses and the Rembrandts, noting that they seemed brighter and better preserved than the ones in the Ringling Museum. Found one painting we both liked very much, "The Threatened Swan" by Jan Asselyn, painted in 1610. And finally, of course, they took us to a diamond cutting and polishing place. Just like the cameo factories of the Mediterranean: "Ees run by my brother's second cousin by marriage. Ees good stuff very cheep." The old hustle. A little percentage rake-off for the bus operators.

Back to the ship for lunch, and then into town on the shuttle bus to do some shopping. The bus went right to Dam Square, where hippies congregate on the shallow steps that surround the war memorial in the middle of the traffic circle.

Even in 1977 they had begun to look like the relics of times past. Little burned-out girls with their dumb doleful faces, sticky spill of hair, buttocks humble under the pale caked denim. Hairy desperado types, khaki and sweat, knapsacks and Aussie hats, their planned air of savage freedom compromised by an uncertainty around the eyes, a vague look, a listless way of moving. There was a constant motion, a shifting around, a perpetual slow investigation of one another, and among the hundreds were the old predators, trying to look young enough for credibility, and the very youngest victims, trying to look old enough to be with it, because this was one of the places of the world where it was all supposed to be: all the grass, all the badly played guitars, all the crotch crabs and stubborn clap and raggedy philosophies anybody could ever dream of. Each evening these drifters of the western world would slowly gather up their gear and obediently vacate their central refuge long enough for the local civil servants to hose the area clean with lots of high-pressure water. And then they would amble back to damp concrete, spread out once more, and continue their endless investigations of one another.

Shopping: a camera strap, a Timex battery, two canvas and leather carryons for the Russian trip, pair of cotton gloves, and two of my titles in Dutch with cover art I had not seen before—to take back as gag gifts aboard. Shuttle bus jammed on the way back. SRO. Found the *Royal Viking Sun* anchored just astern of us. Decided to look it all over after dinner. Most cruise ships have an open-door policy as regards people from other ships. Possible future business.

This was our second night at the captain's table. We had resisted it strongly. The two of us never want for conversation. I tense up with groups, can't enjoy what I'm eating because am only semiconscious of what it is. We liked our banquette corner with Sandy, the great young waitress, and Beth, her co-worker. But John Kilpack had extended the invitation himself, saying, "Please, you guys. Just from Zeebuggy to Scotland, okay? I want to have one table where I can have some fun."

So the captain's nine table guests were the MacDonalds, Al and Emily Morgan, Rugh and Addison Moore, Evelyn Cox, Edra Brophy, and Waynette Schmidt. And it did indeed seem to be a lively enough group.

I can remember the worst table I ever had. It was so bad it was almost unbelievable. There was a mother-and-daughter team. The daughter had been very overweight, apparently as the result of some domestic problems. She had eaten herself up to about a hundred and eighty. The mother had told her that if she would lose forty pounds, she would take her on the cruise, never dreaming the daughter could do it. But she did, and there they were. Then there was a big couple from the Midwest—not fat people, just very big people—Barbara and Bill, both heavy on the booze. Barbara was six feet tall, and she apparently had the money, because she ran things and her husband had very little to say. She was the type who, back home, would reorganize the country club, join a lot of other clubs, and set the agenda. Almost every night she showed up at the table smashed.

Then there was this fantastic couple from New Zealand. His name was Fred Hayes and he had made his fortune in the scrap business. After making it, he was given some minor political appointment, and he liked to be known as the Magistrate. So we called him Freddy 'Ayes, the Magistrate. When he took it upon himself to talk, he would beat on the table to emphasize the major points he was making, and when he finished, he would lean back in his chair and turn his hearing aid off. He didn't like argument or rebuttal. He traveled with his mistress, Mildred, a woman of about fifty. Her function was to back him up on his stories and opinions. Am I right? Yes, dear. Isn't that the way it was? Yes, dear. And what was that chap's name? Jones, dear.

Then there was an English doctor, Dr. Norman Nagle. He looked like Woody Allen. One tuft of hair fell across his forehead. His glasses tilted one way, and his bow tie titled the other. He wore a yellowed old tuxedo jacket. He was a slim, wiry type, but he could eat everything on the menu. He went down the list and ate everything in sight. It took hours for him to do this. Every once in a while he would have something he wanted everybody else to try; if necessary, he would get up and run clear around the table with a dripping forkful for the person across from him. Finally there was a retired Air Force colonel and his wife who went to very extensive cocktail parties every night and arrived bombed out of their skulls.

You can imagine what it was like. The mother and the daughter snarling at each other, Freddy Hayes making political speeches and banging on the table, Norman Nagle running hither and yon with his dripping fork, Bill and the colonel bellowing at each other, and Barbara and the colonel's wife trying to outdo each other at the top of their lungs.

It was total confusion. And sometimes they sang. That was worse. Norman would order fritters with that gooey sauce, and we had to tell him over and over to keep eating, because by the time the rest of us were through, he was just getting into high gear.

At the table nearest us were four ultra-conservative people, two straight-laced couples. They would look over at us and glower all the way through the meals. I could hardly blame them. When Barbara was sitting at my right, she could look right at that other table and glower back at them. And she would say in a stage whisper, "What's the matter with that old bitch over there?"

And I would say, "Now, Barbara, hold it down. Please.

Nothing is wrong. Don't agitate yourself. Just eat your dinner and enjoy."

One night, inevitably, the two tables stood up at the same time to leave, and Barbara and the scowling lady met face to face. Barbara looked down at her from six feet tall and said, "What's the matter with you, honey? Is something bugging you?"

"As a matter of fact there is. I think you people are way out of line over at that table. It is really disgusting."

Barbara tapped her on the chest and said, "Are you paying for my ticket?"

"No, of course not."

"Well, in that case, mind your own goddamned business."

This all went on night after night. They would get very bad. They would be so noisy. They sang. They beat on the table. Norman Nagle ordered everything. I would plead with them. "Please. Let's hold it down. No singing tonight. No more 'Wild Blue Yonder.' Let's maybe just tell some nice quiet jokes, and everybody behave."

They knew when they had gotten to me. I would give up. I would just skip dinner. I would stay away for a couple of nights and ask the waitress how they behaved.

She would say, "They were beautiful. They were really fine."

So I would take a chance and go to dinner again, and it would all blow up in my face.

The way the seating at my table was arranged, I would be given a VIP list from the company and a passenger list. I would look through the passenger list, and if there were people I had sailed with before and had a pleasant relationship with, naturally I would want them at my table. Some of the VIPs might be on the first sitting. Quite often with all the bustle and activity of sailing, I didn't have a chance to make up a table, so I would depend on the advice of the purser and the maître d'.

The trouble with that situation was that some of them—a maître d' named Manny, for example—were very susceptible to a tip. And there are people who lust to sit at the captain's table. They believe it indicates some special cachet of approval.

I would go to Manny after I had picked out two or three

couples from the list I wanted at my table and give him their names.

"Oh, no," he would say. "I know the Robinsons. They always want a banquette. They always sit by themselves."

"Well, ask them. All they can do is say no."

When I forced him to ask them, they would say yes. But while all this was going on, he would keep throwing names at me. "Wonderful people. Charming people. And they always sit at the captain's table."

"Well, they aren't going to this time. I don't want them."

Sometimes I would follow his advice, and the results would be disaster. It was better to fight him off and get the people I wanted.

On one trip I had a good table outward bound, but I was going to lose all of them at Sydney. As we neared Sydney, Manny would grab hold of my arm every night as I came out of the dining room and say, "Can I talk to you?"

"No, I'm busy right now."

"It will only take a minute."

"Okay, what is it?"

"I've got a really nice couple for your table on the way back. The Forresters."

"I don't know who they are."

"They are very very nice."

"Where are they? Can you point them out?"

"Right over there."

"Forget it."

And from the shattered expression on his face, I could tell that he had virtually promised them that they would be moved to the captain's table.

"But they are wonderful people, Captain!"

"No, Manny. Forget it."

"Well, in that case, if you don't have them at the table, if you have a cocktail party will you invite them?"

"We'll see. We'll see."

Every night he kept furnishing these names. Sometimes I would know the people. I knew he was taking tips from them to place them at my table. They were invariably people I didn't want. He kept mentioning the cocktail party, and I would not commit myself. I finally worked out a decent table for the trip *back, and I had forgotten about the whole thing. One night on the way in Manny handed me a list. I looked at it and said, "Who are these people?"*

"These are the people for your cocktail party, Captain."

There were eighteen people on that list, all of whom had thought they were going to make it to my table and didn't.

"Manny, you have got to be kidding! What is this affair going to be called? The losers' cocktail party? No way!" He was terribly crushed because now he had a new problem to lie his way out of. He had, in effect, been selling tickets to my quarters.

Another time there was a mother and two daughters aboard. The mother and one daughter were fairly nice, but the other daughter, who lived in Cleveland, liked to talk about her husband's Mercedes and the chauffeur who had taken her to the airport and the executive top brass they hobnobbed with. I got stuck with them for a little while one night up in the Poly Room. The daughter that was a turkey wore high-heeled spike shoes and tended to wobble around a lot after the eighth drink. Also, she wore a wig that was a little loose, and when she was gassed she tended to turn her head so suddenly the wig faced sideways.

On the way down to Sydney, the three of them sat at a table for four with one of the junior pursers, and near the end of that leg the turkey asked me who made the selections for the captain's table. I told her it was the maître d'. So she went to Manny, and he told her he had nothing to do with it, that the selections were made by the captain. She came back to me and I said, "Oh, no. Manny makes the selections. Everybody knows he is a big liar. You'll have to see him."

So she went back and hit him up again, and he did not know she had been talking to me. The next night when we came out of dinner, Manny intercepted me.

"I have some very nice ladies for your table. Three nice ladies."

"Manny, I can't take three ladies. I need couples. I can take one lady, or two at the most, but not three."

"These are really nice ladies and they would be an asset to your table."

"Who are they?" He pointed them out. "You have got to be out of your mind, Manny. Forget it!"

The next day she went to Manny and asked him how the project was coming along.

"I am working on it, but it is very very difficult."

"Would fifty dollars make it a little easier?"

He promised he would really get to work on it. The next day he approached me and said these ladies were very high class, and her husband was so and so, and they really expected to sit at my table.

"Manny, that is your problem. And there is no way you can solve it."

She hit him again the next day and he said he was working hard on it, and she upped the offer to a hundred dollars. I was getting this information from the junior purser at their table, a nice fellow who was very amused by the whole scene.

I kept brushing Manny off. He kept insisting. The offer went up to two hundred dollars. After he had tried every other way, he came to me and insisted that because of the seating arrangements in the dining room, he was going to have to find a place for those three ladies at my table.

I said, "Fine. Put all three of them there, because I won't be eating in this dining room on the way back." He looked close to tears.

By this time the three women had told everybody on the ship they were being invited to sit at the captain's table, and it had become a matter of saving face. When he hit me with a final desperate reason, I said, "Manny, I understand the price is now up to two hundred." He looked as if he wanted to sink through the floor. Needless to say, they never made it.

Once I had a very classy table. Miguel Alemán, the ex-president of Mexico, and his wife, and the president of Aero Mexico and his wife, and William H. Sullivan, ambassador to the Philippines, his wife, and a couple they were traveling with. To fill out the table they had given me a surgeon from Vancouver and his young wife. This was a high-brow table, with lots of interesting talk about international tensions and relationships, with everybody pausing politely to listen closely to whoever was talking. Except the doctor's wife. She was a jolly, rattle-brained girl who talked just about all the time. She would be carrying on and then notice that the ambassador and the ex-president were talking across the table and she would say, "Hey, what are you two guys talking about? I missed the first part."

I could see her husband wince whenever she did that. But he seemed compassionate. I guess he had been enduring it for a few years.

This went on night after night, and one night she was sitting on my right, and the ex-president's wife, Señora Alemán, was on my left, with her husband on the other side of her. The surgeon's wife suddenly leaned across me and said, "Mr. President, what do you think of the wetback situation?"

Before she finished the sentence, I was under the table, tying my shoe.

Tour No. 25: Volendam and the Isle Of Marken

Morning by motorcoach and ferryboat.
Leave the pier at 9 A.M. on Sunday, May 29.

Leave by motorcoach for an interesting excursion to Volendam, a picturesque old fishing village on the shores of the Zuiderzee. The inhabitants all wear the colorful local costumes that are imagined to be the normal Dutch dress. Then on to Marken, an island now joined to the mainland by a dike, where the fisher-folk are even more gaily attired. You'll return by ferry and visit a farm where Dutch cheese is processed, then return to the ship for luncheon.

Up early to go on bus tour No. 25. This is not a travel book in the usual sense of the term, so there will be little mention of the traditional and inevitable canals and canalboats, windmills and swans.

Marken Island was strangely unpleasant. Small, high-peaked, black-and-green houses with white trim. Very close together, with duckboard walks. A religious sect lives there, a group akin to the Amish. They stay in, behind their lace curtains, on Sunday. From time to time a face would look out at the three busloads of foreigners clumping by, chattering loudly, trying to see into the houses. And the face looking out would wear an expression of malevolence and contempt. Evidently they receive some recompense for this constant invasion of their privacy. Evidently it is not enough. We regretted having been taken there. We saw some of the women of the village. They wore ugly costumes of black skirts, upholstery-fabric corselettes, printed blouses, and off-white pillbox hats, and wooden shoes, which are made one pair at a time on an automatic lathe and a router.

The marina at Volendam requires a quantum of patience and consideration that yachtsmen at Marina del Rey or Bahia Mar would find impossible. The marina is very crowded and opens out into an artificial lake so broad the other shore is invisible. The power boats and sailboats are tied off the dock four and five deep. The Sunday boat people were arriving with their families, extricating their boats from the pack, carefully making fast once again all lines disturbed by their escape. It was a monstrous nuisance, time-consuming but accomplished with good cheer. All other boats were treated just as carefully as they treated their own. Perhaps this same consideration could be found in the States at a private sailing club. But at a public marina like the one at Volendam? Never. Callousness, indifference, and vandalism would spoil it quickly for everyone.

Back to the ship. Sailed at four. Watched us back out the dirty North Sea Canal and out into the North Sea, cold and rough in a gray daylight that lasted well past nine o'clock.

20

|||||||||||||||||||||||||||||||||||||||||||

Monday and Tuesday, May 30 and 31
Hamburg, Germany

The change of time zone between Amsterdam and Hamburg caught a lot of people unawares. The worst sufferers were those who got up at what they thought was 4 A.M. to see the pilot come aboard and found they had a cold, dark, windy hour of waiting.

For me the big scene in Hamburg was going up the river. It is a busy harbor and there is a lot of it. Miles. The German pilot and I discussed the various navigation hazards, and he told me where to slow down because of damage a wake might cause, and where I could pick up again. We went up the river at several different speeds, and finally they had to turn us around with tugs and back us into a slot inside a floating pier arrangement. There was a ship moored outboard of the floating pier. The pilot did a pretty good job, but he brought us in a little fast and scraped us along one side where there were some big I-beams holding the floating pier.

I said to him, "Well, you got us in here all right. That was a nice job."

And he said, "Ya, dot's the first time I effer do dot."

Everybody trooped ashore that night, and the next morning I got word one of our Hawaiian sailors was being held in jail on a rape charge. There was a lot of debate and conjecture and speculation aboard as to how anybody could have committed rape in Hamburg, especially in that section of town devoted to open cribs, sex shows, sex shops, and a lot of aggressive solicitation. It seemed like a very novel offense. Possibly a first.

The authorities did not want to make a big fuss about it, and for the sum of $860 they would return our Hawaiian to us. This was the bail. They would send him back and forget the whole thing.

That sounded okay. I could go for it. I asked the paymaster to deduct this amount from his wages, only to find out that he was one of the high rollers and had taken so many advance draws he only had $200 on the books.

So I changed my mind and said they could keep him. The crew heard about this executive decision and took up a collection and raised the remaining $660. The officials said they would bring the sailor to the ship around noon, and they wanted their money in German marks. The purser went ashore with the cash and came back with a big roll of marks and handed it over to me.

I waited around near the gangplank, and when nobody showed up I went back to my room. At about one o'clock the agent came in with a German officer. He was all dressed up like a storm trooper and was introduced to me as Captain Oberstauffer, or something similar.

I shook hands with him and went into a ten-minute monologue on how much I appreciated their cooperation in this matter of the Hawaiian rapist, and I was very sorry that it happened, and I wanted to apologize on behalf of the ship and the steamship company, and I didn't want them to think that this was typical of the kind of clean-cut young seamen we had on board. "I've complied with your request, and here is the entire amount of the bail in German marks."

I held it out to him, and both the agent and the captain looked at me with strange expressions. The agent said, "Captain, I think you are making a mistake. This man is not from the local police. This is Captain Oberstauffer from the Hamburg Harbor Police, and he is here to arrest you for speeding in the river."

I looked down at the money I was holding and put it back in my pocket.

He went into a lengthy discussion of my activities coming up the river, and how I had gone too fast in this place and that place, and these limitations were all made quite clear in the Hamburg Harbor Regulations, of which I had to have a copy on board because it was required. "And now vy did you disobey these regulations?"

"Well, I am very sorry that I haven't read the Hamburg Harbor Regulations. I haven't read them because they are in German. I can't read German. Secondly, I hired a German harbor pilot, and it was on his instructions that I proceeded at these various speeds coming up your river."

"Ve vill deal with the pilot. Now ve are dealing with you. You are the captain, and you are responsible."

I said, "Okay, okay. I'm a big boy and I've been there before, so okay. Let's get this straightened out. I'll have them bring down the logbook and the bell book, and we'll see what we can work out on this thing."

As is the custom with ships in harbor, and probably with most other kinds of negotiation, if you pour a few drinks, you have a chance to soften up the situation a little. So I turned to this German and I said, "While we're waiting for the logbook and the bell book, let me fix you a drink. What will you have?"

"I do not drink. I am a Mormon."

My God! I thought. A German Mormon. I didn't know they had any.

I thought I was really in bad shape, but after a lot of negotiation he fined me $270 for speeding up his river. I had to ask the purser to bring up more cash.

Later on, the local police brought the Hawaiian back to the ship and we handed over the bail money. The Hawaiian said that it had been a frame-up. The police told us that if the woman in question had any past record of solicitation, they would refund the money. Needless to say, we never heard from them again.

The local authorities are always a pain when they think you are out of line. Several years ago the Monterey was going into the Bay of Islands, a small port in northern New Zealand. You go through a very narrow passage before you get into the *harbor where it opens up. Along the narrow passage, on the shore, are signs saying* DO NOT ANCHOR *and* CABLE CROSSING. *Only after you clear this area can you drop your anchor and use it to turn around on.*

On the pilot's advice, when they assumed they were well clear of this cable area, they dropped the Monterey's anchor. But either the cable had drifted and shifted underwater, or more probably it collected some kind of trash and the tide got a purchase on it and moved it, but anyway, they snagged it pretty good, snapped the power cable, and blacked out the entire north end of the island. This created a lot of problems. Deep freezes were knocked out. They had no lights and no television, and this increased the birthrate.

There was a lawsuit pending, with the company maintaining it was not the Monterey's fault because the New Zealand pilot had told them where to drop the anchor. About a year later I went in there as first officer under Captain Y, a very reserved and dignified fellow. I was up most of the night because we left Auckland in the afternoon and arrived at Opua, the Bay of Islands, in the first faint light of day. By the time the ship was secured, there was not much time left for sleeping.

At noon I went back to my quarters to take a little nap. I left my door open and stretched out with my clothes on. At one o'clock I heard voices in my little entrance hallway. I was just getting up when Captain Y came into my room with two gentlemen. He said, "Oh, I'm sorry. I didn't realize you were sleeping. But is one o'clock. I would like to introduce Sheriff So-and-so and Magistrate So-and-so. It looks as if we are in a little trouble, Kilpack."

So I stepped quickly over to the bulkhead and leaned against it with both hands and spread my legs apart as they do in the movies when the cops shake them down, and I turned and said to them over my shoulder, "I'm innocent. She told me she was eighteen."

The two Kiwi officials thought that was pretty funny. But it didn't strike Captain Y as remotely humorous, and with a pained look he said, "These gentlemen are here to put an eighty-five-thousand-dollar lien against this vessel for the Monterey's cable episode."

We did eventually bail out of that one. But I didn't know

how well we would have done if the two officials had reacted the same way Captain Y did.

On Memorial Day afternoon, Dorothy and I took a cab to the Hamburg Zoo. A holiday in Germany as well. Through the empty and drab-looking downtown, a wild ride with an impetuous driver. Zoo paths packed with families. One of the great zoos of the world. More variety though in less space than San Diego. Creatures clean and content. Good coats. One very unhappy one, a variety of fox or wolf we had never seen before. South American origin. Very thin, small feral head, extremely long legs. Grotesquely long. A swift and unhappy beast, trotting back and forth, behind the wire, endlessly ready to leave.

A pretty redheaded woman taxied us back to the ship, mostly by sign language.

Next morning we walked up the dock area to an elevated train station. They have a splendid system that would never work in our own society. You study a wall-sized color coded route map. When you decide where you want to go, you put coins in the color-coded slots in the indicated amount and get your ticket. You walk onto a broad clean platform. No turnstiles. No ticket takers. You get on your train, get off where you please, and, when leaving the station, drop your ticket into a bin fastened to the wall.

Try that in any large American city and within a week the maps and coin slots would be vandalized and no one would be making the slightest attempt to pay a fare. Municipal services are fair game for all. The very orderliness of the German acceptance of the obligation to pay without coercion results in better service, cleaner facilities, and, to that extent, a better life-style than we have.

We have a barbarous society. Along the Amalfi Drive near Naples, blind hairpin turns have large mirrors mounted on poles to provide a way to look ahead. The road is so narrow that if one sees a bus coming in the mirror, the procedure is to pull over and stop far enough short of the curve to enable the bus to round it, and to back and fill if necessary. No one seems to molest the mirrors. They are for the safety of all. A similar mirror was erected at a blind corner on Siesta Key in Florida, two blocks from our home. Within days the sub-human young who infest the neighborhood had smashed it to bits. A new one was mounted. Within another few days the same group of retards, or another group, smashed it again. There was one final try, and when that too was vandalized, the officials gave up. There is an ugly mindlessness about destructive violence in the United States.

Anyway, our overhead train ducked underground and we got off in the heart of a large shopping area. After we picked up some odds and ends and stowed them in that indispensible traveler's friend, the string bag, we found a street with no vehicular traffic. It was lined with shops and had a long line of back-to-back stalls down the middle. They were selling herring, wool socks, bicycle clips, rug cleaner, and everything in between.

We had a roaming lunch. We ate our way down the street, down several blocks. Hot dogs, crepes, beer, sausage, shish kebabs of alternating chunks of cheese and cucumber on wooden skewers, vanilla ice-cream cones, and a terminal beer. Waddled to a cab stand and rode back. Ship sailed at six. After dinner went on deck and saw the simultaneous full moon and sunset from where we lay at anchor at the mouth of the Elbe, waiting to enter the Kiel Canal.

When we left Hamburg, another German pilot came aboard to take us down the Elbe. I told him I was in absolutely no hurry at all. I told him we could really take our time going down the river. And I told him I did not want another speeding ticket, even though I had already established credit.

When we reached the entrance to the Kiel Canal, their headquarters computer wasn't ready for us, so we had to anchor for a couple of hours. At this time they made a change of pilots. I didn't take to the new one who came aboard. I had no reason for it. He just didn't strike me as being the best around.

It takes a very sharp turn to get into the canal. We had a tug ahead and a tug astern to help us make that turn and get into the locks. The pilot was giving instructions to the tug captains. Just as we entered the locks and were getting secured in there, the after tug released his line, which allowed the stern of the Mariposa *to swing over and strike the walkway along the side of the locks. It made a heavy thump, so when we were secured, Chief Mate Coco and I walked down to take a look. There was no damage to the ship except for a small scratch near the side port, but the impact had buckled and lifted some slabs of cement on the walkway on the side of the locks.*

I immediately put the pilot on notice and made an entry in the log. I said, "It's your fault, or the tugboat's fault. You should have held us off until we got the ship secured."

"Oh, that's all right, Captain. No problem at all. The people on the docks aren't concerned. All it is is a few broken slabs of cement, and it'll be no problem whatsoever." So we forged ahead under very foggy conditions.

Halfway through we changed pilots again. When we reached the other end to go through the locks into the Baltic, a whole battery of legal flegals, shysters with briefcases, boarded the ship, wanting to know who our insurance carrier was. I said I couldn't tell them because we have several carriers, several policies, and they'd have to be more specific.

They said we had smashed up the other end of their canal and done thousands of dollars' worth of damage, and they couldn't let us proceed until they found out if we were solvent and had assurances that we would pay for the damage.

After a lot of hassling around, the agent got in touch with San Francisco. I told the agent to add a special message from me: the same one I'd been sending back now and then: NOTHING CAN GO WRONG. *The agent was puzzled, but he relayed it. After negotiations, they let us proceed. I had said to them, "Why don't you go back and talk to the first pilot? He told me there was no problem whatsoever."*

"Ve vill take care of the pilot. Right now ve are dealing with you."

21

||||||||||||||||||||||||||||||||||||||||||||

Wednesday, June 1

En Route to Leningrad

Up by five to go up forward on the Boat Deck and watch the slow canal transit. It is a very special sensation riding a ship through a narrow waterway. Because of the slow speed, it happens in spooky silence. We were going through farmland rich with the colors of spring. Over the sound of our wash moving against the banks, we could hear cocks crowing, bird songs, cattle lowing. It was bright and sunny and very cold.

We would watch the swans ahead, very cool about oncoming ships, waiting until the last minute to pick one side or the other for their slow escape from twenty thousand oncoming tons. We saw wild deer bounding across the fields toward the hedgerow thickets. Families of rabbits gave us casual glances from the grass patches on the banks where they were feeding. Heard my first cuckoos. Absolutely astonished to find out that their cry was exactly that: *coo-coooo*. It seemed terribly oversimplified. It sounded far too much like a cuckoo clock.

There were great bright hillside fields of yellow rape. Small lateral canals led off the main channel. Saw a stir of fish from time to time. Passed ships in sidings, headed the other way: Greek, Panamanian, Brazilian, Indian. Lots of small local freighters, mostly tidy and freshly painted. Slept hard after lunch and then went to a briefing on Russia in the Theater, down below the Main Deck. The briefing was for people who had signed up for tours. We had signed up for the "Red Arrow":

Tour No. 34: Moscow, Russia's Capital.
Two days, by train and motorcoach, including all meals. Leave the pier at 11 P.M. on Friday, June 3. LENINGRAD-MOSCOW. In the late evening, drive to the Leningrad railway station and board the "Red Arrow" sleeping-car express for Moscow.

Saturday, June 4: MOSCOW. Upon arrival in Moscow in the morning, transfer to a leading hotel for breakfast. A morning and afternoon drive by motorcoach will be offered in the Soviet capital. Among the highlights to be seen are Red Square, Moscow University, and the Kremlin—including the churches, buildings of state, gala reception halls, the huge outdoor bell, and the world's largest cannon. In the evening, entertainment will be offered at a Moscow public attraction. At the conclusion of the entertainment, drive to the railroad station and board the "Red Arrow" express for the return journey to Leningrad.

Sunday, June 5: LENINGRAD. Arrive in Leningrad in the morning and rejoin the *Mariposa* for breakfast on board.

Membership limited.

Many words of caution. The questions from the audience indicated various degrees of anxiety.

A formal night. Found the captain at his table for a change. Is now known to us as His Irreverence. Dorothy toasted him. "Here's to the captain. He got us out of another port." Broke him up.

As I had hoped, it was turning out to be a pretty good table, reminiscent of good ones in the past.

When I first became captain, it took quite awhile for the staff and the much-traveled passengers to catch on to my sense of humor and the way I operated, particularly in the dining room with the waiters and the waitresses.

Myrna was a tiny little waitress, quite well up in years, a frail lady who looked something like Grandma on The Beverly Hillbillies. She was very feisty and really on the ball. Very very good at her job. She had finally realized that I liked to come in and kid all the waitresses and the help, and that I was fairly human.

One time a woman told me a story about Myrna. This woman was very rich, quite portly, and had traveled all over the world for years, staying at the very best hotels and traveling on the best ships.

She said she came to dinner one night and after she was seated at the table for only a few minutes, Myrna came in with one of the woman's sweaters, a cardigan, and slipped it around the woman's shoulders, saying "It's getting a little chilly this evening, and I thought you might like to have this."

The woman didn't think it was chilly but didn't want to make an issue of it. She accepted the sweater and kept it around her shoulders. When she returned to her room that night she discovered that her zipper was broken in the back. She said she had never been so impressed with anyone's tact in her life. Myrna could have come over and whispered to her that her zipper was broken, or even made a unsuccessful attempt to tug it up, but she decided it was best not to say a word. She just sent the bellhop for a sweater. The woman said, "I have been in most of the world's best places, with the best and most sophisticated service money can buy, but I never saw anything as smooth and as thoughtful as that."

When Myrna finally retired, they had a special party for her in the crew's mess, and on the last night before we reached San Francisco, I had them bring me a mike in the dining room, and I got up and told everyone that one of our most valued employees was retiring, and because she had been serving all of us for twenty years, I was going to serve her. She turned beet red, but I made her come over and sit in my place, and I put a napkin over my sleeve and served her coffee and dessert. She protested, but I knew she was enjoying it.

The next morning I got one of the women passengers who knew Myrna well to tell her some kind of fib and lead her up to the bridge early in the morning. It worked, and Myrna rode under the Golden Gate bridge and on up to the dock, right *alongside me on the bridge. That was the first time she had ever been up there, and she told me that, to her, it was the high point of her whole career. Nobody had ever thought to ask her before, and she was really thrilled by it.*

Among a good group I had at the table one time was a couple from Hollywood. The woman was a writer, and her husband had some sort of position with one of the studios: a very attractive couple.

From my table in the Pit, we could see a three-quarter profile of an older man with gray hair in a mod cut. He sat at one of the corner tables on the upper level.

On the second night out, the Hollywood woman was on my right and she said to me, "Captain, isn't that . . . look up there . . . isn't that the retired jockey, Johnny Longden?"

"Gosh, I wouldn't know. Sure, I've seen him ride. He was a famous jockey, but I wouldn't really know him if I saw him."

"Well, I'm positive. Just look at him."

"Anyway, I can check it out," I said. When Myrna came by I told her, "Don't make a special trip and don't be obvious, but when you go by, take a look and see if that fellow at the corner table in the gray jacket might be Johnny Longden, the famous old jockey."

She made a sweep around there and came back and said, "Captain, that is an old lady."

That started a whole series of jockey jokes and horse jokes. One of the room stewards was a short stocky Chinese we called Dr. Lee. He had the damnedest bowed legs you ever saw in your life. He wore baggy pants in an unsuccessful attempt to disguise them. One day the little guy came through the dining room holding a tray up in the air.

I nudged the Hollywood writer and said, "Do you see that man over there?"

"Yes, yes, I do," she said.

"Well, he was once a very famous jockey in Hong Kong."

People would rack their brains to come in to dinner with a horse joke. Finally I remembered the one about the fellow who had a very promising stallion which had only one fault. If there was a little filly in the race, he would always drop back and come in second behind her.

The owner talked to the horse several times. "Look, knock

this off or I am going to send you to the vet and have you fixed. That'll get these notions out of your mind. I'm putting you in the big race Saturday and I want you to win, and I am betting a bundle on you."

So the race started and the horse was doing well. He was a couple of lengths ahead when he looked back and saw this little filly coming up, so he dropped back and came in second.

So the owner said, "Okay. This is it. You have had it." He took him to the vet's and had him taken care of. He rested the horse up in the pasture for a few weeks and then he asked how he felt.

"Oh, I feel great. Those notions are all out of my mind. If you put me in a race now I will really do a job for you."

"Okay, I am putting you in the big race on Saturday and I am betting a bundle again, and you had better win." The horses were all in the starting gate on the last race on the Saturday card, and there was a lot of excitement and screaming and yelling. The bell rang and the gates opened and the horse came plunging out and fell down right away.

When the jockey led him off, the owner went over to the horse and said, "What the hell is the matter with you? I had a lot of money on you. You promised me you were going to win today. What happened?"

The horse said, "I was all set to go, boss. I was going to win that race for you. The bell rang and the gates banged open and I came charging out and the starter yelled, "They're off!" and I was so embarrassed. I crossed my legs and fell right on my ass."

The Hollywood couple got off in Hawaii. On our next stop at Honolulu I had a lot of people up in my room when I got word that the same couple was down in the lobby and wanted to see me. I had them come right up. They were both trying to stifle laughter, and they had this gift package for me about the size of a shoe box.

I said, "I know this has something to do with horse racing." She started giggling. "Probably this box is full of old racing forms." They said it wasn't. "Maybe jockey shorts in my size?" No, not that.

I opened the box and there was an exquisite little racehorse made of hand-blown glass. He was wearing the winner's horseshoe wreath of flowers, and his back legs were crossed. They said the man who made it was pretty puzzled about those hind legs, but he crossed them on request. I still have that little glass horse at home.

In contrast with splendid waitresses like Myrna, there will always be a Gretchen. Gretchen was a tall buxom German girl, and she was problem prone. I heard about her early efforts aboard. When she was first hired, she cleaned up her table one night, went back to her room, read about a function going on up in the Polynesian Room, put on her best dress, and went up and joined the passengers.

They fired her. But she had found out she liked ships. She persisted and wangled a job as a library stewardess, taking care of the library and the writing room and helping out with tea in the lounge. She became very aware of the grand piano in the lounge, and because she was a fair pianist, she thought she could practice when nobody was around. Nobody is around at three in the morning. She played with a lot of muscle.

They fired her. Later she managed to get back aboard as a room stewardess. At that time they had those small pantries off the corridors, with a toaster and refrigerator. It was their job to keep the refrigerator stocked with orange juice and ice and so on, and the pantry stocked with bread and rolls and cocktail peanuts and pretzels. Her station was up forward, and somebody kept taking the orange juice out of her refrigerator.

She got hot about this, and she made a few inquiries, but nobody admitted stealing it. So she filled the orange juice container and hid around the corner and waited. Sure enough, a figure ducked into her pantry with a pitcher and stood bent over, head in the refrigerator, pouring out her orange juice. So Gretchen snuck up behind him and gave him a healthy kick in the behind and knocked him into the refrigerator. He came out roaring; it was Captain X.

They fired her. But she kept at it and finally made her way back aboard as a dining room waitress. As a matter of fact, when the mother with the two daughters were sitting with the junior purser, Gretchen was their waitress. This purser got very tired of listening every night to those women scheming how to get to sit at my table and talking about how great things were in Cleveland. So he called the dining room one night and *said he wouldn't be in to dinner. Apparently that word did not get to Gretchen, and the three women waited a long time for the purser before ordering their dinner.*

The next morning I was having breakfast in the officers' mess when Gretchen came charging in, braids flying around, and started chewing out the young purser, Phil, for not coming to dinner. "Ve waited for you an hour and you didn't show up. It is not right!" she said in her German accent.

Phil said, "Gretchen, I called the bell stand and informed them I was not coming to dinner."

She continued to stand there and chew him out until Kelly, one of the other pursers, said, "Get the hell out of here and let us enjoy our breakfast."

"Haff a nice day!" Gretchen said through clenched teeth, and flounced out.

The next thing I knew, a written complaint came from Phil through channels to me. It was a complaint about unauthorized people frequenting the officers' mess. I called Phil up and said, "This complaint doesn't say anything at all. If you want to make a complaint, make a complaint. Be specific. If not, forget it. I was there. I witnessed the thing. As far as I am concerned, it was definitely conduct disrespectful to an officer. If you want to go ahead, write it up and I will take it from there."

So he rewrote it, and I got Gretchen and the stewards' delegate and the chief steward up to my quarters. In the course of the investigation I found she had been warned before to stay out of the officer's mess. She would go in there all the time when she had eyes for one of the ship's officers.

I proceeded to log her, and I read off for the official log book that she was being reprimanded for frequenting the officers' mess after having been previously warned and for conduct disrespectful to an officer.

When you begin an official logging, you say to the person, "This logging has been read in an audible manner, etc., etc., etc., and her reply is—" and the person being logged has the opportunity to reply. So, knowing Gretchen, before she had her chance to speak, I said, "I don't want to go into all the past details of this thing. We know what happened, and I do not want some kind of dissertation on it, and I do not want it to go any further than this room. I don't want you discussing

*this with the passengers. I want it to end right here. So now
you just tell me what you did or didn't do and we will drop it
right there. Go ahead."*

She took a deep breath and said, *"I have known Phil for
a very long time and he is like a young brother to me and I
am always—"*

*"Whoa, Gretchen. I do not want to hear all this. It means
that the purser has to copy all this crap down. If you have
something pertinent to say, say it, and let's get this over with."*

*"Well, does this mean I am fired? Mr. Lubin hates me and
Mr. Ayres hates me, and I have been fired off the* Monterey.
*And when I was fired, it wasn't fair. It wasn't right. What
happened was—"*

*"Whoa, Gretchen. Did I say you were fired? I have logged
you and reprimanded you, and whatever action is taken will
have to be taken by the company and the union. It is up to
them. All I am doing is putting it in the official logbook."*

So she started crying and trying to go over the whole thing
again, and finally her delegate said, *"Sign the thing and let's
get out of here."*

So she signed it and they left. Later the chief officer came
and told me that Gretchen had been to see him and asked him
to intercede with me, because we were good friends, and ask
me to strike the whole entry from the log. He told her there
was no way I could do that even if I wanted to. Which I didn't.

Her next step was to hustle the passengers on her behalf,
trying with tears and sighs to get them to intercede. Then she
started trying to play footsie with Phil again. So, two or three
times or more, she would try to snag me when she saw me
going through the public rooms, so she could talk about it.

And I would say, *"Gretchen, I am busy. I don't want to
talk about it."* But she kept trying to get the whole thing taken
off her record.

On the final Sunday of that trip, little Father Kern, who had
brought us all the good weather and cured the rainsquall problem, held the service. Gretchen attended often; she would always get there early and plop her big behind right in the middle
of the front row, forgetting all the times she had been told not
to sit up there but to sit over on the side, inconspicuously,

leaving the good seats for the people who were paying for their passage.

The little priest did not preach a sermon that last Sunday. He just recapped the high points of the trip, and told us what it had meant to him. He had worked for underprivileged people all his life, and this was a dream which had come true for him. I have a pretty thick skin, but I can tell you that it was so moving, so warm and decent, that I had a lump in my throat. And I could hear sniffles all around me. I don't think there was a really dry eye in the place.

After it was over I went up and shook Father Kern's hand and told him how much I enjoyed it, and turned to go up to my room. As I went to go through the passage way toward the stairs, Gretchen must have figured, now is the time to hit him up. He is in a sentimental mood.

She came trotting over to intercept me.

"Captain, can I talk to you?"

"No. Not now, Gretchen." I wanted to get out of the uniform. I had one of those chokers on.

"Captain, it will only take a minute."

"No, Gretchen. I haven't got time to talk now." I kept walking.

I started up the stairs, and she came after me. "But Captain, Captain, you have got to do something. Mr. Ayres hates me. Mr. Lubin hates me. They are going to fire me." At this point she actually caught hold of my leg. I turned and looked down at her. She was yelling, "You are the only one who can help me! You are the only one who can help me!"

And I was saying, "Back, Gretchen, back! Down. Down, Gretchen."

I finally pulled away from her and fled to my room.

No, they didn't fire her.

Firing people had been a lot easier when I first started working the White Ships. Toward the end, it became almost impossible. And that, of course, hastened the end.

It became a stronger union situation over the years. You had to have something specific. I couldn't fire anyone aboard just because I didn't happen to like him or her.

We had an arrogant bartender for several trips. He was

often nasty to the cash customers, and people came to me to complain about what he had said to them or to their wives.

And I would say, "I don't like him either, but I can't fire him just because I don't like him. Go down to the purser's counter and make a complaint in writing. Make it specific, and maybe we can get him fired."

"Well, I don't think I want to go that far. I just thought you ought to know how he's been acting."

"I already know, and there's nothing I can do about it unless you want to put the complaint in writing."

Crew members would come to me to complain about someone, and even though they were not required to sign their name, they were just as reluctant to make a written report. So there was an increasing number of people aboard the White Ships we weren't happy with, and who weren't doing a good job, but we couldn't get rid of them.

Also, we had a problem with the new people. We had to report a vacancy to the union, and they would send people down from the hiring hall, and we almost always had to take them.

One case involved a young doctor we had on board. He had been in the army, and I believe he went back into the army after he left the ship. He was young and husky, with prematurely white hair. He was good at sorting out the malingerers and turning down people he didn't think physically capable of handling the job.

We were in Hawaii and there was an opening for a scullion, a pot washer in the galley. They sent this young Hawaiian down, and when he reported for work the first day, he was using a cane. You can imagine what happened when the executive chef saw this. "What the hell are you doing with a cane? How can you work on a ship and expect to carry big pots and pans and lots of hot soup and roasts and stuff around hot stoves and ovens in a heavy sea, using a cane?"

"I don't really have to use it. It just helps me get around."

"Hey, I don't want you under these circumstances. You go see the doctor."

The kid went in to see the doctor, protesting that he had ridden down to the ship on his ten-speed bicycle, saying that he really didn't need the cane.

The doctor had him strip and found a terrible-looking scar, a wide thickened vertical scar, down his whole torso. In addition there were three scars on either side of the big scar, like big buttons on either side, giving the impression the kid was wearing a strange vest.

The doctor said, "What is this mess?"

"I was shot," the kid said.

They had done extensive surgery on him to repair his insides and remove bullets. The three button things on either side were where they had wired him together while he healed.

"You're not in good shape. You're going to have further complications with that. That is an unhealthy mass of scar tissue called keloid formation. I don't think you should be on this ship."

"No, doctor. I'm in good shape. I just made a trip on a freighter and I was okay, and I've been passed by the union doctor and the public health service, and I'm fit for duty."

"I'm sorry. I've got enough people here already to take care of. I don't want to take on any more responsibilities. I feel you are definitely going to have problems with that, and I think you ought to go back to the union and try to get a job elsewhere. You should be on shore where you can get medical attention when you need it."

So the kid left and went back to the union. The union hates to be turned down on anything. So they told the kid that they had sent him down for the job, and the job was his, and he better go right on back and claim it.

The kid came back, and the executive chef dumped the problem onto the chief steward, and he dropped it in my lap. Every problem that gets out of hand is referred to me. I assembled everyone in the chief steward's office: the chief purser, the chief steward, the doctor, the union representative, and the chef, as well as the kid with a cane.

The doctor said, "I have no animosity toward this young man at all. I don't really even know him. I do know we're not doing him any favor sending him out to sea. He's got a medical condition called keloid formation, which means an uncontrolled growth of scar tissue, and he should be ashore where he's close to medical care."

The union representative said, "No, this guy's been checked out, and we've got a good report from the last ship he worked on, and you're gonna have to take him. He's perfectly all right."

The doctor turned to the kid, who was a gangling teenager, and said, "Young man, I've nothing against you at all. I'd like to see you get a job and go to work. But I've got over three hundred passengers and two hundred and seventy crew members to take care of, and I don't want to take on something I anticipate is going to be trouble for me. Would you take off your shirt and show these gentlemen what we're discussing here?"

The kid took off his shirt and slid his belt down a little. It was my first look, and it was really a terrible-looking mess. The doctor said it was an example of the kind of condition he had named.

"Is this giving you any problem right now?"

"Well, not particularly."

"You are definitely going to have problems in the future. You are going to have to have additional surgery to correct this situation. It really does not look good to me at all." And then the doctor said, "I'll show you how a scar in that area should look." He took off his shirt, and he had a nice neat scar right down the center of his stomach where he evidently had some sort of internal surgery. And he stood there, a few inches away from the kid, both of them facing the union rep, who finally said, "Okay, kid, go on back to the hall and we'll work something out for you."

Incidentally, this was the same doctor who took the fishhook out of the boy's eye at Christmas Island. And never heard another word. He came aboard when we were in Hamburg, in uniform, to say hello. He was stationed in Germany. I should have kept him around to talk to Captain Oberstauffer.

After dinner we went to Susan Cashman's show. As any shipboard entertainer will attest, it is very difficult to do a show when they have been putting the clock ahead for a long period of time. We had been losing an hour every day, and to most of the people at her 9:45 show it felt like three in the morning.

Going the other way, everybody turns into night owls. But Susan made them listen. She did well.

When we made some comment to Captain Kilpack about the time changes, he told us that it was the date line which makes the real trouble. He said that on one Pacific cruise a blushing young wife had gone to the ship's doctor and asked him what she should do about taking her pill for Friday, when there hadn't been any Friday.

22

||||||||||||||||||||||||||||||||||||||||||||||

Thursday, June 2

En Route to Leningrad

A clear, cold, and sunny day in the Baltic Sea. The sea had long slow mild swells and an oily look about it. We were in a lot of traffic, up to five ships visible at times. There was increasing anticipation aboard regarding the docking at Leningrad tomorrow morning.

Hal Wagner's indoctrination talk was well attended. Leningrad is as far north of the equator as is Juneau, Alaska. Most of Russia lies north of the 50-degree-latitude line, which is that of Winnipeg. Moscow is on a line with Southern Alaska.

There will be two gangways, one for the passengers, one for the crew. In Leningrad we will find no taxis, no city maps. Stick with bottled water. Except for the smallest purchases, use U.S. currency. Take no pictures at all as we come into the harbor approaching the docks. No pictures on the docks. No pictures of railway terminals or airports. No pictures from moving vehicles. Be prepared to wear scuffs over the shoes in museums, especially in Leningrad.

Passengers who had been to Russia, or who had known someone who had been to Russia, were very busy handing out erroneous bits of information. This is one of the curses of the cruise-ship traveler, to be forever assaulted by inside information from nonofficial sources, 98 percent of it useless.

The other subject of conversation that day was tipping. This had been stimulated by the distribution of the shipboard accounts, up to date. The protocol of tipping is murky indeed, and a source of anxiety to new passengers.

There is no tipping at all aboard Russian cruise ships. It is a firm rule.

Holland American advertises "no tipping," but it does exist.

For all other lines, the simplest rule of thumb is $2.50 a day per person for room-steward service, and the same for table service. For a couple, it can be rounded off to $35 a week for the room steward or stewardess, and $35 a week per couple for the table steward and his assistant. And it is best to do it by the week. When you have been aboard a week give the money in an envelope to your waiter, and leave money in an envelope for your room steward in your room. Those people are traveling too and prefer to have the money in transit rather than all at the end. Incidentally, service people aboard ship do much better on short cruises than long cruises. On a long cruise, when passengers tip at the halfway mark, or at the end of the voyage, they tend to cut way back, percentagewise.

On the Sun Line, tips are pooled, and the travel brochures suggest that $6 per day per person be left in an envelope at the purser's desk upon debarkation.

For wine stewards, bar waiters, lounge waiters, and the like, it is easiest to put the tip on the chit when you sign it. For moving you to a more desirable table, the amount of the tip to the maître d'hôtel should bear some relation to the length of the voyage. From $10 to $40 is within reason. If your table captain cooks special dishes for you at your table, tip him from $5 to $10 a week, depending on how much you use his services and how many people are at the table.

Usually, on any lengthy cruise there is so much discussion among the passengers of how much to tip, to whom it should be given, and how often, it tends to average out. Passengers who have the more expensive accommodations aboard tip more than the average passenger, but on the other hand they require more service.

A couple budgeting a trip of, say, eight weeks can safely anticipate that tipping will require less than 5 percent of their total fare. If their double outside stateroom costs $30,000 for the cruise, they can anticipate spending $1,500 on tips—*as a maximum*. And a weekly tip-as-you-go plan will not inflict as surprising a bruise as if you wait until the end. On short cruises, $3 or $4 a day per passenger is a reasonable estimate. A couple on a three-day cruise can figure on about $25 to $30.

Aboard the *Mariposa* on the North Cape cruise, nearly everyone had sailed aboard the White Ships on previous voyages. Patterns had been established. The service personnel knew the ones who were inclined to be difficult and stingy. It was a credit to the staff and the steward's department that there was no perceptible difference in the service given to each passenger.

I was leaving the ship one day in Honolulu. I was in uniform, and I think I was going off to buy something in the shop on the dock. I don't recall. Anyway, about halfway down the gangway I met this little old lady coming aboard. She was carrying a big purse and a small suitcase.

She said, "Pardon me, sir, are you one of the pursers?"

"No, I'm not."

"I wonder who I can get to help me with my bag?"

"Give me your bag. I'll take it aboard."

So I escorted the old lady back through the lobby and down to her room. As we passed through the lobby all the bellhops raised up and looked at me, and the pursers stared from behind the counter.

We went down to her room, and I put her bag down and came back to the lobby to go ashore. As I passed the purser's desk one of the young pursers said, "Captain, what is going on? What are you doing carrying a passenger's luggage on board?"

And I patted my pocket and said, "Hey guys. Don't knock it. I just made myself a dollar tip."

We had one steady passenger I'll call Tootsie. A very good tipper. She was kind of a limp, pale, drawly old gal with thick glasses and rumpled blond hair. She sort of sagged and teetered around as if she was slightly smashed, and she usually was. I think she owned a big drive-in in Texas someplace. Whenever she traveled with us, she would bring aboard a complete cowgirl outfit for the costume party: cap pistols, white boots, twelve-gallon hat, and all. The cap pistols were loaded, and so was Tootsie.

On the South Pacific trip, there was always one night when they would put on a show based on excerpts from South Pacific. The entertainment staff and the passengers would do it. It was a traditional thing. They would have one of the younger passengers dress up, and the planter would sing "Younger than Springtime" to her. All she had to do was look up into his face with rapture.

On this one trip there wasn't any young person right for the part, so they decided to put Tootsie in there as the sweet young thing. The fellow who was to sing the bass was Russ, the pianist. Russ is a rotund guy; for a long time I thought he wore a rug to cover the top of his head, but actually he had a method of letting the hair grow very long in the back and on the sides, and then have it teased and combed forward and sprayed into position at the beauty shop, so that it only looked like a rug.

At the rehearsal they worked out a costume for Tootsie, and they told her all she had to do was look into Russ's eyes, and maybe once in a while give his cheek a little stroke or a little pat. Rehearsal went fine.

Before the actual performance, Tootsie took on a pretty good load to prepare herself for her show-biz debut. The booze gave her a compulsion to improvise. After some cheek-stroking, she decided she wanted to reach up a little farther and run her fingers through Russ's hair.

When she made a pass at it, Russ yanked his head away in panic and tried to back off. Tootsie thought he was just being coy. She came floundering after him, and Russ backed around in a panic under the spotlight, singing, "Younger than springtime—don't touch the hair!—are you—for God's sake, don't touch the hair!" It was one of the all-time great renditions. It broke everybody up.

In Fiji, Tootsie went ashore with one of the women passengers—the one who told me this story about Tootsie the tipper. One of the cabs hustled them at the dock, and after some negotiations they settled on a price of $20 for a tour of the sights and a little shopping.

Tootsie told the cabdriver she wanted to buy some Indian

saris, so the cabdriver took them to one of the hindu shops. There Tootsie bought a dozen or so, "For all the girls at the drive-in."

After they were bought and wrapped and paid for and put in the taxi, they went to another shop and Tootsie found she had really been hustled. The same quality saris were available for about half what she had paid. It was obviously a rake-off situation for the cabdriver.

They finished up the tour and the shopping and got back to the dock and got out with their packages, and the driver said, "That is forty dollars."

They said, "You told us it was only twenty!"

"I said it is twenty each. Twenty each is forty dollars."

Tootsie told me the next part of the story herself. "He told me it was going to be twenty, and he charged me forty. I don't think that was neighborly."

"Tootsie, why didn't you just tell him he said twenty, and twenty was what he was going to get, and toss it through the cab window to him?"

"Well, I just couldn't do that."

"Then you should have called the police. Twenty dollars is twenty dollars."

"Well, I didn't think of it, and I couldn't do that anyway."

The other passenger finished the story the next day. "Yes, when we got back Tootsie did give that driver a pretty good argument about it being just twenty dollars, but he kept saying forty, so finally she paid him forty and tipped him five."

23

||||||||||||||||||||||||||||||||||||||||||||||||||

Friday, June 3

Leningrad, U.S.S.R.

On a cold and overcast day, we burbled slowly along past miles of industrial port installations and activities. Fields of little identical tan automobiles. Whole cities of warehouses. Mountains of crates and containers. Forests of cranes and derricks. There was no contour to the land beyond the dock area. It looked flat and drab.

We docked on schedule at Berth 33, Yuzhnaya Damba. Those travelwise crew members and passengers who intended to go about on their own in downtown Leningrad carried with them a postcard showing the ship, with the number and name of the berth written on it in Russian.

The immigration officers who came aboard were uniformed, expressionless, and quick. This time there were very few laggards who had to be blasted out of the beds to get in line so the ship could be cleared. The laggards are the reverse of the first-in-liners. They are hypothyroid, dim of wit, usually wearing an expression of benign stupor. They seem astonished to learn they have inconvenienced anyone, astonished but not remorseful. They are the ones who drift around unaware that

215

everyone else has gotten onto the bus and is sitting there, waiting. A round of sardonic applause from the other bus passengers does not faze them. They respond with small dopey smiles.

Jack Stanton, the Thomas Cook tour manager, told us that when he was conducting bus tours of the Orient, he would stand up in the front of the bus when they arrived at a hotel and say, "Your suitcases will be outside your room tomorrow morning by seven A.M. Breakfast at seven fifteen. You will be aboard the bus by eight. We will leave at eight. We are not baby-sitters. If you are not aboard, you will have to arrange to catch up with us or fly home."

He said, "They wouldn't really believe you until you left poor old Charlie stranded in Bangkok, but from then on they shaped up. It isn't fair to the others to have to wait for the tardy few."

After the ship was cleared, we had to go down the gangway, passport in hand, and give the passport to a young armed soldier who stood unsmiling, silent. He would look at the photo in the passport, look at the person who had handed it to him, then hand the passport to a second soldier seated at a small table on which were a couple of cardboard boxes a little bigger than shoe boxes. The seated soldier would repeat the photo check, though not as thoroughly, find the proper niche in one of the cardboard boxes, file the passport, and take out a numbered permit card and hand it to you.

Even if you were just going to walk across the dock to the passenger pavilion and buy something at the little Beriozka (Birch Tree) store, you had to follow the procedure. It never varied.

The composure of the soldiers at the foot of the gangplank was fractured only once. We had identical twins aboard, two plump white-haired ladies in their middle years. They looked exactly alike. They dressed exactly alike at all times. Almost everything they wore was flowered.

Probably what broke up the soldiers was the fact that one of them had been married, and so the names on the two passports were different. The standing soldier studied the face of the first one, handed the passport down, and then gave a little jump when he looked at the photo in the next passport. He grunted something, and the two of them stared first at one twin and then the other. Then their young faces broke into broad peasant grins, quickly stifled as they got back to the sober discipline of carefully checking all these dangerous old capitalist passengers.

A railway siding ran down the center of the concrete pier. The passenger pavilion was small. At nine we obediently boarded our tourist bus. The driver never spoke. The Intourist guide was a young blond woman with adequate English. She explained that she spoke three languages: her native tongue, from one of the provinces, and two foreign languages— Russian and English.

We noticed from the bus window how very many huge floodlights they had in the area of the docks. Bushel-basket size, two to each very high steel pole. Everybody had been made aware of the no-camera-work-in-the-dock-area rule, and the Intourist guide refreshed our memory.

In our ride to the gatehouse we passed stacked piles of big ingots, big strapped crates of what seemed to be heavy equipment. Guards checked us out past the gatehouse and past a wall covered with huge portraits of the leadership.

The planet is overpopulated with instant experts. Nobody, after three days in the world's largest country, should have the gall to try to tell anyone what Russia is really like. But there are impressions, very strong ones, perhaps of some validity. We took a couple of bus rides that day:

Tour No. 31: Leningrad City
Morning by motorcoach.
Leave the pier at 9 A.M. on Friday, June 3.

This drive will include outstanding places of historical and architectural interest, such as the great Winter Palace of the former Czars, the old Peter and Paul Fortress, the house of the poet Pushkin, and the broad avenue known as the Nevski Prospect. Return to the *Mariposa* for luncheon.

Tour No. 32: A Visit To The Hermitage
Afternoon, transfers by motorcoach.
Leave the pier at 2 P.M. on Friday, June 3.

Drive directly to the magnificent Hermitage Museum.
En route, guides will give an explanation of this famous
cultural attraction. Each day hundreds of local and foreign tourists visit the Hermitage to see the outstanding
art collection. Two hours will be allowed for tour members to view the collection according to their individual
preference. At 4 P.M. the motorcoaches will leave the
museum to return to the ship.

On that gray day, the Leningrad world was just coming into
early spring. There were rows and rows of apartment houses, with
double windows to protect against the severe winters. The occupied ones had a few automobiles around them, lots of bicycles and
minibikes. Many new apartments are being built, the guide
pointed out, but to me they had the look of something that had been
begun years earlier and abandoned. Either that or they had per-
fected the art of instant old buildings. Old and new, they sat on land
so bare it did indeed look like construction sites. One saw no Mediterranean flair for individuality—no bright curtains, window
boxes or colorful clothes hanging out on the windy lines.

There were some shattered buildings bombed out by Germans, shelled by Germans, over thirty years earlier. Whether
they were left there as editorials or due to bureaucratic over-
sight, one could not tell. These were in the dock area.

Lots of ornamental ironwork, on elegant fences and on
the abutments to the bridges over the rivers. With every
building the guide pointed out to us, old or new, she felt
compelled to tell us, in careful detail, the very long Russian
name of the particular architect who had designed it. It seemed
a strange quirk. Not one of us could have repeated the name
after her, much less remembered all of it. It was as if the
architects had a union contract with Intourist.

We saw the early lilacs, and some people selling lilies of
the valley. Dress was uniformly drab. Dark, unmatched clothing. Many with dark clothing and white shoes. Some of the
young were wearing blue jeans. Our young cruise hostess

was offered the equivalent of $125 in rubles for the blue jeans she was wearing. But, of course, the value of the rubles offered is a wide-open question. The ruble is valueless everywhere in the world except in Mother Russia. The exchange rate inside Russia for hard currency is by government edict, bearing little relation to reality. According to the goods one can buy, 30 cents would seem a fair exchange value rather than the $1.25 a ruble we were permitted. Thus, in buying power, the hostess was being offered $30—still a good price for used jeans.

We saw other tourist groups, Germans and Japanese (who are everywhere) and U.S.S.R. tourists from distant states. The streets were constantly being swept by men and by women, with brooms made of bundles of twigs lashed to the end of a stick.

And we saw many teenage girls, cute as buttons in white jump suits, wearing hard hats and covered from head to toe with plaster. We saw some on the street and some up on scaffolding, working. Plasterer seems to be an approved profession for the young ladies of Leningrad.

In the afternoon the Hermitage. A huge complex, bursting with people, scores of groups being led about, lectured to in different languages. After a half hour of staring at the same sort of baroque art which fills the Ringling Museum, great muddy masterpieces, portraits of noblemen and angels, we peeled off from our group and went to the top floor and saw fabulous and unfamiliar work by Monet, Gauguin, Van Gogh, Matisse, Cézanne, the best of the best. Room after room. Breathtaking. Apparently the titled classes during pre-revolutionary days, in the period 1890 to 1914, had collected these Impressionist paintings in Paris and brought them back to Russia where, at the time of the revolution, they became the property of the state. We could take pictures, but without flash. When departure time neared and we could not find our group because we could not find where we had entered the place, Dorothy got help from a young Russian couple who had previously admired her Polaroid camera. They had a few words of English and a map, and they headed us in the right direction.

* * *

In the Russian operation the biggest flap, as far as I was concerned, was the fact that they had no visas for the crew. The passengers had made individual applications months prior to the trip and sent them through the PFEL offices for processing, and they were all taken care of. But the crew is usually visa-ed all at one time. You submit what is called a visa crew list which verifies the nationality and vital statistics of each and every crew member, and this sets them up for official shore passes.

At every port we'd received a lot of mail, but in Leningrad there was almost none. And the Russians claimed they had never received a visa crew list. Jim Yonge, the purser, made a big pitch to the Russian immigration officers who came aboard, but they had no sense of humor, no willingness to assist, no apparent interest in our problem. They wouldn't even take a cup of coffee on the house. They just stared at Jim out of cold eyes in those flat faces, and the boss fellow said, "Nyet!"

At that point I was brought into the conversation. The officials asked me if I had a passport, and I told them I did.

"Then, as the master of the ship, since you have a passport, you can go ashore. But the crew cannot go."

"You've got to be kidding. You mean that I'm supposed to head down the dock with my crew leaning over the rail and watching me go? No way. I'm not going to leave the ship until such time as my crew can get their passes also."

"They are not permitted."

"What recourse have I got?"

The boss zombie shrugged. "Perhaps the American consul."

So it turned out I had to make a number of phone calls. We weren't hooked up, of course, so I had to make them from the passenger pavilion. Each time I would wear the whole uniform, with the braid on the hat, hoping this would impress them, and each time I left the ship to telephone I had to turn in my passport and take their little card, and each time they looked from the passport photo to my face and back again a couple of times, to make sure this was the same captain who phoned a little while ago.

I got hold of the consul's office, and they said, "Yes, we know these things happen. It isn't uncommon. We'll go to work on it right away."

"How long do you think it might take to get it straightened out?"

"Well, it usually takes about three days."

"That's just great. That's about the time we'll be sailing."

"All I can say is we'll do the best we can."

Pretty soon we began to hear rumors that something was happening, and sure enough, about six or six thirty that evening they came through with the crew passes. I invited the consul and his wife down to have dinner on the ship, with whomever else he wanted to invite. I asked him, incidentally, if his office knew we were coming, and he said they had been given no notification at all. This is typical U.S. State Department dedication. Here we were, the last passenger ship in service, making the final trip to Europe that would ever be made, and nobody in Washington thought it important enough to notify the State Department people at our ports of call.

The consul and his wife were charming. They could speak Russian, and I thought that was unusual, because the run-of-the-mill State Department person hardly ever speaks the language of the country to which he is assigned. And there is no policy which encourages them to learn it.

The consul told us at dinner that normally it really does take about three days to clear these things. But he had a typist working in his office, a local woman who was obviously charged by her government to keep them apprised of everything that was going on. She was typing a visa crew list for a Russian ship approaching New York, and he said to her, "You can stop what you're doing now and work on this list for the Mariposa."

"But this is for a Russian ship that is going to be in New York the day after tomorrow."

"Fine, I want you to get that done, of course. But first you will do this one. This is an American ship, and I am the American consul. When you get this one finished and cleared, we can go back to the other one."

He said she dropped everything and left the office for a little while, and not long after she came back to her desk the office got word from Moscow that the local immigration people had been instructed to go ahead and issue passes for the crew of the Mariposa. "And that's the only reason they came through so fast," he told me. "Otherwise you would have had a three-day wait like everybody else."

Even though Jim Yonge didn't make any headway with those customs officers, I think he probably saved us from another kind of trouble. We had a klepto aboard who had caused so much trouble on prior trips I was surprised they let her book this cruise. She was heavy, with dyed reddish hair and a lot of dresses with big floral patterns, and a lot of big pocketbooks. I'll call her Marian Richards.

She spoke in a loud angry whine. She had a personality so aggressively unpleasant they made her book a single cabin for herself. As an example of typical Marian behavior, when mail came aboard, the pursers would sort it into the boxes on the wall behind the purser's counter. People would be standing waiting for them to finish. Old Marian would come along and crowd right through the other people without a word of apology and say in that chain-saw whine, "There's a letter in my box. Give it to me."

"Please wait until we finish sorting."

"I see that letter right there. In my box. Give it to me right now."

If some other passenger—who didn't know her—asked her to wait her turn, she would turn that squinty baleful glare on him or her and say, "If you are trying to tell me what to do forget it. Who the hell do you think you are? Just shut up and leave me alone. You, there, give me my letter."

It was easier to get rid of her by giving it to her. When she took a tour bus, she always sat right behind the driver. If somebody else got that seat before she got on, she would stand over them, blocking the aisle, ranting at them, claiming it was her seat; everybody knew it was her seat. If she failed to move them, she would not get off the bus at the next stop. She would just move up to "her" seat.

The other passengers hated to go into a souvenir shop with old Marian. She would just open one of those big purses and start dumping into it whatever struck her fancy. She was so blatant about it, it seemed miraculous they never caught her. If a passenger remonstrated with her, old Marian would swivel squinted eyes and that big bosom around and say in a voice you could hear at a hundred yards, "Are you accusing me of theft? Let me tell you what you are doing. You are slandering me. You are blackening my name and my reputation. I have had legal training. Just tell me what you said one more time, in the presence of these other people, and I will clean you out. I will take your home and your car and your money and leave you flat broke. So help me God. So say it again."

Nobody ever did. In the dining room she had some great moves. She would put an open purse on her lap. She would pick up a spoonful of something, and after she had put it in her mouth she would just let go, and the spoon would fall into her purse. On the way out of the dining room, when she passed the stand, she would load her purse with after-dinner mints. She managed to smuggle big dinner-plate covers out of the dining room. She would take teacups out of the lounge. She stole rolls of toilet paper, soap, sugar bowls, creamers, candlesticks, steak knives. Every few days the room steward would go through her stuff and retrieve the ship's belongings and put them back into stock. When she went into the gift shop, they watched her like eagles.

She used to come up and talk to me, in a kind of flirtatious way, and fondle my brass buttons, at which point I had to hold my hands across my chest. I was always afraid she would try for my wristwatch.

When the Russians were clearing the last few people in the lounge, Jim Yonge spotted Marian Richards drifting in her sly way toward the card table where the Russians had spread out all their paraphernalia, all their fancy rubber stamps. She was looking for some action and slowly tacking her way toward the table when Jim sprang over and got between her and the table and headed her off. If she'd added some of those rubber stamps to her collection, it would have created an international incident.

When the trip was finally over, the purser and the chief steward told Customs to give Marian a complete shakedown, and they arranged to have ship's personnel down there in the shed to retrieve all the ship's stuff from her suitcases and *endless cartons. She said she didn't know how in the world it all got there. She said they were framing her. She warned them of a lawsuit.*

We were back at the ship by four thirty. At 11 P.M. we took off by bus for the Leningrad railway station. There were about fifty pilgrims, split into two groups and shepherded by Hal Wagner, Jan Mazurus, and two Intourist guides, a fellow in his fifties named Mike, who had lived in the States and had a rattling command of English, and Alla, a pleasant dark-haired girl in her twenties.

The station looked like an airport terminal in a Midwest city of two hundred thousand. It was cold inside the station, and not yet dark. All the station lights were on. A gigantic head of Lenin on a pedestal stood flood-lighted at the end of the longest vista.

Our compartment was in a tall, elderly, but well-maintained car. There were two narrow bunks set crosswise of the compartment—very narrow, the top one a startling distance up in the air. The backs of the bunks and the blankets were completely covered by linen sheets. There was a linen-covered table under the window, and linen cottage curtains on the window, and large gray linen towels folded and laid out on each bunk. We shared a lavatory room with the couple in the next compartment. It was a tiny space with narrow doors that could be locked on the inside. There were unisex toilet rooms at each end of the car; also at one end of the car, before the toilet-room door, was a small wood-fired hot-water heater for tea.

The beginning acceleration was smooth, and at midnight we were speeding through a suburban area of stark apartment houses and industrial installations, old and new. There were sunset colors at midnight, and a red rising moon.

A pleasant porter asked us if we'd like tea and brought it in glasses set into filigreed silver holders with silver handles, served with fat gray sugar cubes. The wash water was ice and the compartment was cold. There was one blanket per bunk, so intricately rolled and folded that it took time to figure out how to open it up. Once I was ensconced in the high bunk, I got over the feeling that I could be catapulted out of there by some unexpected change of speed. We learned later that two heavy women who shared a compartment in the same car had taken turns trying to get into the upper bunk and had finally given up and slept, fitfully, head to toe in the lower.

24

||||||||||||||||||||||||||||||||||||||||||||

Saturday, June 4

Moscow

We arose in early daylight in our compartment, a little after four, to watch the Russian land whirling by. I scrounged some early tea and tipped the porter, getting at first a firm refusal and then deft acceptance, indicating I had not been the first to begin the process of corruption.

We had tea and a Hershey bar and took forbidden photographs out the window. The forest scenes shocked us. We were time travelers, looking back into the Middle Ages. These were lovely green forests of pine and budding birch. The villages were in clearings, surrounded by small vegetable gardens. The log and plank cabins were set seemingly at random in rutted areas of black mud. The cabins had steep roofs, for snow load, and were the size of beach cabanas. The doorways were so low the people had to bend almost double to go inside.

These were not joyous primitive scenes but mud, despair, and desolation. This was life at a brute level, at an existence level. The villages looked silent. Some wisps of smoke. A few people in heavy dark garments walking the footpaths. Few domestic animals. Windrows of trash around the huts. Some pieces of hard-worn farm equipment. Water standing in the deep ruts and potholes of the mud roads that wound between the random placement of the cottages. We saw not one paved road.

After endless miles of this, all along the main line between the two most populous cities of the country, one must begin to think that the fearsome face Russian presents to the Western world is a fraud. After reading *The Russians* by Hedrick Smith, one realizes that their laborious and corrupt bureaucracy can never tap the energy of the people to the extent necessary to lift these millions out of the mud. Perhaps their foreign adventures are efforts to draw attention from their exhausted debility at home. A sick child can set fire to a house. Look at me! The noisy and cynical energy of the Muscovites is devoted in the main to circumventing the idiot regulations of the bureaucratic departments so that they can scrounge a bit more living space, transportation, and consumer items. And every week the train rolls down from Finland with the big consignment of expendables for the newspeople and diplomatic groups living in Moscow: crates and cases of Kleenex, soap, shampoo, toothpaste, Coca-Cola, Pepsi, Saltines, hairbrushes, stereo tapes. Corn Flakes, ball-points, paper clips, lipstick, Band-Aids....

The individual Russians on the street, above all people of the world, seem to want to avoid any eye contact with the Imperialists. In the tourist stores and hotels where contact is necessary, the attitude toward this silver-topped tourist seemed to be one of semi-amused, semi-bored contempt. One realizes the hopelessness of trying to tell anyone in a closed society what the world is like. Their government never lets them know that it can not adequately feed, clothe, house, and educate them. Not that any nation is doing these chores well in this world of 4.3 billion.

There is one special stricture on information which I find particularly infuriating. The Russians fought very bravely in World War II. The seige of Stalingrad is a classic, no doubt about it. The Germans came almost to within spitting distance of Moscow before they were driven back. It was close. It was so *very* close that the end result was determined by many interwoven factors.

The Russians were in desperate need of aircraft, aviation fuel, fuel oil, tanks, troop carriers, machine guns, artillery pieces, ammunition of all kinds. They could not replenish their battle losses. Without replenishment, they would succumb.

And so the United States and Britain mounted all those desperate convoys to Murmansk. Terrible waters up there, north of the North Cape. Incredible icing conditions. Big convoys with escorts of small cruisers, destroyers, destroyer escorts, and small escort carriers. Because the German high command knew the significance of replenishing the Russian forces, they put a heavy concentration of wolf packs of their most advanced submarines in these waters. And they made air strikes with squadrons of Condors dropping the dreaded glider bombs.

There was no point in having the crews of the freighters and tankers wear life jackets, or having the men on the naval vessels wear them either. A man in the sea died within three minutes, unless he was on fire.

The losses were heartbreaking. In some cases less than half the escorted vessels limped into Kola Inlet, the gate-way to Murmansk. Hundreds of thousands of tons of shipping went to the bottom of the North Sea. Thousands of men were pushed by fear, tension, sleeplessness, frostbite to the very limit of their resources, and thousands of men died in missions that most of them thought right and necessary. But hundreds of thousands of tons of fuel, parts, ammunition, weapons, ordnance got through.

This has been excised from the history books in Russia, if indeed it was ever mentioned at all. Not one citizen of the U.S.S.R. in a hundred has heard even a rumor of this sacrificial effort. The Russian government promotes a far different emphasis. Their history books claim that Russia stood alone, and owing to the enormous bravery of the common soldier and of the people as a whole, they repulsed the invader.

Maybe this is dandy politics, great for national morale, but I suspect that any nation which excises whole chapters of its history for the sake of some kind of political opportunism imperils itself and its future. Truth has a nasty way of reasserting itself at unexpected moments. And on the floor of that icy sea lie the bones of brave men who came along at just the right moment and saved Russia.

As the "Red Arrow" came closer to Moscow, we began to pass industrial communities where factories had been built, sidings constructed, and perfectly hideous apartment houses spotted around the areas at random.

Arrived at the Moscow station—one of the stations—at eight o'clock. A cold gray morning, raining. (Later in the day it cleared and the temperature shot up to 80 degrees, then faded back down to a chill drizzle in the evening.)

A bus took us to the Hotel National, where our groups were given six rooms and a suite to use for luggage and rendezvous points. Severe-looking matrons on each floor made certain nobody left her floor without turning in the key. We were assigned the suite, along with several other couples. Good bathroom. Very ponderous, dark, depressing furniture. Could look out the window and see a long line of people, herded into a column of four by busy guards, shuffling through the drizzle, heading across the square for a quick look at Lenin's corpse under glass. There seems a ponderous religiosity about these Russian ceremonies. If formal religion is a process of charms, rituals, and incantations, undergone in the hope that some of the goodness and promise of eternity will rub off on one's nasty little unworthy self, then these celebrations of long-dead heroes seem to fit the pattern.

We went down several floors to a breakfast room set up with large tables. A breakfast of baskets of bread and flat rolls, good butter, raspberry jam, with each place at the table preset with a plate containing three large cold greasy slices of sausage and a white tumbler of yogurt. Big bowls of warm eggs were brought in, but when the eggs were cracked into the egg cups they proved to be just that—warm raw eggs. Time to shop after breakfast in the hotel shop. Bought myself a mink hat for a very low dollar, which eventually appeared in a drawing of me on the back flap of *The Green Ripper*. Dorothy bought an umbrella about a foot long that virtually explodes into full shape and size at the push of a button and resists all but the most determined effort to crush it back into its original size and shape.

Then by bus to the Moscow Museum. Going through on a guided tour is much like being required to eat one's way through nine chocolate sundaes.

Crown jewels, fantastic embroidered and brocaded garments from the czarist era (clearly the women they had fitted had to be very very short and very very fat), gifts of silver and gold and jeweled items presented to the czars by other nations, carriages, sleighs, flintlocks inlaid with gold, suits of armor riding on stuffed horses. A dazzling incredible wealth of precious metals and gems fashioned into many items of international kitsch and some of honest beauty. There were acres of this stuff, an overwhelming trove laid out to be admired by the people. And admire they did. It struck us as curious that the objects and the buildings they were most anxious for us to see were all prerevolution. Tender care was given to the restoration of the elegant old castles and country homes. They had gone to great expense to properly display the treasures of the czars. All this was their culture. And afterward, the only culture of the revolution has been the theater art—music, ballet, opera— most of which is derivative of prerevolutionary forms.

We were trundled about in the bus, getting out for special vistas. The pale sunlight was very handsome on the onion towers near the University of Moscow. We walked around in Red Square, enchanted by the fabulously ornate towers of the church. I moved away from the group. I hate guide talks, with their dramatics, oversimplifications, preplanned jocularity.

(Every day Mexican guides take people off down the remnants of a Mayan road to the great cenote at Chichén Itzá and tell them of how virgins were thrown into the big deep evil-looking green pool. "Ah," the tourists say. "Oh, my! How dreadful!" Fact: When the bones were recovered from the bottom, 70 feet below the surface, 135 feet below ground level, some years ago and sorted out, of the identifiable remains they counted thirteen men, twenty-one children aged eighteen months to twelve years, and eight women, of whom seven were well past the age of consent. From the sampling it appeared that the percentage of children might really be far higher due to the diminished durability of their bones. But each day at Chichén the myth is reinforced, because guides dote on glamorous bullshit).

I wandered away from the group and came to a line, a white thick line across the square, much like the middle line on a highway. I wandered across it, wondering what it signified. Then I heard a clomping, jingling sound and a young soldier came running up to me, carbine held at present arms. He shouted angry words and made angry gestures, indicating I should go back onto the other side of that line from nowhere to nowhere. There were no buildings anywhere near us.

It seemed such a childish, asinine performance I had to laugh at him. He was like a little dog out there barking at the front gate. I was in no hurry to move back across the line. He stared at me out of dark slitty little Mongol eyes, and changed the position of his feet a little, and changed the way he held the carbine, and I suddenly realized he was considering slapping me across the face with the butt of that weapon. I popped nimbly back across the line to where he wanted me, with a vivid image of broken spectacles, crushed cheekbone, missing teeth, and lots of blood. After I had gone a hundred feet, I looked back. He was still there, bravely guarding the white line, staring after me.

Back to the hotel for lunch. Big bottles of opened beer standing on the table. Canapé of cold sliced fish, chicken broth in big pot with ladle, meat-filled puff pastries, veal filet, mashed potatoes, carrots and peas in a cream sauce, stacks of rye and white bread, ice cream with blueberry sauce, coffee. Good meal. Service was brusque, fast, impersonal. They thumped the dishes down heartily.

After lunch and more city vistas we went to a large government store, a super-Beriozka, or Birch Tree. Objects of wood and fur and cut glass. Babushkas and jewelry of amber. Canes inlaid with silver, and exquisite little hand-painted wooden boxes.

Departure was a revelation. There were several lines, several checkout clerks. So you picked the line which represented your preferred method of paying for the goods: the cash line (all hard currencies), the American Express line, the Diner's Club line, the Visa line, the MasterCard line, the traveler's checks line. It simplified the procedure of extracting good foreign exchange monies from the tourists who had browsed the glittering aisles. Out in front of the store was a big bed of forget-me-nots. Not to worry. We wouldn't.

Back by bus to the hotel with a limited time to freshen up, grab our belongings, and get back on the bus to be taken to the Bolshoi Theater for the ballet.

It was an extraordinary evening. The performance was to

celebrate the one hundredth anniversary of the first performance of *Swan Lake*. A very famous fifty-two-year-old ballerina named Plisetskaya had come out of semi-retirement to dance the lead, with Bogdanov playing the prince. There were hundreds of people outside the huge modern building, trying vainly to get tickets from those trying to enter, reaching, clutching, crying out.

The giant theater was jam-packed full. Plisetskaya was slender, youthful, vibrant, and powerful. Even though they had removed from the choreography some of the most difficult portions of her role, she was enough to make the breath catch in the throat. Bogdanov was perfect counterpoint, with just enough rigidity to highlight her pliancy of movement. Applause was explosive. We saw among the audience people in their work clothes. Generals in uniform, people in jeans, women in formal gowns, young people in blue denim. The ballet company was, to the untutored eye, superb.

Our group was scattered all over the theater, and we had been told to go to the lobby at intermission and take the escalators up to the fifth floor for a snack. It was a curious and dangerous trip. They were high-speed escalators. I have never seen any that hoisted one as quickly. Everyone in that audience was determined to get to the fifth floor as quickly as possible. One could not pause and pick a step and hop aboard. Everybody pushed. You were thrust aboard to scramble for footing as best you could. And at each floor, you were propelled off the end in a half trot, with people still shoving, roaring, wedging themselves into the next part of the ascent. At one point there were three young Arabs behind us. They were very muscular, very hopped up. I don't know if they were on pills or booze, but their shoving was done only half in fun and could have turned dangerous. We made certain they got by us to brutalize somebody else. I think it was the first escalator they had ever seen.

On the fifth floor we went into a huge room. The oblong center section was dropped about seven steps down from the level of the rest of the room. It was like a big empty swimming pool surrounded on all sides by a broad apron. Up on the apron part were stalls selling food. The fifty or so of us were told to go down the steps into the empty area. There were long tables there, but no chairs. There were place settings. One was supposed to stand at one of the place settings and eat what had been laid out, while beyond the railing that surrounded the pool-like sunken portion, hundreds upon hundreds of Russians ate their purchases and looked casually at the old imperialists in that huge oblong space down there, all by themselves.

At each place was buttered bread covered with red caviar, additional red caviar on a separate little plate, mushroom paste in a silver pot with a long handle, several very eggy crepes, very thin slices of fish on bread, a small goblet of beer, a filled cream puff shaped like a doughnut, and sweetened coffee. Every item was superb. Twenty minutes later we were heading back down to our seats.

The rest of the ballet was very stirring. At the end there were too many curtain calls to count. Continuous deafening applause, as Plisetskaya was given a whole greenhouse worth of bouquets.

Then back on the bus to the station. Rainy evening. Different design of railway car compartments. We had two lowers. No lavatory facilities shared with the next compartment. Two communal bathrooms, one at each end of the car, unclean and high-smelling. White cloth had been spread down the aisle because of the drizzly night and dirty shoes. We broke out the little crystal glasses we had bought in the Birch Tree store and drank little straight shots of Stolichnaya vodka and talked until very late. It was difficult to come down from the high of that evening.

After the ship was cleared, after the crew was allowed to go ashore, the Russians really extended hospitality to them. In fact they did a lot more for the crew than they did for the passengers. They arranged buses at frequent intervals to take the crew members to the museums and the czar's summer palace, and Petrodvorets Park, and to a circus that was in town.

Some of the passengers heard about the great circus from some of the crew members, so the passengers contacted the Intourist people and asked if they too could be taken to the circus. "Nyet!" said the Russians. "It is impossible. There is absolutely no circus in Leningrad at this time."

On that second evening in port, most of the people from my table had gone to Moscow, and Captain Rawles, the British

*pilot, was eating with me and with Edra Brophy, a lady Mariner
with a couple of billion miles' worth of little golden bear pins.
As we finished, Captain Rawles said, "Let's go over to the
seamen's club and have a drink."*

"I'm not really too enthused about seamen's clubs."

*"Well, at least you ought to go take a look at it. It is
special."*

*So we three went down and got on the special crew bus and
were taken over to this club. It was a palatial mansion. I tried
to get the history of it, and somebody said that back in the days
of the czars it had been built by a wealthy brewer. It had a
marble staircase leading up from a foyer the size of a hotel
lobby. Off to the left of the lobby was a bar for dedicated hard-
core drinkers. As a matter of fact they had two bars in that
room. The place was heavy with smoke, and people stood thick
at the bar. Rawles knew his way around in there, and we
elbowed our way in to where a heavy-set peasant woman was
making drinks. Rawles and I ordered screwdrivers and Edra
wanted a beer. That old woman took two glasses the size of
mason jars, dumped about a half a pint of vodka in each one,
filled them with orange juice from a can she held way up high
in the air, and shoved them across the bar to us. Then she
opened a quart of beer, upended a glass over the top of it, and
shoved it over to Edra. They drink big, often, and with dedication. We carried our drinks upstairs to what had once been
the grand ballroom, where one side was solid mirrors, and
overhead were crystal chandeliers. They had a rock-and-roll
band and hostesses.*

*I got into conversation with a fairly attractive Russian girl
who spoke good English and who, someone said, was an accomplished pianist. She sat with us and said how happy she
was to welcome us to the club.*

"It's very nice to be here."

*"We get very few captains here, and we never get a captain
from a passenger ship."*

*I kept telling her what a great club they had here, and what
a beautiful mansion it was, and how glad I was to be here, but
she kept coming back to this fact that I was the captain of the
ship, and I was mingling with the crew.*

She said, "You seem to get along very well with your crew. They all seem to like you a great deal."

"I work very hard at it," I told her. "I want them to like me, and I make an effort to see that they do."

She kept harping on the same thing until finally it irritated me.

"Miss," I said, "I have a large crew on that ship. I have two hundred and sixty people. Every one of them has a job to do, and I need every one of them desperately. I can't really do any one of them much in the way of harm or damage, but any one of them can really screw me up, so I think it is important to get along with them."

She sat silent and thoughtful, mulling my words over for quite a long time, and she finally said, "Captain, I think that's a very nice idea."

Apparently that was the first time such a thought had ever entered her mind. Though I don't really know, I would guess that on all the Russian cruise ships, the officers don't have anything to do with the lower classes aboard.

That same night Art and Dotty Todd showed up. Like a good cruise entertainer, he had brought his banjo, and he did several solo numbers for everybody, and then he played along with the band.

Later we all went down and piled onto the bus. A lot of the crew had had more than enough to drink, and when we rolled through the dock gates on our way back to the ship, they were singing God Bless America at the top of their lungs. I hoped we weren't going to make the morning papers.

At the crew gangway there was a long lineup to go aboard because the guards had to check the documents with great care before letting anybody back on board. Art and Dotty were ahead of me, and I saw them in discussion with the officials, and then I saw him go over to the little Intourist office with some of them. I thought that maybe they were taking offense about his taking his banjo ashore. When somebody asked me if I would go over there too, it sounded like trouble.

When I got there I found he had taken his banjo out of the case and volunteered to give a little concert for the guards and dockworkers and people around there, and they had accepted.

He started, and a pretty good crowd gathered. I had no

idea Art knew so many Russian songs. When Art gets going, he seems to get more and more excited as he goes along. He does his bouncy little steps and walks back and forth, and he can sound like six banjos. He always makes me think of the Pied Piper. When he really gets an audience with him, he could go trotting off and they would all follow him as long as he could keep playing. I looked around at the faces. At first all those people were just as expressionless as the young guards, who are taught never to show emotion when on duty. But he got to them, and soon they were grinning and clapping and going along with the music. He never did get the border guards to smile. But they wouldn't leave. They stayed right there and heard it all.

25

▮▮▮▮▮▮▮▮▮▮▮▮▮▮▮▮▮▮▮▮▮▮▮▮▮▮▮▮▮▮▮

Sunday, June 5

Moscow to Leningrad

We rode the "Red Arrow" back through a cool overcast semi-sunny day, after a quick wash in the little swamp at the end of the car. Tried to get tea from the porter. No way. This one was a female with an iron jaw and no intention of lighting a fire in the water heater.

Birch, spruce, and maple trees. Some apple blossoms. No paved roads. Lots of electric wires into the villages, with insulators shaped like white porcelain ink pots. One strange aspect was the concrete fencing along the tracks. Open diamond pattern, untold miles of it. Most of it very old. A lot of it broken. It was not high enough or uninterrupted enough to be a barrier for man or beast, so its sole purpose had to be decoration. Yet a stupendous effort for a limited decorative effect.

On this day, Sunday, the people looked more dressed up. Many were standing waiting on cement platforms for local trains as we plunged by. Many young boys fishing. The cemeteries had little painted iron fences around the graves, mostly blue. More factories, with dull apartment houses dropped here and there at random. Curious as to why they feel they have to make these areas treeless wastelands.

When we got off the train at eight, there was a woman in the station selling lilies of the valley.

Showered, changed, lunched aboard the ship, and then back onto a bus:

Tour No. 38: Pushkin and Pavlovsk Palaces
Afternoon by motorcoach.
Leave the pier at 2 P.M. on Saturday, June 4.

Drive through the streets of Leningrad and out into the Russian countryside to the old town of Pushkin. The village is named for the famous writer Alexander Pushkin, who lived and worked here. Before Pushkin's day, however, these grounds were owned by Catherine I, wife of Peter the Great, and contain the beautiful Yekaterinsky (Catherine's) Palace. You'll visit the magnificent interior of the royal residence and then continue to the lovely Palace of Pavlovsk. Return to the ship in the late afternoon.

En route saw pansy beds, rows of greenhouses devoted to the growing of vegetables, young girls wearing yellow crowns of dandelions. The palace was jammed with Russian tourists. Pleased me to see an old town named after a writer. Hemingway, Indiana? Twain, New Jersey? Poe, Georgia? Faulkner, Virginia?

Yekaterinsky Palace was a perfect example of the Russian infatuation with their prerevolutionary past. The Germans had looted, smashed, and burned the place. It had been the palace of Catherine I, wife of Peter the Great.

There had been years and years of painful and careful restoration here. Scholars had studied the available documentation, descriptions, drawings, plans; where the background was incomplete, they had designed the portions which might well have been there. The garden statuary, parquet floors, tile stoves, porcelain trim, gilt decorations, latticed windows, ornamentations—all restored, reproduced, or reinvented in the mood of the original.

We all shuffled along in our group, canvas bags tied over our shoes, trying to hear our little blond guide over the loudmouthed guides leading other groups, shouting in other tongues. The attendants, all of them, were silent, sour, fat, expressionless old women.

Back to the ship. Lines were cast off at exactly six o'clock. And suddenly, all over the ship, as we went chugging out to the Baltic Sea, there was an intense feeling of holiday. Everyone was smiling. We felt as if some great weight had been lifted from our hearts.

Passengers who had been to Russia by plane told us that the same thing happens aboard the aircraft. Once you are off and have climbed to your assigned altitude, the plane is filled with that same glad relief.

Once long ago, when leaving Caracas, I'd had that same sense of the lifting of a weight. That was at a time when the Venezuelans were more hostile than usual.

I cannot believe the feeling aboard the *Mariposa* was merely escape from hostility. There had to be more than that. The Intourist people act as if there were some self-evident truth which you cannot comprehend and thus cannot share. Unless one is reasonably fluent in Russian, there can be no contact at all with the people. They will not look at you. Perhaps a black man in a small white community gets this same feeling of apartness, of being at risk, when he comes into town to do his weekend shopping. He knows that something very serious must happen to him before he can seek the protection of the law. He knows there is a lot of unpredictability in the community around him. Maybe he feels that same relief as he recrosses the town line, heading toward his place in the country.

For a couple of million years, we have learned to be wary of strange environments. When you are in the place you know best, you are at ease because you can anticipate and evaluate every peril. You know what could be hiding behind every tree. But when you travel out of your own domain, there is a hidden demand upon your nervous energy. You have to keep watching, evaluating, anticipating. It is not your turf. You don't know what might jump out at you from where. And what can be a minor drain in other countries can become major in a country so remote in custom, thought, and behavior as Russia. You spend your hours there in a kind of unfocused anxiety, which, of course, is the product of ignorance. But it does exist, and it feels awfully good when you are safe at home aboard your ship and the feeling goes away.

So we sailed off, laughing too loudly at the most feeble jokes.

At the dinner table, Al and Emily Morgan told us of their adventure in the Leningrad subway. They had taken the shuttle bus in and then thought it would be interesting to use some Russian coins to ride just one stop on the subway and get off and ride back. They said it was truly a beautiful thing, that subway: murals and space and effective lighting.

But apparently the train they boarded to come back did not stop at the original station where they got on. They were carried past their memorized exit place, and then they could not find anyone who could understand enough English to help them in any way. People brushed by them, ignoring their entreaties. It was only by the greatest good luck, and good judgment, that they were able to catch the last shuttle bus back to the ship.

We had seen Al and Emily Morgan on a previous cruise. They had been at a table near us, and we became nodding acquaintances. When we began this cruise and saw the Morgans, we had been shocked at the way Al looked. He wore the face of death. The shape of the skull showed. His skin was gray and lifeless, and he was much thinner than we remembered.

Early during this cruise we learned that he did indeed have bone cancer, and they had made arrangements at several ports along the way for him to receive transfusions of whole blood. His condition did not in any way subdue the group at the captain's table. He would wince when he eased himself into the chair and, when it was time to leave, and when he was ready, he would let her know. But during dinner, he was part of the group. We forgot his condition. He had a warm wit and an exceptionally sweet smile. He was a considerate and a courteous man. I believe he wanted with all his heart and soul to be back home in California, where there would not be these social drains on his meager energies.

But it is a pretty problem, is it not? If a man knows he is dying, does he want to pursue that process in the midst of life, amid the bustle and confusion of travel, always at the edge of exhaustion, always in pain, or should he, in the old phrase, take to his bed and let it come? I suspect that his decision was brave and good. The cruise had been planned long before. He was among friends. There were distractions, such as the conversations at table, to keep his mind off himself and his condition. And I believe he felt that it was a good way, for Emily's sake, to wind his life down.

During the early part of the cruise, when passengers were participating in the entertainment, Al played good Chicago jazz piano, and Emily sang with good pace and tone, ballads and blues. They were a team. They knew where they were.

I remember one woman saying that the dying look of him depressed her, was spoiling her cruise. I told her that we were all dying, each in our individual manner, and that Al Morgan showed it a little more than the rest of us. It is strange now to recall that the complaining woman died of cancer herself within two years of the termination of that cruise. Perhaps her depression was triggered by some subconscious awareness of what was just beginning for her.

Sometimes Al would skip a meal and Emily would come and join us and say he was hurting a little too much. But it didn't happen often. I would guess that he was very sparing with the painkillers. I think he valued his mental alertness, his social alertness. I know that Dorothy and I felt good when we came into the dining room and saw that he was already there at the captain's table. He was a good person to be with.

There was a happy mood aboard the ship. I was as glad to get out of there as anyone. It was the same mood you have aboard when the ship is about to begin a cruise, and the bon voyage parties are going on.

I remember one busy sailing when I had been called down to meet some guests and was heading back to my own area when I had to work my way through a very large and happy party. Somebody in one of those modest inside staterooms was obviously having a huge sendoff. It was probably their first trip and they had invited everybody in the neighborhood and all their friends and relatives down to wish them a bon voyage. The stateroom was packed full in no time, so the party had spread out into the forward ship alleyway and way out into the main alleyway. Drinks were being passed along the line, and everybody was having a ball, laughing and giggling and yelling.

Just as I was trying to get through, there were blood-curdling screams from the stateroom, terrible shrieking and yelling. My God, I thought, what could have happened? So I went charging through to the stateroom.

Somebody with a fantastic sense of humor had bought a two-man inflatable life raft as a bon-voyage present and had rigged the little charge cartridge so that when the box was opened, the raft would inflate. They had been unable to get into the stateroom to make the presentation, so they had passed it on in. The host was pretty well gone on champagne by the time he opened it. There was no room in the cabin to inflate it, but it sure made room for itself.

When there is a flavor of celebration aboard, the dancers really go. When I looked in Sunday night after dinner, they were happily swooping around. It made me think of Frank Ellery, the purser. He was the one I mentioned before, the friend Mrs. Suggs invited home.

We often use the pursers as tour directors, riding the bus, counting noses, and so on. We were on special cruise to the Caribbean, and one of the tours in Acapulco, on our way to the Panama Canal, was a nightclub tour. Frank Ellery was pressed into service. I think it was a four-nightclub tour, with dinner at one of them and drinks at all of them. Frank had a few knocks at the Smirnoff before he left the ship, and then they had some cocktails ashore and proceeded on to these various nightclubs, and Frank, feeling like a host to the passengers, probably had more than his share.

He was a flamboyant dancer, known to pick up little old ladies and whirl them around. In fact, he cracked a couple of ribs on one of them one time, doing his dancing thing.

On this Acapulco tour there was a nice woman named Mrs. Lauderdale, with straight white hair, always cheerful and smiling. She and her friends were great bridge players and eager dancers, and they were friends of Frank Ellery. At the last nightclub on the tour, Frank got Mrs. Lauderdale out onto the dance floor to do his version of the tango, which included a lot of very fast sideways running. He raced across the floor with Mrs. Lauderdale but forgot that the dance floor was about a foot and a half higher than the rest of the nightclub—and danced her off into space. They seemed to be airborne for thirty seconds before they came crashing down onto one of the ringside tables. Miraculously, Mrs. Lauderdale escaped without a scratch, but Frank landed on his mod air force glasses and mashed them into his nose. It was a very bloody scene; they had to pack him off to the hospital. He was flown home from there and spent weeks recovering.

Frank tucked his ponytail under a wig aboard ship, but let it hang free when he went off the ship in his ragged jeans and wooden beads. One time Captain Jim Stafford, who liked to run a tight ship, had to fire a junior officer during the course of one of the cruises. There had been a squabble between two junior officers, and he fired the one who had gotten out of line—told him to pack his gear and get off in Hawaii—and notified the agent there that he would require a replacement third mate when the ship arrived. I think it must have been a phone call rather than a wire, because Jim made it clear that he didn't want "one of those creepy young punks with a beard. I want him to have uniforms and no beard and be ready to take over his duties as soon as he comes on board."

When they docked in Hawaii, the replacement came aboard. He was a nice-looking young fellow, and he was in proper uniform and didn't have a beard, and he had a pleasant and respectful manner when he reported to Jim Stafford. Jim approved of him and welcomed him aboard, but when the fellow turned to leave, Captain Stafford saw he had a ponytail and blew up.

"Why are you wearing a ponytail? It looks like hell? Cut it off!"

"Well, my girl friend, she likes it."

They were only in port a couple of hours and no other replacement was available, and the fellow insisted on keeping his ponytail. It was agreed that he could wear the tail tucked up into his hat, and he wouldn't take his hat off in the presence of any passenger.

When Jim jumped the agent about sending him that fellow, the agent said, "You said you wanted a clean-cut, nice-appearing young third mate without a beard and with proper uniforms. You didn't say a word about a ponytail."

26

|||||||||||||||||||||||||||||||||||||||||||

Helsinki, Finland

Up early in the clear cold day to watch the docking. A few fellow passengers, all bundled up, helped bring the ship in. Lots of delicious fresh raspberries for breakfast. When the captain piled fresh raspberries atop his French toast, Emily Morgan told him to take his mess and depart. He said that if we weren't nicer to him, he would eat in the officers' mess from now on.

A department store brought aboard a huge assortment of clothing and gifts and set up shop in the lounge. Great sweaters, knit hats, scarves. Took a cab to Stockman's Department Store in the middle of the city. On the way we noticed a large flower and vegetable market not far from the dock. After shopping, we walked back to the market. It was a sparkling city in the bright clear air. The young people on the streets were smartly dressed.

Helsinki enjoys some of the accidents of history. It had been a Swedish city, ceded to czarist Russia in 1809. After 108 years of Russian influence, Finland won independence from Russia in 1917. A later Russian attempt to reacquire it ended in compromise. In many odd ways Helsinki performs some of the same functions for Russia that Hong Kong provides for Red China.

After walking through the market, we went over to the Palace Hotel and took the elevator to the bar on the tenth floor. The Finns have the best word in the world for "elevator." They call it a *hissi hiss*. We had a beer, an open sandwich of fresh shrimp, and coffee. There was a great view of the harbor from the tenth floor, complete with *Mariposa*, looking very white and clean and happy. Walked back into the city. Went back to Stockman's and bought the things we had only looked at on the first visit; a black knit vest for me, a blue and green mohair poncho for Dorothy. On the way out we bought lilies of the valley and took a taxi back to the berth.

A steward from South America arrived back at the ship on his ten-speed bicycle at the same time we did. We had seen him much earlier, near the dolphin fountain, and marveled at his nerve in confronting Helsinki's formidable traffic. He told us he had covered over twenty miles.

I make an inspection at least once a week of all areas of the ship, and there are some areas I inspect more frequently. So in going through A Deck, where the crew lives, I have gotten accustomed to seeing quite a few bicycles tied or chained along the alleyway there. A bike is a handy vehicle for a crew member, a quick and inexpensive way to get around when we are in port.

On one of my inspections on a trip to the Islands, I went into one of the recreation rooms and there was a small motorcycle.

"What the hell is this?"

"It belongs to one of the crew members."

"No, no, no. No motorcycles on the ship. It's not only against the rules, but it has gasoline in it, which makes it illegal hazardous cargo."

"The gasoline is drained."

"I'm not going to worry about whether it's drained or not drained, because I want that thing off the ship, and you tell whoever owns it to get it off. No more discussion."

I never knew who owned it, but the motorcycle disappeared, so I assumed that the word got to him. A couple of ports later we were in Nawiliwili, where the crew had scheduled a big football game. It was a challenge match, the steward's de-

partment against the engine room. There is a public park about two blocks from where the ship ties up. They had kicked in numerous cases of beer, and some of the deck crew had signed up with one team or another, and it is safe to assume there was some betting going on.

John Anderson, one of the pursers, and I were pressed into service as officials. It was supposed to be tag football, where you have a piece of cloth tucked inside your belt, and when someone grabs it and yanks it loose, that constitutes a legal tackle. But in the heat of the game some of the players were tying that cloth securely, and when a man grabbed the rag he was hurled to the ground. There were some big black crewmen out there, especially in the steward's department, including one big butcher who had obviously played football before, perhaps even pro ball. He could pick up a little guy by the waist and carry him in front like a spear, knocking down the tacklers.

So they changed the rule to touch football, where you have to touch the ball carrier with two hands below the belt. It was a very rough afternoon, but we got by with just one broken wrist and the expected bruises and sprains. I suggested to them they try softball next time. The game was close. And a lot of beer went down the hatch. It was a big success.

The next morning the chief mate came to me and said, "Well, I've got some good news and some bad news." I told him to give me the bad stuff first, and he said we had one man pretty well banged up in the hospital. I thought it was maybe a delayed reaction from an injury during the game, but he said, "No, as near as I can piece the story together, the owner of that motorcycle that was supposed to be removed from the ship sold it to another crew member, without saying anything about the stipulation. So after a lot of beers, the new owner rode the motorcycle over a bank, and he is in the hospital all banged up. A friend of his went out to get the motorcycle. He got it running again, but on the way back he took a shortcut and rode it over a cliff. He survived; he swam home without a scratch and is back on board. So the good news is that the motorcycle is definitely off the ship and we only have one man in the hospital."

I told him I was glad to hear it, and glad it wasn't worse.

But there turned out to be more. The fellow who had bought it decided he didn't want it after all and wanted to give it back to the guy he bought it from. I don't think he had paid for it yet. So they told the third fellow, the one who had ridden it into the ocean, that he had to pay for it. So the third fellow went over with a scuba outfit and some of his buddies and they recovered the motorcycle. The next time I went on inspection there it was again, looking a little worse for wear. This time I tried to find out who owned it, but nobody would admit to it; the ownership was in doubt. I told them I didn't care who owned it. It had to go. And pretty soon it went. I kept looking for it, but it didn't reappear.

Years ago a lot of the crew members used to rent motor scooters in Tahiti. We couldn't order them not to do so, but we made strong suggestions about not renting them. The driving habits of the average Tahitian and the size of the average Tahitian chuckholes made it a dangerous business at best.

On one trip one of the crew members got full of the local rum and rode his rented scooter right off the end of the dock. Another time, one of the quartet aboard, the bass fiddler, had a minor accident on a rented scooter. The only thing he broke was the middle finger on his right hand, but that injury put him out of the music business for the rest of the trip.

Anyway, to get back to the stop at Helsinki, that was the place where the ship's photographer finally caught up with me. He had been after a posed photograph of the various members of the staff. He had taken pictures of Kaui Barrett and Annette Alioto and Alan Scott and the Todds and so on. He would take several pictures of each person and they would pick out the one they liked best, and it would go up on the rotating display rack in the gallery off the lounge. Then the passengers could buy pictures by signing a slip with the picture number on it and dropping it in the box on Kaui's desk.

When I wasn't busy the light wasn't right. But finally in Helsinki we got the job done. He wanted me with the ship in the background. It's a very nice picture. It flatters me. I had my hat on so you can't see I'm bald, and the hat was at the right angle. There was a streak of rust down the front of the ship under the anchor, so he had me stand where I would block out the rust, and the rest of the old ship looked good.

He put the shot up on the rack, and the next day he told me that quite a few people had ordered it. I was flattered and told him that was nice. Every time he saw me that day, he gave me a count on how many had been sold. After several days he caught me and said, "I've been the photographer on this ship off and on for a long time, and this is the most prints we have ever sold of any single picture. You should be very flattered."

"I am," I said. "I really am. It's nice to know so many people would like to have my picture and be willing to buy one."

Later, the ship had the usual costume party. There was a spry little old woman who sat back on a banquette on the port side forward in the dining room, on the first sitting. Sandy the waitress called her "the yogurt lady," because about all she would eat was yogurt and fresh fruit. She went round and round the decks at a half trot all day, and she didn't want anybody smoking anywhere near her.

The yogurt lady came to the costume party as a belly dancer. She had on a very flimsy little skirt really low on her hips, and a tiny little bra, and she did a very up-front belly dance in front of the judges, and the photographer got some good shots of her.

A few days later he said to me, "Captain, I'm sorry, but you got knocked out of first place by the belly dancer. I've sold more copies of her picture than I have of yours."

That's show biz.

27

||||||||||||||||||||||||||||||||||||||||

Tuesday and Wednesday, June 7 and 8
Stockholm, Sweden

On a cold bright morning, a little past five, the *Mariposa* moved up the channel toward Stockholm, passing scores of small islands of tumbled granite and evergreens, much like the small islands in Adirondack lakes. As we neared the city we saw, in addition to the squat white lighthouses on the islands, camps and houses and small piers.

Closer to the city we passed, on the port side, impressive houses built upon wooded slopes, and we were told that this was a residential area popular with the entertainment people of Sweden, the actors, producers, writers, and musicians.

We anchored out in calm water with a striking vista of the city. We did some housekeeping chores and then went ashore by comfortable broad-beamed launch and walked a slow mile toward the city center to the NK Department Store.

Walking city streets, shopping city stores, is the best and quickest way to catch the flavor of the people, their manners and attitudes. In impatience and rudeness the Swedes ranked right up there with the Germans but seemed, on the whole, to be a better-looking people.

From the buildup we expected NK to be something of a cross between Harrods and Neiman-Marcus. But it turned out to be a very ordinary store, with very high prices. The only thing we bought was a Robert Hale edition of my book *The Girl, the Gold Watch and Everything*, for the equivalent of $10 U.S. Took it back for a present. Could find nothing of mine in Swedish, though there are usually some in print. Rewalked the windy mile to the dock and waited in the wind for the next launch. Three of the waiting passengers jammed themselves into the phone booth on the dock to keep warm.

Had lunch and then joined the 2 P.M. queue for Tour No. 47:

TOUR No. 47: STOCKHOLM'S WATERWAYS
Afternoon by motor launch.
Leave the pier at 2 P.M. on Tuesday, June 7.

The motor launch is a popular means of transportation in Stockholm, and this sightseeing trip along the canals is an exciting and interesting experience. The motor launch will sail around Kungsholmen Island, past the Old Castle of Karlborg, and cruise through Arsta Waterway to Hammarby Locks, where the sweet water of Lake Malaren flows out into Saltsjon (Salt Lake). Continue through the Danvik Canal, out into the open waterway of Saltsjon, and around the island of Djurgården, which was once a royal hunting park. Return to the ship in the afternoon.

After standing there for fifteen minutes, we were told that the ship had radioed ahead for space for 168 persons on the tour, but it had been garbled and they had reserved space for 68. "Come back at three," they told us.

When we finally did go, the day was cold and overcast. The trip was not quite worth taking. The most impressive thing to us was the abundance of huge apartment buildings of an architectural distinction similar to those of Russia. We decided that if a sufficient number of Swedes out of Stockholm's 1.4 million lived in those rabbit warrens, it could account for their irritability and their rudeness in the ships and on the streets. One best remembers small things—like some squirrels who had established a family business at the Hammarby Locks, cadging snacks from the launches and posing for pictures.

Back on the ship a tiredness caught up with us, and we turned down an invitation to an evening ashore of smorgasbord and opera in favor of twelve hours of sleep.

The next day was warmer. We went ashore with the idea of walking to the Viking ship, the *Wasa*, which had been raised from the harbor floor and was housed in a long shedlike building, still undergoing restoration and repair. We had a city map, and it seemed to be a long distance from the dock to the Viking ship. But after we had turned right and walked across a wooden bridge, we found we were very close to the Ostasiatiska Museet, the Asiatic Museum, which housed King Gustaf's collection of Asian art and was quite close to the Viking ship structure.

From afar we saw some big bulgy plaster objects and thought they were part of a children's playground, but when we got to them we found it was an outdoor sculpture display, of weird, grisly, and comic objects and strange machinery, some of it in motion, as if, perhaps, by Tinguely, but we could find no creator's name. It had a nightmarish quality, perhaps intentional.

The Museum of Asian Art would not open until twelve, and we walked on through a park, up a slope, to the Museum of Modern Art, which would open at eleven. We passed bright buildings painted Williamsburg yellow, which seemed to be part of a school. Finally we reached the Viking ship, except that the building it was in stood a hundred yards away across a canal. From the map we learned that we would have to walk perhaps three more miles to find our way, bridge by bridge, around to the Viking ship. So we turned back and walked through green spaces, past purple and white lilacs, and arrived at the Museum of Modern Art just as it opened.

It is a fine collection, daring and wide-ranging and handsomely mounted. The most shocking and astonishing piece is a rough table, life size, out in the middle of a wide expanse of floor, with thirteen stuffed figures seated at it, ranged all along one side and with one at either end. The dusty satin and velvet seem to clothe skeletal figures. The first glance at it conveys an instant of medieval madness, prickles the back of the neck, catches at the breath. It is called "La Table" and is by a sculptor named Eva Aeppli.

The museum architecture was splendid. It created lots of airy bright space without intruding. The Museum of Asiatic Art was a far more traditional structure. The collection is huge: bronzes, fabrics, porcelains, ivories, prints. I was especially interested in the king's collection of netsuke on display. It was strong in early nineteenth-century carvers. I could identify a few but was, of course, unable to check the signatures. Mostly traditional subjects. One *very* nice horse, apparently very early.

After we walked out of the museum area, we took a taxi down to the Hotel Royal for B & B—beer and bathroom— and sat at the bar and had two small beers apiece for a total tab of $10. Came upon the ship's klepto asleep in the lobby and wondered if we could find a "do not disturb" sign to hang about her neck so that we would no longer be troubled by her aboard.

We went to Wimpy's for a late lunch. We were hamburg hungry because the ship's hamburgs were always too salty. We had hamburgs at Wimpy's. Too salty. We walked through the park on the way back to the ship. A great park. Flowers, birds, people, children, fountains, chess games—including one huge chess game with a board made of twelve-inch tiles set into the walkway and wooden chessmen two feet high. The spectators were three deep around the board, and some had climbed up on statuary to watch the match. We bought gigantic ice-cream cones and watched too. Made the next-to-last launch back to the *Mariposa.* When you are chugging on out toward the gangway, she always has a look of welcome, growing bigger and bigger as you near her. Friends lean on the rails, calling down as you step out onto the float. You take your loot to the warm cabin. Every purchase looks better than it did ashore. Time to shower and change and go topside to watch the departure, watch the city dwindle astern.

Dinner with the captain. Dorothy saw Emily Morgan popping nitro and took her pulse and found it alarming: very slow, with an occasional fast triplet. They had been under severe strain in the Leningrad subway last Sunday. Emily was upset because Al had chemotherapy today, and it took a lot out of him, spent a lot of his dwindling energies. Dorothy had seen them sitting alone in a corner of the lounge, holding hands in silence, watching the sea go by. Continuing tension and anxiety can distort the electrical impulses which control the heart. They left the dinner table early to go see the doctor.

After dinner, the captain invited us up to the bridge. We saw the radar images of other ships. The captain retracted the stabilizers to show Dorothy how much good they did. The steady ship began a slow rocking that turned her ashen, and he laughed and extended them again.

I can't remember if the general was up there or not that night. He probably was. He was a retired major general, a dignified and cultivated man. He did nice pencil sketches. He was interested in navigation. I think he had a small boat. Maybe he was a frustrated sailor. Very early during the cruise he asked me if he could go up to the bridge.

Maybe he thought I was going to escort him there, but I said, "Sure, just go right on up." He wanted to know when, and I said, "Well, the four-to-eight watch is pretty busy, and the twelve-to-four watch I'm not too enthused about, so go up on the eight-to-twelve watch." He seemed a little insecure about it so I added, "I'll tell them you're coming up. You're free to ask any questions you want. They're nice guys and won't mind having you up there."

So I told the eight-to-twelve watch that this retired general might be coming up, and apparently the next morning he went and really enjoyed himself. He was a pipe smoker. Always had that pipe going. I thought he would go up there for a half hour or forty-five minutes or an hour at the very most, find out what he wanted to know about navigation, and that would be it. But when I went up later in the morning, he was there in the chart room, sitting back in a corner facing the chart table, happily enjoying the whole thing. When I asked him, he said everything was fine and thanked me for letting him come up.

When I went back the next day he was there again. He became sort of a permanent addition to the eight-to-twelve watch. He studied the charts and did his own navigation and checked it against the ship's course. Sometimes if I came up through the inside door, he would be in the wheelhouse, smoking his pipe and telling stories, and the boys would all be yakking away. I could come in and the conversation would break up and the general would fade back into his corner in the chart room.

When I had a chance I asked the fellows on that watch, "Is this arrangement bothering you guys, is it too much of a problem? If so, let me know and I'll tell him he can't spend all his time up here on the bridge."

"No, it's no problem," they said. "He knows when to stay out of things. He likes to observe everything going on, and we talk some when everything is quiet."

"Okay, then, we'll let it continue. But if it does turn into a problem, just let me know."

It was my usual practice after dinner to take a quick run up the bridge to see about our speed and our position and what was going on at that particular point. It's always dark, and all the lights are out on the bridge. They would hear me coming. I never like to sneak up on people. I would bang the door, take a look at the chart first, then go on out to the wheelhouse. I had no fast rule about gossiping or telling stories. It's a long stretch up there, four hours at a time, and as long as the work was done and they kept a good lookout I was never tough about this. But, of course, whenever I walked in, the gossip would stop. As soon as my eyes were accustomed to the darkness, I would see the glow of the pipe over there in the corner, where the general held court and did his navigation.

Now, on a passenger ship, I have two complete vocabularies. In dealing with the crew, especially when I am annoyed about something, I tend to use expressions which have been known to blister the paint and start small fires in the ashtrays. I get a lot of attention from the crew that way, and I have seldom used the wrong vocabulary when dealing with the passengers.

On this particular night we were behind schedule. When I had gotten my eight-o'clock position report and speed report, it looked as though we were in good shape. But after dinner, about nine thirty or thereabouts, when I went up on the bridge, looked in the chart room, checked off our position, I found we *were considerably behind what I had been told on the eight-o'clock position report. Whereupon I cut loose. "Goddamn it, what's going on around this____ing place. You____s told me at eight o'clock we were in good shape, and now you____me up with this____ing____, ____report. Can't you find out where the____ing ship is on this____ing ocean?" I walked into the wheelhouse. Over in the corner I could see the glow of the pipe. He wasn't saying a word. After ten minutes of venting my emotions I said, "Oh, good evening, General! How are you tonight?"*

"Very fine, very fine," he said stiffly. I knew he didn't approve of my method of handling my troops, but he wasn't about to say anything because he enjoyed the privileges of the bridge too much.

So after that, whenever I went up and found him there, I would cut loose with a little barrage of paint-peelers and fire-starters and then turn to him and say, "Don't you agree with me, General?"

And he would go, "Haw, harrumph, haw, hum," and that would be it.

I told him not to tell anybody he was spending this much time on the bridge, because it wasn't fair to other would-be navigators. He swore he wouldn't mention it, that he would slip up there like a thief and study his navigation and stay out of sight.

One day he approached me and said, "Captain, I think we're in trouble."

And I said, "Haven't I had enough trouble on this trip? What have we got now?"

He said he had been up on the bridge doing his usual navigation and one of the more important high-rent-level passengers had been looking for me, had come up on the outside and looked in the wheelhouse, and had seen the general there.

"He's probably going to have something to say about my being up here."

I said, "General, I think we can handle that. With retired general officers of the army or flag officers of the navy, it is traditional military etiquette to offer them access to the bridge at their pleasure."

This is the way instant tradition is born. He smiled and

said, "Captain, if I am cornered, that is my story." And he managed to last out the whole trip on the bridge. He was never a problem.

I had an admiral one time who was making a South Pacific trip, and he asked to come up onto the bridge sometime because he wanted to make a search of the charts. It seemed that during World War II he had discovered a sea mount—that is, the top of a mountain or coral crag or something. They call them sea mounts. He thought they might possibly have named it after him, and he wanted to see if his name was on the charts.

He was a charming man. I took him up on the bridge and he reminisced about how the convoy he was escorting was steaming south through some straits off New Caledonia, and he could almost come up with the position. So we looked over the appropriate chart very carefully, but we couldn't find anything with his name on it. He was disappointed.

We told a couple of World War II stories. The second mate had been doing some navigation, and his sextant was on the chart table. Our visitor looked over at it and said, "Oh, my gosh, I haven't seen one of those in years."

"Admiral, be my guest. See what you can do with it."

The old boy picked it up backwards, so I said, "Admiral, you've got it backwards."

"Oh, yes. I believe I have. Well, you know it's been many years since I handled one, and after all, I did have a very good quartermaster."

And I said, "I bet you did, Admiral."

When we were swapping World War II stories, he told me one I really liked. Some time after the war, he was Admiral of the Seventh Fleet when it was stationed in Hong Kong. At night they would dress the ships, run strings of light bulbs clear to the top of the masts and down the other side, making an outline of the ship's rigging. They thought to carry this a bit further, and since it was the Seventh Fleet, they put together a big circle of light bulbs and hoisted it up there, with a big seven made of bulbs in the middle. They were all very proud of this.

About a week later the admiral was invited to a very posh cocktail party. There were diplomatic people there, and quite a few Chinese officials. One of the Chinese officials complimented him on the decorations and asked, "How come you navy people are plugging 7-Up? Why don't you give some advertisement to Coca-Cola?"

28

|||||||||||||||||||||||||||||||||||||||||||

En Route to Copenhagen

A day at sea. The fog began at forty thirty in the morning. The captain was called to the bridge. Proceeded at dead slow, hooting the mournful horn, keeping a close watch on radar.

On a subsequent journey on the *Royal Viking Sea,* we were shown how the satellite navigation system works. Captain Kilpack had had this same system on the PFEL's largest freighter, the *Golden Bear,* when he was assigned to her.

Once a known position, an exact position, verified by landmarks, has been programmed into the computer, the continuous transmission from the transponder enables the satellite computer, when queried, to give the position of the ship with a precision previously impossible, especially when far from land-based navigation aids.

One of the more fascinating aspects of this control system is the way it is keyed into a separate radar installation. This radar scans a 360-degree circle and transmits the blips to the satellite. The computer reads the blips and, if it should discover that a blip is on a converging course with the ship, it will sound a warning in the wheelhouse while there is still time to take action to avoid collision. A supertanker of a quarter million tons, moving at cruising speed, will travel at least eight miles after the signal for emergency stop is given before all forward motion ends. The interval before the warning is given can be programmed into the computer.

After prolonged spells of overcast lasting for days in mid-ocean, when traditional navigation by the taking of sights is impossible, a ship with satellite navigation will often be asked for position reports by passing vessels, so they can check their dead reckoning against the truth.

From the Vikings' use of captive birds, released to find the direction of the land, to the astrolabe, the compass afloat in whale oil, the octant, the sextant, loran, and now the satellite navigation system, there yet remains a flavor of man's early history on the sea. When, after the moon flights, and men came scorching back into the atmosphere to swing on the great chutes and land in the Pacific, a giant aircraft carrier was there to make rendezvous. In a locker on the bridge was a box of oak chips. After the command to come to a dead stop, dead in the water, the captain would take a handful of the chips, walk out to the wing of the bridge, and drop them into the sea to observe how they rested there relative to the ship. The test is simple, truthful, and quick.

When you hoot your slow way through heavy fog, you can only hope that there are no small wooden boats out there, boats which will not reflect any signal to the radar screen. To anyone aboard a small wooden boat in heavy fog, the sound of an oncoming ship, sounding its foghorn, is terrifying. Fog does something very strange to the transmission of sound; it is almost impossible to tell from which direction it is coming. Only when the sound begins to diminish can you know that it has passed you, unseen, and soon the diminishing wake will make you pitch and rock and, from its direction, tell you on which side the ship has passed.

Once we were out in a man-made fog, feeling our way from the Bahamas to Fort Lauderdale in a small cabin cruiser. The Everglades, victim of ruthless agribusiness and land exploitation, was afire, and the smoke was drifting far out across the Gulf Stream. A small bird blundered aboard and flew into the cabin. We let it stay there. Half an hour later, a great blue heron came flapping down out of the murk and perched on the small safety rail that extended around the outer edge of the transom. It rode there in solemn unconcern. After a time the small bird flew out of the cabin and perched beside the heron. The heron seemed unaware of it but suddenly reached out with one big gray scaly foot, grasped and crunched the small bird, and dropped it dead on the transom. We were four, and two of us saw it happen. It had a ghastly indifference quite appropriate to heavy fog. Fog always wreaths the castle towers when the vampires awaken in their coffins.

People talk more quietly in fog. The vibration of the ship seems more pronounced and more audible. Bridge players quarrel with their partners. People drink too much before lunch. The deck walkers pursue their discipline glumly indeed.

The scheduled "Midnight Sun Captain's Champagne Party" went well, but the captain seemed to be forcing himself to be the jovial host. Later he was listless and quiet at dinner, and without appetite.

There are always bugs being passed around a ship, especially when you stop at many foreign ports. People go ashore and spread out and bring back everything they encounter, from intestinal parasites to the common cold. I usually throw things off pretty well and seldom ask help from the doctor.

One time in Tahiti I was coming down with a touch of the flu. It had been going around the ship, and we were getting ready to sail from Papeete. All the French Tahitians came up to my room to get their papers signed and have the customary farewell drink. I had felt a little squeamish but thought I was fighting it off until they all crowded in there. They aren't too heavy on the deodorants and they are very heavy on the garlic, and they had come in from some very hot weather. When they left, I barely made it to the head. One of the mates heard me in there and decided to do me a favor by telling the doctor.

He sent a nurse up with a shot. She was a big square-looking no-nonsense girl from a small town, very straight, named Rosemary. This was her first trip with me. She came to my room with a bottle of medicine and a towel folded over, and I knew what was under that towel because I had seen that trick before. She was sympathetic with my condition and told me how much medicine to take and when to take it, and she said she had been told to give me a shot.

I said, "Rosemary, do you think that is necessary?"

She said, "Yes, I think it will make you feel better."

"Well, whatever you think."

So I stood there. We were about three feet apart. She stood there looking at me, and began to sort of fidget, and finally she said, "Captain, would you drop your trousers?"

"Rosemary, I hardly know you. Can't we shake hands first?"

She turned beet red. I turned, laughing, and let the trousers down, and while I was laughing, before I could get ready, she nailed me with that shot. And then she laughed.

On one trip I broke a tooth off—a tooth not quite in front, but almost. It had been a full cap, and the thing came off and just left the little prong sticking down, so I was going around the ship all day trying to talk out of the other side of my mouth. There was a nice dentist on board, a little guy named something like LaFlora, from the Midwest.

He came to me and said, "I understand you have a problem."

"Yes, I broke off one of my teeth."

"Do you have the tooth?"

"Yes, but it's broken off almost flush, and I don't think you can do much."

"Let's take a look. Maybe I can do something."

We went down to the doctor's office and the guy looked it over and said, "I think if I could drill this tooth out and get more retention, I could cement it back in so that it would at least last you the trip."

"That would be fantastic."

"Well, I'll need a drill."

"There are lots of them down in the engine room. Why don't we go down and see what they've got?"

So we went below and it was really hot, with guys working at drills and lathes. It was very noisy and steamy and everything was greasy and oily. I said, "Fellows, this is Dr. LaFlora. He is going to fix my tooth and he wants to borrow a drill."

So of course one of the wise guys down there said, "Sir, if you put your head in this drill press right here, we can drill it out."

They got LaFlora a hand drill, and he picked out the small bit that he wanted. He couldn't put the tooth in a vise, so he *put the drill in the vise and hand-held the tooth and drilled it out. Then he turned to me and said, "Now open your mouth and we'll see how it fits."*

He seemed to have forgotten where he was, he had gotten so interested in the tooth. He'd been handling the drill and the vise. I said, "Doctor, it isn't that I don't appreciate what you're doing for me, but would you mind washing your hands first?"

Everybody in the engine room enjoyed that. So we went back up to the doctor's office. The dentist's wife was there. She had laid out the instruments and she was mixing up the cement on a little marble slab. They washed the tooth off and tried it, and it felt fine, and he said he was going to cement it back in.

"That isn't the way to do it," she said.

"That is the way we are going to do it," he said.

They got into a big loud discussion about the procedure. He turned to me and said, "Captain, I hope you realize that my wife is also a dentist, and you are now seeing why we don't practice together. Her office is clear across town, and that is the way it is always going to be."

They reached agreement and put the tooth back in, and it stayed there with no problems for the rest of the trip.

A lot of impromptu medical work can happen on a ship. One night on one of the island trips, a fairly heavy woman was getting dressed, and in zipping up her zipper, she got her skin caught in it. This was very painful. She rang for the room steward who soon found out that it was a real calamity. Every time he tried to touch the zipper, she screamed. He called the nurse and the doctor, and they came and looked at her. They saw it was not a medical problem, it was a mechanical problem, so the only person to call was the joiner.

The joiner is the crew member who does all sorts of odd jobs in the passenger areas, fixing door locks, replacing a towel rack, repairing luggage, putting a broken heel back on a shoe, even mending eyeglass frames.

So the joiner came up. It was the peak of his seafaring career. They put a mask on him, like a surgeon's mask, and the doctor stood by, and the joiner would call out, "Wire! Screwdriver! Tweezer!" and they were passed to him, and in a minimum of time, with a minimum of discomfort, he got the woman out of the zipper so the doctor could fix the wound. This joiner had been around a long time, and he was well known to the crew, and he was not averse to having a little drink or, if conditions favored it, several little drinks.

From then on, after the first little drink, he always told about the lady and the zipper.

29

||||||||||||||||||||||||||||||||||||||||||||||||||

Friday and Saturday, June 10 and 11
Copenhagen, Denmark

We were on time at Copenhagan, having gone at top speed after the fog cleared. We took the shuttle bus into the city, to the Hotel Royal, and walked from there to the mouth of the fabulous "walking street," more than seven blocks of straight-away shops with no wheeled traffic, either on that street or on the cross streets. Hundreds of shops. The sun came out. The world warmed up. Lots of people carrying coats and capes and sweaters. The young people were very attractive and lively, fresh-faced, smartly dressed, and having fun. Went into a gigantic sweater store and bought a bunch of sweaters to send to the New Zealand branch of our clan.

Went shopping in Illums, a very fine store, for small gifts and such. Had a department-store lunch: mushroom omelette or broiled hamburger, salad of Boston lettuce with red pepper strips, chopped onion, marinated cucumber, and then some good Tuborg. Back foot-weary to the hotel for the shuttle bus, with string bags chock full and camera full of people-pictures. Drove past the little Mermaid, symbol of Copenhagen, recently beheaded by hoodlums and restored.

That evening taxied to the Tivoli, the vast amusement park. Crowded. Millions of bright lights. Rides. Music coming from all directions. It wasn't full dark until after eleven.

On the way back to the ship in the taxi, we argued with friends about the pronunciation of the name of the city. There is a myth that one must pronounce the a as in hay, instead of as the o in hog, based falsely on the idea that the Germans, when they held Denmark, pronounced it Copen-hog-en.

I told them of Mackinlay Kantor's tale of his instruction by a man in the city when he was buying pipes. "Tell me," said Mack, "is it Copen-hay-gen, or Copen-hog-en?"

"Mr. Kantor," he man said, "it is really Kyerpin-haahn."

Back to the walking streets on Saturday morning to buy camera film, Scotch tape, a couple of loaves of rye bread for the captain's table. Expected to have lunch at Illum's but came out of a shop into the first drops of a cold rain, darted away from the walking streets, and found a cab just as it really began to come down. Drinks and lunch aboard, then afternoon chores, including packing the carryon bags we bought in Amsterdam with warm clothing for the Norway tour. We were to leave the ship the next morning.

Hal Wagner lectured on Oslo and the fjords at quarter to ten. Very detailed. As always.

In Oslo we picked up Captain Olav Tviet (pronounced Schwett), who turned out to be an asset to the trip. He was our Norway pilot for the fjords and the North Cape. He was, in addition to Captain Rawles, our North Sea pilot. Whenever we took on a port pilot, that made four of us up there. Nothing could go wrong.

Olav was an imperturbable guy. He would stand there, smoking his pipe, giving a little instruction now and then. I remember one day we were going up this fjord. It was very narrow, with high cliffs on either side. Each time we would go around a bend it seemed to be narrower. Sheer cliffs on either side, with waterfalls dropping all the way down to the water, winds blowing the water into mist as it fell.

I finally turned to old Captain Tviet and I said, "Olav, now dammit, don't con me. I think we're lost. Do you know where in the hell we're going?"

He waited about twenty seconds and then he took his pipe out of his mouth and said, "Vell, we joost go as far as ve can, and then ve stop and ask somebody."

Very funny. By then it was too narrow to ever get her turned around, and with that single prop and the torque we sure couldn't have backed out of there. And who is going to be living at the bottom of three thousand feet of sheer naked rock, waiting to be asked directions?

When at last it opened up ahead, I sighed with relief.

30

||||||||||||||||||||||||||||||||||||||||||||||||||

Sunday, Monday, and Tuesday, June 12–14
Oslo to Bergen

After the red tape of departure, we boarded the second and smaller of two buses making the Oslo-to-Bergen tour. We went to the back and found that we could each have a huge window, with space alongside for cameras and carryons. A fine little bus. Mint condition. Hal Wagner was aboard. The guide was a middle-aged woman with an accent to which we soon became accustomed.

As we went through downtown Oslo, we narrowly escaped being broadsided by a city bus. Great wrenching and shrieking of brakes and rubber.

TOUR No. 53: THE FJORDLANDS
Three days of motorcoach and ferry, all meals included. Leave the pier at 10:30 A.M. on Sunday, June 12.

Sunday, June 12: OSLO–LAKE TYIN. Drive up the Sollihogda Pass and through the beautiful Begna Valley to Fagernes. After lunch ascend to the mighty Jotunheimen Mountains to lovely Lake Tyin, arriving in time for dinner and overnight.

Monday, June 13: LAKE TYIN–STALHEIM. Cross the reindeer-inhabited mountains to visit a 12th Century

273

Stavekirke. Cross over to Laerdal. This afternoon cruise on the majestic Sognefjord. Spend the night at Stalheim.

Tuesday, June 14: STALHEIM–BERGEN. Drive via Voss, through exciting mountain passes and past roaring waterfalls, along the lovely Hardangerfjord to Norheimsund, arriving in time for lunch. Then drive directly to Bergen and rejoin the ship.

Membership limited.

Rather than some kind of orderly travelog, I will try to give impressions, mostly of the unexpected. First fine day after long days of rain. Oslo residential areas mostly houses, very few apartments. Lilacs, chestnuts, and dandelions everywhere. Lots of marinas. Still have salmon in the river near the city. Many ski slopes, and much construction going on in the area of the slopes. Construction prosperity, probably from North Sea oil money.

Narrow winding road up into the hills. Birch and very tall spruce against rocky landscape. Many places where rock slides have narrowed the road further. Signs warning of rock slides. Signs warning of moose-crossing area. The ferns are opening. Many campers in trailers on lake shores. Green rolling country, with red Adirondack barns. Grain farms. Rock gardens. Apple trees. A Viking mound, burial place of a king. Wild strawberries. A mink farm. (Norway big exporter of mink, silver fox, blue fox.) Small towns and villages and a small city, streets quiet on a Sunday.

The law says that anyone who cuts one tree must plant ten trees. Splendid law. The forests are both public and private, but closely controlled by the state, along with the sawmills. Big paper plant. Enclosed flumes running down the side of a mountain, natural power for the paper mill. Blueberries and cranberries. Little red and brown cabins, as by Catskill lakes. People taking the sun after many dark days. Few tents in camping areas. Perhaps still too cold.

Made rest stop at roadside café at Nesiadal. Big sign outside said "P-Busser." Drank Brugg, a low-alcohol beer. Those who couldn't wait for lunch bought cookies.

Country getting higher and rougher. Very few domestic animals. Guide pointed out the town of Bogn, a small place perched on the slope of enormous mountains, and said there was a big battle here in World War II. One cannot imagine why anyone would want to waste the men it must have cost to take that little place. The Nazis liked total control and clung to Norway from 1940 to 1945. Our guide said, "They behaved terribly."

Beginning to see snow on the peaks. They are from 6,000 to 9,000 feet high. More buildings with slate roofs. Stopped for a smorgasbord lunch at Fagernes. I am dubious of tour-bus food stops. Usually it consists of something the kitchen can whip up in short order without spoiling it too badly.

But this was crackers, jam, bread, rolls, smoked salmon, marinated raw salmon, baked salmon, egg custard for salmon, lamb stew, smoked lamb, mild sausage patties, hot vegetables, reindeer steak, an assortment of cheeses (including one dark-yellow goat cheese with a caramel taste and peanut-butter texture), beer, coffee, and an assortment of desserts, including a feather-light chocolate soufflé.

Went to outdoor museum after lunch. Reconstructed houses of the fifteenth, sixteenth, and seventeenth centuries, moved here to lakeshore to form a sort of improbable village and furnished in keeping with the era. Some older ones with sod roofs, now freshening with spring grasses. All dark as pockets inside. Windows create heating problems.

Found "violets" in the field nearby. They were wild pansies, called here "forget-me-nots." This is West Zealand, a pretty country of small farms, woodworkers, mink farms. Saga Mink comes from Norway. A month ago the lake had still been frozen.

Climbing higher. Air chillier. Many Norwegian flags flying. Discovered it is the custom to fly the flag on Sundays.

In this high country a thirty-acre farm would go for about 450,000 kroner, or about $7,500. Short growing season.

We are up to 3,500 feet. The birch leaves are just coming out. Birch are the only trees at this level. There are great green blankets of moss over the rocks. Different-colored mosses. Reindeer eat the white moss. Reindeer hunting season opens September 1. Now no trees at all. Patches of snow. Cabins with sod roofs placed over birch bark. Passed a place which the guide stated was opened as a tourist hotel in the year 1384.

Passed fierce torrential rivers, banging spray high into the air, fed by melting snow on the heights. Valley after valley after valley.

We finally came winding down to a wide shallow river flowing through a quiet valley. Sheep and goat herds. For some reason, a dry valley. We saw rain guns turning slowly, irrigating the fields. Looked at Stave Church at Borgund. Little high round windows. Stone altar dating back to 1050, when the Maya were still building temples in Yucatán.

The farmers own the river. It is a salmon fishing place so famous that people come from all over the world and pay $100 to fish there. The farmers make more out of the river than out of their crops. Stopped between stone tunnels at a narrow fast slant of green water, where the salmon were appearing now and again, heading up against the current. Much reindeer moss near river. Saw old Viking road on the other side of the river, most of it just a trace of tumbled neglect, some of it in surprisingly good shape, stone pavings. All birch. No evergreens.

Strawberry, apple, and potato country. Saw sea gulls working their way through a field of strawberries. Reached our little Hotel Fjordstven at Laerdal at eight thirty. On broad bank of a fjord, across from the far rocky shore.

Found to our pleasure that the bigger busload was housed elsewhere. This was a small clean modern hotel. Shocked to find bodies in our beds in the small room. Only an illusion. Huge down comforters had been folded into sleeping-bag shape and covered by thin cotton bedspreads. Went down to the lobby and bought beers (nothing else available on Sundays) and carried them out to tin tables on the banks of the fjord. The sun seemed to be setting into a V in the far rim of the fjord wall, but on steady examination it proved to be going mostly sideways, and very little downward.

It did not become dark until after eleven. Dinner was fresh broiled salmon caught that very day, the best we had ever had. Slept warm and well, awoke to light rain and a strange smorgasbord breakfast, light and dark bread, packaged butter, five different fruit preserves, boiled eggs, corn flakes and puffed rice, four kinds of cheese, liver loaf, hot kidney beans in tomato sauce with bits of meat, three kinds of sliced cold sausage.

Of course, among our group was the usual big-mouth complaining woman who, staring at this gracious and interesting spread, with the English-speaking assistant manager of the hotel right beside her, yammered, "What kind of a breakfast is this, anyhow? No juice, even. It looks like a lot of leftovers from last night's dinner."

Many U.S. passports should be stamped: NOT VALID OUT-SIDE THE CONTINENTAL LIMITS OF THE UNITED STATES.

The rain had stopped. Before we checked out, the bus took us down to the village a little over a mile away. The bank was in a frame house painted lavender. There were two gift shops and a supermarket among a lot of small frame houses, and red, white, and purple lilacs, tulips, tuberous begonias, and some little sod-roofed outbuildings. Bought some small presents for the people at the captain's table and, in the supermarket, bought four heavy brass animal bells of different sizes for us.

After a hotel lunch, the bus took us from Laerdal to Stalheim, where we walked aboard a ferry called the *Førdefjord* to tour down the Sognefjord, a fjord 110 miles long and 4,000 feet deep at its deepest part.

We found a sunshiny sheltered place out of the icy wind, took far too many pictures of overpowering scenery. Spidery waterfalls tumbled from the fjord rims thousands of feet overhead. I found myself wondering about the people who lived in little clusters of houses down at the water level in places where the sheer drop did not reach all the way down to the water. You could make out faint and precarious winding trails that climbed up and up to the top, but it was obvious they would seldom be used. These lives had to be attuned to water traffic. They did look snug and out of the wind, but there would be a perpetual gloom there except during those very few hours when the sun might shine directly down into the fjord.

No electricity, no commercial entertainment, with the possible exception of radio used with a generator. Books and silence. Fish and bread and bed. Are they secure in their awareness of who they are? What are their social and emotional values? How do they endure the long iron winter? Are they mad, by our standards? We saw their little gardens, their goats, their children. One could readily accept a winter there. Or a year. One year might have a flavor of novelty. But a lifetime down at the bottom of a deep incredible gash in the earth, next to frigid water? It stuns the mind to contemplate a willing acceptance.

· The ferry stopped at Gudvangen, which means "Nice Place," and we took the bus from there to the Stalheim Hotel, up 1,000 feet in thirteen alarming hairpin turns. It is a luxury hotel. The steep long view down the valley is fascinating. The Germans manned observation bunkers there during World War II, built into the side of the cliff face, just under the level of the high ground where the hotel is. Dank little rooms with a view. Tiresome boring duty. Because no one ever came. But better, of course, than the Russian front. Or Italy. Or North Africa. Perhaps these were old men they used here. Or those incapacitated by wounds. A bad post in winter. The hotel is closed all winter.

Lovely flower gardens. An exhibition of antiques behind glass. Good food, good shop, good bar, pleasant service people, good rooms. People from both our buses converged here, along with some who had arranged to make the trip by private car.

Dinner, and nightcaps of aquavit, and off to the feather beds and down comforters.

After the morning smorgasbord we—thankfully—took a different road than the one we had climbed the evening before. Passed endless waterfalls. Stopped and took pictures of an especially grand one called Tvindefoss. Stopped in Voss, a big ski area, a small city heavily bombed in World War II, birthplace of Knute Rockne. It has a nice stone church with wooden steeple dating from 1277, with neat beflowered graves in the churchyard. We walked through town and down to the lake.

Passed, later, fields of dandelions and buttercups, villages with boats and garden plots, and potato patches for aquavit. Passed salmon nets, and the mountains along the Hardangerfjord, and a glacier called Jostedalsbre, which covers a hundred square miles, and on into a town named Norheimsund for a smorgasbord lunch: cold salmon, herring, cheeses, hams and sausages, tomatoes, toast, jams, hot sausage, stews, fish, vegetables, beer, coffee, chocolate and vanilla pudding, raspberry cake with whipped cream, cookies, and another assortment of cheeses. Coming down into lower country, the day became hot. After the heavy lunch we drove to another waterfall called Steindalsfossen, where one can walk on a narrow muddy path under the great smashing roaring fall of cold water which comes from thirty feet over one's head and crashes with great tumult onto stones about twenty feet below the path.

In the late afternoon we drove through miles of tunnels, with four closely spaced at a place called Tokagjetlet. There was a stop for cold Brugg and time to watch twin lambs at play in a field. As we neared Bergen, going pellmell down the long slopes toward sea level, traffic grew heavy on a road which was, by all normal reckoning, but a lane and a half wide. As we skinned past the trucks and buses coming the other way, there seemed only inches to spare.

After an abortive attempt to leave us on the wrong pier, the driver found the ship. The big golden bear on the stack looked welcoming and comforting. We were all warmly greeted aboard. Our departure was slightly delayed as they waited for a shipment of whole blood for Al Morgan. As we moved out in the bright evening light, we had a good view of Bergen. It looks older than Oslo because of the bomb damage Oslo suffered, and the subsequent rebuilding. Against a far shore was a giant drilling platform with a name painted on it. Big John.

Without knowing it, we were leaving Bergen without one of our less-than-tightly-wrapped crew members. He worked in the engine room, and nobody missed him until we were on our way. It wasn't even a nighttime sailing, when you expect to lose somebody. We were only there for a few hours in the afternoon.

The next port was Geiranger, and as we were only going to be there a couple of hours, and it is a very small place, I didn't expect him to catch up with us, but he did. I was going to log him and fine him for the time missed, and let them decide back in the States whether to fire him. But I hadn't begun those details yet, as I was busy with the departure. We were beginning to pull away when I noticed a dude in a bright funny hat and a shiny funny jacket, running toward the dock. I told Coco to take a look at the local hotshot in this little out-of-the-way place. As we were busy getting turned around by the tugs, I was told there was a crew member who missed the departure and was now in the pilot boat and wanted us to lower the ladder or open the side port so he could come aboard.

I said, "Don't do it now while we're maneuvering. When we get turned around, let him come aboard. And let me know who the hell it is."

When everything was settled down, I found out it was the same fellow, the one in the fancy garments, who had caught up with us after missing the ship in Bergen.

After we got clear I had him up in the office with the chief engineer and the union representative, and I logged him for the time he missed.

I stared at him and said, "What is going on? You miss the ship in Bergen, and you nearly miss it again here. If I hadn't opened the side port for you, we could have left you there."

"Well," he said, "I met this girl in Bergen and I fell madly in love with her, and that's why I forgot about the departure time and missed the ship. She loaned me the money to get back up here to meet the ship again, so when I came aboard I went to the purser and drew some money and went back into town to telegraph the money to her, and it took so long that's why I was late and nearly missed the ship."

I guess he was keeping his credit good.

After we were clear of Bergen, we went to dinner. We had time to bestow our gifts, and the captain had time to order, but not receive, a steak, when they called him back up to the bridge.

More fog.

31

|||||||||||||||||||||||||||||||||||||||

Geiranger, Norway

We went up the coast in the brief night and nosed into the Geirangerfjord, one of the most spectacular. It was overcast and very raw on the weather decks. I was thankful I had brought along a watch cap.

The geology of the fjords is unique. During the Ice Age a million years ago, the glacial ice moved down the old riverbeds toward the sea. The ice cap was relatively thin at the seacoast, but inland the massive weight and slow movement of the ice burrowed it as deep as 4,000 feet below sea level. When the ice retreated as the ice age slowly ended, the sea broke through and filled these deeps with salt water. Though some are a hundred miles long, Geirangerfjord is only nine miles long. It is an average 1,500 feet wide. The abrupt side walls are 5,000 feet high. This gives a height-to-depth ratio of better than three to one, which intensifies the sensation of being very small and very vulnerable, way down in the bottom of that slot.

These steep-sided fjords create a strange impression. Sometimes, in a long straight stretch, you can see the distant snow-capped mountains ahead, but most of the time all you can see is the light sharp edge of the fjord walls. There is a profusion of waterfalls rushing over that edge and falling down to the waters of the fjord. Where the wall is irregular, sometimes a thin high waterfall will descend in two or three or even four separate segments. Where the volume of water coming over the crest is large, it will come down in a gray-green column to explode into a vivid white foam where it hits the rocks. Someone was counting waterfalls aloud, and I heard them give up at a hundred and eighty something when we rounded a bend and saw dozens more ahead.

In autumn, after the freeze and the snows have begun, the waterfalls dwindle and die. In the spring they are at peak. At one place seven of them came bursting over the high cliff, thousands of feet above us, in a distance of perhaps a quarter mile along the rim. There is an everpresent roar of water, audible above the sounds of the ship.

We had tickets for a bus ride from the little town of Geiranger up some 4,000 feet to Djupvasshytta (which sounds remarkably Hindu) on Lake Djupvatn, from where we could look down upon Geiranger and the *Mariposa*. But the day was too overcast for viewing, and the memory of the thirteen dreadful cutbacks to climb only a thousand feet was too vivid. So we gave our tickets to young friends. They were pleased and we were relieved.

The mountains behind Geiranger were huge. This was the end of this particular branch of the Geirangerfjord, and we would have to go on back past the Seven Sisters and all the other waterfalls to the Norwegian Sea to go north to Trondheim. At Geiranger a sprinkling of small pastel houses climbed the lower slopes. There was a small downtown area that led to the left, away from the dock, to a waterfall and a country road. We went into a grocery store and bought pumpernickel bread and goat cheese and a yarn winder. We walked past lilacs and blue columbine to the waterfall, and there we found painted on a big rock, "Aloha, *Mariposa* 1977."

We walked back in the cold, in a light sprinkle, to stop at the gift shop and buy large picture postcards taken in 1974 from Djupvasshytta of the *Monterey* at anchor at Geiranger, a white toy ship on a watercolor bay by a pastel village.

As we sailed away, we could see, astern, the high white country of the Norwegian Alps. The village slid around a corner of land behind us. We headed down the wet rocky trough, back to the sea.

* * *

The purser, Jim Yonge, told me that right after lunch an old man had come up to him, hopping mad, demanding to know why there was no afternoon movie way down there in the theater. It really makes you wonder. Some of the most fantastic nine miles of the trip, and that old boy wanted to spend it watching an old movie called The Amazing Dobermans, *a dog movie with Fred Astaire.*

The choice of movies aboard is never all that great: The Big Bus, Cougar Country, Silent Movie, Swashbuckler, Robin and Marian, Midway, Singing in the Rain, *and all those scratchy old travelogues. I guess they just aren't making many great movies. The film supplier furnishes us with a certain number of movies for a trip. We get an audience reaction right away, and if a picture is terrible we'll get rid of it. If there is a good reaction, as with* Patton, *we'll keep it aboard for several trips.*

We never get any X-rated movies. They are usually G or PG. Sometimes they'll put a horror movie aboard. I remember one a few years ago. The food situation on the ship is heavy. Everybody eats three or four meals a day. You have buffets. You have cocktail time with the hors d'oeuvres, and you have the eleven-thirty buffet at night.

A lot of people, even though they aren't heavy eaters at home, never miss a meal or a course in any meal, just because it is there and part of the ticket.

The first time this movie showed I went down to see it. It was titled Solent Green *and it had Edward G. Robinson and Charlton Heston in it. It was a good production. It was set in the year two thousand and something, and the United States had gone to pot. No gasoline. People living in broken-down cars. Food was such a major problem nobody was allowed to leave New York City and go out into the countryside. They were encouraging people to commit suicide. They had a suicide method all planned. You signed up and they took you to a theater and showed you beautiful films of the countryside and gave you a last big delicious meal, with a poison chaser at the end.*

When Charlton Heston investigated the suicide method, he found out they were taking the bodies out to this plant and rendering them into little green wafers, and the government through advertising was extolling the nutritional value of these little green wafers, pushing them hard as a food substitute. During the course of the movie, people were getting up and leaving.

When the lights went up, there were only six of us left, and they jumped on me for showing such a horrible movie. I said, "Hey, I didn't make the movie, and we won't show it again, okay?"

I guess that after eating four meals a day they didn't want to see a movie about people being ground up into little green wafers of nutritional value, so it went ashore at the next port.

I became a self-styled expert on production quality years ago when they made an episode of Hawaii Five-O on the ship. I was Chief Officer at the time. It had been the idea of Doug Green, one of the directors. He had been an old-time traveler on the White Ships, riding them back and forth long after air travel had become the fashionable and economic way to go. As a boy he had traveled with his family on the Matson ships. He wanted to do an episode on the Mariposa or the Monterey.

Jack Lord Enterprises had been lukewarm about Doug's idea. They didn't think it could be done, taking the entire cast on board and filming en route from Honolulu to the mainland.

When Doug finally got a green light he rode the ship several times, studying and learning all the routines, fire and boat drills, how the crew operated, ship's laundry, chief steward's department, the whole thing. I was instructed by our company to give him complete cooperation as he figured out what and where to shoot. He spent a lot of time with me when he made these research trips. He would ask me how we would handle a certain problem and I would tell him and he would ask, "Well, could you do it this way?"

"We wouldn't normally do it that way, but I guess we could."

"No, I want this thing to be factual. I don't want anybody who has ever ridden these ships before saying that you don't do things that way. I want it to show the ship in a good light, and I want it to be factual."

I appreciated his attitude. They make a lot of pictures about, for example, medicine or the army or industry, and people in the know think those pictures are ridiculous. They have technical advisers, but they don't listen to them. They want the stuff to be dramatic rather than dramatic and factual.

Doug roamed the ship until he knew every inch of it. He was interested in things like watertight doors and the laundry and the shop, and all those places he could utilize in the story line he was putting together. He wrote what I thought was a good episode. It was submitted to the studio and they flew a writer out who started from scratch, utilizing only a few of Doug Green's ideas, and changed the whole treatment around.

They decided to go ahead and make it the final show of the season. They shot it in December when a lot of their people were leaving Hawaii to go back to the mainland until the next year's schedule would begin. The cast and the cameramen and the lighting people and the script girls came onto the ship, with four and a half days in which to shoot the episode.

Doug Green and I had become close friends, and he asked me if I would like to work for them as a technical adviser and coordinator between the crew and the ship's personnel for the shooting. My bosses were enthused about this, and they flew me out to Hawaii to spend ten days prior to sailing, working on the problems they anticipated.

The electric supply problem was a big one because our power on the ship was not compatible with their lights and cameras. They had a trailerized generator they towed around the island to power their equipment when they were doing location shots, and there was another trailer with room for their cameras, lights, booms, and miscellany. We finally decided that they could put their two big trailers out on the after deck near the pool. They just barely fit, and they were too heavy for the ship's cranes, so we had to hire a heavier one to come down and hoist the trailers aboard.

When I began, I thought it would be fun hanging around these showbiz people, taking care of a few details. They told me I could have a small part in the show, and being a real ham I was very pleased. But when I began to see these problems coming up, one after another, I had second thoughts. But I had agreed, so I was stuck with it for the duration.

Our chief engineer was not the most jolly person in the world to deal with, and when he and I went to the studio to discuss how we might modify our power output so the production team could use the ship's generators, it wasn't ten minutes before he got into a quarrel with their lot electrician, a technical genius with frizzy hair and thick glasses who used scientific terminology way over the chief's head.

The chief answered him by saying, "It just won't work, and I won't let you try it anyway." They finally put their own transformers on the ship so they could hook into our power. They had already done the early filming of dock scenes, departures, and people throwing streamers while the band played, and they had hired a chopper and filmed stock shots of the ship, filming from the land side so that it looked as if the ship were out at sea.

When they were doing this, I got on the horn at their suggestion and told the passengers that there was a chopper coming out to take shots of the ship, and he might do quite a bit of circling, and it was for television. "So when the chopper comes over, folks, please don't pay any attention to it at all. Don't look at it and don't wave at it, because we are supposed to be out in the middle of the ocean."

I should have known better than to say that. As soon as it arrived, they all rushed to the rail, waving frantically, and when it went around to the other side, they all rushed over there, waving and yelling. It took a lot of time and effort to get them thinned out until it looked like a normal day at sea.

When the day arrived, the TV people all piled on board and took thirty rooms. Jack Lord, James MacArthur, the producer, and the director had the best rooms, and the low folk on their totem pole got the inside rooms.

We saved one of the Lanai Suites to use for shooting interior scenes in connection with several incidents in the script. One little actress got an inside room by herself, and as soon as we sailed she found out nobody was in the Lanai Suite. She came to me and said she would like that suite. I told her to talk to the producer, a man named Bill Finnegan. I told him he might have a little trouble with her.

She went to speak to him and he took her out in the corridor and when he came back in alone, three minutes later, he said, "It's all settled."

"Does she get the suite?"

"I told her she was lucky to have a room by herself. Lots of people were doubled up. She said she had claustrophobia and had to have an outside room. I told her, In that case, forget the whole thing; we have someone else on board who can handle your part, so if you don't think you can hack it, let's just forget it right now. Then she said she thought she could probably get used to the inside room."

They planned to shoot from eight in the morning until six. They knew how many feet they had to shoot a day. The dining room didn't open until eight fifteen. I told Si Lubin to have breakfast at seven o'clock for the television team, and he began sobbing about overtime and how much it would cost and so on. So I told him to keep track. The film company would pay it.

Whenever I asked for anything from the ship, I would get negative reactions. The passengers weren't too happy either. I was right in the middle. One of the technical people went and asked the chief engineer about something, and he said, "God-damn it, don't bother me with any of that crap. I don't have anything to do with the film business. Go see Kilpack. He's the big hot-dog show-business person." I had to ask them all to please come to me first with everything.

They planned to use the passengers and crew to fill in as extras, the way they do when they film in Hawaii. They looked around and picked out the people they wanted to use, and then the casting director came to me to tell me who he wanted and how many people he wanted, and when and where he wanted them. That made me the heavy. If anybody wasn't asked, I was standing between them and instant stardom. Also, they had brought along somebody to play the part of the captain, and this made Captain X unhappy. It was a lengthy part, and they thought he would be too busy running the ship to be on call. When I asked him to please have the passenger fire and boat drill and the crew fire and boat drill one right after the other, he said they couldn't do it that way. Sorry. I explained why they wanted it that way and how much money it would save, and he finally agreed to do it.

I went to the producer and the director to tell them all the P.R. problems I was having, so they said they would let the *captain introduce Jack Lord to the passengers at the regular champagne cocktail party.*

This brightened the captain's spirits, and he introduced Jack Lord. Lord made a fine presentation, saying he was happy to be on board and hoped that he would be able to make a good production, and a lot of people would be involved in the episode. He apologized for the disruption, with wires strung all over the ship and corridors blocked off from time to time. "I realize a lot of you people think of this as almost your home at this point in your cruise. We do apologize for the inconveniences and we hope it will be a good show. I would like to try to answer any questions you might have."

One old lady with about six glasses of free champagne aboard yelled, "What's your room number, honey?"

"At this point," he said, "I'd better introduce my wife, Marie."

The first day we fell an hour behind in the shooting, so the next day they had to start shooting at seven. I had to go back to Si Lubin and break his heart again with a special six o'clock breakfast. We split up into two units, and I went with the unit that filmed all the action shots when they were running around the ship chasing each other, and the other unit did the dialogue, where they seem to have to shoot things over and over and over.

I was picking up film lingo, and when we had a meeting the next day they told how much film they had in the can. Unit One had shot so much and Unit Two had shot so much, so I broke in and said, "My God, those guys in Unit Two are way ahead of you. If you guys in Unit One will get off your ass and get the job done, we can finish this turkey on schedule." That broke them up. The fearless amateur.

They were going to shoot a scene in the captain's room where Jack Lord is talking to the department heads. He wanted the chief steward, the chief engineer, and the chief mate all in there with their uniforms on. The chief mate was hot to do it, but they had an actor playing his part. Hal Wagner played himself as chief purser, and he had some lines to speak.

I went to Si Lubin and I said, "I know you're probably too busy for this kind of nonsense. These people have been complicating your job. But they want all the department heads in there for this shot. It won't take long and they want you there in uniform, but I understand how you feel, and if you don't—"

Whereupon he grabbed me by the sleeve and said, "John, you've got to put me in that show. My kids watch it all the time. You've got to get me in there for that shot." So he wasn't any problem.

Next I went to the big grumpy chief engineer and said, "You've made it pretty clear how you feel about show business, but there is a scene coming up where Jack Lord wants all the department heads in the captain's cabin while he tells them all about there being a crook on the ship. I knew you would be against it, so I have been trying to locate somebody about your size to play the part, but I would appreciate it if I could borrow a good uniform from you. Of course, in the interest of realism, Mr. Lord would like to use the real people—"

"If they want me up there," he said, "I'll do it."

"Okay then. I can't give you an exact time as they are running behind. It might be one o'clock or three. I'll give you the last possible call I can."

He called me once and asked how it was going, and I said I'd get back to him. Finally they were ready and soon he was on the upper deck with a towel around his shoulders, getting made up. One of the cruise hostesses went by and said, "Gee, chief, it looks great on you! You ought to wear it all the time."

When they shot it, Jack Lord wasn't satisfied with the first takes and wanted the furniture moved around and rearranged; then they tried some test shots. I'd been busy with the other unit, and I came back to see how things were going. There was a lot of confusion with the lights and cameras and cables. They had moved everybody out of the room. I passed by this very small bathroom and looked in, and there was the chief engineer sitting on the john and Si Lubin sitting on the floor. It was the only place they could be, having been crowded out of the main room and having to be available as soon as they were needed.

As I passed by I said, "Well, that's show biz."

The whole experience seemed to mellow the chief. He had said there would be absolutely no shooting in his engine room. But when I asked him again, he said, "Why not? Tell them it's okay."

The crew and the passengers kept trying all kinds of dodges to get into the various scenes. People would hang around for hours at a time, hoping they could duck into a mob scene and grin at their friends and relations. At one point I noticed the lighting people had stuck a great big hot floodlight in the dining room, aimed at Jack Lord's table, right under one of the sprinkler heads, and by good luck I got it turned off before they had a cloudburst in the dining room.

We had very good weather for December, and they got some beautiful shots coming into the bay, under the bridge. I have since seen some of those shots used in other pictures, so apparently good general stuff goes on file at the studios.

The biggest problem was not being able to develop the film aboard each night so they could see rushes of the previous day's shooting and know what had to be done again. They tried to solve it by shooting a lot of the dubious stuff several times, and on the last day, after going from six in the morning to eight at night, everybody was exhausted. It turned out to be a good episode, and they gave us a copy to show on the ship. For a time it would be shown once or twice every trip, and occasionally they would show it for the crew. That was more fun, because everybody cheered or booed for the people they knew.

Doug Green and I remained good friends, and later on he came back to try to work out a series that would all take place on a cruise ship. At that time the networks were trying to get rid of TV violence, and they wouldn't stand for any knife fights or shootings on the ship. While things were still in the talk stage, somebody asked if it would be okay if we had maybe a small fire on the ship. I think right there PFEL lost interest. Too bad it didn't go, as it would have come in ahead of The Love Boat.

32

||||||||||||||||||||||||||||||||||||||||||

Trondheim, Norway

The ship was docking at Trondheim before we got up. After breakfast with the Morgans and Edra, Al looking much better, we went to the foyer and asked the gangway guard what it was like out there. A sour fellow at best, he said, "It's cold. There's no shuttle bus and no taxis."

So we bundled up for a long cold walk to town. The pier smelled of apples arriving from Argentina and salt fish waiting to be shipped out. We came to a big bridge with lots of traffic and crossed it on a wooden walkway. Walked up some old streets on the far side of the bridge and found an antique shop. The nice young owner spoke good English. Changed some money in a bank across the street and bought some small items: inkwells, a little white vase with a golden chicken on it, a little flat oil lamp, a carved black brooch with flowers painted on it. A cruise ship had been in port yesterday, and some Americans had come to the shop and purchased a lot of items for a museum of Norwegian Antiquities in Minnesota. The man's mother had three lovely antique dolls with porcelain heads which had belonged to her grandmother when she was a child. The woman hoped to sell them for two hundred dollars and buy a car.

They recommended an interesting walk. We walked long

blocks up a quiet street of houses that fronted on the sidewalk. Few pedestrians. Much interesting detail in the architecture, in the occasional glimpse of the yards behind the houses. When we reached the top of the hill, we could look down on the whole city and see the harbor area and the ships beyond. We went down a steep unpaved road to a pedestrian bridge with a red arch over either end of it, and a system of gears and chains painted black to enable it to be opened for river traffic. Along the river, toward the harbor, stood old warehouses on pilings.

From the bridge we walked to the center of the city. The window displays in the shipping area were stark and unattractive and seemed to carry the same order of "useful" merchandise one finds in the stores in New Zealand.

At a newsstand in a department store Dorothy spotted my name on a book written in Norwegian. Bought that and a *Newsweek* and a Paris *Herald Tribune*, and soon it was time to take a taxi back to the ship.

In a curious way it was a memorable day. The bright cold, the stillness of the streets, the flower and vegetable stands in the town plaza. The only other choice ashore would have been to visit Trondheim Cathedral and the Ringve Musical Museum, on Tour No. 57, with a brief stop at the Stiftsgaarden, the largest wooden building in the country and the king's royal residence when he visits the city.

I have a very low tolerance for gothic cathedrals, especially when visiting one takes time from the primary pleasure of watching the people, listening to them, seeing how they live. I always remember a cartoon in *The New Yorker* showing two plump middle-aged ladies outside a cathedral. They have cameras and guidebooks, and one is saying, "We don't have much time, Martha. You do the outside and I'll do the inside."

Additionally, we are not intrigued with museums of historical gadgetry: old cars, old music boxes, the farm implements of yesteryear. They seem to amuse tourists. There is an increasing emphasis in Sarasota on this sort of thing, and, I suppose, all over the Sun Belt. Each such museum is far less instructional than what your local research librarian can dig up for you to read. The pert and chipper guides are more interested in amusing you than in instructing you. These museums seem to deprive one of the sense of being in a foreign place. They are large cubicles to hold tourists and contain no sense of place, only a vague sense of the past. We found our own sense of Trondheim, especially on the little walking bridge, looking at the warehouses where river trade had been brisk not long ago. We saw office girls buying flowers from the stand in the plaza on their lunch break. We heard an old man saying terrible words to his broken bicycle. We bought a lavender glass bud vase with gold trim and can see and smell the cramped little antique shop where we bought it.

Watched the ship break loose and leave. Beautiful and clear by then. Just about everybody out on the deck. Once we were under way, the wind of passage drove everyone inside. Cocktail party for the forty-seventh anniversary of a pleasant candy mogul and his wife. After dinner I went to Casino Night in the lounge. Played with the total abandon typical of playing with funny money, and did not take long to lose my last chip. Standing by the tables, I could feel the leg weariness of the long Trondheim walk, possibly no more than three miles, but a lot of it uphill.

Left the games marveling at how cross and touchy some players become when faced with a competitive situation. Glad to go to bed.

I remember one night when I wandered down to the lounge just as they were beginning to wind up the games. People take this chance to win some sort of Mickey Mouse prize very seriously.

The cruise director got on the mike and said, "There are only five minutes left in the competition, folks, so bet a bundle."

I was watching a noisy blackjack table. There was a lot of activity, and the dealer had been having a few drinks. There seemed to be a lot of good-natured rivalry at the table. A man pushed all his chips out in front and said, "I'm betting the whole thing, pal."

The old lady next to him was taking it all very seriously. She turned to him and said, "There's a five-chip limit in blackjack. You can't bet all that. It's against the rules."

"Lady, the man said bet a bundle and that is what I am doing. I am betting a bundle. Let it ride."

The dealer dealt the cards and the man won. Everybody else at the table was laughing, but the old lady was very grim. "That was cheating!" she said.

"Let it ride again!" the man said.

"It's a five-chip limit at blackjack."

"I don't care. I'm letting it ride."

The dealer dealt the cards and the man won again. The table was in an uproar. The dealer had another drink and scooped out enough chips to roughly match the pile the man had bet.

She turned around and spotted me and said, "Can he do that?"

"I don't really know. I'll go ask the cruise director."

I sauntered over and said, "Ted, did you take the limit off?"

"No, I didn't."

"Well, some guy over there is doubling up and betting thousands of dollars and if he wins a couple more times, he'll own the ship."

"Go tell him the limit is five chips."

"You go tell him. You're the cruise director."

I went back to see what was happening, and by this time he had won another hand and he had a huge mountain of chips in front of him, and at that the dealer picked up his ice bucket of chips and dumped it alongside. The table was getting a kick out of it, except for the old lady. Steam was coming out of her ears. She was still insisting that five chips was the limit, but nobody was paying any attention to her.

The man let it ride one more time and lost. He lost the whole mountain. Everybody—almost—at the table laughed, and the dealer scooped all the chips back into the big bucket. The loser couldn't have cared less.

The old lady turned on him, and with her face all squeezed up, she chanted in this little singsong voice, "Cheaters never prosper! Cheaters never prosper!"

It broke me up. I hadn't heard that since I was in grade school.

33

|||||||||||||||||||||||||||||||||||||||||||

Friday and Saturday, June 17 and 18

Norwegian Sea and Honningsvag

During the night we crossed the Arctic Circle, and by morning we were working our way up the inside channels along the coast. The water was bright blue instead of the gray-green of the fjords. There were very high, rough, jagged peaks quite close, covered with snow, and on the stony slopes near the water were little green farms, looking dwarfed and lonely with such tangled and inhospitable country behind them.

I well remember, when I was very young, my sense of confusion and dismay upon learning that there were many mountains in the world without names. I had thought a name indispensible to any mountain. Or at least, as in the Himalayas, a number. Here were too many for names, and too wild for such a civilian indignity.

Though the sun was out, it was thermal underwear time on the Flying Bridge, up there with the fur-hat, warmup-suit Nikon folk, huffing on their fingers and changing lenses and saying, "Wow!"

Later in the day we moved on and out away from the land, but the big white scenery kept unrolling off to starboard, the upthrust of sharp white ridges and peaks brutal and mysterious. One knew that man had never, and would never, set foot on those places. There was nothing there but a lifeless silence.

295

They were neither destination nor passage to a destination. Between the snow and the sea was the dull brown strip of the stony coast.

After dinner we went to a small party to celebrate the birthday of the cruise director, Alan Scott. John Merlo baked him a balloon cake that exploded handsomely. We then went to Alan's show and, after that, up onto the Pool Terrace for the dance. Still daylight, of course, and very cold. The first and perhaps last time in my life the ends of the sleeves of my thermal underwear showed below the cuffs and cufflinks of my formal shirt. The sun performed as had been promised. It did its sideways thing, slanting toward the horizon, and then touching it and beginning an upward slant, moving away from it, in effect a simultaneous sunset and sunrise. When the sun was close to the horizon, there was a muted quality to the light, much like the light that shines on the earth during a total eclipse of the sun. But at a little before one in the morning, after it had started up, the day became perceptibly brighter and we could see the sunlight on the distant white mountains. Dancing and drinking fended off the cold. There were maniacal smiles. It was a good place to be, and a good time to be there.

I had a little trouble with one of the important passengers about how we were going to come into the North Cape. We were going to come in from the southern side and go out over the top. He had been there once before and they had come in over the top and gone out the southern side, and by God, he wanted to do it that way again because it was best.

When I went through the bar he was with a big bunch of people, and he summoned me over and asked me how we were going to go in and come out, and I told him the plan. He became very agitated. He was going to get up a petition right then and there. He wanted it done his way.

"I don't see what difference it would make. Either way, you're going to see both sides of it."

"It isn't the same!"

"Tell you what. If it will make everything okay with you, I'll go out backward." This made the other people laugh, and didn't please him at all. But there was no petition signed.

We spent a long time docking at Honningsvag, a few miles

southeast of the North Cape. In my book of instructions it said that on the previous trip they had anchored out and had a launch to go back and forth. But in the meantime, the book said, they had built a nice dock, and that would make it a much better operation.

It didn't mention that the dock was only half as long as the ship, the wind blew from three directions at once, and they had no tugs. It was close quarters in there. We finally ended up dropping both anchors and backing in. It was almost as much of a hassle getting out.

Honningsvag is one Godforsaken barren dismal little town. Captain Olav Tviet told us he was up there one time when he was an officer on a Norwegian submarine. He had a faraway look in his eyes as he remembered how it was. The submarine was on a tour of the coast, he said, and they stayed a couple of days. While they were there, there was a local wedding, which is about the biggest event that can happen there. The town has no bars and no liquor. This was a community decision, arrived at by vote. Anybody who wanted booze would write to a friend farther down the coast, and the friend would mail it up to them in a package.

Olav said that because they were in town they were all invited to this wedding. When the party was in full swing, they ran out of liquor because of the extra guests.

This created a problem, so the postmaster got several fellows to help him, and he went down to the post office and unlocked it. They went in and proceeded to shake all the parcels, setting aside all those that gurgled when shaken to carry back to the party.

Olav said thoughtfully, "I don't think that was very honest. But it kept the party going."

Slept in the thermal underwear for four hours and got up at six for the docking at Honningsvag, and to be ready for the tour at eight thirty. There was a loud cold wind. What there was of the village was just beyond the end of the pier: some stark buildings with minimal windows. Not a tree anywhere, either there or up in the steep hills beyond. Took a short walk and hurried back, shuddering with the cold, as the rain started.

After breakfast we bundled up and they directed us to several spavined old buses. We got in and the buses went banging and bouncing up into the gray and dismal hills, sliding on wet clay, bounding over the rocks and potholes. As we climbed up out of the town we saw houses painted in pastel colors tucked into folds of the hills. Not a tree in sight. Rocks, mud, and here and there, in the shadows, a remaining scum of gray ice. The road swung around the bay, and we could look down into deep valleys with water below and hope the driver would go no closer to the crumbly-looking edge. The young driver went much too fast and ignored all entreaties to slow down.

We stopped at a hill where, a hundred feet off the road up a crude path, were some primitive tents in tepee style. There were Lapp women and children in native costume, looking like Eskimos, asking money from anyone who took pictures of them. A small round old woman came out of a tent and beckoned to us to look inside. She had reindeer hides on the floor, surrounding a pit with gray ashes in it. Even in the cold and the wind, a fierce smell came wafting out. Then she held her hand out for a tip for letting us look. There was reindeer dung all around the tents, and we saw several small herds of reindeer. They were the color of dirty sheep, and the size of very large sick skinny awkward dogs. They moved in a resigned, dispirited manner, and their antlers looked like afterthoughts, stuck on in a forlorn attempt to improve a badly designed beast.

After we piled back onto our bus, there was a lot of bitter wit about the garden spot where the Lapps lived. By then the windows on one side of the bus were covered with brown mud, and the sprinkle of rain had frozen on the windows on the otherside. At the top we stepped out under a gunmetal sky into a sustained wind of such great force that people were in danger of being knocked down. We crouched and leaned into it, clothing snapping and rattling, and plodded carefully to a big long concrete gift shop full of souvenirs of the North Cape.

One could go around the gift-shop area and out toward the edge of the cliff. There was a handsome monument out there, dedicated to the protectors of the North Cape in World War II. Dorothy did not trust her footing on the windy rubbly slope. I went out to take a picture of the monument with our waitress friends, Sandy and Beth, sitting on the edge of it, holding on, their hair snapping so smartly in the wind that it was stinging their cheeks. I had never before experienced a wind like that. It was absolutely steady, a constant thrust. Reliable sources estimated it at between sixty and eighty miles an hour. I would tend to guess toward the high side.

One of our dingalings, the tall thin languid Tootsie, she who had overtipped the Fiji cabdriver, was caught off balance by the wind, and suddenly she was running with long strides toward the edge of the cliff, bending forward from the waist, arms flailing, trying in vain to recover her balance. She was either going to stumble and pitch headlong at full speed onto rocks the size of softballs or she was going to run right off the edge of the mile-high cliff. By great good fortune Alan Scott was in the right strategic position to angle over and intercept her. He thought quickly and caught her by the arm as she was going by. She came whirling around like Raggedy Ann and fell to her knees facing the wind. He helped her back to the concrete building.

There were few salespeople in the big souvenir shop, and customers three deep trying to get rid of their kroner before it was time to board the buses. They wanted to buy things made of reindeer hide and reindeer horns, shoulder patches, fur hats, trolls, dolls, certificates of having been there, bells, carved polar bears, pennants, bracelets, and all kinds of clutter. Anyone who could get a clerk's attention relayed orders from friends close behind him. One woman yammered loudly, over and over, "Give me forty-eight of those bells! I want forty-eight of the little bells. Sell me forty-eight bells." Finally somebody quieted her down by telling her to write it on a piece of paper. It worked and she got the attention and the bells. Dorothy and I fed the last of our Norwegian coins into a slot machine sponsored by the North Cape Red Cross.

We went slewing down the mountain, the trip made more nauseating by being unable to see anything out of any window. Spent the last of the paper money in, of course, a gift shop in Honningsvag. A bell, an ivory polar bear, a cheese knife with a reindeer-antler handle, postcards.

The ship honked everybody back aboard, and we left and went up the coast and turned so that we were around in front of that great black cliff. There was a gray sea banging against its base. The wind was just as fierce at sea level as at the top, so constant that it had flattened the sea. Dorothy had a wool cap she bought in Finland, a knitted cap that came down over her ears. It had a tassel on top, quite a long one. She stood in that wind on the Promenade Deck, and the wind held the tassel absolutely straight out, motionless, as if it had frozen. When we were farther from the cliff, we could see the tiny cement structure up at the top. I wondered how Tootsie must have felt, looking up there. She would not have run off the front of the cliff, but off the east side of it, had it not been for Alan.

An hour after we left the cape area, the sea became very lumpy, the worst of the trip. Dorothy was laid low. I took Dramamine. In the early evening I went alone to a cocktail party given by an eye surgeon and his wife. (I must give his name: Dr. Snip.) I gave Dorothy's regrets. Quite a few others were missing. It became a sitdown cocktail party, with the occasional big shuddering heave of the ship that made people hold their glasses out away from their bodies so the drink would not slop out onto their clothing. A few guests left hurriedly. The late sitting was but lightly attended, and some of those left abruptly.

On that evening there was a perceptible change in the emotional flavor of travel. We had reached that far point. We had turned. We were heading for the barn. There was Scotland, the Azores, and Saint Croix still to come, but one sensed that relish would be diminished by regret that it was all beginning to end.

We had a cadet along on this cruise—a deck cadet, no engine cadet this time. They are young men who attend the United States Merchant Marine Academy at King's Point. As part of their program they spend so many months at sea. It is a very competitive program, and the kids we get are sharp and well-mannered, good with the passengers, and an asset to the ship. I had begun to wonder if the one we had aboard was wondering if I was conducting a course in Unexpected Problems.

We did get one very memorable cadet on a South Pacific cruise: Steve Harris, a good-looking dark-haired kid about nineteen years old, and a hustler, a real goer. His only problem was that his voice seemed to be still changing, and under stress he would break into falsetto, an odd sound coming from a husky young male.

On duty he wore his hair in a sort of mod wave across his forehead, but when he went on the prowl ashore, he would part it in the middle and flatten it back. He had a fantastic knack for creating problems for himself. I think after he got back to the academy, they must have retired his number.

On that trip we had a family who'd been on several of my cruises before. They had a son about eighteen and a fourteen-year-old Lolita, with a sly sultry smile and one very ripe body.

On the second night out, the mother came up to me in the Poly Room and said, "Captain, is the cadet under your jurisdiction?" It was eleven o'clock at night.

"Yes, more or less. Why?"

"We can't seem to find our fourteen-year-old daughter."

I stammered something about being sure there was some reasonable explanation, and let me check it out right away. So I went running around the ship to all the places where I thought the little bastard might be. I tried the rooms first, and then I went up to the Pool Terrace. There were several young people aboard and they had a record player, and they gathered up there at night. I checked them, and then up on the Boat Deck in all the quiet corners, and as I came down across the Pool Terrace, the door of a locker back over in a corner by the bar, a locker where they store tables, opened and out came Steve and the fourteen-year-old girl.

I took him away, well out of earshot of anybody, and said, "God damn it, you dumb bastard, do you know how old she is?"

"Well, sir, she said she was eighteen," he said, his voice cracking.

"She is fourteen, and she is very bad news. You stay the hell away from her. I don't want you taking any of these kids into your room. Furthermore..." And in great detail I told him the ground rules, which I had assumed he already knew.

That girl from then on tried to drive Steve crazy. She wore thin little cotton halter tops, and she would come up beside Steve and sort of sway into him. He would gulp and turn pale. Everybody on the ship knew what was going on. One day I was standing in the hallway in front of the lounge, and little Lolita came up and said, "Are you mad at me, Uncle John?"

"No, should I be?"

"You haven't talked to me for days."

"Do me a favor. Just stay the hell away from that cadet. Leave him alone. He's got enough problems."

"Everybody treats me like a kid."

"You are a kid. You are fourteen years old, and you are bad news. Just leave him alone and everything will be fine. There are enough other kids on the ship for you to have fun with, and enough activities going on."

So she leaned against me and said, "What are you going to do now?"

"I am going to go down to the movies."

"Okay if I go too?"

"It is included in the price of your ticket," I said, and started up to my room. She followed me. I said, "I thought you were going to the movies."

"Well, you're going too, and I thought I'd go with you, okay?"

So she followed me into my room and started looking at my pictures and souvenirs and things. She was barefoot, and she walked across the davenport and down across the other side, looking at things. I said, "I'm ready. Let's go. Come on."

Whereupon she jumped over onto my swivel chair, and as she did this, the chair swung and tilted and she let out a scream.

"Kid. Hey, kid. Please don't scream! I'll do anything, but don't scream. Just don't scream! Let's just get the hell out of here, kid."

She kept on harassing Steve, but he had acquired another problem. Here's the way it was finally reported to me, long after the event. The crew was having a party out on the fantail, and Steve was there. A waitress had her eye on him. She was a Basque. We all called her Carla. She had long black hair which she kept wound up into a bun when she was on duty, and which she let hang down her back when she went ashore. She was in her early thirties, and she had a habit of taking young officers and young sailors under her wing. She began to put the arm on him, and in the course of the conversation, Steve was coming on very strong, and she finally said, "You talk a lot, kid. I would like to take you to my room and show you how."

Steve said, "What makes you think I don't know how already?" But his voice cracked and spoiled the effect. Carla took Steve over, and I guess she thought she was going to really work on his education aboard. But Steve liked to go ashore with the young kids on the passenger list, so they worked out an arrangement where he agreed to come back on board at midnight, when, one might assume, she gave him a bed check.

In Tahiti Steve went ashore with a couple of passenger kids, and when he got downtown where they have open-air restaurants, he was walking along looking for action, hair parted in the middle. He saw a tall girl half a block away ahead of him with black hair hanging down her back. He thought it was Carla, so he ran up behind her and gave a playful tug on that black hair and said, "Hi, Carla!"

She spun around and it was a big tall Tahitian girl, and her boyfriend who was eight feet tall was suddenly there beside her, moving toward Steve with the intent of doing him some damage. Steve was trying to back away and explain the whole thing, trying to get out of the situation as best he could, when he suddenly decided to spin around and take some long steps out of there. He was too close to a telephone pole and ran into it and got a bloody nose. So his passenger friends helped out. They got the bleeding stopped and Steve cheered up and started to look for some action. He found a good-looking Tahitian girl and she smiled and she led him down an alley, and in very short order he found that he had made overtures to a very good-looking Tahitian fellow in drag. That was one of his typical days ashore. In the morning he would always start out saying, "Hey, wow, you won't believe what happened to me last night."

And people would say, "We believe it. Just tell us."

One time in Auckland, I was in the officers' mess having a quick solitary dinner when one of the pursers came in all excited. He had a little stammer when he got excited. You had to quiet him down to follow what he was trying to tell you.

It seemed that some woman had called the ship to get in touch with an officer who was no longer aboard, and the call

had been turned over to Stammering Jim. After a long conversation, she said she and her girl friend were coming down
to the ship to say hello.

Jim was convinced he had a couple of live ones, and for
some reason he wanted to deal me in on the action. "This g-
gal is about five foot f-five and a b-brunette and well built and
really s-sharp."

"Who said so?"

"She d-did."

"Jim, you haven't got a brain in your head. You should
have volunteered to meet them out on the street someplace.
Then, if they look like I think they are going to look, you could
have taken a walk, no harm done."

But he was convinced everything was fine.

I said, "Thanks for thinking of me, but no thanks."

I happened to be standing where I could see about halfway
down the gangway an hour later. Jim was busy at the purser's
desk. I saw those two turkeys coming up the gangway. One
wasn't really all that bad, but the other one reminded me of
the late late movie where Charles Laughton plays the part of
Quasimodo, the hunchback bell ringer. They went to the desk
and asked for Jim, not knowing they were talking to him. He
stuttered something about just a minute and came running to
me and leaned close and whispered, "What are we going to
do?"

I said, "I'm going to go have a drink with friends." I got
into the elevator and, as he hesitated, the door shut. I rode up
to the Upper Deck, and when the door opened, there was Jim.
He was panting hard. He had run all the way up the stairs.

"What are we going to do?"

"What is all this we business? I don't know what you are
going to do. I am going to have a drink with friends, who are
even now on their way to my cabin."

I found out later he ran from there to his room, locked the
door, and would not answer the phone. The two women found
their way to the bar, and there they managed to fall into conversation with a purser named Billy Burton Pool, an old southern gentleman quite partial to bourbon. They explained that
they were there by Jim's invitation but nobody seemed to be
able to locate the fellow. That gave Billy Burton Pool carte

blanche to buy them, and himself, drinks for the rest of the evening, signing Stammering Jim's name to the tabs.

In time Quasimodo began to feel unwell, so she went home. The other one, who was supposed to meet Jim, was not budging. She began to get loud. She began to make scenes. So somebody in authority told the watchman to escort her off the ship. She refused to go, so they called the local police.

At about this time Steve the cadet returned from his evening ashore and somebody told him that there was a great-looking woman up in the bar looking for action.

So his voice went up an octave and he said, "You know me. That's what I'm looking for too."

He went racing up to the bar but she was not there and he learned she was in the process of being thrown off the ship. So he ran back down the gangway and there she was, making a scene. She was in trouble because the police were on their way, and if they had to haul her off the ship, she would go to jail. Steve agreed to walk her off. She was quieting down by that time. If she was gone when the police arrived, she would be in the clear. So she and Steve were walking together late at night down that long cavernous warehouse structure in Auckland, which is the only way to the street. It was very quiet, their footsteps echoing, and who did they run into but Carla, on her way back to the ship. Before Steve could explain everything, she went into a tirade, giving him hell. "You rotten little bastard, after all I've done for you!" The girl turned on Steve and she started yammering at him too. Finally Carla went stomping off, and the girl realized she was wrong about Steve; he was only trying to do her a favor. They went out to the road to catch a cab, and she told him, getting a little more sober each minute, "This was very nice of you, kid. Come on, I'll take you to my apartment."

"I don't have any money."

She said that didn't matter. She took him home. Steve later said the place had wall-to-wall carpeting made of fur. He got back to the ship in a cab she paid for, at about six in the morning. At that point he was staying in a passenger room—he had to be moved around as space became available. Carla had gotten in there and she was waiting for him. When he walked in, she went at him, hollering at him and trying to belt

*him. He was trying to explain. Finally she picked up a whole
big carton of Life Savers. Steve liked them, and she had given
him the carton. She threw them at him and he ducked and they
hit the bulkhead and burst open, and spilled all over the cabin.
She had her boots off, and she grabbed them and started trying
to bash him with the boots. He took them out of her hand,
opened the door, and threw them out into the alleyway. When
she bent down to pick them up, he put his foot against her rear,
shoved her out, and slammed the door and locked it.*

*When he told the whole story later on, somebody said, "You
sure lead an interesting life. Was that the end of it?"*

*"Well, no. I could hear her out there crying and I felt sort
of sorry for her, so I let her back in the room again."*

*One day Steve came to me, very concerned, and said, "Sir,
I have really got a problem."*

"Such as?"

"Carla has missed her period. What am I going to do?"

*"Steve, what you can do, you can look on the brighter side.
Just think, when you graduate from the academy, and it's a
beautiful spring day and you're all dressed up in your formal
uniform, and your mom and dad show up, you get word that
Carla is at the gate. You go out there and she has your little
one with her, and you bring them into the academy and you
say, 'Mom and Dad, I want you to meet Carla.' They might
look pretty shocked, so then you say, 'Mom and Dad, don't
worry. She is really great. She can handle a table for eight.'"*

*We had an audience by then, and Steve looked around and
said, "You guys think this is funny. Everybody picks on the
cadet."*

*He was a fantastic kid. One time in Samoa, we were there
just a few hours. We arrived at seven and were due to sail at
noon. Everybody went off to ride the cable car. We had a lot
of cargo to move and only five hours to do it in. There were
all the customary foul-ups. I had Steve working with me. Tell
him to do something, and he would do it quickly and correctly.
He was better than any mate I had on the ship. He would follow
through. He and I were really going at it all morning. We were
up and down that gangway fifty times, chasing down the way-
bills, making sure all the cargo got out, and taking care of all*

*the details involved in working general cargo. It was a suf-
focatingly hot day, and our shirts were wet through.*

*We went like tigers, and at the end of it, I said, "Steve, you
really hustled all morning. This is the way you have to work
on a general cargo ship. It is really worthwhile. When we
finish here in a couple of minutes, you will really feel that you
have accomplished something. You will really feel that you
have done something. Now, wouldn't you really rather be doing
this than be out there trying to ball the natives?"*

*And he said in that uncertain voice, "Well, if it is all the
same to you, I would like to go out and try to ball the natives."*

*On that trip people were sitting around the Pool Terrace
one day, talking about their purchases, the souvenirs and junk
they had bought during the cruise. Pam Cavan, one of the
entertainers, was there. Steve had bought a great big batch of
horrible-looking wood carvings in Fiji. He piped up and said,
"Miss Cavan, I've got some real neat wood carvings in my
room. Would you like to come and take a look at them?"*

*She whirled around and stared at him and said, "Kid, I've
heard all about you. Don't give me that wood-carving jazz.
I'm not, repeat, not going to your room."*

*"Everybody picks on the cadet," Steve said, with a hurt
look.*

34

||||||||||||||||||||||||||||||||||||||||||||||||||

Sunday and Monday, June 19 and 20

En Route to Scotland

The system of seas and oceans is a confusion. Above the North Cape I suspect that we were at some vague midpoint between the Norwegian Sea and the Barents Sea and not quite up into the Arctic Ocean. But we did come on down through the waters of the Norwegian Sea and into the North Sea.

Our turn, Sunday before lunch, to have a cocktail party. We'd grabbed the date far ahead. Sixty-five people. Arranged it through Ken Yoshinaka, the second steward, and Dottie, the girl in his office. For the sake of historical accuracy, the menu was a large shrimp bowl, egg halves with caviar, ham curls, and little toast squares with peanut butter and bacon on top. The drinks were Black Velvets and Bloody Marys. Pretty fair party. A few underestimated the impact of a mixture of half champagne and half stout and got attacks of the blind staggers and the empty laughter.

It was a dark choppy day on the sea. After lunch it began to get rougher, and Dorothy decided it would be best to take to her bed. In the evening, the dining room had thinned out again. Al and Emily Morgan had made it to all meals that day and had come to our party. But at dinner he looked not at all well, and it took him two slow difficult attempts to get up from the dinner table to leave, creating that Emily-look of sharp-focused concern.

Dorothy was well enough to have an evening snack brought. I ordered a nightcap in the room of two small bottles of champagne, but the bell man brought two splits instead. So we read for a time and drank his mistakes, thus ending the day.

Monday was sunny and cold. Hal Wagner gave a short and very informative talk on Edinburgh, telling us that the natives speak quite a bit of English. We packed up a big cardboard box of odds and ends for the room steward to stow for us until San Francisco departure.

Lots of sea traffic. Many giant oil platforms on the horizon. I played four sets of paddle tennis, then showered and changed for a large cocktail party before we went to dinner. Dorothy ate Norwegian elk. Al Morgan wasn't there.

After dinner we went on deck to watch the sunset. Saw a trace of the green flash as it went down. Saw a very small moon, and a ship, and the distant Orkney Islands.

Went back to the room and tried to make an objective analysis of why we felt so relieved that the next-to-last session at the captain's table was over. We had become fond of the captain. Very amusing, but at the same time quick and sensitive to the feelings of others. Considerate.

It was not, we decided, that we were particularly antisocial. Just that a dinner party three times a day overstresses the social mechanisms. There were some very strong egos at the table, requiring constant care to keep any discussion from becoming too abrasive. When conversation did become intense, one tended to be unaware of what one was eating—a shameful lapse with John Merlo in charge. Also, there was a great deal of unavoidable dawdling. One could not leave until the late arrivals had finished their dinner and their coffee, which meant too much time spent at table. We looked forward with a sense of holiday to getting back to our hideaway, our banquette corner with Sandy the waitress, our private conversations, our own schedule for arriving and leaving, and the kind of wine we wanted when we wanted it—instead of a sort of wine grab bag each dinner hour.

Speaking of wine, I remember one short trip where my table list was made up for me by the company office for the leg from

San Francisco to Honolulu. I didn't make dinner the first night, which is not uncommon when leaving port. The second night one couple was missing. There is nothing too unusual about this. Maybe they were a little seasick. I didn't think much about it. The next night they were absent again, and I became concerned and asked their room steward if they were ill, so I could send sympathy. I found out they were both in good shape. When I found out what they looked like, I tracked them down and found out the husband spent all of every day at the bar, on the end stood, and his wife sat at a table just around the corner from the bar, and they hit it pretty heavy all day long. They were strange looking. I remember he had his hair cut short on top like a butch cut, and worn long on the sides. They looked well and healthy and seemed to be enjoying themselves, so I didn't worry about them any more.

The last night before we arrived, they showed up for dinner, and she was seated at my right, with her husband just beyond her.

When the others had arrived, I turned to the couple and said, "It's sure nice to have you folks here at dinner."

The man yelled, "What did he say?"

And his wife turned to him and yelled, "He said they missed us."

It made people at nearby tables give a little jump and then stare at us. I realized we had acquired a deaf alcoholic. It certainly started the dinner off in great shape.

I was going to order the wine that last night, and I turned to him and yelled, "Would you like some wine?"

"What did he say?"

"He wants to know if you want some wine."

"Of course we want some wine."

Rather than go through a shouting match about what type of wine they might like, I passed him the wine list and he perused it for some time and then yelled his choice at the wine steward, driving him back a step.

Since he had made the selection, I let him taste the wine. I had bought the wine for the table. Everybody had the appropriate wine glasses in front of them. The steward poured a little in the man's glass and he tasted it and nodded, and the *steward started to go around the table to fill the glasses, but the man reached and grabbed him and said, "Put the bottle down right here, son." The wine steward shrugged and did as he was told. "Give me that cork, son." He put it down. The man filled his wife's glass and his own and turned his attention back to the food on his plate. Everybody at the table just stared at him. He didn't notice. I ordered more wine. When they were through, there was about a third of a bottle of wine left. The man corked it, stood up, and without a word took his wine and his wife off to the bar.*

One trip I had a very good table. The people were a lot of fun. We lost one at Honolulu, but a new passenger was coming aboard who had written on his table assignment request, "I always sit at the captain's table." The agent told me he was a retired executive from some big important conglomerate, and he was traveling with his nanny, a nurse who pushed him around in the wheelchair he used most of the time. He had told the agent it would not be necessary to have the nurse at the captain's table. She could sit somewhere else. But he was going to sit at the captain's table as he always had and always would. He boarded in Hawaii as I was coming out of the dining room, and they called me over to meet him. The nurse folded the footrest on the wheelchair and he got up. Before he could make it, he had to rock back and forth a few times, the way Harvey Korman and Carol used to do when they played the ancient couple on the Carol Burnett Show. He made it up and teetered back and forth until he got his knees locked, and we shook hands.

"Very glad to meet you. I understand you want to sit at my table."

He was a very tall, thin old boy, with a long thin face. "I always sit at the captain's table," he said in a shaky old voice.

"I'd be happy to have you there, but you've probably traveled a lot more than I have on passenger ships, and you may have a preconceived idea about a captain's table. Mine doesn't always run the way you're probably used to."

"What are you trying to tell me?"

"I'm not an old passenger skipper, and my table sometimes gets out of hand, especially the table I've got at the present time, the one you'd be joining. The people have been there *quite a while. They're very relaxed, and I don't think it is going to measure up to what you expect from a captain's table."*

"I don't understand what you're talking about. I always sit at the captain's table."

"Okay. You're welcome to join us. But if you can't take a little needling and a little raucous behavior, I'd suggest you'll be happier at a nice table for two with your nurse."

The night after we left Honolulu the table picked up full steam again, and we were going on with things that had happened before Honolulu, like the night I had borrowed a passenger's monocle and lost it in the French onion soup when I couldn't hold it in place. They were all pretty loud, and the jokes were good but off-color.

After dinner the old boy said, "I can't believe this! I've been traveling all these years and I . . . I can't believe this! I've never seen a captain's table like this before."

"Sir, I warned you. This is the way it is, and this is the way it's going to be, from here to Sydney."

For two or three nights he kept telling me that he couldn't believe it. Then he started believing it and actually started enjoying it. He even ended up by taking part, as best he could.

If it had been that world's worst table, the one with Freddy the Magistrate, Norman and the fritters and the drippy fork, and big Barbara, I don't think the old boy could have adjusted.

That table came to an end at New Zealand. Freddy the Magistrate had told me many times during the trip that he was going to take me to his club, and I kept telling him that I appreciated the thought but my time was never my own in port, and I didn't think I could get away.

After we got the passengers off in Auckland and I had more or less forgotten about the Magistrate, I was paged and told somebody was having trouble with a car. I suggested they get hold of the chief mate, but the operator said the party wanted to talk to me. It was old Freddy, over on the dock, double parked, waiting for me to come out. I said, "I told you I don't think I can make it. I've got some other people coming down on business, and I'll have to take a rain check."

"Fine. We'll only be gone a little while. I'm waiting right here doubled parked on the dock."

There was no use arguing with him when he had his hearing

aid turned off, so I decided to get it over with. I expected to see a big Mercedes with a chauffeur. The pier there is double deck, and Freddy was up on top with a yellow British sports car about eighteen inches high, eight feet wide, and seventeen feet long. And nobody to drive but Freddy, who I had guessed was almost eighty and had frequent attacks of the shakes. I shook hands with him and told him that I really had to take a rain check, and I would make it next trip.

"Fine," he said. "Get in and I'll have you back in no time at all."

He had trouble climbing down into it, and he had trouble finding out how to start it. "It's a new car," he said. "My nephew has been breaking it in for me."

When he got it going I grabbed a big handle near the windshield and he went zooming backward, almost off the top of the pier, scaring the hell out of me, and then he went forward. I think you are supposed to go down that ramp to the street at ten miles an hour. Freddy the Magistrate went down there at thirty-five and hit the street and went right on out into a bunch of traffic. Brakes squealed, horns honked, people yelled, but Freddy drove right on like Mr. McGoo, trying to light his pipe as he drove.

"Freddy, let me light your pipe for you. You watch out where you're going!"

"What did you say?" He had his volume turned down.

We sped through town on a busy boulevard. I could see ahead that a light was red and imagined an eighteen-car pile-up when we drove into the cross stream of traffic at sixty-five miles an hour. But so help me, just as we got there, the light changed and the traffic opened up, and Freddy went shooting through. We were getting farther and farther away from the ship, and he was keeping his foot jammed down on the gas pedal. I think he had it in one of the lower gears.

I yelled, "Fred, I've got to get back to the ship! I've got some people I have to meet. I really think I should get back."

He was still trying to light his pipe. He looked over at me and said, "What did you say?" I gave up because I didn't want him looking at me at all.

He yelled at me that we were sightseeing, and then we were going to his house. We drove to a nice section of town and pulled up in front of a mansion. We went in and I found out he hadn't even been home yet. He'd gone from the ship to his office and transacted some business. We got out in the driveway and Freddy said, "This is my house and this is my view." A middle-aged woman came out to greet us, and he embraced her and gave her a pat on the behind and said, "And this is my housekeeper."

We went into the house and Freddy started showing me the library, the gallery, and the portraits of his ancestors. Soon a nice elderly lady came downstairs and was introduced as his wife. We had a little chat and I kept looking at my watch and talking about going back to the ship. Freddy pushed a button, and a whole section of library wall slid aside and there was the bar. He asked me what I wanted to drink and I said I had to get back to the ship, no thanks, so he smiled and fixed me a drink and handed it to me. I saw I was going to have a problem trying to get back. I was making conversation with his wife and with Freddy, and I was saying what a good time we had aboard. Then I said we really had a good time at our table at dinner. And stepping up the volume a little in case Freddy had his turned down, I started to name off the people at the table, starting at the other side and working my way around toward Freddy and his mistress.

Freddy froze and stared at me and then said, "I think I'd better get you back to the ship." He hustled me right out of there, telling me that it was only twenty minutes back, because he had brought me the long way around.

On the way back I found out it was twenty minutes by air, and also twenty minutes in that yellow car. He got the same break from the fates on the way back, with a miraculous parting of the traffic whenever there was an intersection. I held onto that handle near the windshield with both hands, and a lot of the time I kept my eyes closed.

When the ship stopped other times at Auckland, there would be a message from Freddy that he wanted to pick me up and show me the town, but somehow I never made it.

Shore-side hospitality can be an illusion. I remember one time when Manny, the Hungarian maître d'hôtel who hustled tips for the chore of sitting people at my table, overreached himself a little.

During the course of a cruise you meet a lot of people and everybody exchanges cards, and they are always saying, "You must look me up if you ever get to Phoenix," or Tulsa, or Albany. "I'm a member of the umpty-ump country club and we'll play a little golf." And there I am with their card. I've got three and half pounds of cards by now. Maybe I could go freeload for a year, but I can imagine how shocked some of them would be if I suddenly showed up on their doorstep.

On one trip Manny met some wealthy people from Shreveport, Louisiana. They had an attractive older daughter, and Manny was trying to make a few points in that direction. He hovered around them for the entire trip, and during the course of some after dinner brandy, Manny mentioned he might be taking a trip down that way. They said, "Manny, if you're ever in Shreveport, please be sure and give us a call."

Two months later they were in their palatial mansion and the phone rang and it was Manny.

"Nice to hear from you," they said. "Where are you?"

"I'm right here in town."

There was a silence, and maybe some whispering, and then they said, "Well, you must come on out and visit us."

"I'll be right out," he said.

Half an hour later the door chimes rang and they went to the door and there was Manny with two suitcases, smiling. After they let him in and had a couple of drinks with him, they recommended a nice motel, called and got him a reservation, and then drove him over there.

I have often wondered about this. If I pursued this thing, in how many homes would I be welcomed? And how many of them would take me to the motel?

Nothing ever seemed to work out too well for Manny. But he tried hard. He tried to make out with any eligible unattached female, be she passenger, crew, or whatever. I remember one time he met a girl in New Zealand who really wasn't too bad looking, and he arranged with her for her to fly over to Sydney and board the ship. He set it up with the purser and bought her ticket.

She came aboard while Manny was on duty, and after she settled in, she went up to the bar and had a couple of drinks.

Manny had the whole thing planned, a nice table back in a corner of the dining room with flowers and champagne.

While she was up in the bar having her drinks, one of the pursers told one of the young engineering officers, who had some of the same instincts as Steve the cadet, that there was a good-looking unattached girl in the bar who had just come aboard.

He charged up and introduced himself and poured a few more down her, and apparently she couldn't handle the sauce too well. She kept telling the engineer she had to go down to dinner, and he kept telling her there was lots of time. In no time at all it was too late for dinner, and he said to her, "That's okay. We can go have something in my room."

He took her up there, ordered some food, poured some more booze into her, and in due course the two of them went to bed. In the meantime, Manny had gone up the wall. He couldn't find his girl friend. Everybody had left the dining room. He couldn't get any answer from her room. He was charging all over the ship looking for her. He couldn't find her.

In the wee hours of the morning, she went back to her own room, and Manny got hold of her the next day. She told him she'd had too much to drink in the bar and had gone to bed and passed out. She hadn't heard the phone. He halfway bought this story, but when he checked with the bar stewards he found out she had been up there drinking with the young engineer.

The next night he planned a more elaborate thing. He hired a waitress, made a special menu up with one of the chefs, and they were going to have a candlelight dinner after the passengers were gone and Manny was off work. Once again the engineer met the girl up in the bar, once again they had drinks, once again she said she had to get down to dinner, and once again they headed for a room. He knew if he took her back to his room, Manny would be a problem. The bar stewards had told him Manny had checked on what happened the previous evening.

So they went to her room. She had an inside room, one of those rooms where, as you walk in, there is a chest of drawers just inside the door. The door opens inward, and if you pull one of those drawers out, there is no way anybody can get in the room. It blocks the door like a big latch.

After drinks and love, she went sound asleep. The engineer took the phone off the hook and went to sleep too. Manny was really irate. He had paced back and forth waiting for her until it was too late for the special dinner. He ran all over the ship. There was no one in the engineer's room. The operator said the phone in her room was off the hook. He went up there and banged on the door until the passengers complained about the noise and they ran him off. Finally, he got hold of a passkey somehow and went up and opened the door, but it only opened a half inch on account of the drawer being pulled out.

"I know you are in there!" he yelled. "Come out! I paid for your ticket!"

But she was dead to the world, and he made so much noise they had to roust him out of there again.

When we got to the next port, the girl disappeared. It was as far as her ticket went. Manny hunted high and low for her. He was in a fury. The son of one of the pursers had flown down to the port with some friends, and there was a big party, lots of young people. Somehow the girl got caught up in this party, which lasted all the time we were there.

When the ship was pulling away from the dock, everybody was out on deck, and Manny looked over toward the dock and there was the young son of the purser, on leave from the army, and he had Manny's girl friend braced up against a post, and neither of them was aware there was a ship within fifty miles.

"That's my girl!" Manny yelled. "There's my girl! I paid for her ticket! I paid for her ticket! There she is!"

He was practically foaming at the mouth as we moved on out of sight of the happy pair. And Manny was such a well-beloved sweetheart aboard, everybody really enjoyed the whole thing.

35

||||||||||||||||||||||||||||||||||||||||||||

Tuesday and Wednesday, June 21 and 22
Leith and Edinburgh, Scotland

Overslept, and at breakfast we seemed to be the very last passengers in the dining room. But there were several tables of the usual port moochers: official types, gangster types, clerical types. A ship can be very sturdy in the winds and the seas, but very fragile when dealing with the shore people.

The first time we traveled on the *Mariposa*'s sister ship, the *Monterey*, we arrived in Sydney to find out that the dockworkers would have nothing at all to do with us. We could not dock. They would not supply launches. They were in this tizzy because Nixon had announced a heavy bombing program for Hanoi. There were passengers leaving the ship there, and new ones coming aboard. And so the ship's motorized lifeboats were pressed into service.

Hal Wagner was the chief purser on that trip, and I remember standing near him as a smallish, stocky, very excited Australian, who was leaving the ship there, complained bitterly. He was about to go ashore in the lifeboat with his wife and suitcases, but he was leaving behind an item that would not fit into the lifeboat.

"What about my Mercedes?" he demanded. "What about my Mercedes?"

Hal, who was trying to do nine things at once, looked down

upon him and smiled and patted him on the shoulder and said, "Look at it this way, sir. Your car is going to be a little bit better traveled than you." And it was off-loaded at, I believe, Fiji, for shipment back to Sydney by the agent there.

After dithering about and phoning the home offices, New Caledonia was added to the schedule, and we took off. Within a couple of days all passengers were given certificates making them members of the Sydney Bridge and Opera House Watchers Society.

The U.S. maritime unions decided that this high-handed procedure was unfair to the working seaman and avowed that no more Australian ships would be serviced at U.S. ports until they mended their manners. It so happened that a refrigerator ship with $6 million worth of Australian beef was entering New York harbor at the time this retaliation was announced. There was an abrupt change of policy.

The freeloaders having breakfast that morning on the *Mariposa* were people who had it in their power to delay the ship and make the port stop a lot more expensive than had been projected. So they ate the gargantuan breakfasts, enjoyed speedy service, and found the world to their taste.

We missed the ten-o'clock shuttle bus and took a taxi to St. Andrew's Square, Edinburgh, where I changed some money. We did not expect much of the weather, as the city is actually more northerly than Goose Bay, Labrador, but it was sunny and reasonably pleasant out of the wind. We took the obligatory and expensive walk down Prince Street. It has long been famed as a place of elegant shops and wonderful merchandise, but it was our impression it was beginning to curl at the edges. Honky-tonk was elbowing its way in. The junk stores were taking over, and some of the better places were pulling out and moving a few blocks up the slope. Doubtless there were others closing for good.

But we did find things we coveted. Tweed jacket, turtle-necks, cashmere ties. One department-store display window had Dorothy shaking her head. The elegant plaster models in the window were dressed in thin lavendar and white voile and eyelet ruffles, but they also wore tan pumps with heels, with white bobby socks.

Walked to the end of Prince Street and had lunch at a

somewhat dubious-looking hotel called the Caledonia, where they made excellent Bloody Marys and where Dorothy won ten pence from a slot machine.

After lunch we took a cab to the Grassmarket area, where we were told we would find antiques. Found nothing attractive in antiques. Most of the stores were closed. This was a very old section: old buildings, roads winding off in narrow confusing directions, a small park packed full of skid-row drunks. Came upon a shop called the Portcullis, which seemed to be half bookstore and half souvenirs, art objects, and oddments. I found several of my titles in stock in hard and soft covers and had a long talk with the book partner while Dorothy was prowling through the other part of the store. It is an unusual store where one can buy: charms, heather pins, reproductions of ancient prints, a mohair lap robe, stationery, neckties, postcards, a small bronze Shetland pony, and fieldstones with elegant paintings of wild life on them, otters and mallards and raccoons.

Kept careful track, as usual. I translate every price back into dollars and enter everything on the customs forms. I do this as we go along. Sort of fussbudgety, but it pays off. If they poke around in your luggage, nothing has been overlooked. There is no point in stinting on the purchases of items you see and want, because the duties on the stuff over the duty-free limit will average out at from six to nine percent. I am not talking about making major purchases—diamonds and furs and automobiles. I don't know how duties run on such items. I speak of what we buy, and what most travelers buy: gifts and gadgets, souvenirs and clothing items and luggage items, and small art objects and handicrafts.

When we walked back from the Portcullis, we walked through the long park beside Prince Street, which slopes up toward the somewhat gloomy array of castles on the ridge. It was, they said, the first warm afternoon of the season, and all over the expanse of rolling green the bodies were sprawled, faces upturned to the sun, fishbelly flesh of the clerks and shopgirls and secretaries striving for that first pink flush of the outdoor season.

We hurried to St. Andrew's Square, saw the bus pulling away, and took a taxi back to the ship. We were heavy-laden with packages. Rested, changed, went for cocktails in the captain's quarters. A mob scene. We gave him a grouse-claw cockade for his civilian hat.

During one of the special Mariner cruises to the Islands, we had a series of Hawaiian parties ashore at the major hotels. When we stopped at Maui, the party was at the Intercontinental. I went over there early to participate in the reception for the cocktail hour. I had on a brand-new Hawaiian sport shirt and slacks. The shirt was so unusual, I was sure I'd never see anyone else wearing that pattern. So of course Chief Steward Jack Abramson showed up in the identical number.

People were just getting off the bus and milling around after they got inside. I was talking to a group when a lady backed into me. I turned around and said, "Pardon me." She did a double take and then said in a very loud voice, as I think the dear old thing was slightly deaf, "Oh! It's you captain! I didn't recognize you with your clothes on." I kept hearing about that for the rest of the cruise.

Down to the final dinner at the captain's table and said goodbye to the group. Al Morgan was at dinner, looking very bad, moving with difficulty. Emily was furious. They'd had a confirmed appointment with a local specialist, but his office told them that the doctor had had to go down to London. So he had received no attention, no transfusion. The ship's doctor was suggesting that they fly home from there. But they would be able to see the specialist tomorrow.

On Wednesday morning we made the ten-o'clock shuttle bus, standing room only. Went back to Dunn's and bought tartan vests as gifts for the men in the family, and a Black Watch cap and tweed hat for me. Bought mohair material and a mohair cape at Jenner's and had them sent to New Zealand. Almost noon when we left there. Edinburgh is dirty, very noisy, and very pretty. Heavy bus traffic. Diesel stink and air brakes. Lots of public flower beds. Nice vistas. Walked up to George Street looking for netsuke. Found only some Hong Kong junk. Walked over to Queen and Hanover to case the Chinese restaurants, but the menus posted outside were more Scottish than Mandarin.

Finally ended up in a pretty little hotel called The George. Flowering window boxes across the front. Walking gives the tourist multiple choice. If you use a taxi, you have to have a destination. If you have gotten your destination from a guide-book, a restaurant perhaps, the odds are in favor of it being on the way downhill. Every year thousands of innocent tourists take taxis to Raffles in Singapore to enjoy the bad drinks, slovenly service, open contempt, and indifferent food. If you are a durable walker you can make your own choices, take your own risks. The George had a buffet of typically coarse Scottish food. We were served by a Chinese waitress and a Spanish waitress from Madeira. Canned corned beef, cold legs of an unidentified fowl, scrambled eggs, very lumpy quiche, corn and rice, sardines and herring, sour raw cauliflower, chunky hunks of potato salad, good beer, good coffee, good vegetable soup, and some absolutely great cheese, and a small piece of chocolate cake.

Walked back to Prince Street and replaced the grouse-foot cockade, tried and failed to find a tartan dinner jacket, and then went into the park and took pictures. Took one of the memorial statue to a clergyman-humanitarian named Guthrie, on the off chance he was one of the Scots forebears of our daughter-in-law. Again all the white hide was asprawl around the gardens, soaking up sunlight, having shed everything legally sheddable. Took the transit bus back to the ship in time for a cold beer before the Edinburgh Police Pipe Band began playing at quayside at twenty to five. Very slow and solemn, with stately marching back and forth by the bagpipers. Even the baton and drumsticks seemed in slow motion.

Watched the lines being cast off. We chugged out through watery sunlight, past old harbor installations, and on out into the open sea, lifting and subsiding in the ground swell. Then below to change, reread the mail we had hastily scanned.

Learned that my novel, *Condominium*, had moved from eighth to fifth place on the *New York Times* best-seller list. Odd to be off doing so many things and having that book back there, plugging away, asserting itself. And paying for the cruise.

Learned that Al Morgan had seen the doctor, that his blood

count had improved. He was given chemotherapy, and the ship's doctor approved his continuing the voyage.

Went up for cocktails. Lots of conversations. It is odd how everybody seems to find it necessary to assert that what they did was absolutely the very best choice of all available. The motorcoach set bragged about their three tours. The golfers could see no earthly reason for coming to Scotland except to play two of the most famous courses in the world, one each day. Gleneagles was, they said, the better.

Down to dinner, back in our corner. Glad to be back, and were welcomed back warmly. Very good spirits. Three sea days coming up. We always welcome long stretches of travel with no ports. There is a lot of input to be sorted out. Impressions to be nailed down. On every cruise there are people who have but the most vague and general idea of where they have been. And those are the ones who never correct their strange notions of geography by studying a map. At the other end of the scale are the fanatics, who read nine books before arriving at each port, correct the mistakes of their guides, and do their sightseeing with a small tape recorder held close to the lips, thumb on the on-off button, muttering their impressions onto the tape for later transcription. Theirs is a deadly earnestness as irritating as the torpor of the totally uninformed.

So, the book was doing well, we were back where we belonged, sea days that would take us to warmer waters were coming up, the letters told us all was well at home, and Chuck, the wine steward, had recommended a dry white that turned out to be extra delicious. From what we could see of the captain's table, he now had a more dignified group than before.

36

Thursday, Friday, and Saturday, June 23–25
En Route to the Azores

Awakened at five thirty by the foghorn, and soon thereafter the seas became bumpy. A few hours later when the fog lifted, the lumpy sea turned into a long slow swell.

We are adjusting to Azores time by setting the clock back thirty minutes each morning at 1 A.M. for four mornings.

Jim Yonge, the chief purser, had apparently been stampeded into designating these three nights at sea as formal nights. One unfortunate aspect of this was that with no dry cleaning available aboard, the men who brought one evening jacket for the trip were beginning to waft a stale and acrid aroma, a splendid reason for not riding the small elevator in the evenings. The other and better reason is that if you use the stairs each and every time, you stay in better condition. The people who most obviously need stair-climbing are the ones you see waiting for the elevator.

In the late morning there was a little sun at the pool end of the Pool Terrace, with less wind and less motion there. Consommé and conversation. Looked out at the Hebrides off Ireland, locale of that fine book *Ring of Bright Water*. Waves were smashing at the stony shores, below the soft and misty mountains.

The Stanley kids, Eileen and Scott, were seasick green and

soon retired from view. Those long swells which move the whole ship as a unit, and cannot be quelled by any setting of the stabilizers, tend to thin out the public areas.

With Kaui's help, people were working away in the bar area on their costumes for the party on Saturday.

After lunch there was an announcement of whales off to starboard. Hurried over and spotted them. Or it. A very few, at any rate, and quite small. Looked like some variety of grampus, like those we've seen in the Tongue of the Ocean in the Bahamas. Nice to see, though, as they tend to jump all the way out of the water and fall with a mighty splash.

We were now aimed at the Azores, and everyone was hoping it would get warmer and the sea would flatten out. Tried to play paddle tennis, but too rough, court too slick. Poor time to be breaking elbows and hips.

Cocktail party on the Pool Terrace. Cool. Women in formals and wraps. Everybody eating too much because of the cold. Snacks were pizza, hot Japanese shrimp, bacon and peanut butter on toast. Still daylight there when a four-motor propeller aircraft with British and NATO insignia started buzzing us and dropping objects on both sides of the ship. They repeated this six or seven times. The captain told us they were dropping sonar devices and using the ship to check their antisubmarine gear and measuring devices. At dinner Sandy told us they had orders to secure the ship, string the lifelines, tie things down. So skipped the Stanley concert, took pills, went to bed, read Stegner's *Spectator Bird*. Crusty, wry, and deceptive.

Dorothy bought six yellow iris and two big white roses in Scotland. Jess, the room steward, found a tall stable vase for them. Flowers look especially fresh and good at sea. These were lasting well. Sea not much quieter. Periods of gray rain all day. Good day for sorting, recording, reading. Good day for the bridge players.

Emily Morgan reported to us that Al is much better physically, and his spirits are good.

We had no party to go to. We were grateful that we were not invited to the one large cocktail party held that evening. We heard later that the hostess, a lady of years who fancied herself a vocalist, had led her guests in song. In fifteen songs, to be exact. Someone counted.

* * *

I had to hit that one. I think I got there about the third song and left at about the seventh. One time when I had a birthday party she was aboard and came to the surprise birthday party because somebody had invited her. She brought her ukulele along, and she sang about twenty-seven verses of a song about me, which she made up as she went along.

She was a good-hearted person and a dedicated Mariner. On each cruise she would organize a choir and rehearse them and they would sing at the church services aboard. She conducted with great big motions. She insisted that they dress all in white, and she would have these eight or nine ladies trained to stand up when she made a certain gesture and sit down when she made another gesture.

It wasn't that they were bad. It was just that they were never very good, and they tended to sing a lot of hymns. It made the services too long.

On the North Cape trip she started asking Jim Yonge about her setting up one of her choirs as soon as she came aboard. He kept ducking it and came to me and said, "What are we going to do?"

And I said, "You are running the entertainment side. It's your problem."

So finally he went to her and said, "Every cruise you've been on, you've organized these choirs, rehearsing and all. You don't have any fun and you don't enjoy the trip because you have to spend your time whipping these people into line and organizing this choral group, so we all think that this cruise you should really relax and enjoy yourself and not be working yourself to death like you always do." I guess it worked, because we didn't have one.

So instead of another stand-up-and-sway party, we had a quiet sit-down drink in a corner of the bar, with a friend. But along with the first drink order arrived a bore and hemmed us in, one of the ladies who causes Dorothy to come back from the laundromat room with gritted teeth and fire in her eye. She claims that there is nothing like an overused laundry room to bring out the ultimate in stupidity, hostility, and aggression.

This woman's specialty was stupidity. The bore is one of

the hazards of the seafaring life. Were they sensitive enough
to realize you are trying to escape, they would no longer be
a bore. They cannot imagine anyone wanting to escape from
them. At stand-up parties it is often simple to get rid of one
by simply moving inside their space. Everyone has a distance
at which they feel comfortable. The average in head-to-head
conversation is about thirty inches. Media people seem more
comfortable at twenty. This space is a part of the territorial
imperative. Different varieties of birds space themselves dif-
ferently on phone wires. If your bore is comfortable at two feet
distance, you just keep moving into his space. This will make
him uncomfortable without his being able to figure out why.
And soon he will see someone across the room he would rather
afflict.

Big rolling swells, and another cool and misty day. Got up
early to go to an "eye opener" party scheduled for 8 to 9:30
A.M. About half the ship had been invited. Champagne, gin
fizzes, Bloody Marys, screwdrivers, with hors d'oeuvres of
bacon, sausage, melon balls, etc. Finished off with sweet rolls
and coffee. One couple came in pajamas and nightcaps, and
the chef gave the man a chicken from the kitchen to serve as
a substitute teddy bear.

Had a touch of normal breakfast after that debauch, then
went to Hal Wagner's talk on Ponta Delgada. I got snagged
to be a judge for the parade of contestants in the costume
competition. Should have stuck by the lesson I learned long
ago when I agreed to be a beauty contest judge in Sarasota.
You make one friend and thirty-five enemies. But I guess I
agreed because of my sense of guilt at never participating in
these group events aboard. Lots of people like to dress up.
Thirty-two out of two hundred plus aboard. Three categories.
Most Colorful, Most Original, Most Humorous. Humorous and
Original tend to overlap. Good thing that the contestant makes
the choice.

Caught a lot of static from the passengers afterward because
we three judges had not given a prize to the little old belly
dancer. One of the judges absolutely adamant in declaring her
act in very bad taste, saying he would disassociate himself from
the whole thing and give his reasons to the assembled multitude

if we dared give her any kind of an award. He took it all very seriously.

It turned into a very late evening. Everybody seemed all hopped up, overly jolly. Everybody ready for a port tomorrow.

37

||||||||||||||||||||||||||||||||||||||||||||||||||

Sunday, June 26

Ponta Delgada, Azores

Another misty day, with some warmth in the occasional sunshine. The fog had caused a delay we could not make up, so port time was changed to arrival an hour later than the originally scheduled 10 A.M., and departure moved an hour later as well.

We asked another couple to share a cab with us, and after the appropriate dickering, we hired a very imaginative and resourceful driver named Arturio and his seven-year-old Mercedes sedan.

When we left the town there were low clouds resting on the higher hills. Most of the buildings in town were painted in very soft, worn, faded pastels. The churches were in the black and white colors of Madeira. Off and on, all day long, we were reminded of Madeira. The gardens and terraces were very distinct in the distance, as they were marked out in black lava rock. We went to a high place overlooking a lake and a town, where we could see, off along the slopes of the hill, citrus orchards bordered by hedges made of taller trees, to protect them from the cold sea winds. From the overlook we could hear the individual bells of the cattle grazing on a slope far below, each bell of a slightly different tone.

Arturio took us to a very weird place where hot springs bubbled, steamed, and stank, scattered in random order over a flat trampled place, infested by tour buses. From there we raced to what he said was a good luncheon place, the Hotel Terra Nostra, but found we would have to wait because Tour No. 64 from the *Mariposa* got there first.

On some tour situations, hotels don't take it well if the tourists going around on their own get in on special things arranged for the groups that come by bus.

We had a very funny Australian fellow who made a lot of trips on the ship. He had made his money running a trucking line through the outback, from Darwin to a lot of nothing places. He was what they call out there a jolly good bloke, the type that whacks you on the back, and when he laughed you could see all the way down to his tonsils. He wore a baggy old pair of swimming trunks. His hair was pretty thin on top, and he always wore a towel wrapped around his head in the day-time.

The Jolly Swag Man, as we called him, had something stirred up all the time on the ship. At Bali Hai, Moorea, we'd anchor in the bay and the three Americans who ran the hotel would take the tour group over there for a local floor show, fried chicken, and rum drinks and bring them back to the ship. Since they could only handle a certain number of people, it was always made clear to everybody aboard that people who did not buy the tour ticket were not entitled to go to the hotel. The food was served buffet style. If you wandered in and saw the show for free, it irritated the people who had paid for tickets.

One trip a couple of the pursers conned me into going over there. I went in and met a couple of the owners who were there at the bar having a drink, and as I was talking to them, in walked the Jolly Swag Man and one of his buddies. One of the owners had bought me a drink, and suddenly the bartender gave me another drink when I was only halfway through the first one. I asked him where it came from and he pointed over to the Jolly Swag Man. At this time the pursers were discussing with the owners the problem of people coming in without buying a ticket.

So I waved to the Jolly Swag Man and acknowledged the drink and he waved back. The purser noticed this and said,

*"There's an example over there. Those two guys didn't buy
any ticket. What should we do?"*

"No problem," I said. "Throw them out."

*So the owners went over and asked them to leave. They left
under protest. That night back on the ship, as I was walking
through the bar area, the Jolly Swag Man accosted me and
said, "You bloody bloke, I bought you a drink and you have
me thrown out of the bar!"*

*"Sure, Jack. You bought me a drink and I was compelled
to buy you one back. The drinks over there are two seventy-
five, so the cheapest thing for me to do was to have you thrown
out. If you want your drink now, I'll buy you one right here."*

We waited in a pleasant little bar for the tour to finish eating.
They had a very nice wine called Dao for 36 escudos, or $1,
a bottle. When they called us in, the lunch was adequate:
vegetable soup, a fish course with salad, scalloped veal, and
a very good domestic cheese.

After we were back on the road, the overwhelming impression of the island was one of lushness. Bright new growth in
all the fields. Fat hedges of blue, white, and pink hydrangeas,
seemingly growing wild. Blue stalks of agapanthus. And an
unknown tree, dark gray-green, with very dark red flowers.
Nasturtiums, climbing roses, wild calla lilies, cornfields, to-
bacco plants, greenhouses full of pineapples, groves of fruit
trees, vineyards, potatoes, sweet potatoes, sugar beets, sugar
cane, chicory, tea. With the sea deeps as additional larder, they
can grow and catch everything they need.

A lovely place, facing change. Not much tourism as yet
because air travelers have to land at the big airport at Santa
Maria and take a smaller plane to São Miguel. But new hotels
are being constructed. Arturio took us down a quiet street and
pointed out the way the door keys to the front doors are left
in the doors in plain sight, an affirmation of trust rare in our
world.

We saw the initials F L A painted and spray-bombed onto
walls, fences, buildings. They stand for *Frente Liberdad
Azores*. People are restive, the driver said, because the Por-
tuguese mainland government levies big taxes and provides no
services in exchange. They send over police types and big shots

to run the island affairs, he said, and the people do not need or want this kind of patronizing administration.

In the town we saw very few young girls, but lots of young dark daring-looking fellows taking furious risks on noisy motorbikes.

Downtown they were having a small fiesta. Many of the older women were dressed from head to toe in dull dead black, from their stockings to the shawl over their heads, and most of the older men wore dark felt hats of an ugly shape.

Arturio said that parents still exercise strict control over their teenage children, but that the old ways are beginning to change, and he said that in a few years it would all be different.

Back to the ship. Had a phone call from the captain. He wanted to show me something.

In the Azores was where I really started getting hexed. There is no tugboat at Ponta Delgada, and after we took the pilot aboard he said we would come in and drop the anchor, not an uncommon practice, turn the ship on the anchor, and then ease her up to the dock, paying out chain as we went. Then when we left, we would use the anchor to pull ourselves away from the dock.

He told us when to drop it and we dropped it, paid out some chain, and got the ship swinging around. I told Coco as we approached the dock to let the anchor slack off. He did so, and then the chain didn't come tight again as we moved. I thought maybe it was dragging on the bottom, but we had about three slots of chain out by then, and the flukes should have grabbed.

Very soon it became obvious that the anchor was not holding because the chain did not pay out at all as we moved. I thought, Well, we've lost the anchor.

The first link right at the top of the anchor is called the patent link. It is the one you can take apart by knocking a pin out, and it is the weakest link in the anchor chain. I thought the patent link was probably broken.

When we got tied up at the dock and secured, I said, "We might as well pull it up and see what we've got." Coco started to bring the anchor in. I expected to see the patent link broken or no patent link there.

Finally through the murky water, Coco saw it and said, "Hell, we didn't lose the anchor. We've still got it." But when he heaved up a little bit more, he said, "No, we haven't."

That anchor had broken at its very strongest point, right down at the base of the stock. We brought it all the way aboard to get a good look at it. That great thick area of forged steel looked as if somebody had cut through it. I have never seen or heard of an anchor breaking in that manner.

So I had to go ashore and find a phone and try to call the office and tell them what had gone wrong. As we drove out through the port area, I noticed that they had landscaped the drive with some ship antiques, and we passed a huge anchor set in cement, about the same size as ours. Somebody suggested we send Marian Richards, our klepto, out to pick it up as a replacement.

Aboard, among the officers and staff, we had a disease called telephonitis which I was trying to control. When I sailed on freighters you never called the home office unless you were on fire or sinking. But on the passenger ships they call all the time. I told them it was ridiculous and they were running up an unbelievable bill. After I heard that in one day the chief engineer had phoned his boss, the chief purser had phoned his boss, and the chief steward had just finished a call to his boss, I put a stop to it. I told them to let me know when they were going to call, and we would check with the others and consolidate these calls and pool our information and our questions.

This new system started in Southampton, and when we made the first consolidated call, I found out it was not going to work too well. I talked briefly, and then the chief purser had a little chat, and then the chief engineer talked quite a while about bearings, and then the chief steward talked a long long time about buying wine in France.

Once I got Vice President Price on the line, he said, "How's everything?"

"Everything seems to be going along okay."

"Well, what's new?"

"Something went wrong with the anchor."

"What do you mean?"

"When we came in here, we dropped the port anchor and

swung on it okay and docked, but when we pulled it up, all we got was the top half."

"What do you mean, the top half?"

"From the patent link all the way down to the base of the stock. The rest of it is down there. Good thing it took enough strain to get us stopped and turned before it broke. We were coming in here pretty fast."

"There's the spare."

"I can't get it out of where it's stowed without help from a heavy crane on shore. It weighs seven tons. And there's nothing like that here. Or at St. Croix. What'll I do?"

"Well, get it up out of there and get it rigged in Panama. Nothing else can go wrong between where you are and Panama. Remember, save that top half for the underwriters."

Went to a small cocktail party that evening in Booth Three in the bar area. Had a quiet dinner and went to sleep thinking about the beautiful countryside, all the colors, all that intense green.

38

||||||||||||||||||||||||||||||||||||||||||||||||||||||

Monday, June 27

En Route to the Virgin Islands

At last, the first beautiful warm sunny day of the trip back, with the blue sea as calm as one ever sees it. At noon we were 337 miles from Ponta Delgada and 2,055 miles from St. Croix. At close to 20 knots, the white wake stretched out behind us as far as we could see.

I was on the Pool Terrace reading a *New Yorker* article on the Azores which a packrat friend had squirreled aboard with all his other reading miscellany back in Los Angeles. The article was from a November 1957 issue.

A woman came stomping onto the Pool Terrace, absolutely flaming with indignation because she had looked over the rail and seen a crewman hurling garbage out of one of the side hatches. "Into this clean and beautiful sea!" she declaimed. We wondered where she had been hiding aboard ship until now.

One of the perennial problems was garbage disposal. In the old days they just threw the garbage over the fantail and it trailed out behind the ship, and the sea gulls and the gooney birds would swoop down and have a feast. A long time ago the seabird union settled a jurisdictional dispute by giving sea gulls the scavenger rights for the first hundred or so miles out from land. The albatrosses take over from there until the ship nears land again, when they peel off and leave it to the gulls.

When the ecology thing became popular, some passengers began to lodge very strong protests about our dumping garbage over the side and littering the ocean. They complained to me and to the pursers. So we started paying overtime to some of the crew members to dump the garbage overboard at night. It would be saved up in garbage cans out on the fantail and thrown over after dark. Even then, a few staunch ecologists would be out there at night listening for it, so they could come and complain that we were littering again.

So somebody got the idea we should buy a big heavy trash compactor. We installed it out on the fantail and had several trial runs to see how it worked. It turned out a big square box of garbage or trash that was too heavy for one person to lift up over the rail, so we still had to pay two people overtime at night to throw those things overboard. The second problem was that unless a box contained enough glass and mashed cans and heavy things, it would float. We were leaving a trail of boxes floating along there way behind us, and the birds couldn't get into them. So we went back to the old system of dumping most of it at night, putting up with the abuse of the red-hot ecologists, and trying to explain that all we were doing was feeding the birds and the fishes.

What the lady had seen was a no-no. Things are not supposed to be dumped from amidship. But they do it: the new ones, and the ones too lazy to walk back to the trash cans on the fantail who decide nobody is looking. I remember one time we were having some kind of function on the Pool Terrace, perhaps the Equator-crossing festivities, and some very ambitious hard-working young kid walked out on the lower deck amidship and dumped a wastepaper basket into the wind. It was full of very small pieces of torn-up paper and carbon paper, and it got caught in the updraft and blew right back across the Pool Terrace and pool area. Si Lubin was the chief steward, and he vowed he was going to have somebody's hide, but I don't think he ever found out who did it.

One time after they started using the big plastic bags for trash, a crewman on janitor duty filled a bag and, rather than tote it all the way to the stern, stepped outside and tossed it

*over. It was about two in the morning. It made a pretty good
thump when it hit the water. A couple who had spent the evening
in the bar and then stepped outside to the rail, to watch the
stars, caught a glimpse of this thing and both insisted it was
a body. They started yelling* Man overboard! *and it got passed
up to the bridge and they got the ship turned around and started
back down the same track, using the searchlights and counting
noses. They finally found out nobody was missing, and added
two and two, found out who had thrown the bag over, and
logged him for it.*

Took a few turns around the deck on this beautiful day.
Played paddle tennis and got a sunburned face. The sun was
setting as we got to our table on the Pool Terrace for the prime
rib dinner. Very pleasant indeed.

After dinner we went and listened to Art and Dotty Todd
do their show. And during it, Art brought out his balalaika
class. They had all bought their instruments in Russia. Dozens
of them, all playing at once. Art took the lead; they were the
chorus. After two lessons and one rehearsal, they were wonderful. We stayed right there after the show and had nightcaps
until I managed to semi-disgrace myself by getting out there
at the mike and singing, along with a woman who had also put
in time in the Far East, that old Limey marching ballad called
"Ragged but Right." Went to bed with a solid guarantee of an
upcoming hangover.

39

|||||||||||||||||||||||||||||||||||||||||||||

En Route to the Virgin Islands

At six o'clock in the morning I got a call from the bridge saying that the ship wasn't steering well. They had it on automatic, so I told them to put it on manual and try it, and I would be right up. Joe Coco and I arrived at the same time. It was a half hour past sunrise. It was taking an awful lot of wheel to hold the ship on course, and as a result we were leaving a wake that wandered from side to side.

I hoped it was a malfunction in the steering engine, because we have two different setups we can use. We switched to the other one, but the problem remained unchanged. By then I was almost sure what had happened. It had happened to two previous ships of the same type of construction: to the Monterey, *several years back, and to one of the company's freighters in the Far East. These ships have an offset rudder, which breaks at about the midpoint, so you lose the bottom of it, the deepest part.*

But we had to make sure. So at midmorning I got on the horn and told the passengers that we were going to do some maneuvering and we were going to stop the ship. I said we were testing the steering mechanism. I knew they were probably all talking about the funny-looking wake we were leaving.

I went back with some of the others, when we were at a

341

dead stop, to a place where you could lean out and look down into the clear water. Sure enough, the bottom half was gone; you could see the torn edge where it had broken.

To get an idea of scale, imagine a hollow steel structure about two stories high, twelve feet wide, and three feet thick in the middle part, tapering in all directions for a streamlined effect. This thing is hung on a massive vertical round steel bar, just behind the big propeller. When you turn the rudder, it presents more of a flat side to the push of the water past the prop, so the stern moves to the side, away from the flat side, and the bow turns in the other direction. Only the top half of the rudder is hung on the steel bar. The bottom half is offset. It broke off at a point a little below the center hub of the propeller.

We fooled around on the flat-calm sea, trying to see how much control we had left. From dead slow up to almost full cruise, we had nothing. In fact, at dead slow we had less than nothing. The torque caused the stern to keep swinging slowly to starboard.

After we were back at speed on course, I told one of the passengers we'd lost half the rudder, and he suggested we take a look in the klepto's room. I put a call through to the company offices.

"What now?" they asked.

"Well, I'm about seventeen hundred miles from St. Croix, and it's a bright clear calm morning."

"What's new?"

"Well, about six this morning, half the rudder fell off. Same break as on the Monterey that time."

"Can you get to St. Croix?"

"If I don't have to slow down for weather. Forecast looks okay. But I can't get in."

"I can get a couple of tugs over there from San Juan. What's it going to do to your ETA?"

"We'll be on schedule."

"Somebody will fly over there. I'll tell the Coast Guard and the underwriter and the Bureau of Shipping."

"Where are we going to get this thing fixed?"

"Everything will be worked out. You don't have to worry. You won't have any problems."

"What!"

"I mean more than you've got already."

"Won't we have to fly all these people home?"

"Good God! Don't even think it."

"I only said it once."

"We wish you hadn't said it at all."

We noticed the zigzag track we were making across the blue morning sea, and it caused a lot of discussion. We guessed that maybe the automatic steering was out, and the manual steering was suffering because our best Hawaiian helmsman had flipped halfway through the trip and had been flown home.

By eleven in the morning, when we were invited to go have a drink in the chief purser's quarters, a few of us knew that we had lost a piece of the rudder and that we would steer pretty well at cruising speed but would be endangered by any rough weather. Seas pounding against the rudder and surging up inside its hollow structure could damage the rest of it or remove it entirely. There were four crew members, another passenger couple, and us, drinking Silver Fizzes. Then John Merlo arrived with a big delicious pizza. He was the star of the show, with his broken English full of pieces of Italian, French, and Spanish. He is from Trieste, studied at the Cordon Bleu, and cooked in China for four years. The captain stopped in for one drink, but he looked almost sick with worry and had nothing to say. We all knew that the fate of this cruise was being decided in the Vatican, as San Francisco headquarters of PFEL was frequently called.

After lunch, the more people who knew about the rudder, the wilder the rumors became. Our most probable destination was Norfolk, or Fort Lauderdale, or Jacksonville, or Havana. Puerto Rico seemed a good possibility: good air connections for the people getting off and getting on at St. Croix. We'd need a dry dock, tugs, Coast Guard inspection. Somebody said the *Monterey* was back in service in three days. They were there at the time. It would cost a fortune to fly all the passengers and their overweight luggage back to the West Coast. Charter airplanes were being lined up. Old ones. We were going to skip St. Croix and go right down to the canal, and tugs were going to take us through. Tugs take dead ships through the canal often. There were good facilities for repair and replacement at the other end of the canal. No, they were going to have an oceangoing tug meet us at the other end of the canal and take us up to San Francisco. At 10 or 11 knots, that would take over two weeks. An oceangoing tug was on its way right now to take us in tow and take us to Jamaica, Havana, San Juan, St. Croix, Jacksonville, Norfolk, the St. Lawrence Seaway—take your choice. By dawn we'd be in tow.

By tomorrow we might know what was going to happen, but we all suspected that any decision which came out of the Vatican would be based on a computer analysis of expense rather than on the safety and comfort of the passengers.

Before dinner we went up to the Pool Terrace to a cocktail party given by Waynette Schmidt, Edra Brophy, and the Morgans. After some urging, Al played the little piano up there and Emily sang some ballads. Very touching. A beautiful warm calm evening at sea.

After dinner we were standing outside the purser's office with a little group, talking, and Dorothy noticed the legal document which was permanently posted there. She suggested we read the fine print concerning liability. It said, ". . . not responsible for prior damage to equipment if previously unknown."

40

||||||||||||||||||||||||||||||||||||||||||

Wednesday, Thursday, and Friday, June 29–July 1

En Route to the Virgin Islands

The official word is that we are indeed going to proceed to St. Croix. Can't understand the thinking behind that choice, except that it does make it a lot cheaper to drop off and take on the passengers scheduled at that port.

There was a big Mai Tai party for the Mariners in the lounge in midmorning. The captain made a speech about our situation, dissembling for the sake of morale. He had recovered his aplomb. He made a personal presentation to each Mariner of a good-looking smoked-glass plate with a picture of the *Mariposa* and of a Viking ship incised into the glass. After it had gone on for some time, he paused and looked back at Allan Scott and said, "Couldn't we just slip these under their doors?"

One important gentleman passenger who sat near us said in a confidential, gassy whisper, "We're going to be met later today by a U.S. gunboat to protect six hundred imperiled citizens!"

At lunch the captain came over to our banquette corner, sat with us, and had Sandy bring him some iced tea. He told us that at the moment weather was the big factor. Dorothy said,

"I remember we've had two hurricanes in June, but they're not really very common this time of year."

He stared at her and said, "I was going to send you a Christmas card, but now you're off my list." I told him that if he had to hide at any time, we would give him shelter in our stateroom.

Quiet afternoon. After dinner we walked the deck in bright moonlight. Inspected the wake. Fairly straight. Helmsmen were getting the knack of holding it dead on. On automatic it wandered all over the ocean, because it undercompensated for the drift off course and then overcompensated.

On Thursday the gods of the sea were still on our side. Hot, clear, calm. Not much talk among the passengers about our dilemma. We just ask each other what will happen at St. Croix, and nobody knows.

A long hot quiet day, good for eating, sunning, napping, and some paddle tennis. When we had drinks before dinner, the bartender was slightly smashed, and he loaded our drinks. We did not realize it in time and thus it made for a very short evening.

NOTICE

There may have been a satisfactory reaction to the letters and petitions forwarded to Representatives and Senators on behalf of the *Mariposa* and *Monterey*, as a Congressional hearing into the fate of these vessels is presently scheduled for late July. Whatever the outcome, we will at least have our day in court.

On Friday, July 1, the incredibly good weather continued. Hot, clear, and calm. We trundled along across the sea, steady as a cathedral. A long lazy day, much like yesterday. After dinner we went to a special show in the Poly Club put on by passengers and staff. These are never what you expect. They do a lot of rehearsing. The end result is either much better or much worse than anticipated. This one was better.

41

||||||||||||||||||||||||||||||||||||||||||||||

St. Croix, Virgin Islands

An overcast day, with the sun shining through. Flat calm. Got up early to watch us come in. A batch of Immigration people came aboard off the pilot boat, set up their dumb fussy little tables, and afflicted us all with their dumb fussy little routines of inspecting the passports and stamping over landing cards. All this before breakfast.

We could see St. Croix dead ahead. Mostly flat, with some little hills back of the flats, glaring in pale sunlight.

Two small, ratty-looking, elderly tugs had come over from Puerto Rico to tow us to the dock. At a little past seven we could see the dock way ahead of us, sticking straight out from the nondescript harbor structures.

From that point, it took two hours to work us all the way in to the dock. The pilot was not used to working with tugs. The tugs were not used to taking orders from that pilot. Everybody was being extra careful not to let the ship pick up any momentum because, with so little rudder and so much torque, there was no way to stop momentum by ordering full astern. The stern would merely swing to port.

The scrofulous little tugs were constantly changing the angle of push and pull. At one point one of the tugs was pulling at a line which was made fast to the port side aft. He was pulling us along, and he was about amidships with the line extending out at maybe a 20-degree angle from the centerline of the ship. The pilot noticed that the ship's stern seemed to be swinging too far to starboard. He wanted the tug to increase the angle to about 40 or 50 degrees to correct this swing, while still moving the *Mariposa* forward at about .5 knots. So he called to the tug and told its captain to aim toward a misty point of land visible off the port bow. This would have given the proper angle.

The tug merrily dropped the tow and went bucketing off toward the distant point of land, with everybody on the wing of the bridge yelling to him to come back, waving their arms and using crude words. He hesitated, then came back and picked up the tow again, but he had to pull at right angles for a time to get us aimed properly.

After an interminable time we were close enough to hear the steeldrum band on the dock. Forty minutes later we were tied up, starboard side to the dock, bow aimed at the island.

A PFEL executive came aboard with other officials, a man from the American Bureau of Shipping stationed in Tampa, Coast Guard representatives, and others from PFEL. As we knew it would take a long time to make a decision, we might just as well spend the day in Christiansted. At a little past ten we shared a ride with several other people in a microbus taxi. Aside from some poinciana in bloom, the island was unattractive. It looked parched and dead and dusty. A dry island, more littered even than Curaçao, which we had thought—until we saw St. Croix—would take international first prize for the bulk and weight of trash per square foot.

I have often been puzzled by these welfare islands, by the Virgins and Puerto Rico, and by the urban areas of the United States. People seem to live among squalid and depressing litter with no thought of ever cleaning it up. Kurt Vonnegut once suggested, in an effort to increase the amount of reading in America, that people should have to turn in a book report to get their unemployment check. Would it be too strange to require people to bring in a trash bag full of trash once a week? Singapore is spanking clean. It sparkles. Any citizen can make a citizen's arrest of anybody who drops even an empty cigarette package on the street. The fine is $500. People take pride in that city. St. Croix is obviously full of people who take no pride in the place. Perhaps, under some circumstances, St. Croix is a nice place to live. But it is a depressing place to visit. It has been stomped into the ground by too much tourism, too much indifference, too much indolence.

The main shopping area of Christiansted is dirtier and less scenic than Nassau. Downtown seems to be one extended gift shop, with a few Arab and Indian stores thrown in.

We walked ourselves footsore, then met with friends at a second-floor restaurant in the center of town. Conch chowder, good hamburgers, and hot fudge sundaes. Found a Mexican shop with very good embroidered shirts, skirts, and tabards at extremely reasonable prices. Found a fair netsuke at a place called the Compass Rose. Bought other odds and ends at Cavanagh's. Found a cabdriver who, for a little extra, brought us back to the ship via the "scenic drive."

He took us through a dusty jungle, where thigh-thick vines hung, draped from scraggly trees. Termites had built nests as big as wheelbarrows in the trees. I could not believe so many of them were all active and occupied, so I had him stop and I went to a tree and brushed away one of the mud tunnels leading up the trunk to the nest. The little white fellows came boiling out, agitated and indignant.

The driver showed us some of the "deluxe houses of the very rich," and though they were certainly large enough, the architecture was without distinction. Saw low hills and sugar plantations. Back at the ship it was the consensus that this had been the only ugly island on the entire trip. And the only place other than Paris and Stockholm where people had been actively rude and insolent.

While we had been gone, a team of diver-technicians had done some underwater torch cutting and welding. They had cut off the torn edge of the break and had cut a flat piece of steel to the shape of the rudder in cross section, and had welded that in place, so that the hollow rudder portion was once again sealed from the pressures of the sea.

Based on this "repair," the decision was to let us proceed to the canal. It seemed to me then—and still does—that this was a curious and dangerous decision. It is 1,007 sea miles from St. Croix to Cristóbal. The ship would have been helpless in any bad weather. We could maintain course by going at cruising speed. If weather forced a speed reduction, they could not hold her into the wind. There was some nonsense along with the permission, saying, "accompanied by an ocean-going tug." At the speed we had to maintain in order to steer the ship, no tug could keep up with us. And if we slowed down to the speed of the tug, the ship would not steer. Certainly the Coast Guard and the American Bureau of Shipping and the PFEL management and the captain understood this.

They made the decision and told Captain Kilpack to take it to Panama. He could have refused. They had certified the ship seaworthy and hedged it with a nonsense provision about the tug. Captain Kilpack knew it was not seaworthy. It is quite possible that by refusing to take the ship further, its condition would attract so much attention no other captain would take that chance either. If the ship had to stay there, passengers evacuated by air, portion of passage refunded, ship taken under tow to a port where she could be repaired, crew flown home, that expense would bankrupt Pacific Far East Line. (It was not known then, of course, how near bankruptcy the line was, even without another financial blow.)

The captain made a decision he did not enjoy making. The long-range weather forecast looked good. We could be ready to leave a little after ten on Saturday night and reach Cristóbal early Tuesday morning.

I will never understand why the Coast Guard and the American Bureau of Shipping let us continue with only half a rudder. I have nice underwater color prints of the damage, taken in St. Croix, and I have had them mounted, with the date and the name of the ship and the voyage and a copy of the permission to continue. The next time I am told my ship is not seaworthy for some chickenshit reason like we're missing one life ring, I am going to show them the picture and ask them if they think that ship is seaworthy, and when they say, "Hell, no!" I will point to those underwater fellows who are pointing at the rudder and I will say, "Those guys are your Coast Guard people, and here is the permission to continue, and I brought that donkey all the way from St. Croix to Panama." It ought to be a lot of fun.

Maybe as much fun as the time we were missing a lifeboat. We were scheduled to make a fifty-day South Pacific cruise around the South Island of New Zealand and over to Tasmania and other ports we don't normally hit. This was billed as a Mariner cruise, and it filled up quite well. We had a full house.

Just prior to this cruise the ship went into its annual dry-docking in San Francisco, a ten-day lay-up period they have once a year. During the inspections they test all the safety items aboard the ship. One of the things they do is take off the lifeboats and test the davits. They put sandbags in the lifeboats to see if the davits will handle the load with the boats full of people. Well, they tested one motor lifeboat filled with sandbags, the Number 4 boat, and when they went to put it back aboard, they let it swing too much and it struck the side of the dry dock and its steel hull buckled quite badly, rendering it unseaworthy.

This threw everything into a big turmoil, and they immediately started repairs on the boat, which was pretty badly banged up. We left the dry dock and, after a lot of delay, got permission to proceed to Los Angeles without the motorboat. In the meantime they were feverishly trying to complete the repairs, and at the same time, just in case, they were looking for a substitute boat. They could find ones that would fit but they were not motorboats, and the Coast Guard would not certify us as seaworthy without a motorboat.

When we reached Los Angeles we found that Matson had a motorboat from a freighter, and it was supposedly the right dimensions. They brought it over and we tried to put in in place, but the davit placement on the freighter was different. When we tried to bring it up we could only get it as high as the Prom Deck and then the falls started to pull in and we couldn't get it any farther.

We saw there was going to be a delay. We were going through various plans of action. The cash customers were beginning to mill around, so I went onto the P.A. system and said, "You are all invited to a special cocktail party." That stopped the grumbling. After all, it was a cruise and nobody was trying to get to any given place at a special time, and we had only a very few passengers booked just to Hawaii.

At the end of the eight-hour postponement of sailing, things were as screwed up as ever, and the passengers were milling around again, so I told Jim Yonge to make the announcement of the delay this time. He wrote it out first and tried it on me and I said it would have to do.

Meanwhile, we had been phoning San Francisco, the office and the shipyard, and kept getting different stories about the progress they were making repairing our motorboat. The Coast Guard indicated that they would accept the motorboat that didn't fit if we could lash it solidly in place and secure it level with the Boat Deck. Then we could go to Hawaii with it, and by the time we got there the other boat would be repaired and could be airfreighted over. I was not happy with this idea, but it looked like the only way, so they proceeded to make this temporary lashup. We used to carry boats over the side like that in wartime, but I still didn't like it.

By then so much time had passed we had to respot the sailing board, and there was more milling around and grumbling. During the two-day delay, when we had to repost the board seven times, we put on a champagne party, a Bloody Mary party, and another cocktail party, trying to keep them all either stoned or occupied.

Finally, word came that our boat was on its way down from San Francisco. It was an overload, and we learned that overload trucks are not permitted on California highways on weekends. Maybe the Aliotos used their political clout to get a special highway permit.

We waited and waited. We could not get any word about where the truck was or when it would arrive. We couldn't reach anyone at the trucking company. Soon we were going to have to post the board again and change the sailing time.

The engineering vice president had the idea that because

it was an overload truck on special permit, the State Police might well know where it was.

He called State Police Headquarters and got some sergeant on the line and said, "Sir, I'd like to ask you for some help."

"What is it?"

"We are expecting...we are waiting for a lifeboat that's coming down Highway Five, and we'd like to get a progress report."

Click.

The V.P. called him back and said, "Sir, please don't hang up. Let me explain this to you. My name is C. J. Smith and I'm a vice-president of Pacific Far East Line and we've got a problem here. Don't hang up! We have our lifeboat loaded aboard a flatbed truck coming down Highway Five. It's an overload, and we'd like to know if you've had a report on it."

"Negative. No overloads move on the weekend."

"Sir, we have special permission from Sacramento, from the Governor's Office, to move this boat."

"It might have moved in the daytime, but I can tell you right now that no overload is going to move anywhere at night, no matter what."

We had visions of the driver in some all-night coffee shop waiting for dawn to start driving again.

Somebody else had a bright idea. He said he had a friend who was a real CB radio nut and he said, "Those guys love something like this. I'll get on my radio and call him and he'll get a chain reaction started and pretty soon they'll all be up and down the highway looking for the boat and telling each other when they find it, and they'll get the word back to us where it is."

He tried to fire up his hand-held set but his batteries were dead. We woke up the gift-shop woman and got some fresh batteries, and to my surprise he got hold of his good buddy in the valley. The friend relished the idea and started calling up all his CB friends. But they never did find the truck with the motorboat, and it showed up at three in the morning.

Coast Guard inspectors had been sticking around and had been pretty cooperative, but they were adamant about our not sailing without a motorboat. They wanted the one tested which

*had come down from San Francisco, and said that if it was
put in the water over in the shipyard and ran from there to the
side of our ship—which was about a mile—we could then hook
it up and be on our way.*

*Everybody rushed out to their cars and roared over to the
shipyard. We forgot to bring the engineering vice-president,
and left him fuming because everybody went off without him.*

*After they got the boat off the flatbed and into the water,
it wouldn't start. They couldn't get the diesel to kick over.
The problem was diagnosed as a depleted nitrogen charge.
There is an inner tank that holds gas under pressure, and
when that is released, it kicks the engine over so that it will
start. The tank seemed to be empty. So in the middle of the
night they drove over to Torrence and got a scuba diver out
of bed to open his shop to recharge the tank, only to find
out that he hadn't any connection that would match the one
on the tank.*

*By the next day we were beginning to lose customers. We
lost about six or seven, I think. Honolulu passengers. Finally
they let us go to Hawaii with the lifeboat that wouldn't run as
cargo, and the one that didn't fit lashed over the side. We had
instructions not to go one inch past Hawaii without solving the
problem.*

*Everybody was talking about the lifeboat situation when
we took off. When we had the first boat drill, the passengers
and crew assigned to Number 4 boat wanted to know if they
should assemble down by the one tied over the side or back
by the cargo hatch. They formed a group—the Number 4
boat people—and had their own parties.*

*Ironically, after we were at sea two days and the engineers
were caught up on their chores below, they turned their
attention to the motorboat, blew out some fuel lines, made
some adjustments, and in a couple of hours had it running
perfectly.*

So, after ten o'clock, after the young waitresses had swum
off the far end of the long dock, admired by the sailors
aboard the navy service ship parked on the other side of the
dock, the lines were cast off and our ratty little tugs pulled
us away from the dock and turned us around.

Art Todd started playing his banjo up on the open deck aft of the bar. He played all the way out of there, up until past midnight, ending up with a medley of Augustin Lara melodies, and then *Rhapsody in Blue!* By then the lights of St. Croix had faded from sight astern.

42

||||||||||||||||||||||||||||||||||||||||||||||||||

Sunday and Monday, July 3 and 4

En Route to the Panama Canal

Sunday was hot, with a greasy sea and those long slow rollers that fell the queasy.

A fine Chinese lunch on the Pool Terrace. Much talk about the condition of the ship. Many rumors about the rudder repair, one of the most attractive ones being that there had been a spare in San Francisco and it was even now being rushed by high-speed freighter down to Balboa to be installed there. Many jokes about scanning the horizon, looking for our escort, the oceangoing tug.

I played paddle tennis in the afternoon but quit at five because it got too hot. We had a following breeze. Came down and showered. No way to take a cold shower. Water is very hot from the hot-water tap, and medium hot from the cold-water tap. Many warnings in the *Polynesian* about conserving the air-conditioned air aboard. Finished shower and stretched out and read *Time* magazine until I was cooled off enough to dress. *Time* had *Condominium* fifth on its bestseller list. Hang in there, book!

A sweltering evening. Uncomfortably warm on deck at dusk. The captain stopped by and said hello in the lounge before dinner. Imparted absolutely no information and looked thoroughly worried.

The next morning was windy and hot, with a good sea running, but we were running along in front of it, easing the motion. A strange place for Fourth of July to happen. Debauched with morning waffles in celebration, while reading the news in the morning *Polynesian*. The news said that the State Department would neither confirm nor deny that the United States will offer Panama fifty million a year in tolls as an inducement to go along with a new Panama Canal treaty. The canal can only continue to exist as a facility, I think, through some strained exercise of good will, or at least tolerance. It can be knocked out temporarily in twenty minutes, or permanently in a day, leaving nothing at all to defend.

The day before yesterday seemed increasingly unreal. All those sailors on that weird-looking vessel parked near us, out on deck watching a movie in the warm night. Waitresses swimming in traces of green phosphorescence. The interminable steel drums, whanging away for hours on end during the daylight, while dark children marched and danced up and down, making twisting black shadows on the surface of the pier.

I heard more of those steel drums that I needed that day. Like a cat did once upon a time. There were kennels on the ship. From time to time we carried pets. We didn't like to do this. We discouraged it, in fact. But sometimes we had people, whole families, moving to or from the South Pacific, and they would have dogs or cats or both. Then it was a necessary evil.

On one of the Caribbean cruises, a wealthy couple booked a nice suite on condition they could bring their cat along with them. The company wasn't enthused about this, but on the other hand maybe the bookings weren't too great either. It was the only pet on board, and nobody was going to make a big fuss if they brought the cat up to their room frequently.

Everything was going fine until we came to Martinique, where they have a steel band on the dock playing all day long. The couple put the cat in the kennel and were gone all day. The cat could not stand that sound. When they got back to the ship, the cat was out of its mind. It didn't even know them. It was soaked with sweat and panting.

They were so distressed about the whole thing, they canceled out and took their cat and flew home where they could get psychiatric consultation for the animal. And that was the end of their cruise.

My first experience with pets aboard was with two strange ladies and their two big red dogs. I believe most dog owners are a little freaky anyhow, and I always told the crewman who took care of the dogs to bend over backwards to humor the owners. I said, "If they want to go down there at night to say good night to a dog, let them do it. But I don't want them going down there by themselves."

The kennels were back in from the fantail where the male crew members had their recreation area. It didn't amount to much. The mooring lines and other miscellany were stowed back there. The dog handler would go and take one or two dogs at a time, tie one to the rail and feed him, exercise the other, then reverse the procedure and put them back in the kennel.

I heard that the ladies were complaining about the food being given to their big red dogs, and they were making up doggy bags in the dining room and taking them down to the kennels. The dog handler was feeding them regular dog food, and the women were augmenting this with food they had taken from the dining room. Of course, very soon the dogs had stomach problems. The women tried to get the ship's doctor to go down and treat their dogs. Next they wanted to order special tidbits à la carte for the dogs from the galley, ground top sirloin and such.

The dog handler would take the ladies down for their last good-night trip, but he found out they were sneaking back at ten or eleven at night to see their dogs again. It is not a well-lighted area, and I did not want them going down there alone. They were on the early sitting, so I told the dog handler to tell them that their eight-o'clock farewell was it. It would have to last them the rest of the night.

The next night at dinner I had to go rushing out to the purser's desk for an emergency phone call. The purser told me that it was from a lady in a hysterical condition. She went down to see her dog and found the kennels had been locked up, and she was demanding they be unlocked.

I told him I would handle it and asked him to get her on the phone.

She did sound hysterical. I said, "What is your problem, madam?"

"Our dogs. Our dogs. You have locked up our dogs! They are locked in."

"Yes, we do this for their own safety. What if somebody went down and let the dogs out and one of them jumped over the side?"

"Oh, our dogs would never do that."

"We have to lock them up as a precaution."

"Our dogs have never been locked up before. If they knew they were locked in there, they would become hysterical."

"We can solve that," I said. "We can give the dogs the key."

"Young man, you are not listening to me."

"I am trying."

"I will tell you something else. You have got to stop treating our dogs like dogs."

Those two ladies were a problem for the whole cruise. Our last three ports were Honolulu, San Francisco, and Los Angeles. Once they opened up the kennel in the daytime and one of those big red dogs got loose and ran through the galley. We had very hairy arguments about dog rules before we reached San Francisco, their last port before leaving the ship in Los Angeles. They made inquiries about Golden Gate Park. They engaged two taxicabs and took these two big dogs to Golden Gate Park so they could get a little exercise and meet other dogs. We were happy to wave goodbye to the dogs in Los Angeles.

One time, coming back from Australia, there were several dogs on the ship. One diplomat had a plain old hound dog. Like Old Blue. A woman owned some kind of a spaniel, and there was a gigantic German—he must have been at least six foot six—who owned a great big German Shepherd. There were a couple of other nondescript dogs in there, and one lonesome cat.

The dog owners got into a squabble about who should have the biggest kennel. The German demanded it, saying it was fair, because he had the biggest dog. Actually there was about two inches difference in the size of the kennels, and that difference was due to the contour of the ship. The person who had the biggest kennel said they were there first, and they were keeping it. I made it a point to stay away from dog owners and dog quarrels.

I got a call one day that the German, a Mr. Rauchenstauffer, had brought his dog up on deck and tethered it outside the bar. I went to take care of it in person. The German had lined himself up with an attractive woman, and he was impressing her with the fine points of his big wonderful dog.

"Mr. Rauchenstauffer," I said, "We have rules on this ship about animals. Dogs are allowed outside on the fantail, nowhere else."

"Well, everybody likes my dog, and they enjoy seeing him and petting him."

"That's fine. It is a very nice-looking dog, but it might bite somebody."

"My Schatzie has never bitten anyone and never would."

"You know that and I know that, but Schatzie doesn't know that. So put that dog back in the kennel and do not bring it up here again. Do you understand me?"

Reluctantly, he took the dog back to the kennel. Two days later I heard that he had the dog back in the bar. I got hold of Hal Wagner, the purser, and said, "Go tell that son of a bitch his dog stays in the kennel, and if there is any more of this nonsense, Rauchenstauffer and Schatzie get off at the next port. And I am coming with you to see that the message gets delivered."

We went down to the bar and sure enough, there they were, the dog all sprawled out, and I wait for Hal to deliver the message. But Hal gives a cry of pleasure, goes over, starts patting the dog and telling the man the Latin name of the breed, and remarking on what a fine-looking dog it is.

"Hal!" I said.

"This is really an exceptional dog," Hal said.

"Hal, tell him! Tell him!"

"Look at the shape of his head!"

"Enough of this," I said. "You, Mr. Rauchenstauffer. I have the authority to put you and your dog off this ship at the next port. If you bring that dog up here again, I will do it. Clear?"

And that settled it. Several days later I heard the story of Schatzie and Old Blue. The dog handler brought out a couple of dogs to feed them and exercise them. He tied Old Blue to the rail on one side, and one of the other dogs he tied on the other side. At about this time, Rauchenstauffer came down and let Schatzie out by himself, without a leash. The dog came charging out full of vim and vigor and rushed over to Old Blue, barking and barking. These dogs had been caged side by side for a couple of weeks, barking at each other.

Old Blue was eating. I don't think his desposition was improved by being in a kennel on a ship. He was an outdoor dog. When Schatzie came bullying up to him, he stopped eating long enough to turn and chomp off a big hunk of Schatzie's left ear and drop it on the deck. Schatzie went screaming back to Rauchenstauffer, and Old Blue went back to his dinner.

The big German had been telling everybody Schatzie was a $10,000 show dog. All of a sudden he had been a $25,000 show dog and was now worthless because of the carelessness of the ship's handler and the refusal of the ship's doctor to treat the damaged ear immediately. That was another suit that evidently came to nothing, because I cannot remember having to give a deposition.

We went to a Fourth of July party before lunch. In the afternoon the two of us were invited up to the captain's quarters for a drink. He and I made the final decision then and there to write a book about cruise ships, format unknown. Told him it would take some time. He never believed it would take *this* long. Gave us a little silver ingot with a design of the *Mariposa* etched into it. Handshake contract.

Holiday drinks on the house at cocktail time. Festivities all day. Captain said the weather is holding. We'll make it okay on our half rudder. That is worth being festive about. At ten thirty in the evening, an icecream social up on the Pool Terrace. Make your own sundae. Orchestra. Art and his banjo. Cloudy moonlight, breezy deck-walking.

43

‖‖‖

Tuesday and Wednesday, July 5 and 6
Cristóbal and the Panama Canal

Though the crippled ship left St. Croix late, it arrived at Cristóbal on time and thus was able to put tourists ashore for the two last tours, No. 70, a full day by plane, launch, and canoe, including lunch, to the San Blas Islands to see the Kuna Indians, a virtually untouched pre-Columbian culture—untouched, that is, except by several years of tourists who have come to haggle over the purchase of hand-sewn, design-covered panels called molas—and No. 71, a full day by motorcoach across the isthmus, including lunch. The Thomas Cook representatives had to make no cancellation refunds.

A very humid morning. We were inspected by the canal authorities and pronounced suitable for canal transit, with tugboat assistance. Spent most of the day topside, seeking shelter on the Prom Deck and under cover at the Pool Terrace from the frequent heavy rainstorms, some of them thunderous. A Texas party started at quarter to noon. Once again it was a pleasure to the eye to steam through the narrow cuts and wide lakes of the inner isthmus, past the intense tropic greenery. It was a silvery day, without glare. The canal P.R. man aboard broadcast over the P.A. system. Lots of statistics about people dying digging the canal, cubic yards of earth moved, and so on. The beautiful scenic quality of the inner canal is seldom mentioned. It is a lot of miles, a lot of hours of a placid beauty.

At one point we did not turn with sufficient agility and rammed our nose into a mudbank, but a pair of tugs quickly yanked us off and put us back on course.

At quarter to five I was up on the flying bridge with camera, overcast darkening the day prematurely, the breeze of passage almost chill. All over the ship people were packing, writing the last batch of postcards, filling out customs forms, finishing their squares for the cruise quilt. In spite of the long haul ahead, up from Panama to California, there was a flavor of ending.

During the cocktail hour came the announcement we would not be leaving from Balboa for Los Angeles at ten o'clock tonight. It astonished me how many people, because of the flawless transit from St. Croix to Cristóbal, believed we were in shape to go up the Pacific Coast, which can be anything but pacific. The announcement said we would not leave before 8 A.M. Wednesday. The next announcement turned the 8 A.M. promise to nonsense. It said there would be a gratis tour of Balboa and Panama City tomorrow, leaving the ship at nine and returning at noon.

Soon after we had tied up at Balboa, a big work platform was lowered at the stern and floodlights strung. When we went down onto the dock after dinner a diver was inspecting the rudder, and I heard the boss man of the work crew tell someone else that there was too much play in what was left of it. I gathered that they were going to take the half rudder off, put it on a flatbed, and take it all the way across the isthmus where there was a place which could weld a big extension on it to take the place of much of what we had lost.

There were rumors all over the place. We were going into dry dock. They were going to fly a new rudder down. Everybody was going to be transferred to another cruise ship, Greek registry. Everybody was going to be flown home. All I knew was that I was not taking this turkey anywhere else the way we were. And the Vatican wanted it brought home somehow, with the cash customers aboard.

They flew a rugged-looking engineer type down to take charge of the repairs. His name was Frank Bradford, and he looked a little like John Madden, the ex-coach of the Raiders. He arrived at two in the morning. He had flown from San Francisco to Florida to get connections to Panama, and he was exhausted. I told them to wake me when he arrived, so I went down onto the dock and talked to him about what he thought had to be done.

At first light we went up onto the Pool Terrace for coffee. They were just setting up, so we got our coffee from the urn, carried it over to a table, and sat down. Two little old ladies came out and sat near us, and leaned so far toward us they were nearly falling out of their chairs, trying to hear what was going on. Everybody on the ship knew something was up. They had been asking me all day long and I would say, "I can tell you what's going on right now, but that will all be changed in the next couple of hours."

When our cups were empty, one of the old ladies came over and said, "Would you like to have more coffee?"

Bradford looked up at her and said, "Yes, we would, thanks." She took the cups and filled them and brought them back and went and sat down. "Who is she?" he asked. "She work here?"

"No. Just one of the passengers. She thought she might pick up the word about what we're doing."

He was amazed at the passengers. He thought they would be complaining bitterly about the schedule, the danger, and so on. But they just seemed intensely interested.

By then he was certain we could get the damaged rudder off the rudder post in a matter of hours. But it had been warped in such a way it turned into a longer job. They thought they would get it off at six that evening, but another problem developed and it was midnight before they freed it and lifted it onto the dock.

At nine o'clock that night an old lady who had been watching the action confronted him down on the dock and said, "Mr. Bradford, when are you going to get that thing off?"

"I don't know, ma'am. We're hoping to have it off pretty soon."

"Well, my feet are killing me. Do you realize I've been on my feet for thirteen hours today?"

"Why don't you go back onto the ship and go to bed, then?"

"*No way. I've waited this long, and I'm not going to leave this dock until you get that rudder off. And that's final.*"

Bradford couldn't get over the way the people would come down off the ship and watch the big rudder show. He told me he was thinking of setting up a concession down there, selling iced tea, cold drinks, and beer and renting folding chairs.

Part of the big rudder show was the cutting of the fare plate, a big steel plate in front of the rudder. It had to be torched off to provide access to the big locking nut which, when removed, would free the rudder.

It was a big rusty steel plate, and when the crane lifted it up out of the murky water and swung it ashore, people kept asking him if that was part of the rudder, and he said it wasn't really part of the rudder itself, but you could call it part of the rudder assembly.

He told some of the repair people there he wanted the fare plate taken over to the shop and cut into three hundred little pieces. They wanted to know what for, and he said, "Just do it. Okay?"

The pieces were about an inch and a quarter square and three eighths of an inch thick. Kaui and Alan cleaned them up and glued green felt to the bottom of every one. Later we gave them to the passengers along with a certificate saying they were true members of the Rudder Watchers' Society. It was all Bradford's doing, because he had overheard one of them saying he wished he could have a piece of that rudder.

This tough engineer thought he was coming into a hornet's nest, with people in a state of panic and confusion. Instead, he found it was an interesting experience for them, and they wanted to watch every moment of it because it was memorable.

On Wednesday morning we walked out to the dock gates and took a taxi downtown to the Hotel Panama. We had expected something we could call Scranton South, but it was a reasonably good-looking city. A lot of Spanish colonial influence in the architecture. If there was any question of my not enjoying the day, it went away after we bought the new *Time* and found that *Condominium* was in third place on the list. I had not thought it had the wind for that kind of distance.

Found a shop where they had framed Molas hanging in the

trees. Bought a couple of very old ones for framing. They had been part of dresses, washed a hundred times to great softness and subdued colors. One design was of butterflies, the other of a Picasso-like cat. Had lunch at the hotel. Loitered in a large camera store, one of my compulsive habits. Have taken and filed enough boxes of 35-mm slides to anesthetize the entire population of Youngstown, Ohio.

When it began to look like rain, we caught a cab at the hotel, and just as we started back, the rain came down in great roaring silver sheets. The cabdriver was permitted by the gate guards to let us off at the entrance to the shed, where we could walk in shelter to the ship.

The scuttlebutt was that we would be tied up there for at least two more days. They were going to bring the spare anchor up out of stowage, and they were going to mount a new rudder. Nobody seemed particularly upset at the prospect. The few people who definitely *had* to be back in California by the twelfth were being assisted by the Cook travel group in making air reservations and were putting their excess luggage in storage aboard so that they could come and get it after the ship arrived.

Dorothy got her pet plant, brought from Hamburg, out of the room and carried it outside and put it down in the rain, near the pool. The rain had turned gentle and steady. We sat in the shelter of the Pool Terrace and talked with others who had been milling around town that day, about what they had found and the attitude of the people. Because of the increasing agitation for a new canal treaty, we expected the same sort of obvious hostility we had once experienced in Caracas: people glaring, shaking fists, blocking the sidewalk, making audible comments.

But no one experienced any of this. The Panamanians seemed pleasant and courteous, though not overly warm. One cabdriver had told us his particular view of reality. He said the politicos and the students were the ones making the big fuss about the canal, and the general public did not really care that much. The thing they cared about was that the canal keep operating, because it brought in a lot of money in wages, and it brought tourists. He said he thought Panamanians could run it okay if they took over, but probably wages would go down and tolls would go up, because that is always what the politicos do, everywhere.

In all Latin countries one sees, of course, those quick dark glances from the slender young men. Scorn, disdain, challenge? A look is only a look. Without accompanying word or gesture, it can be interpreted incorrectly. Instead of thinking about plastique and machine pistols and assaults on the embassy, he may be wondering where you bought the funny hat or pondering what he is going to wear to the evening disco. Many travelers have acute attacks of paranoia in foreign places. Drawing the most generous conclusions is the way to retain balance and sanity. Fear spoils the view.

44

||||||||||||||||||||||||||||||||||||||||||

Thursday, July 7

Balboa

A MESSAGE FROM CAPTAIN KILPACK

As announced, our departure from Balboa has been delayed at least two days for further inspection and repairs to our rudder.

I personally extend my sincere appreciation for your understanding and patience during these trying times.

Another day of steady downpour. Dorothy put her plant back out by the pool. We and another couple decided to brave it, found a taxi at the gate, and went into the city. We separated and arranged to meet at the hotel for lunch.

After they joined us there, we decided to try a Chinese restaurant they had seen. Full of locals. Food okay, decor on the dingy side. Cabdrivers scarce in the rain. Found one who, for a flat fee, agreed to take us to a store called Casa Tokyo for a limited period of time and take us back to the ship.

Should not have let him limit our time. Great store. Full of junk and good things too. Found beautiful blue hand-embroidered guayaberas made in Red China, on sale for $14 each. Cabdriver soon came in and started making a nuisance of himself, hustling us. Couldn't tell him to go away for fear of being unable to find another cab in that neighborhood, in the rain.

We were trying to get waited on. Soon he began bellowing at us. Very surly fellow.

Went to a nice party on the Pool Terrace. Very steamy and rainy outside. Four of us men appeared in our blue $14 Chinese guayaberas, Red Lion brand, and were immortalized by the ship's photographer, wearing our manic tourist smiles.

After dinner found an announcement under our door for a free trip tomorrow to an offshore island, and so signed up at once.

I had wondered whether the foolhardy ride of the Mariposa *from St. Croix down to Panama on half a rudder, with one anchor unavailable, might become a news item. I knew the company didn't want anything made of it. But if the media wanted to interview me, I was ready.*

On a subsequent short trip to the Islands, before the roof fell in for keeps, we had some very bad weather. A big storm sweeping across the Pacific passed through Hawaii and hit us on its way to the West Coast. We bounced around, utilizing both stabilizers, and by five thirty or six one night it got so increasingly rough I decided to heave to. I changed course, slowed the ship way down, headed it into the sea, and just kept steerageway. I decided I would do this until after dinner and then get back on course. It made everything fairly comfortable for the people, but I was aware of how much time I was losing.

After dinner there was entertainment scheduled, but I had the cruise director cancel that out and get everybody into the lounge—everybody who was still ambulatory—and have some kind of sing-along so they would all be sitting down.

At ten o'clock I decided to bring her back on course. I went up to full speed and swung the ship around, and let me tell you, she really rolled. She went over to about 20 degrees, and that is one great big tilt when you've got a lot of brittle bones aboard. It slid people around, tipped over all the barstools, dumped the drinks, skidded the chairs in the lounge. I saw that it wouldn't work and went back to a course directly into the waves. We were very fortunate. Absolutely no injuries at all, practically a miracle. It was some time before I could safely make my turn and get back on course. It was a rough and tiring trip, and when we got into Honolulu twelve hours late,

I was happy to have the ship tied up at the dock and the people getting off.

The next morning I got an early call from the chief purser to tell me that the police had just called up to advise us that two fairly young fellows from the steward's department had been found dead of overdoses in a fleabag hotel.

"Oh, great!" I said. "That's all I need at this point."

"It shouldn't be too hairy. It didn't happen on the ship. The officer I talked to says they have a pretty good rundown on where they got the heroin, but the police will have to come down and search their room and make an investigation."

Hours later, one of the TV stations in Honolulu phoned me and said, "We understand that two of your crew members died of an overdose."

"That's right. I don't have all the details yet."

"We'd like to come down and do a story on this, a few minutes on film."

"No, friend. Hell, no. I don't know whether the next of kin have been notified. I don't know all the details. It didn't happen on the ship. And I won't give you an interview on something like that."

"Well, I understand you were pretty late in getting in?"

"Yes, we were."

"That same storm did a lot of damage here on the island, and one of the container ships lost some containers over the side. Could we maybe come down and do a little story on how it affected a passenger ship?"

I didn't want to do it, but I realized if I turned him down, I couldn't stop him from doing interviews on the dock, and that might come out worse than if I controlled the situation. I said, "You are welcome to come down and I'll be happy to cooperate, but I want to control how this thing is going to look on film. I don't want it to look like the Poseidon Adventure." *He agreed and said they'd be down at noon. In the meantime my old friend Doug Green, then the producer for* Hawaii Five-O, *and his wife were coming down for lunch. I met them in the main lobby and I was chatting with them when the TV people arrived, and there were introductions all around.*

I asked them if they were in a hurry, or could they come

in and have lunch with us. They said that lunch would be really fine, and sure, they had the time.

After we were all seated and had ordered, I said, "Now about this interview you want to do, I definitely want to control what type of questions are going to be asked and what this script is going to be like."

"Well, I guess we're agreeable to that."

"I also want my choice of the background of where this will be shot, and my choice of lighting. I have Mr. Green here, my own director whom I always work with, and he will direct the sequence."

They were staring at me, obviously wondering what kind of nut they had happened upon, who wanted a director for a three-minute news story.

The interviewer turned to Doug Green and said, "Are you in the television business."

"Yes, in a small way." Doug is a soft-spoken, self-effacing man.

"Like what do you do, sir?"

"I'm connected with Hawaii Five-O."

The light dawned, and when the young interviewer realized he was with the producer of a network show, he eliminated me from the conversation. He began rattling on about the film and television people in Hawaii and trying to make a big impression on Doug.

When we finished lunch we went back out into the lobby and I said, "Now I assume you would like to talk to some of our passengers and get their reaction?"

"Yes, Captain, with your permission I would like to."

"There are two lady passengers who went through the storm sitting over there. They're both shy, but if you handle them right, they'll probably say a few words."

I knew those two old gals. They never stopped talking. One of them was a character, the type who comes running up and grabs the mike away from the M.C. and starts telling dirty jokes or doing her imitation of Sophie Tucker. The other one was almost as bad. They had just come back from a shopping tour and were arguing about who should have paid the cab fare.

He went up to them and said, "I'm with Channel Two, and

I wonder if I could ask you two nice ladies about your impression of the trip coming over—"

The two of them jumped up and started fighting each other for the microphone, one of them yelling, "No, Ethel, let me talk, I've had more experience at this."

"But I'm the one that fell down, right?"

He had a hard time getting his microphone back. One of them wanted to tell a couple of very funny jokes. Doug and his wife and I were around the corner, doubled up laughing.

When he shook loose he came to us and said, "My, those ladies were certainly cooperative. They're extroverts. They're quite talkative."

"No, they hardly ever have anything to say. You must have handled them just right. And now I assume you'd like to go up and see the bridge?"

"Yes, we'd really like that!"

Everybody who comes on board wants to see the bridge. I don't know what's so fascinating about it. They gathered up their gear, and we went on up. They were interested in looking around at all the gadgets, the wheel and the compass and everything. The interviewer said to his cameraman, "Do you think we could shoot in here?"

I interrupted, saying, "Yes, you can shoot in here, but you're going to have to watch out. If you shoot against the after bulkhead, a lot of those panels are highly polished and glossy and you're going to get a kickback in your film. Normally when we shoot we spray them with laquer, and that reduces the glare. Also, watch out because you've got intense light streaming in through the portholes."

By then they were both looking at me strangely.

I said, "Now, what I would suggest, first we go out on the wing of the bridge." They followed me out. "Take your camera and zoom in on the Aloha Tower, because that's going to identify the set and people will know where we are. Right?"

"Right."

"Then take your camera and pan on down the lifeboats. Let your film run right on down the whole row because this will give a feeling of depth and dimension and make it look like a much larger ship. How does that sound?"

"That's great."

"Then we'll get over here and I'll be out on the wing of the bridge by the compass repeater, and I'll be up on this platform. That is going to make me six inches taller than you, but it will make me film well. I'll be wearing a hat, so watch the shadow on my face. I'd like you to shoot the left side of my face because I've got this scar here, and it films well."

They are giving me that stare.

I said, "Now, when we work, I like to have my director, Mr. Green, kneel down in front of the camera. That's the way we always work together, and it comes out quite well. Now let's run through it once. Give me an idea of what your questions are going to be, and we can try it for size."

They seemed stunned. At this point the interviewer looked back over his shoulder and saw that Doug Green and his wife were doubled up, trying to stifle their laughter.

He looked back at me. "Why, goddamnit, you're putting me on!"

"Sure."

"I do interviews all day. I interview politicians and I see through their act right away." He turned back to Doug with a look of vacant wonder and said, "So I come aboard a ship and meet the captain, and the son of a bitch snows me!"

From then on we got along fine. They did a quick little TV sequence, and when we were all saying goodbye down in the lobby, he was still shaking his head.

Anyway, the Panamanian press and television did not leap to cover this great news story we had brought them.

45

|||||||||||||||||||||||||||||||||||||||||||||||||

Friday and Saturday, July 8 and 9

Contadora and Return

You are going to an island considered one of the most beautiful in the Gulf of Panama. The hotel and casino were opened in late December of 1976.

Your complimentary tour will include a three-hour cruise on a brand new Gulf Cruiser. Drinks from the bar on the ship are complimentary.

A buffet lunch will be served at the hotel. You will receive your lunch tickets from the Panama Tours representative aboard the cruiser.

There will be changing rooms available for those who wish to swim and, if you enjoy tennis, courts are available.

Set the alarm and had breakfast and boarded the Gulf Cruiser at eight. We met a woman coming down the gangway as we got on, leaving either in fury or panic. It was difficult to determine. By and large she made a pretty good choice.

It was a chunky boat, all clean and new, with low freeboard. It looked somewhat like a ferryboat, with a big exposed upper deck and a central stairwell down to the big lower deck where were the restrooms and the bar. There was another deck below that, dark and gloomy, for stowage of gear and access to docks and small boats.

It would have been crowded with a hundred passengers aboard. But there were more than two hundred of us. There were nowhere near enough chairs and benches to go around.

We found a corner on the top deck near the stern where we could sit on the round sides of a big life raft. By the time we came aboard, all the chairs and bench spaces were long gone.

At eight thirty we went chugging out past the *Mariposa*. People waved and shouted at us from her decks. The Gulf Cruiser had been moored ahead of our ship. The *Mariposa* looked fine as we started out, but as we reached a point opposite her stern, we could see the platform, the extra lines they had rigged, the equipment strewn about. She looked helpless indeed, like someone having a major operation.

The trip to Contadora was interminable. They had said three hours, but it was four and a half before we anchored off that pretty island. There are huge tides in the Gulf of Panama, as much as twenty feet, so there was no dock where we could tie up. We anchored out, and a tiny outboard motorboat arrived to ferry us to shore. It could carry fifteen at a time. We timed the first round trip to the beach and back, and it took twelve minutes. That translated to seventy-five people per hour, or nearly three hours to unload us, three hours to reload us, and it was already one in the afternoon.

The whole thing seemed so incredibly bungled that we pitied whatever entrepreneur had put his life savings into this dumb vessel. Then we found the real reason for it all. The Gulf Cruiser and the hotel and the whole works were owned and operated by the Panamanian government. It is to laugh—or cry. We were at the mercy of a seagoing civil service.

At last they hauled anchor and moved the boat around a corner, to a place where they could get closer to the beach, and pressed another small boat into service. We had almost decided to try to stay aboard, but when the new system began to work we went ashore, very tired, very sunburned, and very sick of the Gulf Cruiser.

The hotel was handsome, an island-type structure with steep shingled roofs and big ceiling fans. There were several separate two-story buildings housing the rooms. We heard there was air service to the mainland, a seventeen-minute ride. As soon as we heard that, we vowed never to go back aboard the Gulf Cruiser. I made room reservations and plane reservations at the desk. So did a friend who was as fervently glad to be deprived of the pleasure of the trip back as we were. She was almost teary about it.

Contadora means accountant in Spanish. Not a romantic name until you realize that this was the island in the Pearl Island group where the pearl fishermen brought the pearls to be paid off by the accountant. And as a later temporary refuge for the Shah of Iran, the name is still not entirely inappropriate.

There was a nice bar by the outdoor pool, and we had drinks there while all the others had their lunch and filed down to the side beach to be taken back out to our vessel. We were the last served, and it was excellent. Broiled filet of fresh fish. After lunch we walked on the beach and then bought the necessary toilet articles from the hotel shop.

At six we went to the terrace for a free cocktail party given to hotel guests by the management every Friday evening: weak rum drinks and hors d'oeuvres of hot spiced fish. At dinner all seven of us who had made the same wise decision ate together. The other guests seemed to be mostly Panamanians—the usual few silver-tipped businessmen entertaining their lovely daughters, and some families with kids. Dinner was splendid ceviche and more excellent fish, chablis, and coffee.

Aboard the Gulf Cruiser they had handed out certificates for $5 each, good only for chips in the casino. So we went there from dinner. I played the roulette thirds and Dorothy played the dime slot. She hit a jackpot that took an endless time to spit her money out, two and three dimes at a time, all the while ringing bells and making siren sounds: $22.50 in dimes, with a long pause between little spits. I made enough on the thirds so that between us we cleared enough for the hotel, the food, and the flight back. And I won an extra $11 for a lady who had turned her certificate over to me when she went back aboard the Cruiser. It took less than an hour, so we went to bed early in the new, bright, tidy air-conditioned room.

After breakfast the next morning, I walked over to the combination airport and marina about a hundred yards away and rented a VW Thing so the three of us could take a look at the island.

The road followed the perimeter of the island. We stopped at the little bays and walked around. We passed many luxurious homes, nestled back on slopes above the water, half concealed by tropical plantings, and decided that because this was a government operation, they were probably the vacation homes of important Panamanian politicians. There were interesting vistas from the road, and when we came back around we stopped at the airport to photograph two large iguanas and two tethered grazing camels! They were, I believe, a present from the King of Saudi Arabia to the President of Panama and had been brought out to live on Contadora.

After we went back to the hotel for a cold beer, we started out again to see if we could find a new road, but we had covered the whole thing on our first try. I would say it is a ten-minute ride around the island if one does not stop anywhere.

Had rum screwdrivers at the inside bar, after stopping at the airport to buy the tickets we'd reserved. Then lunch in a surprisingly full dining room. Drove back to the airport and turned in the car. Plane a half hour late. Were given the biggest boarding passes I have ever seen. Big slabs of orange plastic, cut into the silhouette of a fish. It was a twin-engine twenty-passenger plane, and we lifted off, past the camels, and came back across a misty sea, over the small Pearl Islands.

Felt so euphoric I neglected to nail down the cost of the taxi ride with sufficient exactitude and thus took the well-deserved screwing when we got to the docks. Nothing to do then but smile and pay. When it is your own fault, there is no need to get agitated.

There was a big crowd of passengers and bystanders around the stern. They were getting ready to fit the repaired rudder onto the ship. It had been repaired by welding on a large flange arrangement but was still not back to the original dimensions, as it should have been.

The departure time was posted on the board as 8 P.M. We showered and changed and went to the bar early and were joined there by the captain and Mr. Bradford, the marine engineering specialist.

Mr. Bradford was very interesting, but they were both a

little evasive as to when we might get away. We did learn that the captain, after looking the repaired rudder over, had refused to take the ship into Los Angeles. "I am not going to go winding up that narrow distance through all that traffic," he said. "It is always bad enough with a good rudder."

They left us, and when we started to go to dinner, the captain intercepted us and took us down a back stairway to the officers' dining room. We went through the room behind the bar, down a circular staircase, and through one end of the galley. Seldom had we ever seen such noisy confusion as in that galley. Waitresses were shrieking their orders. Chefs were yelling back. People were scooting through with loaded trays. No place for a shy girl or one with laryngitis.

The officers' mess was a spare but snug room. The door closed out all the galley racket. There were just the three of us in the room, and the steward to take the order. The captain took the dishes over to the sideboard, and then he and I went back out into the tumult and shouting and got our dessert from the pastry chef. Our wine waiter, Chuck, brought some wine. Every trip to the kitchen must be a traumatic experience for those young waitresses.

The board had been changed to a 10 P.M. sailing, but it was obvious we wouldn't make that either. Dorothy went to the desk to try to get a call through to her brother and his wife to tell them about the delay, and I, wanting to see if the luck was still holding, took my first shot at Bingo and came out with $10.50, just enough to cover the overcharge levied by the cab driver.

And so to bed, amid rumors we might take off at one in the morning.

Well, we didn't leave at 8 P.M., and we didn't leave at 10 P.M. We didn't leave at 1 in the morning, and we didn't leave at 8 A.M. the next morning either. They'd tell me it was just about done. All they had to do was invest the frammis on the squintle, lock it on with the mirching key, and we'd be off.

I had begun to feel like a loser. You run into quite a few of those on the White Ships.

I remember one heavy-set old lady who always wore those caftans. I call them Batman outfits. She was a loser. Everything happened to her. She always had somebody helping her hunt for her glasses or her purse. She was on the clumsy side. Occasionally on the Pool Terrace she would try to sit down quickly when the ship rolled and miss the chair.

Being a loser had turned her into a pessimist. She'd go to the travel desk and say, "I guess Tour Twenty-seven is all sold out, isn't it?"

"No, I think we still have room if you would like to go."

"I guess not. It will probably rain."

Everybody adopted her and tried to cheer her up. On this particular trip, we had lost time, and the only place to make the time back was in Honolulu. We thought of getting back on schedule by eliminating Fiji entirely, but then realized that for many people aboard it would be their one and only chance to see that interesting island, so we decided to cut Hawaii down to the minimum, just giving ourselves enough time to get the people off and get them on, and then sail. Also, a big contingent of people were leaving the ship at Honolulu, ending their cruise there, so that helped us decide to cut Hawaii short.

But the Lady Loser was one of those continuing on to California. She had never been in Hawaii, and from what she said, this was her one and only chance to see it.

The day after we left I saw her and said with tongue in cheek, "How did you enjoy your stay in Hawaii?"

She said, "Well, we weren't there very long, were we? All I bought was this here package of macadamia nuts." She held them out to me. "This is all I bought, and I think there's worms in it."

There was another loser who took a memorable cruise with us. He was a middle-aged, mild, nondescript fellow from the Midwest, traveling alone. He would misplace his glasses and the book he was reading and his room key and his towel. He checked often at the purser's desk to see what stuff of his had been turned in.

Somewhere along the line we had an overnight stay, and there was a shore tour, and he worked out a deal with the travel people that instead of staying with the rest of the group at a resort hotel, he would save money by staying at the YMCA. So he did, and somebody mugged him in the hall and took his wallet and wristwatch.

In New Zealand he went on one of the tours into the caves, and a stalactite which had been hanging up there on the cave roof for tens of thousands of years let go and hit him a glancing blow on the back of the head as he walked underneath it.

When he took an excursion boat around Sydney harbor, a sea gull let him have it on top of the head.

After he got off the ship for good in Honolulu, one of the ship's entertainers was walking through the dining room of one of Honolulu's better hotels and saw the Loser sitting at a table for four, alone, with four chicken dinners. The entertainer stopped and stared and said, "Hey, what goes on?"

"Would you care to join me for a chicken dinner?"

"What's happening here?"

"I contacted these three friends I have in Honolulu and invited them to meet me here at six and have dinner with me. At six o'clock I arrived and they weren't here. I waited and waited. Our reservations were for seven, and the maître d' called me and said my table was ready. I came in here and sat down and the waiter asked me for my order. I was sure they'd be here any minute so I ordered four chicken dinners because they're not very expensive. It's quarter to eight, and I don't think they're coming. I'm about to eat mine. Would you join me in a chicken dinner?"

"So sorry, pal. I'm meeting some people. Thanks anyway." And that was the last anyone heard of him.

46

||||||||||||||||||||||||||||||||||||||||||||||

Sunday, Monday, and Tuesday, July 10–12

Destination: San Francisco

As you were advised earlier, the S.S. *Mariposa* is steaming directly to San Francisco, where a new rudder will be installed.

There are many reasons for by-passing Los Angeles, one being the time factor necessary for drydocking and meeting our commitment for the following voyage.

While we are not able to give you an exact Estimated Time of Arrival at this time, we expect to arrive in San Francisco on Saturday, July 16.

A party had been planned by management to celebrate the departure of the *Mariposa* from Panama. Fizzes and Marys, it was called. Scheduled for 11:30 to 12:30 in the Poly Club, when, presumably, we would be well out to sea.

But we were still tied to the dock. A good party nevertheless, with the orchestra, with the captain and the chief purser making little speeches, telling us we would soon be off. And then they passed out those chunks of the fare plate from the old rudder.

At 13:22 hours we cast off and moved away from the dock, under the big bridge, and out past the ships waiting for transit, on out into the Gulf of Panama.

383

It became evident in these sea days—from almost one thirty in the afternoon of the tenth, until midmorning of the seventeenth—that we had become a village, a web of social structure. There were tribal chiefs and would-be chieftains. We had our clowns and troublemakers, our scandals and disasters. We had our recluses, seldom seen in the public areas. Witches sat around bubbling cauldrons; old men drowsed the days away in deck chairs. We had been through a lot together for a long time. There were passengers who knew every other passenger aboard. But there were others who were as bad at names and faces as I am, such as the woman who had been on the entire trip, who asked me in St. Croix if I had come aboard there. People moved in their own orbits. The great tribal function was the giving and attending of parties for friends. Because people of similar interests tended to bunch up, the final seven days of parties was pretty much a constant gathering of the same group. But not boring, because by then we knew each other well enough to be able to get well past the weather-health-diet gambits of compulsory social conversation.

Between parties I settled into my routine of deck walking, backgammon, reading, paddle tennis, and naps. Dorothy was into her routine of journal keeping, exercise class, deck walking, sunbathing, plant tending, laundromating, and reading—plus various oddments. At one point I found her using a crochet hook to dig small dead Cloroxed critters out of a piece from her driftwood collection, after soaking it in a bucket supplied by Jess, the room steward. A person whose daily activities at sea involved swimming, bridge, shuffleboard, and quilt-making could pass an entire voyage without encountering either of us.

Were guests at a splendid Chinese luncheon in one of the Lanai Suites. First time we had ever been in one of them. Attractive. Chef Merlo stopped by for a glass of champagne and congratulations. (Rice cooked in broth with egg and bits of ham, sweet-and-sour shrimp with pineapple in a shiny red sauce, roast duck cut into pieces in a sauce, chicken wrapped in foil triangles, beef with onions and peppers. Red, white, and rosé wine. Fortune cookies.)

Cocktail party given by some of the backgammon group. Joe Coco in attendance, full of inside wisdom about Las Vegas.

Went to a birthday party for a recently retired publisher. Had been passing Wallace Stegner's *The Spectator Bird* around the group. The age and aging theme of the book, and the illness of Al Morgan, and the substantial age level of our group, led some of us into intense discussion. One frail conclusion: In *any* given age category, 95 percent of the people are dreary because their opinions are all second hand, their prejudices predictable, their conversation largely anecdotal and boring. In the younger categories, the essential dreariness can be concealed by fad and fashion, by having all the right moves, catch words, and haircuts. In the sixties and seventies one is deprived of these simple masquerades and thus inevitably grouped with the drearies of one's own age category. The exceptions are the ones whose appearance is secondary to their office—from Fred Astaire to Barry Goldwater. For all the rest, who are not dreary, the solution is to avoid platitudes and conventional statements. Get out front quickly. Fight back when patronized. Flaunt your most outrageous opinions. Only thus can an older person escape from what one woman in the group termed "the negritude of age."

On Tuesday, a warm and lovely day, I spent too much time in the writing room straightening out my customs declarations and receipts, working up the totals, dismaying myself, as usual, at the amount spent. There are parsimonious people who spend rarely and reluctantly. There are people who spend gladly and willingly and never give it a second thought. My Scots heritage leaves me in some uncomfortable middle ground, awash in anxiety. I spend willingly, and then worry about it a lot. After planter's punches and a Chinese lunch on the Pool Terrace, I went back to the accounts. Next paddle tennis, then shower and change for a stateroom party, given in honor of the necessity of polishing off their extra booze before arrival in San Francisco.

After dinner we went to the entertainment in the Poly Club. This was the show put on by the passengers and rehearsed by Art and Dotty Todd. As they were going to do it only one time, the place was jammed. One passenger reserved our big table by putting a bottle of champagne in an ice bucket on it. I had done one little script for the show, for the Sugar Plum Fairies, and I hoped it would play.

All us villagers enjoyed that show. It was well staged. There were some goofs, as expected. The high point of the evening was Al Morgan doing a solo, several piano numbers up there on the low platform. He had to have a thick cushion on the piano bench to pad his skeletal frame. He wore a straw boater and a bow tie, and with astonishing energy, and his customary skill, he played Dixieland and Chicago jazz, hitting a good rolling bass, spotlighted, fingers flying, bending intently over the keys.

When he finished and stood up, there was loud, long-lasting applause. He smiled around at all of us and sat down again and did an encore. Again, to lots of applause, he came down off the platform more nimbly than I would have thought possible and stood in the middle of the dance floor, spotlighted, and took the straw boater off and made a low, smiling half-circle, boater held in salute, including us all. It was teary-eye time, because we knew the special gallantry of the man, the incredible durability of his good humor, his grace in the presence of pain and despair.

Later, as we were going to bed, we realized that today, July 12, was the day the ship would have docked in Los Angeles.

47

||||||||||||||||||||||||||||||||||||||||||||||||||

En Route to San Francisco

The thirteenth of July was the day we would have landed in San Francisco, and here we were off the coast of Mexico.

At breakfast Sandy gave us an interesting rundown on what indecision over sailing means to the crew. No one knew how long it would take to replace the rudder in San Francisco. That meant indecision about hiring as well. No fun, she said, to sit around the hiring hall or the dock area for hours and hours when they may be your only hours ashore, your only chance to see your family, pay your bills, do your errands.

Went up to the Pool Terrace after breakfast. The liar's dice game seemed, like some variation of the Peter Principle, to be extending itself in both man-hours and personnel.

Had a nap after lunch and then went up to play paddle tennis. Finished about five thirty and on the way back down to the room, I heard that Al Morgan had lost consciousness about an hour earlier and had died shortly thereafter. Went down and told Dorothy.

I really believe, trite as it may sound, that Al, many weeks ago, had set his mental, emotional, and physical clock to July thirteenth. He had vowed in some way to last until then. To last until the thirteenth, when he would be home. And he did.

Through so many of those days he had ached to be home. The mind and the body are mysteriously interwoven. I can believe that a person can indeed hang on until a task is finished.

Emily had her close friends near her. We sent her a note expressing sympathy and our sense of loss, enclosing a Polaroid picture Dorothy had taken of him last night during his act. Though he was quite tiny in the picture, we had learned at noon that in his first serious goof of the trip, the reliable ship's photographer had lost all the pictures he had taken of the show by dunking them in the wrong solution.

We went up and joined a subdued group in the bar. Later we had roast beef on the Pool Terrace, and when we went out on deck after dinner the night was as beautiful as we had seen on the trip. We were close to the Mexican shore, north of Acapulco. We could see some scattered lights on the shore. We could see thunderstorms over the land. The offshore breeze brought a scent of summer and things growing. The black sky was crowded with stars. We took one turn around the windy bow, watched the night for a little while, feeling the steady lift of the ship, and went off to bed.

After breakfast, on our way up to the Pool Terrace, we met Emily with Edra and Waynette. We gave her a hug and she hid her face and said, "But it was so quick!"

Yes, it was. And so slow too, over months and months. There can never be any sort of valid preparation. Fantasies of death, expectations of death, bear no relation to the actuality. He will die. She will die. Empty phrases. He is dead. She is dead. That is the reality, the sick shock, the wonderment that you could not have ever guessed how it would be. The ache to have life all over again.

Okay, he could have been flown home to lie abed and watch the walls. Or he could have forced himself to endure the grinding demands of travel. For the death-marked it is not a marvelous choice to have.

But he left us something. I think many people treasure that memory of him in the spotlight, holding that silly hat out at arm's length, shoulder high, turning slowly, smiling at us as we applauded. His show was over.

Aside from the quick, brutal, irrelevant nonsense of wartime, I have known only two men in my life who have died well,

George Sumner Albee and Albert T. Morgan. They died with full knowledge of what was happening to them, and with the desire to make it just as easy as possible on everyone around them. I wish I had the assurance that when my turn comes I shall do as well.

Prior to our getting up on Bastille Day, the clock had been turned back for the final time of the voyage. In midmorning we went to see the five hundred and fifty paintings on display, student work selected from the nineteen hundred they had done. An immense and interesting show. If R. C. Stanley did nothing other than to get them to look at the world, at light and shadow and pattern and color, with fresh new eyes, it was worth the effort. At the Pool Terrace lunch, a school of Pacific dolphins played in and beside the wake, falling steadily behind. Lots of packing during the afternoon. Went to the White Elephant Auction of unwanted purchases after dinner. Dorothy put in a ring, which no one bought, and bought a balalaika, and thus we ended up with two elephants instead of one.

Went to the memorial service for Al at ten thirty on Friday morning. It was a very special and unusual event on a cruise ship. Deaths on cruise ships are handled much like deaths at resort hotels; they are hurried down the back stairs during the off hours, and nothing more is said. Don't spoil the fun. Don't depress the cash customers.

It was so unusual that I do not doubt there had to be a conference between Hal Wagner, Jim Yonge, and the captain to talk it over. And I have the suspicion that had it not been the last long cruise of the last American passenger ship, it might not have happened, no matter how much we all thought of Al Morgan.

The lounge was crowded when the service began. Almost all the passengers were there, and many of the crew. Hal Wagner read scripture, had us all repeat the Twenty-third Psalm, made some personal remarks about Al's courage, and led the group in "Till We Meet Again." Susan Cashman and Alan Scott each had a solo, and I did not really think Alan was going to get through his. It was Al's favorite, the beautiful Hawaiian song "Beyond the Reef," and just so damned apt that it came very close to breaking me up, and it did break up quite a few.

That night was a formal night. The captain's champagne party was the first of the voyage where there was absolutely no need for introductions when the passengers moved through the reception line.

After dinner we went to the lounge and heard a piano concert by the Stanley's daughter, Joyce. She was cool, elegant, and precise. She does not look as if she could impact the keys with that necessary concert-level strength. It was the right sort of entertainment for that night. The music was moving and very professional.

We went on deck later but did not stay long because the weather had turned very cool very suddenly.

Saturday was the last day at sea, hazy and cool, with long heavy swells. No more chits. Pay cash for everything. The statements of accounts were distributed, and there was a little throng at the purser's desk, paying off, most of the day.

At noon we were 394 miles from San Francisco.

Easy packing. No decisions. All must go. Paddle tennis in the afternoon, and it turned out to be one of those rare days when I won some singles sets. I am not fleet of foot, and my reaction time leaves much to be desired. I very much enjoy winning, at any game there is.

At cocktail time we went to a birthday party for the youngest member of the Stanley family, young Scott. Ice cream, cake, and Hawaiian punch. From there to a birthday party for our friend Forrest Daggett, arranged by his wife, Toni—a surprise, with us as the fake hosts. John Merlo provided an exploding cake. Then to the last dinner aboard, final odds and ends of packing the carry-offs, a last turn around the chilly deck to look at the night sea.

Fog the next morning. The horn started braying at six thirty. The fog lifted just as we came through the Golden Gate Bridge. This was the seventy-seventh day. And there was all of the city, glinting in the misty morning sun. The fog, and a lot of maneuvering in order to get docked, made us late. Then all was total confusion. Every passenger was debarking; we had aboard all the ones who would have gotten off in Los Angeles. Customs, of course, had prepared for far fewer people.

We were the very last to clear Customs. It happened this way. As a certified, guaranteed nit-picker, I had listed everything. I had a pile of receipts and forms as thick as the *World Almanac*. And for a Customs inspector, we got a plump Japanese lady who was also a certified, guaranteed nit-picker. It was her mission and her pleasure to check every single purchase against the "book," find out what it was made of, and make a prolonged calculation on her little machine. "Ah!" she would say, "I have saving you seventeen cents duty on this item!"

People kept staring into the empty lounge at us while she went on and on and on. The other Customs people left.

When at last she finished, we carried our hand luggage down to the pier and I paid my duty. We met our friends, gathered up our gear, and left.

And that was the last big one. I do not want to wind this up with some kind of whimpering, but I do want to make a point about the ship's captain versus management.

In twenty-five years of going to sea, I'd never had to be hospitalized or taken off a ship until one trip to Alaska when, on my way up, I developed a kidney stone, and it was very very painful. When we reached Vancouver they rushed me to the hospital. The ship's doctor, who had made the tentative diagnosis, had to give me a shot at four in the morning before we got in, the pain was so intense.

When I got to the hospital and they did their tests and confirmed the diagnosis, they said I should stay right there. Had I done so, the ship couldn't move. There was no one else to replace me at that time. The office was desperately trying to find someone. By this time it was late in the afternoon, and we were getting set to sail.

I talked it over with San Francisco on the phone and listened to their problem and said, "Okay, I'll go ahead and take the ship to Juneau and fly back from there, and you can fly a replacement up there." They were very pleased with this because it meant the ship could continue on schedule. The doctors in the hospital and the ship's doctor told me that if I went ahead I was going to experience some real pain, more than before. They told me that if I stayed they would not operate right away but would wait to see if the stone moved down. They told me nothing really bad would happen to me, but that the pain would be very severe.

It was. I had a couple of good attacks on the way up, and had some shots when it got impossible. The replacement skipper was waiting at Juneau. I got off and missed the flight by a couple of minutes, and had to sit in the airport until five or six that night, then got a local and arrived in San Francisco at midnight, popping aspirin and codeine all the way.

The point, if any, was that I never heard one word about that trip to Juneau from the company, even though it got them off the spot and saved them one hell of a good piece of change.

Now, back to the rudder situation, looking at the pros and the cons all over again, I don't think I should have brought the ship down from St. Croix to Panama with half a rudder. I think it was a bad decision on my part. I was getting the company out of a financial hole by doing it, but I was endangering the vessel, regardless of that Coast Guard and American Bureau of Shipping decision.

After they installed the temporary extension in Panama, which did not give me full maneuvering on the ship, the company wanted me to go to Los Angeles and then up to San Francisco, and I told them flatly that I would take the ship to one port or the other, but I was not going to go in and out of any more ports with a ship that didn't handle all that well even with a whole rudder. They were very miffed at this, very cross about the whole thing.

When we finished up in San Francisco, I didn't get the time of day from them. It bugged them to have to pay the expenses of shipping the Los Angeles passengers down the coast from San Francisco. They never stopped to think of what it would have cost them had I refused to take the ship down from St. Croix. I stuck my neck out, and as a result our relations went right down the tube because I wouldn't stick it out again. My feeling was we'd had all the luck we were going to get, and it was time to head for the barn.

The twin White Ships were kept operating until the Monterey took a final Pacific cruise in December of 1977 and the Mariposa went on one last Island cruise in April of 1978.

On the way back to San Francisco for the last time, Si Lubin kept hoping they could hang onto enough silverware to feed the people. The souvenir hunters had picked up about everything they could lift. And on the very last night, crew people, facing unemployment, got smashed and threw all the deck chairs over the side.

*   *   *

From the *Los Angeles Times*, Monday, April 3, 1978, by Staff Writer William Endicott:

The *Mariposa* is the third ship to bear the name of that historic California county. The first was built in 1883 and was in service until just before World War I. The second was completed late in 1931, became a troop transport during World War II, was sold to a foreign firm and now sails as the S.S. *Homeric* in transatlantic service.

The current *Mariposa* was built at Quincy, Massachusetts, in 1951 as a cargo ship for merchant service during the Korean War. It was known as the *Pine Tree Mariner*.

But in 1956 it was converted to a luxury liner for the Oceanic Steamship Company, a Matson subsidiary—built to carry 365 passengers and a crew of 276.

It was christened the *Mariposa* in Portland, Oregon, on October 16, 1956, by Electa Sevier, daughter of the late Randolph Sevier, who was then president of Matson Navigation Company.

In keeping with tradition, she broke a bottle of champagne over the bow. President Dwight D. Eisenhower sent a telegram.

"The christening of this ship," said the President, "is a splendid signal of our economic strength and of our faith in the future. The reconstitution of vital American flag passenger ship service provides a new link with our friends and allies in the Pacific and strengthens men of good will everywhere."

In command of the *Mariposa*'s last voyage is Captain R. Caldwell, 64, who has put in forty-three years at sea.

Pacific Far East Line officials said the federal subsidies for the ships, which amounted to $17.6 million last year, were necessary to keep fares competitive with those of foreign ships, many of which are heavily subsidized and aboard which labor and service overheads are much lower.

Legislation was offered by several California and Hawaii lawmakers to grant extensions to the *Mariposa* and the *Monterey*, but there never was much enthusiasm for the extensions from Pacific Far East Line officials.

Nobody from the financially troubled company bothered to attend a hearing on the legislation called for last July in Honolulu by Senator Daniel K. Inouye (D-Hawaii).

The company appeared primarily interested in selling the cruise ships to a foreign line and using the money to shore up its more lucrative cargo service.

From the *Honolulu Advertiser* for April 12, 1979:

Multimillionaire Edward J. Daly, who purchased the *Monterey* and *Mariposa* at auction in San Francisco this week, was asked what he intends to do with the $2.7 million luxury cruise ships. "I might park them in international waters off New Jersey and make them floating casinos," replied Daly, owner of World Airways. "Or I might put one of them in the Oakland Estuary as a cathouse and put West MacArthur out of business." West MacArthur is a notorious San Francisco red-light district.

On November 7th, 1980, a new story in the San Francisco *Chronicle* reported that Ed Daly had sold the two old luxury liners, the *Mariposa* and the *Monterey*, for $6.1 million, for a tidy profit of $3.4 million, less his costs of holding them for a year and a half.

The *Monterey* was purchased by the International Organization of Masters, Mates and Pilots, an AFL-CIO union, with the intention of getting her refurbished and put into service under the U.S. flag with American crews as "an absolutely first class operation."

The mysterious C. Y. Tung's American World Line bought the *Mariposa*, and she was taken immediately under tow, headed for Hong Kong. Tung owns more ships than anyone else in the world. The rumor most likely to succeed was that it would be towed to Shanghai to be turned into a waterfront hotel, by arrangement with the Chinese government.

Should any of us ever see her again, it will wrench the heart.